Praise for Heat

"Utterly riveting, sheer magnetic brilliance. Best book ... g

"The author really knows his subject and has used this
to maximum effect. This would make an excellent movie."

David Hough was born in Cornwall and grew up in
the Georgian City of Bath. He spent forty years working as
an air traffic controller in Northern Ireland, Scotland and
England before retiring early in 2003 and becoming a writer.
David has written over 30 novels and enjoys writing
"a rattling good yarn with a dose of hard grit".
He now lives with his wife in Dorset,
on the south coast of England.

www.TheNovelsofDavidHough.com

Also by David Hough:

Danger in the Sky aviation thrillers
Prestwick
Heathrow

Secret Soldiers of World War I spy thrillers
In Foreign Fields
In Line of Fire

Historical Adventures in Cornwall series
In the Shadow of a Curse
In the Shadow of Disgrace
In the Shadow of Deception

The Family Legacy series
The Legacy of Shame
The Legacy of Secrets
The Legacy of Conflict

David Hough

HEATHROW

Danger in the Sky (Book 2)

Cloudberry

Published by Cloudberry, an imprint of Luscious Books Ltd 2016
Morwellham, Down Park Drive, Tavistock, PL19 9AH, Great Britain

ISBN 978-1-910929-03-2

A CIP catalogue record for this book is available from the British Library.

www.cloudberrybooks.co.uk

Author's Note

In order to make the existence of one of the key characters chronologically credible, I have set this story in 1995. In that year, the Heathrow control tower — built in 1955 — was located in the central area, opposite the bus and coach station. It was demolished after a new control tower was opened in 2007.

It's a similar story with the London Air Traffic Control Centre which is no longer at West Drayton. The En-route Control element moved into a new building at Swanwick, near Southampton, in 2002. The Terminal Control element followed in 2007.

Air Traffic Controllers used the words 'Terminal Control' for the control of aircraft in the vicinity on the London airports. In this story I've called it Terminal Area Control to make it clear that this has nothing to do with terminal buildings or assisted dying. I ask the indulgence of controllers who may read the book.

I have described in some detail what went on inside those older buildings. If you have any thoughts of using that information for nefarious purposes, forget it. The buildings no longer exist and the air traffic control system has changed. However, if you are interested in the way aircraft were once controlled in the London area, read on.

David Hough
February 2016

Chapter 1

November 1995

Commander Colin FitzHugh's telephone rang shortly after midnight. He was not expecting a call, but he was awake. He was always awake at that hour in order to give Angela her medication.

He picked up the receiver in the lounge and said, "Yes?" in a dull, resigned tone. His senses became sharply alerted when he heard the voice of Sir James Heatherley, Permanent Under Secretary at the Home Office.

"How are you, Colin?" It was the same calm, well-educated voice FitzHugh had heard so many times before. Heatherley didn't identify himself and didn't need to.

"Well enough, thank you, Sir James." FitzHugh responded calmly, but he sensed that something was wrong. Seriously wrong. Since his retirement, no one from the Home Office had seen fit to contact him, and certainly not Sir James Heatherley. Why was he calling now, and at this time of night?

"And Angela?" The voice was clear, but held a hint of tension.

"She has her good days and bad days." FitzHugh avoided saying that he had only moments before given Angela a powerful painkiller. It didn't seem appropriate. They both knew that his choice of early retirement had been motivated primarily by his need to look after his wife.

"Yes, I understand your problem." Heatherley paused and coughed. "I fully understand, but, the fact is, we need your help."

"Really? What's happened?"

"A bomb in London. A big one."

"Another IRA attack?" FitzHugh winced at the thought of yet another outrage on English soil. He pulled anxiously at his well-trimmed beard. The Baltic Exchange bomb, three years ago, had caused eight hundred million pounds' worth of damage, as well as ending the lives of three people. Two years ago, two children were killed by a bomb in Warrington. Would it never end?

"It seems likely," Heatherley paused ominously. "The bomb exploded inside the Air Traffic Control Centre at West Drayton. Figuratively speaking, this has the IRA's fingerprints all over it." Heatherley's voice took on a sad, almost hopeless tone. It was the voice of a man who had more problems than he felt able to handle. "We're going to try to put a complete security cloak over it for the time being. The press have been told it's an equipment fire inside the building. We'll hold onto that line while we try to figure out a strategy. The trouble is, Colin, we haven't the manpower to deal with this in the way we'd like. You know how hampered we've been since the Anglo-Irish Agreement. Good men have been posted elsewhere and inexperience is crippling us. You're still one of the most experienced men in the country when it comes to Irish Republican terrorism. We need you back again, Colin."

FitzHugh took a deep breath before replying calmly, but insistently. "You know I can't help you now, Sir James. Angela needs me here."

Heatherley's words came back a little too quickly, as if he had been expecting the rebuff. "I know, I know. We've thought of that. We're sending over a nurse. Someone to take care of Angela. She's already on her way." He paused for a brief moment, as if allowing time for the message to sink in. The nurse was *already on her way*. When he continued, his voice was hesitant. "We're... *asking* you to help us, Colin. We could insist, but... we're *asking*. We badly need you on this one."

"How will others feel about that?" FitzHugh deliberately avoided mention of any names in the chain of command at the Home Office.

This time, Heatherley came back fast and aggressive. "I've already spoken to all the relevant people. Obviously, the PM is on our side. He wants quick and decisive action on this, and the rest of them know they can't guarantee to provide it. Like I said, they don't have the experience, and they know it. No one is going to stand in your way, I can promise you that."

"Do I have a choice, Sir James?" FitzHugh spoke with an air of resignation.

"As I said, we're *asking* you, Colin." The short silence that followed was pregnant with gravity.

When FitzHugh replied, it was with an element of irony. "You're asking me, but you've already sent the nurse."

"We hoped you would agree."

He sighed deeply. "Very well. I'll do what I can." What else could he say? He replaced the receiver and went back to where Angela lay in the dimly-lit bedroom. His heart felt heavy.

"Who was it?" Angela's voice was muted and her eyes dull.

"Sir James Heatherley."

"What did he want?"

"Me."

A glistening sheen began to form over her eyes. "Oh, no, Colin. Not now."

FitzHugh sat down on the side of the bed and took Angela's hand in his. It felt cold and he rubbed it to help her circulation. "I'm sorry, my love. I shall have to go out for a while. A problem has come up and they want my help."

"You're leaving me alone?" A sudden sense of alarm showed in Angela's voice.

"No. A nurse is on her way. You'll not be alone."

"But you're retired, Colin. By now they should have learned how to cope without you."

"Yes, I know." FitzHugh turned his face away so that she would not see the guilt in his eyes.

He wondered whether she would forgive him if she ever learned of the regrets he harboured, regrets for what he had put her through in their life together.

And there was something else.

He felt guilty because he secretly wanted to go.

*

In the quiet of early morning, Peregrine Fraser-Murdoch strode across Connemara Airport and breathed in the cool, fresh air. It felt so good after the years he had spent inside a secure hospital. It was the smell and taste of freedom. It wouldn't last, of course. When this was over, he would have to go back to that place from where his friends had released him. His enemies would see to that. But, by then, the world would be a different place, and he would have made his mark.

As he walked, an arthritic pain stabbed through his left hip. It happened often these days, a factor of age, but it hadn't always been like this. He briefly recalled the time when he had been a lean, muscular student at Cambridge University, with the world at his fingertips. Time had played badly with him since those days. Now seventy-five, his head was bald and most of his muscles had turned to flab. He was well aware that extra weight gave him a dumpy appearance, but that no longer mattered. His carefully-planned endgame would wipe aside all his previous sense of degradation.

In a quiet corner of the airport, he paused alongside an old Fokker F27 twin turbo-prop. A nervous twitch began to affect his face. Like the arthritis, it was nothing new, just an irritating sign that his excitement was getting out of hand. He breathed deeply in an effort to ease his mental strain.

A few minutes passed before he felt calmer. Then he climbed aboard the aircraft, carrying a small torch to guide him into the cabin. He paused in mid-stride when a dark figure rose from a seat near the entrance hatch.

He called out, "It's me, McQuarrie. Only me."

Padraig McQuarrie emerged from the gloom, a short, dishev-elled-looking man, grey-haired and wearing well-crushed combat jacket and trousers.

"You're early," the Ulsterman answered in a broad Belfast accent. "What're you doin' here at this hour?"

"I couldn't sleep in the hotel. You should have found me a more comfortable place." Murdoch eased his stubby body into a seat and breathed heavily. His immaculately tailored lounge suit was crushed under his weight and his podgy hands clasped at the chest of his fine silk shirt. The tightness he felt there wasn't just the effect of flab: he'd been warned by his doctors that any form of exertion was a strain on his heart.

"It's secure enough, is that place. They know how to keep their mouths shut." McQuarrie had the grim, gnarled look of a man who had experienced nothing easy throughout his fifty odd years of life. He acted as if he expected nothing easy in his remaining years. "That hotel's been good enough for better men that you."

"The room is not to my liking," Murdoch snapped. "I don't like sleeping in a tiny bed with insufficient bedclothes."

McQuarrie adopted a scornful tone. "You surprise me. You're supposed to be the product of an English public school, aren't you?" He sniffed loudly, further emphasising his scathing opinion.

Murdoch ignored him and leaned forward to sweep his torch beam over a metal container sitting on the floor in the gangway. The device in that box was his chosen ticket to fame. Something that would ensure the name of Peregrine Fraser-Murdoch would never be forgotten.

A cockroach scuttled out from beneath a nearby seat. Murdoch put his foot over it and slowly pressed down. The faint crunching sound gave him some small satisfaction. He put a hand to his face to contain another nervous twitch. It seemed to last longer this time.

"Give me a cigarette," he demanded. He tried to sound calm, but the excitement made him on edge.

McQuarrie threw a pack across the gangway. "Buy yer own in future."

"Shut up!"

"Please yourself."

"I usually do." Murdoch lit up and drew the smoke deep into his lungs. It did nothing to suppress his rising sense of eager anticipation, and the nervous twitch returned.

Chapter 2

It had been raining heavily during the night. When Simon Hudson awoke, he thought he could hear the sound of it still splashing against the bedroom window. It seemed to be running down the glass like a mountain stream, bubbling constantly.

He lay on his back with his mind only half-concentrating on the rhythmic sound, the legacy of a vivid dream occupying the remainder of his thoughts. He had been running from something. He wasn't too sure what, but it had been something terrifying. A long trickle of sweat dribbled slowly down his face and was soaked up by the sheets.

The bubbling sound of running water continued. Some minutes passed before he realised that it was not the sound of rain; it was the urgent dribble of a tap left partly on. It came from the direction of the bathroom. He turned in the bed towards where Michelle should have been and saw an empty space and sheets hastily thrown aside.

He called out, "Michelle!"

Getting no response, he levered himself out of the bed and staggered to the bathroom, rubbing his face to clear away the traces of sweat. He had slept barely an hour since Michelle's last screaming nightmare and his head ached.

"What are you doing?" he gasped.

Michelle was sprawled across the floor, her back against the tub, her ashen face staring up at the ceiling. The small room smelled foul and there were traces of vomit splashed down the front of her nightdress. In the corner, a small steady stream of tap water bubbled into the sink.

"You've made yourself sick again, haven't you?" He knelt down in front of her and clasped his hands together to stop himself from shaking her. God! How he wanted to shake her violently and drag her to her senses. But their family doctor had warned him to take it easy.

"Answer me, Michelle."

"Uh?" She raised her gaze and looked over his shoulders. These days she never looked him in the face. Most of the time he spent trying to communicate with her was wasted because she simply stared into the space beyond him and she said nothing. Her painfully thin body was shaking spasmodically, as it always did after these events, and her wide, unfocussed eyes were like two black holes in space.

"Get up, please, Michelle. I'll put your nightie in the wash before I leave."

"Leave?" Her eyes flickered as if a measure of understanding had seeped into her brain. "Don't leave. You mustn't leave. I don't want you to."

"Michelle, I have to go to work. I'll leave you at your mum's place on my way. Just like I always do. Remember?" He stared at the outline of her withered breasts beneath the wet nightdress. Once, not so very long ago, they had been full and rounded, sensual to his touch. Now, like the rest of her wasted body, they were a pitiful residue of the past.

"I don't want to go to mum's. The house is empty without dad." She twisted a strand of hair across her face. "I don't like it there without dad."

Of late, when talking about her father, she became slightly more coherent. Perhaps it was a good sign. She had been devastated when he died of cancer. It came too soon after their baby died. Her father had been a stable influence, helping to keep her off heroin for so many years. Now he was gone and the drugs were back.

"I'll have to leave soon." Hudson stood up resignedly. "I have to go to work, you know. I'm on an early morning watch. And I can't leave you on your own. Your mum will look after you."

"I hate you," she mumbled. "I really hate you."

He flinched. Did she mean it? Or was it the illness speaking?

He went out to the kitchen and filled the kettle. The room was physically warm, but it held a cold aura, just like the rest of the house.

A mug of strong black coffee would ease his fatigue, he decided. Maybe it would take away the taste of anger from his throat. While he was waiting for the kettle to boil, he switched on the radio. A news reporter's voice droned out at him.

Hudson quickly flicked to another station, one that was playing soft classical music. The last thing he wanted to listen to this morning was a rundown on the usual gloom and doom that seemed to fill radio and television news reports.

He made his coffee to the soothing sound of Vaughan Williams' *Fantasia on Greensleeves*, one of his favourite pieces.

*

Helen Mayfield was barely awake, only half-conscious of the sound of bare feet padding across the hardwood floor towards her bed. She felt dreamily warm as she pulled the duvet tighter about herself and moaned softly. All she wanted was another hour of rest inside the cocoon.

"Mummy?" Judith's voice crept out of the darkness, like a tiny cry for help. A cry that was almost impossible to refuse.

"Oh, Judith," Helen brushed aside a curtain of her own long blonde hair. It caressed her cheeks as it fell to the pillow. "What do you want at this hour, sweetheart?"

"Can I come in with you?"

"But what's wrong with your own bed?"

"I'm lonely."

Helen instinctively rubbed a hand across her eyes, sat up and switched on the bedside lamp. The sudden burst of light blinded her for a second. Then she saw Judith standing at the side of the bed, prominent in her bright red pyjamas, with her favourite teddy bear clasped tightly in her arms. Even at five, almost six, Judith would not relinquish her teddy bear at night. She called it Mr Wobbles, but Helen had no idea why.

"Oh, come along." Helen lifted up the edge of the duvet and Judith clambered in without a second's hesitation. With her daughter's warm little body pressed tight against her own, Helen switched off the lamp. "You have to be quiet and let mummy sleep a bit longer. All right?"

"Yes." A short pause, and then, "Will daddy be back today?"

"Yes."

"Will he have a birthday present for me?"

"I expect so."

"Where's daddy been this time?"

"America."

"Is that a long way?"

"Oh Judith!" Helen sat up in the darkness and suppressed an urge to continue her angry retort. Instead she took a deep breath, wrapped an arm about her daughter and said, "Please, sweetheart, let's get some sleep, eh? It's early and I've got a busy day ahead of me."

"Very busy?"

"Yes, very busy."

In fact, every day was busy, very busy. Helen had been the ATC Executive Officer at London City Airport for only six months, but already she was wondering if she had been wise to take the post. Always, there seemed to be an intense urge from higher management to reduce staff and increase workloads. It didn't help that she also had to run a home and a family while Dan was away on flights to foreign places. It was the downside of being married to an airline pilot. Nothing in life, she thought, was totally un-burdened by problems.

Judith shuffled in the bed, snuggling closer. A warm arm reached across Helen as the child whispered, "Do you think daddy will remember my birthday present? Will he, mummy?"

Helen sighed. Consciousness had now been thrust fully into her mind, cutting off any remaining chance of getting back to sleep. Past experience told her that her best bet now was to get up and make an early breakfast. Inevitably, while she was doing that

Judith would fall asleep in her bed. It just didn't seem fair.

"I'm sure he will, love," she said. She glanced at the alarm clock. It was 5.15 and she would have to be out of the house by 7.30. She would leave Judith with a childminder before driving to the City Airport in London's docklands. In the meantime, she had more than two hours to kill. Damn!

Maybe she could dash off some ironing. It would be a way of using the time to good effect. She got out of the bed and went to the wardrobe. Now fully resigned to the task of ironing for the next hour, she wrapped a silk gown about herself. When she looked back towards the bed, she saw Judith cuddle down beneath the duvet and close her eyes. Mr Wobbles had his head on the pillow.

Helen went out to the hallway and turned up the thermostat. It had been a cold night and the air was still chilly, even inside the house. She ambled through to the kitchen, filled the kettle and set it to boil. Then she put a generous spoonful of coffee into a mug. Finally she switched on the radio to catch the early morning news broadcast. At the same instant, as if the two devices were somehow linked together, her telephone rang. She turned down the radio volume and lifted the receiver, expecting to hear Dan announce that his flight was very early. Or a message from the company's operations clerk saying he would be impossibly late.

"Helen? It's Seth Jones. Were... um... were you awake?"

Helen frowned. She had never before received a call at home from the head of the London Airports Executive Group. Why was he calling now? And at this early hour? And what was causing that ominous tone in his voice?

"What's the matter, Seth? You sound as if something's wrong."

"Haven't you heard the news this morning?"

"No."

"Switch on your radio and listen, Helen. The press are telling people there's been a major fire at West Drayton. In fact, it's a bomb. The Terminal Area Control room has been wrecked."

"Oh, no! Was anyone—"

"Killed? Yes. It's carnage over there."

16

"Oh, my God! Who? And why?"

"I'm sure you can guess who would do something like this, Helen. Remember what happened at the Baltic Exchange and Warrington? In the meantime, all the London airports are going to have major problems. How soon can you get to your office?"

*

The atmosphere inside the En-route Area Control room at West Drayton was tense, far too tense, but the controllers were doing their jobs despite what had happened next door.

FitzHugh spoke briefly to the watch manager. It was more to offer some reassurance than to gain information. "You didn't evacuate this room?"

The manager shook his head and pointed upwards. "And risk the likely chaos up there? Collisions... hundreds... maybe thousands killed. Balance of risks, old boy. The emergency room at Heathrow won't take all of us, so we stayed."

FitzHugh noticed a deep sadness in the manager's eyes. It must have been a difficult decision.

He tried to put some emphasis into a promise that the perpetrators of the explosion would be found, but that wasn't easy, either. Then he strode along the narrow corridor to where the bomb had exploded in the Terminal Area Control room.

Until last night, the airspace around the London airports had been controlled from here. FitzHugh steeled himself as he stepped into the wrecked room, but he could not prevent a nervous flinch when he saw the carnage. Bodies, and the remains of bodies, still lay where they had been flung by the blast. Blood, flesh, charred pieces of equipment. Smoke still spiralled up into the already foetid air, escaping through a hole in the roof. Fire hoses trailed across the floor. The stench of death hung in the atmosphere and it upset him more than he had expected. That secret longing to be back at work vanished in an instant. Self-recrimination took over. He was retired, dammit! He had a dying wife at home — he didn't need this!

He forced himself to study the details in the scene. He should be able to cope with it, he told himself. He had a long history associated with warfare, or legalised killing as Angela used to call it. He had served ten years in the Royal Navy, including three years with the SBS. Unusually for a Northern Irish Catholic, he had given ten years' service to the RUC, which was as near to war service as you could get in a civilian environment.

When he left Northern Ireland, he tried to convince himself that it was purely to further his career, a career hampered in Ulster by his Catholic background. But that was not the real reason. He left because he had grown overly sick of the death and carnage that was a part of the everyday life of an RUC officer. He left because he could no longer stomach the sight of innocent men, women and children blown to shreds by political psychopaths. He left because he was convinced those same psychopaths enjoyed considerable support within the Northern Ireland community. He left because it had just got too much for him.

The arm-twisting which ensured his transfer to the Yard's Anti-Terrorist Squad was an inevitability he should have foreseen. His experience in Ireland made him an ideal candidate for the work. It aided his rapid promotion, but it also threw him right back into that sickening world of terrorism. The world he hated.

And now, when he should have been able to put it all behind him, he had to face it all again: the blood, the gore, the senseless killing on a grand scale. Bile was rising in his throat as he turned away from the scene. Why on earth had he harboured that private wish to take on this job? Was he growing inhuman? Or was he tired of looking after Angela? His sense of guilt intensified.

FitzHugh had never adopted the mantle of a run-of-the-mill policeman, any more than he had acted like a run-of-the-mill naval commander. A little over six foot tall, he liked to pull at his dark grey beard when he was thinking. In conversation, he spoke slowly, choosing his words carefully, because he was aware his Irish accent did him no favours.

Breathing deeply to calm his nerves, he left the bomb scene

and continued the process of setting up a system to deal with the atrocity. In the past couple of hours, he had consumed endless cups of black coffee, trying to suppress his guilt.

He forced his black feelings to subside by engrossing himself in his work. When a young uniformed constable brought him breakfast — a thick, greasy bacon sandwich — he was past the worst of his emotional reactions. Or so he thought.

"I'm going to visit some people at the Yard," he told the local Scene-of-Crime Officer as the first hint of daylight began to light up the scene beyond the windows. "I'll probably be there the rest of the morning. Call me immediately you find anything significant."

His head ached because he had slept little that night and he knew he would have to get home sometime during the morning to check on... well, just to check. He finished the bacon sandwich, grabbed another cup of black coffee and then took one last look inside the Terminal Area Control room.

It was marginally easier to cope with the horror this time.

Chapter 3

It took Hudson three attempts to get his car engine started. At some time during the night icy cold rain had seeped into the engine compartment, soaking the electrics. He stood at the side of the road, his upper body bent beneath the raised bonnet, and wiped around the electrics with a rag. He coughed as a damp drizzle bit through his worn outer coat and penetrated his chest.

He tried to shrug off the inconvenience of the car's temperamental engine, but it wasn't such an easy thing to do, not when his mind was filled with a festering sense of anger that no one could do anything better to help Michelle. He wondered at times if the medical profession had given up on her, left it all to him.

Eventually, the car started, but it didn't sound healthy. It was ready for the scrap heap and Hudson couldn't afford to replace it.

He left Michelle at her mother's house and, yet again, expressed his appreciation to the older woman for the effort she put into helping her daughter. His words of thanks were genuine. Without Michelle's mother, he would have been at a complete loss.

He stopped at a filling station and put ten pounds' worth of petrol in his tank. He had no more cash in his pocket, his bank account was overdrawn to the limit and both his credit card accounts had been in debit to the maximum limit for some months. When he walked into the shop to pay for the petrol, he heard an early-morning news broadcast blaring out from a radio at the cashier's desk. He stopped abruptly to listen. It was the first he knew of a fire at West Drayton.

*

Helen Mayfield drove her bright red BMW fast along the Woolwich Road towards Silvertown. She had her screen wipers running at half-speed to wipe away a light drizzle that refused to vacate the early-morning sky. Although she was a fierce critic of loud car radios, this morning the volume of her own radio was turned up high. She had it tuned to a pop music station and the quality of the news reporting annoyed her, but she stuck with it. She habitually listened to that station on her way to work, more for the music than the news, and she had not programmed in any other quick select frequencies. It was too late now, the traffic was too busy to allow her to reach across and seek out another station.

"*Our correspondent, George Hills, is ah... is at the scene in West Drayton,*" the announcer said, rather too laconically for the occasion. "*Hello... can you hear me there, George?*"

The answering voice conjured up an image of a junior reporter on a provincial newspaper. Wet behind the ears and easily convinced. "*Yes. I'm here at the air traffic control headquarters in West Drayton where things look pretty bad at the moment...*"

"It's not the headquarters," Helen mumbled out loud. Badly briefed reporters irked her. "Get it right, you miserable little worm."

Apparently unperturbed by Helen's words, George Hills went on with his report. "*The police and fire service are here in large numbers, as you'd expect in this sort of emergency and... um... a big, um, emergency rescue plan has swung into operation. The police are... um... they're backed up by military police. There's smoke coming from inside the compound and the fire looks rather serious from where I'm standing...*"

"Of course it looks serious!" Helen spoke out loud to give vent to her annoyance. "What the hell do you expect it to look like?" She pressed down hard on her brake pedal as a white van emerged from a side road close in front of her. "Stupid idiot!" She wasn't sure who she was addressing.

Like the radio reporter, the white van driver ignored her.

Helen turned her mind back to the radio, promising herself that she would tune in a proper news channel at the first opportunity. She was approaching the entrance to the London City Airport when the announcer interrupted the news reporter by asking, "*Have you been inside the building, George?*"

"*No, I haven't. No, um... no journalists have been allowed inside the headquarters complex... as you would expect... but we do anticipate a briefing from a senior official within the next half hour. That's when we should learn more about what exactly caused the fire.*"

"*So who... I mean... well... just what do you think happened?*"

The reporter took a moment to consider his reply. "*We don't know for sure, and that's the truth. According to what we have been told by the fire brigade authorities, there... um... there was a small explosion which may have been caused by an electrical fault. After that, the fire took hold in some important parts of the building.*"

"*Really? Well... ah... tell us more about it. What exactly do they do in that building?*"

"*As I understand it, they have people here who talk to pilots of aircraft arriving at London airports and give them weather information. They also have guidance systems for getting the planes down safely. It's all linked to the control tower at Heathrow.*"

"Tell us something intelligent for God's sake!" Helen's patience was at full stretch. She pulled into her car parking slot and switched off the engine. Then she leaned forward and switched off the radio. "Ill-informed drivel," she muttered. She hurried out of her car and made her way to the control tower building. This was not going to be a good day.

*

Porters Way in West Drayton was bounded on one side by a council housing estate and on the other by the country's largest Air Traffic Control complex. This morning, the road was lined along its entire length with police cones to prevent parking. In addition, there were barricades across the main entrance to the complex. Armed military police stood with their weapons at readiness.

Television and newspaper crews were crowded close to the main entrance, an amorphous mass of semi-constrained cameramen and reporters. Behind all the exterior activity, a cloud of smoke rose up from the main building. At lower level it was lit up by light spilling up from the street and the site complex. As it swirled higher into the early-morning sky, the smoke became enveloped in cloud. Hudson felt his throat go dry as he eased his car up to a barricade across the site entrance.

An armed military policeman leaned in at his open window. "Your pass, sir."

Hudson held up his plastic security card. "What's happening?"

The policeman checked his clipboard list. "Mr Hudson? You're a Terminal Area Controller?"

"Yes."

"You should report to the tower at Heathrow, sir."

The security barrier was raised and Hudson pointed to where another vehicle was waved through. "But other people are going in here."

"Only en-route controllers are allowed in, sir. Terminal Area Control has been transferred to the emergency control room over at Heathrow."

"Oh. Okay." Hudson stared at the smoking pyre as it rose up into the dull, drizzly air. The instruction made sense: Heathrow was equipped with an emergency control room for use in the event of technical problems here at West Drayton.

The policeman straightened up. "Just get yourself over to Heathrow as quick as you can, sir." He took a step back and waved Hudson through a reversing loop and back out onto Porters Way.

Hudson shook his head sadly. If they had opened up the emergency control room at Heathrow, things had to be bad inside the Terminal Area Control room at West Drayton. As he drove away, he felt his flesh tingle.

*

The demons came to him while he waited. They always came to him at moments like this. Moments when he was off guard.

"They're out to get you!" they screamed at him.

Peregrine Fraser-Murdoch clenched his fists and closed his eyes.

"They're all out to get you! You know that! All of them. They're all going to get you one day!"

The demons were right, of course. They would get him one day. The British, the Americans, the French… anyone with a nuclear capability… anyone who feared Russian intentions. They would get him. But the screaming demons made it so much more painful.

He unclenched his fists and reached into a pocket for his pills. He swallowed two. Then another. It should be enough. It usually was.

He waited until the demons began to fade and then slowly opened his eyes. The F27's two Dart turbo-prop engines were motionless and silent. Inside the aeroplane it was dark and cold and that didn't help him combat the after-effects of the attack. But it was all right now. The demons had retreated.

He shivered and wished there was some means of heating without winding up the engines. It had often been cold like this in the hospital where he had spent so many dreary years. He was so glad to be away from there.

He glanced at his watch and cursed that the hands were moving so slowly. The take-off time had to be accurate if they were to arrive exactly on schedule and it was too early yet to get away from Connemara.

His short, stubby legs were stretched out across the bare metal floor of the cabin, his shoes close up against the metal container on the floor.

The Ulsterman, McQuarrie, had gone up onto the cramped flight deck to talk with the pilot and Murdoch was glad to be away from him. It gave him time to think, time to reappraise his plans. They were good plans, he was sure of that, even though they might be his last on this earth, if things went badly wrong.

Murdoch breathed deeply at the first sign of his nervous twitch returning. He had to keep calm if he was to stay in control of the operation. He glanced down at the box. The bomb inside was relatively small in size, but it was a viable device. One that would deliver a devastating blow. The military sometimes called them suitcase bombs, but that was a gross misnomer. They could never be fitted inside any suitcase. This one weighed sixty pounds and was properly called an RA-115 two-man portable device. He looked again at it and he felt another inner glow of satisfaction as the incipient nervous twitch faded.

At that moment McQuarrie emerged from the flight deck. He stopped at the front of the cabin and leaned towards one of the large windows. "There's a vehicle coming this way," he announced. "A large covered truck. Reckon that's the rest of the brigade. And about time, too."

Murdoch rose slowly from his seat. "Get them aboard quickly, and try not to draw attention to what's happening here."

"You think we're amateurs?" McQuarrie snapped. "We're professionals, pal. Real professionals."

"I hope you are right," Murdoch said forcefully. "I don't want any mistakes."

*

FitzHugh sipped on a cup of insipid tea and flicked through a thick file on the slate-grey desk in front of him. It was an untidy desk in an untidy office, the only space in the Yard available to him at short notice. He briefly glanced outside at the dull, drizzly view to the rear of the building and then turned his attention back to the file.

He was seated in the office of a Chief Inspector now on a well-timed holiday in some distant land, too remote to bring him back for the ensuing emergency. FitzHugh envied him.

The well-thumbed cardboard file was labelled: MOST SECRET. It was a detailed resume of the Provisional IRA hierarchy. If this job was carried out by a PIRA squad, the leader would be listed here.

FitzHugh sat back and reached out for his teacup. It now felt cold to his touch and he replaced it on the desk without attempting to drink.

He looked again at the file, scanning through a list of names.

They were all here: Cahill, Twomey, MacStiofain, Adams, Mc-Guinness, Toome. FitzHugh knew them all by sight and by reputation. He had even interviewed some of them. Which one of them would have masterminded a job like this? He picked out four names and scribbled them on a pad lying on the desk in front of him. Then he read the file again, shook his head and scratched out two of the names. After some further thought, he scratched out one more name. He was left with one obvious contender: Patrick Toome.

He could be wrong, of course. This might not even be a Provisional IRA attack, but his experience and instinct told him he was right. It *was* them. It *was* Toome. He felt it in his bones.

The name Patrick Toome swirled round inside his mind and conjured up images he would prefer to forget... if he could. Images of riots and killings in Belfast, images of dead bodies thrown aside in quiet parts of the Irish countryside, images of hatred and death on a scale that could only be imagined on mainland Britain. And the name of Patrick Toome was neatly tied up with those images. A man he had long wanted to interrogate. A man who had consistently stayed beyond his reach.

He shook himself out of his thoughts with some degree of annoyance, looked at his watch and then picked up the telephone to call home. He needed to know how Angela was faring without him. That incipient sense of guilt was, once again, emerging into his conscious mind and he could do little to control it.

Chapter 4

The atmosphere inside Heathrow's emergency control room was electric with tension. Hudson had worked here once before when the power supply to West Drayton had been disrupted by a cable fault, but he had never before worked here in a real emergency.

He felt his voice wavering as fatigue washed over him in long rolling waves. His hand involuntarily released the radio-telephone transmit switch before he finished speaking, clipping the end of a transmission to an American 747. He breathed deeply and then repeated the transmission before the pilot could complain. His throat felt tight and raw, causing a rasping pain as the breath hissed from his lips. He forced himself to swallow, hoping it would ease his breathing. Then he looked around anxiously. Murmuring voices crowded in from all sides, but no one seemed to have noticed his tired behaviour.

"Think, brain. Think, damn you!" he whispered to himself. "God help me, think!"

What was the matter with him?

Was it the bomb at West Drayton, or was it the trouble with Michelle? Was it the inevitable tiredness after endless nights without proper sleep? He pulled his old black blazer tighter about his shoulders, as if it would have some positive effect upon his sense of discomfort. It didn't.

It had to be the bomb. God, what carnage! He recalled the confidential briefing from the watch manager: fourteen people killed, thirty-six seriously injured, and for what? So that some bloody terrorist could make a political point!

"Concentrate!" The word slipped out unintentionally and he glanced up suddenly, hoping no one had heard. Seemingly, no one had.

He stared at his radar display and blinked, aware that he was rapidly losing the capacity to picture in his mind a three-dimensional image of what he saw in two dimensions on the tube. The more confused he became, the more he realised he needed help.

'Losing the picture' was a risk all radar controllers lived with. It happened to every one of them at some time or other. It was a hazard of the job, but it was the first time it had happened to Hudson.

A gaggle of aircraft was heading towards the Ockham holding stack, each aircraft appearing on his radar screen as an electronically processed cross with an information label alongside. Farther back down the airway, another group of aircraft was also heading towards Ockham. And beyond them, he knew, would be more aircraft. And yet more. He choked as he felt the bile rising in his gut.

His head ached with tiredness.

God, what an impossible mess!

A young female assistant stepped up close beside him and placed a series of new flight progress strips into his display. He glanced at her and momentarily recognised her delicate perfume. Jennifer White, a recent recruit to the job. Attractive, but far too shy for her own good. Nevertheless, he liked her for her quiet manner. Her sober manner. If only Michelle could be more like Jennifer White.

If only.

*

Daylight was greasing up into the sky as an old green Ford Transit van raced away from London in the outside lane of the M4. The driver kept the needle registering a steady seventy miles per hour, ignoring the insistent flashing headlights of a following Porsche.

Patrick Toome sat on the floor at the rear of the van, quietly watching his companions. It was cold as he blew into his hands and rubbed them together. Most of the team were smoking nervously and, with just one exception, were looking tense. Only the Scotsman, McGovan, appeared outwardly calm, probably because he had been drinking.

Toome wanted to drop McGovan from the team, but it was too

late for that. He needed every man he was given and there were no substitutes. It was a tightly planned operation in which each man had a specific role to play to ensure success. Drop one person and the whole plan was in jeopardy. Toome clenched his fist as he felt his own tension rising. God help them all if anything went wrong.

Turning to look out of the rear window, he spotted the bright red Porsche swinging into the centre lane to get past. Toome thought he detected an angry snarl on the driver's face, and he wondered whether to raise two fingers. By the time he had thought about it, the car had accelerated out of his sight. He grunted and shifted his position.

Within seconds, all memory of the Porsche was erased from his mind.

*

Jennifer White, the young assistant with the delicate perfume, moved away and Hudson forced his attention back to his radar screen. For a few minutes, he thought he might be able to regain control of the situation, recapturing his position as the thinking part of the man/machine system. But, as more and more pilots called on his radio frequency, his sense of command continued to crumble. Bit by bit, his last vestiges of authority over the system were whittled away. He had to call for help. He should have done it ten minutes ago.

He looked first at the support controller sitting alongside him, knowing full well he could expect no help there. A young and very inexperienced trainee was doing that job. In theory, Hudson was supervising the youngster, but theory had long since left the reality of the situation.

Next, he looked over his shoulder towards the desk where the watch supervisor sat hunched over a pile of documents. All it needed was a quick shout, or a telephone call, and the supervisor would be obliged to give him help.

Hudson hesitated. "Don't quit now," he told himself. "You can do this, damn you!"

The next gaggle of arriving aircraft began to check in on his radio frequency. The volume of communication built up until the radio calls were following one another with hardly a gap between. Hudson's mental picture of what was happening in the sky grew even fuzzier. Radar echoes were getting too close and he didn't have time to work out which ones he ought to turn. He didn't know which ones were in danger of collision.

*

At altitude, daylight was already full-blown. It illuminated the mass of cloud hanging over southern England. The crew of a British Atlantic Airways Boeing 747 was tired as their flight neared London. It had been a long and arduous flight from New York. Clear air turbulence at high altitude had not only caused discomfort to the passengers, it had fatigued every member of the flight deck crew. The captain glanced across at the first officer and saw the telltale signs spread across the other man's face. They would both be glad when they were on the ground.

The door opened and the senior steward eased himself onto the flight deck.

"They're having a rough time back there," he announced. "The 'stewies' are complaining again. Passengers are honking all over the place."

The captain grimaced and ignored the remarks. He had enough to worry about without the problem of passengers spewing around the cabin.

"Heathrow, British Atlantic One Seven Six is in the hold and levelling at flight level six zero." He made his report to the radar controller and then selected the flight deck intercom to his first officer. "Seems particularly busy this morning."

"It's always busy at Heathrow these days." The first officer paused before adding, sombrely, "Operations say there's been a fire at West Drayton. We should expect delays."

"Damn!"

They both lapsed into silence until the first officer remarked,

30

"Radar has just cleared American 5874 to flight level six zero. Did you hear that? I'm sure it's in the same holding pattern as us."

"We'll have separation," the captain replied, but he looked ahead out of the windscreen anyway. It was a natural reaction. All he saw was the enveloping layers of turbulent cloud.

"Call flight ops and give them—" The captain's words were suddenly halted by the view ahead. The huge silvery grey shape of an American 767 materialised from out of the cloud. It was closing on them fast from above.

"Oh, my God!" The captain grabbed the control column, deselected the automatic pilot and pushed the column forward. The American crew would never know what hit them unless the British Atlantic flight could be forced down below their aircraft. The British pilots held their breath as their own aircraft began to slide downwards while the Americans raced into the airspace they had just vacated.

"Bloody hell!" The first officer breathed again as they continued to sink away from the other aircraft. "What the hell is going on?"

"Heathrow!" The captain spoke angrily as he pressed the radio transmit switch. "This is British Atlantic One Seven Six. We've just had a close call with an American 767. We're descending to flight level five zero."

"Roger—" The reply was hesitant, uncertain. "Stand by."

"For God's sake! We can't just stand by! Are we safe at five zero?"

"Roger... affirmative... stand-by."

*

The supervisor looked up sharply as Hudson called across the darkened room. He was in the middle of scrutinising a training report before it was sent back to the West Drayton training section. Frowning, he removed his spectacles and focussed his mind back onto the reality of the control room. Then he stood up and hurried across the carpeted floor.

"Not more problems with the radar, Simon," he mumbled. "We've enough on our plate today."

As he came closer, he noticed the ashen look on Hudson's face and realised that it was something far more important than a radar malfunction.

"I've had an airmiss," Hudson replied, his voice hoarse with emotion.

"Oh, God! A bad one?"

"Yes, a bad one. I need a relief, quickly!"

"Hang on there." The supervisor turned back to his desk. "I'll get someone else in there as quickly as I can. Just you hang on!"

"I can't hang on. I've lost the picture. For God's sake, get someone in here fast!"

The supervisor grabbed the telephone and swore quietly.

*

The glass main entrance doors to Heathrow control tower faced towards the central area bus station. Across the road from the tower, WPC Eileen Hamilton stood among the passengers mingling around the bus station. She was watching the control tower entrance, casually observing the staff and visitors arriving at that early hour. She knew about controllers being transferred from West Drayton and she knew that car parking space was at a premium, but the controllers could not be allowed to clutter up the main road with their vehicles. She toyed with her radio communicator and then paced up to the next coach loading bay. She walked quickly to help keep warm. An early tea break would have served even better.

Maintenance work had been going on at the control tower building for some weeks, and WPC Hamilton showed no surprise when a contractor's van pulled up at the entrance. It was an old green Ford Transit, rather rusty and with a somewhat noisy exhaust. The name, McBINNS — BUILDING MAINTENANCE, was painted across the side in big white letters. The young policewoman screwed up her eyes and reached for her notebook. The van was illegally halted on the busy road outside the control tower building, obstructing the flow of traffic.

WPC Hamilton had seen it happen before, especially when visitors were taken to the control tower, but it was still illegal. It was also a chance for her to exercise a degree of police authority.

She began to walk towards the van just as eight men in white overalls climbed out through the rear door. Each had the name McBINNS printed in large black letters across the back of his overalls. While the workmen gathered themselves into some semblance of activity, the driver remained inside with the engine running.

Eileen Hamilton quickened her pace, hoping the driver would not move on before he could be cautioned for his offence. She paused and cursed the busy traffic that brought her to a halt at the kerbside. The men opposite pulled a number of large, seemingly heavy tool kits from the back of the van and slammed the doors. One man banged the rear of the van and it moved away into the traffic. With their tool kits strung between them, the men strode in through the glass entrance doors. It was all over in seconds, and the policewoman was left cursing her luck. She debated whether she should follow the men and give them a warning but, on balance, she decided against it. It was, she reflected, almost time for a tea break and her priorities were strongly weighted in favour of her comforts.

*

Hudson went up to the Visual Control Room to watch the British Atlantic 747 land safely. He'd seen many 747s land at Heathrow, but he hadn't jeopardised the safety of the others. It was only a small reassurance to see the wheels bang down on the runway, but better than nothing.

No one had been killed.

He hurried away from the control tower and reached the staff canteen by walking through Terminal Two and taking the connecting corridor to Terminal One at first floor level. He seated himself at a plastic-coated table, ignored the hubbub about him and slowly sipped from a mug of tepid coffee.

Life was just a pig, he told himself, and it wasn't showing signs of getting better. He was twenty-eight years old and already feeling worn beyond his years. It wasn't just the bomb. It wasn't just the stress of the job. Nor was it just the burden of a hefty mortgage, and a fast crumbling marriage. It was the cumulative effects of all of these things coming together in one amorphous mass.

"You want me to go away, don't you?" Michelle had said that morning, almost as if she half-understood the strain she was putting on him. "That's why you keep taking me to my mum's. You want rid of me, don't you? Well, I want rid of you as well, see!"

He had looked at her through tired eyes while shaking his head. What could he do?

"Mind if I join you?" A deep, resonant voice interrupted his thoughts. Hudson shook himself back into full consciousness and nodded.

"Bloody nuisance what happened at Drayton. Heard it on the car radio. Must have been a bad fire." Vince Trewin sat down directly opposite Hudson and planted his coffee mug loudly on the plastic surface. He was a tall, well-built man with a powerful presence that tended to overawe his juniors. In his early fifties, he had a square-cut jaw, sharp eyes, well-groomed greying hair and a broad chest. All the things women most admire in an older, experienced man, Hudson noted.

"It wasn't a fire," Hudson said quietly, glancing round to ensure no one was listening.

"Oh?" Trewin sipped at his coffee.

"It was a bomb. Probably the Provisional IRA."

Trewin jerked back in his seat. "Bloody hell! Any casualties?"

"Of course. Get yourself on duty and the watch manager will tell you all about it. But for God's sake keep it under your hat. It's not public knowledge."

"Dead?"

"Fourteen."

"Bugger!" Trewin drew a deep breath. "If things are that bad, why aren't you on duty, Simon?"

"I had an airmiss," Hudson said soulfully. He compressed his lips and waited for a sympathetic response. "Now go away and leave me alone."

"How close did they get?" Trewin leaned forward in his seat, his brown leather bomber jacket swinging open.

"Bloody close. They would have hit if one of them hadn't taken avoiding action."

"Nasty." Trewin chewed at his lower lip. "But you got away with it."

"Hell's teeth, Vince! I got two aircraft so close they might have collided. I could have wiped out seven or eight hundred people in one go."

"Plus the ones on the ground," Trewin shot back. "Just pull yourself together and thank God they didn't actually collide."

"But they might have done!"

"Yes. They might have done." Trewin rubbed his chin thoughtfully. "One day they will. But the chances are it'll happen to the other guy." He finished his coffee in one go and braced himself to leave. "In the meantime there's an emergency at Drayton. I'd better get over to the tower. I take it you've been suspended?"

"Of course I've been suspended. But the chances are that I'll have to help out. They can always find something for me to do."

"Seems likely. Anyway, I always thought it best to get a controller back into doing the job as quick as possible after an incident. Helps get the confidence back on line. You coming, then?"

Hudson nodded. What was the point of brooding here? And what was the point in continuing with the argument? Shouting at Vince Trewin was not going to help.

"Come on then." Trewin stood up. "Fourteen dead, you say?"

Hudson rose slowly. "Life's a pig, isn't it?"

*

The watch supervisor raised a hand towards the watch manager as the older man emerged from an office at the rear of Heathrow's emergency control room.

"Over here, Frank." Standing beside his desk, the supervisor steeled himself for a difficult conversation.

The watch manager's onerous responsibility — he was the most senior person on duty — was emphasised by his white hair and deep-set blue eyes. He was the second person to be contacted by the watch supervisor. The first was Hudson's relief, an instructor hastily summoned down from the Heathrow training section.

"I've sent Hudson over to the canteen for a coffee to calm him down. This is as much as I can tell you for the moment." As he spoke, the supervisor pointed to the preliminary details written in the watch logbook. He kept his voice low, almost secretive. His head was bent towards the desk top when the door to the control room burst open.

"Don't anyone move!"

Two men in white overalls erupted into the room, each brandishing an Armalite rifle. The supervisor swung round, stunned by the intrusion. Beside him, the watch manager's gaze flicked upwards, but his body remained bent over the desk.

"I said don't anyone move!" one of the attackers bawled in a thick Irish accent. He aimed his gun round the room so that it menaced each of the occupants in turn. The second attacker moved across to a position directly behind the three controllers who were directing Heathrow arrivals.

"What the hell is the meaning of this?" The watch manager straightened up and began to move directly towards one of the intruders. His hand came up in a defiant gesture. He was almost close enough to touch the gunman's weapon, feel the coldness of the steel before it could grow suddenly hot, but he never knew the reaction which his movement caused.

The Armalite roared once with a shattering bark that reverberated round the dark room. A red stain leaped across the watch manager's shirt, he clutched at his chest, and then fell to the floor. In the tense moment that followed, a young female assistant clasped her hands to her mouth and cried out with a short, high-pitched squeal.

"I said no one is to move!" the first attacker shouted. "And I meant *no one.*"

He was a thick-set man. His black eyebrows met at the bridge of his nose and his skin was unusually florid. Drops of perspiration lay on his lower lip and around his mouth. One large sweaty drop rolled down his chin as he spoke.

The supervisor scanned round the room. The controllers were visibly shaken. Their gazes flittered over the crumpled figure spread-eagled on the floor. No one spoke for some seconds and the faint sound of a pilot's radio transmission could be heard echoing from one of the headsets. The controllers hesitated, wondering, shivering. Then, reacting to the calls they were receiving from arriving aircraft, they each in turn bent their heads back towards their radar displays. Regardless of what was happening around them, they had a duty towards the lives of the hundreds of people flying towards Heathrow.

"Who the hell are you?" The supervisor caught a grip on his tense emotions and took a single step towards the Irish gunman. His voice quavered. "And what exactly do you want here?"

"Get back and shut up!"

The supervisor stopped, looked down at the lifeless body on the floor and drew in a deep breath.

"No one is to say a word to anyone about what's happening here, and keep your hands well clear of your telephones." The gunman waved his weapon in a wide arc as an added reminder of the consequences. "Just continue controlling aeroplanes as normal. We'll be listening to you. And ignore any phone calls."

"We can't ignore phone calls—" the supervisor began.

"I said ignore all phone calls! And don't say a word to any pilot about what's goin' on here."

The effect was incongruous. The controllers sat at their brightly polished hardwood ATC consoles while the attackers menaced them with ugly guns, and the dead body lay on the floor, splattered with blood. The combination seemed to have its intended effect.

"What exactly are you trying to do?" The sharp question came from the London City Airport radar controller. Seated back-to-back with the Heathrow radar controllers, his face was set into a hard expression of anger. "Why are you doing this?"

"You'll find out in time."

The second attacker moved closer to the Heathrow radar controllers and peered at each of the screens in turn. He was a smaller man, more wiry in appearance, with a thin, pinched face. After studying the screens, he looked down at the flight progress strips, the printed paper *aides-memoire* displayed in front of each controller. He picked up one of the strips, gave a short grunt of satisfaction. "It's here, Paddy! It's due in a few minutes." His was a harsher, crueller accent.

The one he called Paddy allowed a satisfied grin to wipe across his thick lips. He swung his Armalite towards the Heathrow controllers. "Just you do whatever my friend tells you. And no tricks now, do you hear?" As he spoke, he began to swing back towards the London City and Thames Radar controllers.

"And the same goes for you—" As he completed his turn, an ugly look erupted across his face.

The London City Radar controller's hand was outstretched towards his telephone. Now it hung in mid-air, caught in the act, while his face displayed his guilty intentions. The thick lips curled again and the sweat rolled down the Irishman's cheeks.

"I told you—" Again the Armalite barked. Once, and the City Radar controller fell, a spurt of blood flying out from his shirt. Twice, and the Thames Radar controller alongside him crumpled down, a look of incredulous surprise set firmly and finally on his face.

"For God's sake! Stop it!" The supervisor moved suddenly towards the big gunman, too quickly to consider the effect of his action. He threw out a hand in the direction of the Armalite, his hand actually touching the barrel before it erupted directly into his face.

*

Daylight had settled over the ground, but many of the vehicles pouring into Heathrow central area still had their headlights blazing. Hudson thought he heard the sound of a car backfiring as he and Trewin left Terminal Two and crossed the road to the control tower main entrance. He shrugged. His own problems far outweighed any considerations of other people's motor car troubles, so he ignored it.

Trewin muttered under his breath. "I suppose West Drayton will be classed as another big news item. The press like to get their teeth into things they don't really understand."

Hudson frowned. A car backfiring could be ignored, but his instinct could not. As they entered the control tower building, he sensed that something was very wrong. Where were the security guards? The door should never be left unguarded, especially not now, not when they were in a state of heightened alert. Where were the receptionists? Of all the airport control towers in the United Kingdom, none was more closed to outside access than Heathrow, none was more tightly guarded, so why was it now totally open to intruders? He glanced back at Trewin who hesitated with one hand still at the glass door.

"What's wrong, Simon?"

"There's no one on duty."

"They must have gone to the loo."

"*All* of them? At the same time?"

Hudson walked towards the lift opposite the reception desk and stopped suddenly. In a dark shadowy corner, behind a screen that hid the lift doors from the main entrance doors, a figure in overalls was bending over a tool bag. In one hand he clutched an automatic rifle.

The man looked up, startled, and he swung the weapon round towards the two controllers.

"Don't move!" The man's voice was high-pitched, frightened, with a broad Northern Irish accent. He swept his gaze around to where Trewin stood at the security guard's desk.

"You! Come over here!" he snapped. His hand came out of the tool bag with a printed sign grasped in his fingers.

"Who are you?" Hudson asked, his throat constricted by a clammy fear. He had a sudden flash thought, mentally conjuring up a gory image of death and destruction in the Terminal Area Control room half a mile away at West Drayton.

The man ignored him and threw the sign at Trewin. "Hang that on the door!" he ordered.

Hudson blinked as his eyes focussed on the sign. It read, 'STRICTLY NO ENTRY — BUILDING WORK IN PROGRESS'. He looked again at the automatic rifle and crossed his fingers, hoping that Trewin would not start any heroics.

Trewin seemed to study the situation for some seconds before he breathed deeply and hung the sign at the entrance. At the same time an older man stepped out from a ground floor corridor dressed as a security guard.

The man spoke loudly with an alarmed note in his voice. "Who the hell are these two?"

The overalled gunman shrugged. "They just walked in."

"Shite! You'd better take them down the corridor to Paddy."

"That's what I had in mind."

With his gaze darting from side to side, the gunman waved his rifle at the two controllers. "Walk slowly in front of me!" he ordered.

He led them down a corridor to the right of the entrance lobby, in the direction of the emergency control room. Hudson noted that he appeared to have an uncanny knowledge of where he was going. When they reached the dimly lit radar room, he pushed the two controllers inside, ahead of him.

Hudson gasped at the scene. The watch manager's body lay sprawled on the floor, and the remains of the supervisor's body lay in a bloody heap beside his desk. In the darkness behind the London City Radar console, the bodies of two more controllers were bundled in a sickening heap. And, all the while amidst the mayhem, the remaining controllers continued to direct their never-ending air traffic patterns.

The gunman who had brought Hudson and Trewin into the

room went straight to another armed man leaning against the supervisor's desk. After a brief conversation, this dark and hard-looking man snorted and pointed a finger at Hudson.

"You! Who are you?" His voice was cold and harsh.

"We're controllers. We work here." Hudson's voice came out choked.

"Where did you come from?"

"We were in the staff canteen—"

"All right." The man's eyes seemed to go dim for a moment. A few moments passed before he swung his finger round to the London City Radar console. "Get over there and make sure the radar is still working properly."

Hudson hesitated and then did as he was commanded. You don't argue with a gun, he decided.

The gunman's face twisted into a snarl as he pointed at Trewin and snapped, "You! Take over the supervisor's desk. If the desk phone rings, don't answer it unless I say so."

"And will you tell me what this is all about?" Trewin asked.

The large Irishman sniffed. His voice held a tone of sadistic pleasure. "You'll soon find out what it's all about, mister. You'll soon find out."

Chapter 5

Patrick Toome glanced at his watch and gave a short grunt of satisfaction. It was 0802 GMT and everything was going exactly to plan. Now the whole operation largely hinged on the second active service unit at London City Airport. And the aircraft from Knock.

"Keep an eye on things here!" he snapped brusquely at the gunman who had ushered in the two extra controllers. It was an act, but he figured it helped if he kept up a brutish appearance. "I'm going to check upstairs."

He forced himself to scan slowly round the scene before he walked away. It would take only one minor slip to ruin the whole operation, and too much was at stake to permit any cock-ups. If anything went wrong here, the repercussions would extend far beyond the influence of the IRA. Much too far, he thought, but then he wasn't running the whole show, just one vital part of it. He nodded to Joe Dillon as he walked away. Joe's Belfast tenement background made him a genuine hard man, not like the act Toome was forced into playing. Joe Dillon's aggro was for real.

An air of calm hung over the corridor outside the control room. Mickey Kearney, who had done time in Long Kesh, kept watch from the reception desk in the entrance foyer. He now wore a security guard uniform. Toome nodded silently towards him and then continued on along the corridor. Another man stood guard outside a telecommunications equipment room, his Armalite raised and resting against his shoulder. The door was slightly ajar and Toome glanced inside to where an anxious mass of bodies was huddled. A further armed man stood just inside the door, toting an M16 which he jerked about spasmodically, menacing the hostages. The capture of all those people had gone too easily. Toome couldn't believe their good fortune.

How obliging the local management had been to install a public address system throughout the control tower building. How thoughtful of them to place loudspeakers on the wall of every office and every workshop. It had been so easy to use that system to summon the non-operational staff here to this equipment room. Every member of the control tower staff not actively engaged in air traffic control — clerks, typists, engineers, managers — had obeyed the security call. They did it because they had been taught by their managers to do as they were told. Like a load of mindless sheep. Now it only needed a minimum of effort from two armed men to keep them under guard.

"Everything all right here?" Toome asked.

"Nay bother," the nearest man replied. He sounded a shade too confident, Toome noted.

"Keep on your toes. The alarm hasn't gone up yet. I mean the *real* alarm."

Toome continued on along the corridor and through a room containing long rows of staff lockers. He went on, through a set of fire doors, until he came into the rear entrance lobby. This was also the entrance to the airport flight briefing unit, situated in an adjacent room. Another man, still wearing his McBINNS overalls was crouched at the glass doors.

"All set here?" Toome asked.

The man half-turned. "The grenades are all in place now, Paddy. This is the last one." He rose to his feet and gestured towards a device taped to the door handles. A chain was looped through the handles and firmly secured with a clasp lock. "If they try to break the chain, they'll go up instantly. Kentucky Fried Brits."

"Good. Stay with it."

The man nodded and walked to the rear of the lobby where he retrieved his Armalite rifle.

*

Hudson stared at the Thames Radar screen and fought down an urge to shout, "This is *not* my job!"

Hell! His rightful place was in the Terminal Area Control room at West Drayton. His job was to direct aircraft approaching Heathrow, not London City Airport. He had no experience of Thames Radar or London City Radar, and little knowledge of the City Airport procedures. It was a different type of airspace, with different rules and regulations; in fact, it was a whole new ball game, one which he had not been taught to play. Besides, the Thames Radar controller also handled aircraft into Biggin Hill and Battersea Heliport and he hadn't been taught to carry out those tasks, either.

He suppressed his momentary anger and bent his head towards the display. He had to make some sort of sense out of the radar picture, one way or another. Preferably without killing anyone.

He ran a nervous hand through his short brown hair and glanced at the London City Radar display alongside him. There should have been another controller sitting in front of the display, waiting to sequence aircraft onto final approach at the docklands airport. But the seat was empty and the radar screen was now unusable, smeared with a large red bloodstain like a gruesome Rorschach test. Everything would have to be done from the Thames Radar screen.

This is not real, Hudson told himself. Any minute now I'll wake up from this nightmare. Why are we still shifting the traffic? Doesn't anyone know that Heathrow tower is under terrorist control? Doesn't anyone have the wit to stop the traffic flow?

The smaller gunman, standing between Hudson and the Heathrow controllers, waved his Armalite in a vague show of aggression. The Irish terrorist called Paddy had disappeared earlier, but he was now back in the room, standing beside Trewin at the supervisor's desk. There were no other gunmen in the room, but Hudson was certain there would be others posted at strategic points around the building. Without doubt, one would be upstairs in the Visual Control Room and another would probably be along the corridor in the telecommunications centre. He had no idea how many others were involved, or where they might be.

He gave the radio-telephone transmit switch a tentative jiggle and heard the telltale glitch of carrier wave sound in his headset. At least the radio was working. Perhaps he could get a message to someone... anyone. The telephone buzzer interrupted his thoughts and brought him back into the reality of his waking nightmare. He looked enquiringly at the gunman and pointed to the buzzing line. The terrorist nodded in return. This was one telephone call he could answer.

Hudson selected the line and said, "Yes?"

"There's going to be a diversion." It was the voice of the training officer sitting only a few feet away, the man who had been brought in after the airmiss. Hudson thought he detected a distinct tone of annoyance in the instructor's voice. But for that airmiss, he might now be somewhere else... maybe in the staff canteen across the road.

"You'd better give me the details," Hudson replied and reached for a blank flight progress strip. Out of the corner of his eye he saw the man called Paddy walking towards him.

"He's calling himself *Nemesis*," the controller began.

"Who is?"

"The diversion."

"*Nemesis*? Never heard of it." Hudson snapped as he jotted the word onto the strip. "Who the hell is *Nemesis*?"

"Dunno. But that's what he's calling himself. He was flight-planned as plain Golf India Romeo, but when he came on my frequency he changed his callsign. Don't ask me why. According to the strip, he came from Knock and he was inbound to Biggin Hill. For what it's worth, our murderous friends here know all about him."

"Do they indeed? And what type of aircraft is it?" Hudson flinched as he detected the presence of a rifle barrel close alongside him.

"An F27, so it says here."

"Can they take an F27 into City Airport?"

"Our friends with the guns think they can."

"Oh, yes? You'd better tell me the rest." Hudson lapsed into an air of resigned acceptance. Who was he to argue with dedicated terrorists? "What's his ETA?"

"His estimate for the field is 0853."

Hudson wrote the information onto the flight progress strip and then asked, "Knock? I've heard of it, but where the hell is it?"

"Connemara. Somewhere out in the bogs of Ireland, I think."

"Why wasn't it flight-planned into London City?"

"Would you flight-plan an unknown F27 calling himself *Nemesis* into London City? If you didn't want to arouse suspicion?"

"Suppose not." Hudson knew that landing slots at the City Airport were strictly regulated and a one-off F27 flight would be unlikely to be accepted without investigation.

"One more thing, Simon."

"Yes."

"Next time you have an airmiss, don't expect me to help."

The Heathrow controller rang off and Hudson flinched. He deserved that. He glanced around at the leering face of the Irish terrorist leader and noted with detached calm how cruel the man looked, so cruel that it could almost be an act. He wondered what sort of mentality made the man resort to indiscriminate killing. It scared the hell out of him.

"There's going to be a diversion," he said levelly. "I'll have to warn them at City Airport. They won't be expecting this aircraft."

"Not yet." The man jiggled his gun as he spoke. "I'll tell you when to phone them. And I'll tell you what to say."

Hudson shrugged his shoulders. "What happens then?" he asked.

"Just keep your mouth shut until I tell you to speak."

Hudson lapsed into silence.

At 0845 GMT, the training officer rang again to hand over the diversion aircraft. It was a set procedure for aircraft arriving at London City.

"He's on a bearing from Ockham one eight zero degrees, range fifteen miles. Altitude five thousand feet. Heading zero eight five degrees."

"I have radar contact," Hudson confirmed. "Tell him to call Thames Radar on one three two decimal seven."

"Can you handle it, Simon?"

"Do I have any choice?"

"Suppose not."

Hudson was about to do a job for which he was untrained, unqualified and unsure, with the added problem of an Armalite rifle close to his head. He gave the man called Paddy a quizzical look. The Irishman grunted in return, pulled a piece of paper from his pocket and set it down at the front of the radar console.

"You can phone the controller at City Airport now. And make sure you read this exactly as it's written."

Hudson digested the words on the paper. This was getting to be a bit of a bugger all round. He compressed his lips tightly and selected the telephone switch.

"Yes?" Hudson recognised the voice. His name was Charlie Kent.

"I have an inbound emergency diversion," Hudson began, reading precisely from the script.

"Emergency! Hang on!" Kent's voice exploded down the line. Hudson guessed the reason. Kent had caused a serious airmiss at Gatwick. He had cracked up and been posted to London City for a rest. Hudson felt no sympathy for him.

"The callsign is *Nemesis*," Hudson continued. "The aircraft is an F27 and it has problems with both engines. It will land in approximately ten minutes from now."

"Christ!" Kent responded. "Who the hell is *Nemesis*?"

Hudson rang off without answering. There was no point in trying to explain to Charlie Kent, even if he had the option. He half-turned to the Irishman who nodded to him.

"You'll be getting an important message back from City Airport shortly," Paddy said, looking at his watch. "You're to tell me as soon as they call you."

Hudson returned his attention to the radar screen as he heard the opening call from the aircraft.

"Thames Radar, this is *Nemesis*." The pilot's voice had the Irish lilt he expected. Could almost have been the voice of a television game show host. Stupid idea.

"*Nemesis*, this is Thames Radar. Continue heading zero eight five and descend to three thousand feet on QNH one zero one two."

Hudson thought it was a reasonable heading and altitude, but it was only guesswork. The difficult bit would be the turn onto final approach when the aircraft would have to be lined up with the runway. The City Radar controller should have done that part of the job, but he was dead. Hudson felt a twinge of tension constricting his chest.

"*Nemesis*, have you flown into London City Airport before?" he asked.

"Negative."

"Roger. The ILS is set for a seven-and-a-half-degree glide path. Can you accept that sort of steep approach?" It suddenly occurred to him that perhaps it was rather a foolish question to ask of an F27 pilot who had never before flown into the docklands airport. He then wondered whether seven and a half degrees in an aged Friendship was such a good idea, even if the pilot had been there before.

"I'd rather not try it," the pilot responded to the question with a calm tone, almost as if he was talking to ATC in a normal traffic situation. "Can you give me a three degree approach?"

"There is no ILS set at three degrees," Hudson replied.

"Roger, in that case I'll take an SRA."

"Oh, damn!" The word slipped out from Hudson before he remembered that there was an Armalite close by. He had no experience of giving Surveillance Radar Approaches into London City. He knew the theory of it and he would do his best to play it off the cuff, but it was not a technique he relished. It occurred to him that the F27 pilot was possibly as unprepared for this procedure as he was.

*

The control tower at London City Airport was built to overlook the King George V dock, like a giant fruit bowl at one corner of a box-shaped terminal building. Inside the glasshouse structure, two air traffic controllers looked out over the dockland scene. It was their job to control aircraft landing and taking off.

Charlie Kent, the support controller, trembled as he stared ahead through the big windows at the dockside runway. Peter Elliot, the executive controller, noticed the obvious signs of stress in his colleague and he leaned towards him with concern.

"Trouble, Charlie?"

"An emergency diversion. An F27 with engine trouble." Kent spoke slowly, hesitantly. Fear was oozing out of him and there was seemingly nothing Kent could do to hide it.

"Okay, Charlie. Keep calm."

"Look, maybe I should go downstairs and tell the boss..." Kent spoke hesitantly, as if searching his mind for some means of extricating himself completely from the control room. The look on his face was unrestrained, it showed Elliot that all Kent wanted was to get out of the VCR as quickly as possible.

"Phone her," Elliot suggested.

"No... no, I'll pop down to her office."

"Okay, Charlie. You pop down and fetch the boss." Despite the probability of an emergency, Elliot was glad of the excuse to get Kent out of the room for a while. The man was a liability. He was also relieved by the suggestion of having the boss there to help him. She was a good controller.

*

Helen Mayfield had the West Drayton bomb firmly in her mind that morning. Any emergency in Terminal Area Control would affect the job at all the London airports, but this one was a real humdinger.

She was sitting in her office with an array of papers spread out on her desk. As the ATC Executive Officer at London City Airport, it was her job to deal with operational and administrative matters, which was why she sometimes wished she had stayed on the shop floor as a working controller. After all, she had joined the air traffic control service to control aeroplanes, not to shuffle wads of paper around a desk. However, no one got to the top just by controlling aeroplanes, and Helen intended to get all the way to the top.

She was young to be an Executive Office — thirty-two in a couple of months — but she was ambitious and determined. There were so many things she wanted out of life, so many goals she aimed to score. It was not that she regarded being the wife of a senior airline pilot as in any way a minor part of her life, nor did she underrate the maternal pride which she felt for her daughter, Judith. It was simply that she felt capable of more, substantially different achievements.

A sudden thought caused a ripple to cross her face as she wiped her hands back through her long blonde hair. It would be Judith's sixth birthday tomorrow. There would be a party for her young friends, a birthday cake, candles, presents...

She sat up with a start and glanced at her watch, remembering that she had promised to pick up the present this morning. Maybe she could telephone the shop and get them to deliver the gleaming new bicycle she had chosen. She pushed the rest of the routine papers into a neat pile and reached for the telephone.

Helen's hand was halfway to the receiver when the office door burst open with no warning. Charlie Kent stood in the entrance, grasping the handle tightly.

"We've got problems upstairs, Helen." he said tersely. "An aircraft diverting in with engine trouble." He stood, white-faced and panting heavily.

Helen's immediate impression was of a man with no remaining composure, a man who had flipped. It was no consolation that she had expected something like this sooner or later. If anyone was going to flip, it was always going to be Charlie Kent.

"Who's up there?" Helen jumped up and strode purposefully towards the door.

"Peter Elliot."

"Who else?"

"No one."

Helen stopped dead. "You mean you left him alone in the VCR?"

"I thought I should come and tell you." Kent averted his gaze from Helen's accusing frown.

She resumed her fast pace out of the office. She would deal with Kent later. Should have done so before now. Damn!

The sound of voices coming from the VCR puzzled Helen. She hurriedly climbed up the steps into the control room with troubled thoughts in her mind. Straightaway, she saw two men standing behind Peter Elliot, two men who should not have been in the room.

"What's going on—" she began.

She took in the name McBINNS on the back of their white overalls. They had been looking out onto the landing strip, but one of them turned abruptly to face her. The move brought his automatic rifle into sudden view. Helen stopped, horrified. She heard a scuffling noise behind her as Kent stumbled up the stairs, tripped and swore loudly.

"Oh, bloody hell!" He had not seen the intruders and was cursing his own clumsiness. The stupid man had knocked his shin.

*

Hudson was giving the F27 pilot instructions to turn onto the final approach path when the telephone line to the City Airport buzzed.

"I have a message for you," the voice from the other end said. "You're to pass it on to the IRA brigade leader over there at Heathrow. The message is: the men here are in position and Operation *Nemesis* is on time."

Hudson looked up at the man called Paddy. "It's the message you were expecting. They say the men at City Airport are in position and... and Operation *Nemesis* is on time."

The man looked satisfied. "Good. Tell them we're exactly on schedule here."

Hudson repeated the message and then rang off. The purpose of the messages puzzled him, but he hurriedly pushed his fears aside in order to cope with the more immediate problem. The F27 was far too low for the published approach path to London City Airport. The pilot of the old turbo-prop aircraft was not happy with the steep seven-and-a-half-degree glide path into the dock-lands airport, he wanted a more sedate three degree angle. Hudson reflected ruefully that the noise of the aircraft coming in so low would be certain to annoy a few people in the vicinity of the docks. To add to the problem, Hudson would have to talk him down the approach path with advisory heights. He cast his mind back, trying to recall the heights for a three-degree approach. Three thousand and fifty feet at ten miles from touchdown, and then... He would have to calculate the rest as he went. This was getting too far out of hand, no job for someone who had just caused an airmiss. Hell, hadn't he suffered enough for one day without this?

"I won't be able to guide him all the way down," he said to the Irishman beside him. "He'll drop out of the bottom of my radar cover sooner than usual because of his shallow approach angle."

Paddy redirected his Armalite towards Hudson's head. "Just make sure he gets down safely. Or else."

*

Helen Mayfield looked up at the intruder who appeared to be the leader and she felt spasms of alarm shiver through her body. He had dark, almost hypnotic eyes that blazed at her from beneath a heavily creased forehead. His mouth was large — permanently half-open to reveal blackened teeth — with a pronounced down-ward curve at each corner.

"Why are you here?" she asked and was surprised at the clar-ity of her own voice. She wondered if he would notice her visible signs of fear, a fear which was bringing the taste of bile to her throat.

"Be quiet!" The Armalite swung round until it prodded against her chest. The man's voice was as hard and cold as ice with a strong Geordie accent. "Get over there in the corner, and keep your mouth shut."

Helen stepped back.

The arriving aircraft had transferred to the aerodrome control frequency and she heard Peter Elliot passing a landing clearance. Helen looked out along the approach path to runway two-eight. At first she saw nothing because she was looking too high, her eyes focussed on the area of sky in which landing aircraft would normally appear. But this aircraft was not making the steep approach stipulated for landing at London City; it was coming in low. She finally saw it at only two miles from touchdown.

It was the unmistakable outline of an aged F27, a venerable old workhorse designed and built by the Dutch Fokker company back in the 1960s. Why all this bother just to get an aged aeroplane into City Airport?

The F27 continued its low and slow approach before seeming to waddle onto the runway like a very rheumaticky old lady. For all the drama of the moment, Helen was impressed by the way the pilot put his elderly charge down onto the concrete, easing the undercarriage into contact with the ground with precision. With her engines whining, the old lady ambled on down the runway and turned in towards the apron.

But no one had yet said why the F27 was there.

*

These people, Hudson decided, were for real. They were not the sort of small-time crooks habitually recruited into terrorist ranks. They were not the petty, sometimes amateur, psychopathic criminals who had bombed and bungled their way through Irish politics for thirty years. Neither were they brainwashed young-sters from the backstreets of Belfast. These people killed for more than just warped convictions. So why, he reasoned, did none of them wear masks? Why were they unworried about being identified? It didn't make sense.

Hudson studied the one called Paddy. Outwardly, he gave the appearance of being a hard man, the sort who would kill without a moment's hesitation, nor a moment's regret: a man for whom human life was a cheap commodity, easily thrown away. His was the appearance of a professional international terrorist, if the appearance was to be believed. But Hudson wondered whether there was something deeper behind that outer veneer. His instincts told him there was.

Glancing across the room at the second man, Hudson guessed that he was a professional in the field of aviation. He seemed to understand air traffic control and he knew what he was looking for as he peered at the radar screens. He was the one who listened intently to what the controllers said to the incoming pilots, ensuring no one passed on information about the hijacking of the control tower. Hudson felt even more uneasy about him than about Paddy, probably because of the appearance of dedicated professionalism in the way he worked. The wiry little man was bent forward now, pointing to something on one of the radar screens.

Hudson drew in a deep breath. He had a good idea what the man was pointing at and the thought sent a tremor through his spine. He should have guessed straightaway. The flight was probably just coming into Heathrow radar cover and a cold sweat broke out across his brow. These people really did mean business.

He looked back at his own radar display. *Nemesis* was now well below London City Radar cover, maybe it was already on the ground at London City. *Nemesis*? What the hell did it mean? He had no idea, but he knew now which aircraft was taking the terrorist's attention: it could only be *Kitty One*.

He leaned forward and stared at the upper part of his radar display. The radar echo should soon appear on the screen as the flight approached from the north. There it was! When he arrived at Heathrow that morning, he had seen the official notice about the Kitty flight — the usual details on routes and levels — but he had not bothered to read it as the flight was not scheduled to pass through his section of airspace.

Kitty was the callsign of all baggage aircraft of the Queen's Flight. This particular flight was carrying royal baggage for the royal family's return from a private visit to Balmoral. It was a BAe146 jet aircraft making its way from Inverness to Northolt. But what on earth did the IRA want with a royal aircraft?

Chapter 6

Sidney 'Squiffy' Quilley had not heard the news of the bomb when he arrived at West Drayton that morning. He was prepared for a normal morning watch in the Terminal Area Control room and was astounded to discover there had been a fire somewhere in the building. The military police were changing shift as he arrived at the main gate and, somehow, in the confusion of the changeover, someone goofed. One of the gate guards waved him into the complex. Worse than that, Squiffy had been allowed to make his way upstairs to the Terminal Area Control room. That was when he discovered the horror of the bomb.

The police had been removing debris, a team of officers dragging rubble and human remains from the room. Most of it was wrapped up in black plastic bags, but two policemen had been carrying out a gory mess inside clear polythene. Fourteen people died, they told him. He had run to the toilets and vomited. Then, still ashen-faced, he had made his way back to the reception area where they took him aside and told him about the contingency arrangements for relocating to the emergency control room at Heathrow.

"But you'd better stay here for now," they went on to tell him. "They've got as many people at Heathrow as they need at the moment. And we could do with your help here."

By the time he arrived in the En-route Area Control room, the engineers had reconfigured a radar suite for his use. It was an old flat-top Mediator suite, a leftover from an earlier age of Area Control. Squiffy sniffed to show his displeasure, but he readied himself to do what was required: a back-breaking shift peering down into an old Mediator horizontal screen.

"The old guy upstairs will have had a tough time this morning," Squiffy told the support controller alongside him.

"The General Manager?"

"No! *God*, you fool! Charlton Heston with a long grey beard, and wearing a white nightshirt."

"Oh." The support controller gave him a look of disapproval. "And holding a scythe?"

"No. That's the angel of death."

"Not funny in the circumstances."

Squiffy sniffed again and got on with the job.

It was getting close to the point where Squiffy could reasonably demand a tea break when something odd caught his attention. He stared at the small CCTV screen set into the vertical wall of his suite. The screen showed a close-up of the flight progress strips in use in the Heathrow radar room. The images were relayed across from the control tower to enable the West Drayton controllers to assess Heathrow's landing rate. By watching the information on those strips, Squiffy was able to sequence his oncoming air-craft into the Heathrow pattern without the need for telephone coordination.

He nudged the support controller and pointed to the right-hand end portion of one of the strips. The words TOWER HIJACKED were printed neatly in the space reserved for routine messages.

"Look at that, will you," he barked. "Bugger me. Either some-one's got a sick sense of humour. Or else... or else they've got a bloody serious problem at Heathrow."

*

Taff Windsor shifted uneasily in his seat in the Heathrow control room. He was a short, thick-set man with a large black moustache and a pronounced Welsh accent. There were two overpowering loves in his life: rugby football and the Welsh valleys. He wasn't too sure which he adored most.

On numerous occasions, Taff had seriously considered getting out of the London rat race and taking a less demanding job at one of the Welsh aerodromes. Cardiff perhaps? The idea rose, once again, to become uppermost in his mind when he heard about the

Terminal Area Control Room bomb. Was this the last straw? Time to get out?

The trouble was, the job of air traffic control at a small municipal airport would be far less interesting, and less well paid. Added to which, he felt a certain underlying sense of personal retreat each time he considered the idea. Once or twice in the past he had put out feelers, and once or twice he had tottered on the brink of a decision to move. But each time he had backed down. He was never totally sure why.

Now he felt aroused by something more serious than a rugby match at his favourite ground. The cause of it was the proximity of the Irishman who now stood between himself and the Number Two Radar Director.

"When I give you the order, you will read this to the pilot of the royal flight." The Irishman pushed a scrap of paper in front of Taff.

The Welshman read it and swore, "Bloody hell!"

"You'll say nothing until I tell you."

The Armalite barrel came to rest at Taff's shoulder. He needed no reminder that other controllers had already died here in the radar room. The words that were struggling to escape his lips were bottled up and swallowed.

Taff knew that he had good reason to keep calm, but he also knew that there was equally good reason to keep the terrorist's attention on him. While Taff had no intention of risking his own life, there was a chance he might be able to save someone else's. Alongside him, the adjacent controller sat at a slightly angled wing of the control suite. A small oasis of light bathed his flight progress strips. Video cameras, which were set into a canopy overhanging the suite, recorded all that he wrote on the strips and took the information away to the controllers at West Drayton. As long as the gunman was concentrating on Taff, he was less likely to notice a pertinent message on one of the strips.

Taff had noticed it some minutes before. His first reaction was to tell the other controller to get rid of that strip while he still had his life. Then, on reflection, he realised that the lives of everyone inside the tower could ultimately depend upon that sort of brave deed. He marvelled at the other controller's courage.

"You want me to read this out exactly as it is?" Taff queried.

The gunman nodded and his rifle shuddered. "When I tell you," he warned.

"The first thing they'll do is to check with the Royal Flight operations centre at Benson."

The Irishman sounded compulsive, his voice tinged with a sharp intensity. "Obviously. But the operations people will know nothing about it, and the pilot will do as you tell him. Wouldn't you?"

Taff nodded. He thought the pilot would undoubtedly follow the obvious suggestion.

"I suppose so," he conceded.

*

Helen Mayfield watched carefully as one of the terrorists swung his rifle in a wide curve round the London City Visual Control Room. The man seemed to be surveying the scene with some sense of satisfaction, as if the hijack operation was going well.

Helen looked down to where the F27 was parked on the apron, its propellers slowly rotating to rest. The fuselage was cheerlessly plain, a bare metal lower half and white painted upper, with a green cheat line down the side. It bore no company name, just the registration letters at the rear. For a forty-year-old aeroplane, it seemed to be in quite reasonable condition.

The propellers were almost stopped when the main hatch opened and two figures stepped out. Helen took a cautious step forward to better see what was happening. She noted that one figure was dressed in military combat uniform, but he walked with a lolloping gait that suggested he was not used to military discipline. He paused briefly and raised a hand to the tower. One of the gunmen in the VCR, the apparent leader, walked to the window and waved back. The second person to leave the aircraft — a much older, well-dressed man — cast sharp glances about him as he walked away. Seconds later, a squad of two dozen or more men in combat uniform filed out of the aircraft. Half of them ran in un-coordinated fashion towards the runway, the others made towards the terminal. The men who were now running onto the landing area spread out into two groups before they ran down the grass strips on either side of the runway.

Helen felt intermixed feelings of shock and wonder. She had no idea who the men out on the airport might be, nor why they had positioned themselves on the grass. The only certainty was that they planned something big.

"What happens now?" Peter Elliot had allowed his headset to slip down around his shoulders and leaned back in his seat in an apparently relaxed style. Outwardly, he presented a calm image, but Helen could see the little clues that told her he was inwardly as tense as the rest of them. She noted the tight grasp of his hand on the arm of the seat, a grip that revealed white knuckles. On top of that was the imperceptible quiver of his lip. They both told their story to the careful observer.

"You'll shortly be getting details of a diversion," the Geordie terrorist leader replied. "When the flight details come through, you're to tell me, and no one else. Got that?"

Elliot nodded and glanced back towards Helen. She grimaced in return.

"What happens then?" she asked.

"Shut up, woman." The man gave her a sharp look that spoke of deep feelings and harsh attitudes. The sort of look she had rarely before met face-to-face. It frightened her.

*

Peregrine Fraser-Murdoch gave orders for the bomb to be moved out of the F27, and then he took a moment to look around at the City Airport. It had been rundown dockland when he left the country. Things had been so different then. Poverty had been rampant here and the communist principles had seemed so obvi-ously right. Not perfect, no system of government was perfect, but it had seemed right. He had given away nuclear secrets to the Kremlin because the ideology appealed to him.

And now?

He looked around at the shiny new dockland scene and wondered if he had been mistaken. He felt a twitch begin to invade his face and he reached up a hand to steady his unsteady nerves. No, of course he had not been mistaken. The glossy veneer of democracy that lay over London was not the answer.

Neither was Yeltsin's loosening of the communist ideal.

Something dramatic had to be done if the Russian Federation was to regain a position of military power. His hawkish friends in Russian Intelligence knew that as well as he did. Why else had they spirited him away from that hospital? Why else had they smuggled him out of Russia? Why else had they found the bomb and put it in his hands?

The answer was clear. He had been right about communism all along. And he would be right in bringing down this decadent democratic veneer. More than that: he would be right in giving the hawks in the Kremlin the upper hand.

It had to be him, of course. Burgess, Maclean and Philby died in the Soviet Union. Blunt died in Britain in 1983 after he had been turned by MI5. Murdoch shook his head sadly. Who else could his friends in the SVR turn to?

This operation had to be headed by an Englishman and carried out by Irishmen if it was to succeed. The rest of the world had to believe that any British or American retaliation against Russia was unjustified. When the war began, as it surely would, Moscow had to be able to claim righteous indignation.

Yes, there was only one Englishman the SVR hawks could turn to when they visualised this operation, and that man was Peregrine Fraser-Murdoch.

What happened to him when he returned to Moscow was irrelevant. Thrown back into the hospital, or put in front of a firing squad. It didn't matter. By then his actions would have changed the world forever.

*

In the En-route Control Room at West Drayton, Squiffy Quilley shook his head and looked around, worried. The hijack message, which was still displayed on the television monitor screen, was both alarming and puzzling. The support controller's telephone call to Heathrow was even stranger.

Squiffy's first inclination had been to believe that someone really was playing a joke; the whole thing had that unreal edge to it. It just couldn't be genuine, he tried to tell himself, not after the horror of last night. In any case, he mistrusted the standard ATC sense of humour because he understood the reason for controllers' jokes. Air traffic controllers led such an intense life of stress that they were prone to silly jests just to relieve the pressure. The people at Heathrow now had one hell of a lot of pressure on their shoulders.

"Are you sure the guy over there said everything's in order?" he questioned the support controller.

"Absolutely. All tickety-boo, according to him. Mind you, he did sound a bit miserable."

"Who did you speak to?"

"Didn't recognise the voice."

"This has got to be someone playing silly buggers," Squiffy murmured.

The support controller scratched at his chin. "Funny thing was, he seemed to be holding back on something. No idea what. He said he'd check it out, but it was the way he said it. It was as if... well, as if he was holding back on something important. You know what I mean?" The support controller leaned back expressively in his seat, crossed his arms and added, "I've got this nasty gut feeling about it, Squiffy."

Even as his support controller spoke, the realisation was dawning on Squiffy that there had to be more to it than a simple prank, just had to be. Suppose this was connected with last night's outrage? Oh my God!

His hand, which had been hovering over the switch to the

watch manager's telephone line, came down sharply.

"What do you think we ought to do about it?" he asked as he waited for the manager to respond.

The support controller looked up for a brief moment, scratched his head and gave a wry look. "That's for the boss to decide."

"Never come across one like this before. Have you?"

"No. Maybe it's just some stupid joker going out of his mind. It's the sort of thing a nutter would do."

"Maybe. But somehow I don't think so. Not this time." Squiffy banged again at the switch to the watch manager's telephone. "Come on... come on. Answer the phone, damn you." If this was only a bit of fun, someone's arse was about to get kicked. Bloody hard.

"Hello." The watch manager finally took the call.

"It may not be anything important," Squiffy said carefully. "All the same, I think you'd better come down here and have a look yourself. There's something really odd going on over at Heathrow."

*

Taff Windsor's hand was shaking as he held the scrap of paper in front of him. At first he couldn't understand why because he had never experienced the phenomenon before. After some minutes of analytical thought he decided that the chances seemed in favour of fear being the cause, or at least a major contributory factor. He realised, with some degree of personal shame, that he was actually afraid of the gunmen. Okay, so most people would be afraid of that sort of bastard, and most people would be willing to admit to the fear. But Taff Windsor was not most people. So why was he reacting so uncharacteristically? Dammit! Why was his hand shaking?

The Armalite rifle prodded him in the back and he compressed his lips.

"Now!" the voice behind the rifle barked.

Taff coughed to clear his throat, licked his lips which suddenly felt dry and sore, and began, "Kitty One, this is Heathrow Radar, do you read me?"

The words sounded hollow and unreal, not at all like his own voice.

"Go ahead Heathrow."

"Kitty One, this is Heathrow. We have just received a telephone message advising us that you have a bomb on board your aircraft. The bomb is set to detonate at 0930 Zulu. The time is now 0921. We suggest you divert immediately to the nearest airport. Please turn left heading one seven zero degrees on a direct track to London City. Acknowledge."

There was a short pause. Taff held his breath, waiting to see whether the pilot would take the bait. He hoped the pilot would have the wit to refuse the suggestion. It was only a very small hope.

"Heathrow, this is Kitty One. I am turning onto heading one seven zero degrees." Taff's tiny little hope crumbled and there was nothing left. "Have you any information on the location of the bomb?"

"Negative, Kitty One. Descend now to two thousand feet on the QNH. You have two zero track miles to run to touchdown. I suggest you keep your forward speed up." He felt angry. There was nothing he could do to prevent the pilot walking right into a trap. But what trap? And why?

"Roger. Wilco."

Taff selected the telephone to Thames Radar.

"What is it, Taffy?" Simon Hudson's voice answered.

"A diversion into City."

"All right. You'd better give me the details." Hudson sounded strangely unsurprised, almost as if he expected the diversion. Taff passed the flight details and noted Hudson's calm acknowledgement. Even the details of the bomb warning failed to elicit more than a slight rise in octave of his otherwise resigned voice. Did Hudson deserve more credit than the rest of the staff had previously allowed the younger man?

"Okay, Taffy. Bring him on down to one thousand feet and turn him right onto one nine zero degrees. Then put him over to me."

Taff read back the altitude and heading. Then he said, "Good luck, Simon."

He rang off and called the royal aircraft again. "Kitty One, this is Heathrow, continue descent to one thousand feet, and turn right heading one nine zero degrees."

The pilot responded with an air of doubt. "Roger Heathrow. Can you give us any information to help us locate the bomb?"

"Negative, Kitty One."

"We need more information, Heathrow," the pilot replied. "Our operations people have no information on this, none at all. At least tell us everything that was said in the warning message."

"Sorry, Kitty One. I can't tell you anything more at the moment. We've only just received the call."

"Well, who made the call? Did they identify themselves?"

"Negative. I've no information on that."

"Well, keep us advised. We're turning right now and leaving two thousand feet for one thousand."

"Roger." Taff breathed deeply and looked again at the paper in front of him. "Kitty One, how many people on board your aircraft?"

"We have four on board."

"Roger. Contact Thames Radar now on one three two decimal seven. They have all the details and will direct you onto final approach."

"Roger Heathrow."

Taff turned to the gunman. "There are four on board."

*

Dan Mayfield smiled, patted the bottom of a tall blonde stewardess, and picked up his leather case. He put a friendly arm about the girl's shoulder and gave her a gentle peck on the cheek.

"That's one for the road, love." He grinned and noticed the responding sparkle in her eyes.

Mayfield's mind was still taken with the past few days. He had enjoyed a pleasant stopover in the States. The weather had been bad, especially on the return flight, but the company had seen fit to roster Janice Wilkins among the crew, and that was all Mayfield needed in order to enjoy his trip.

Now, however, the party was over and he looked forward to getting home to see Helen and Judith. He had an expensive birthday present for Judith. It was probably too expensive, but he adored his daughter and enjoyed spoiling her. He continued to spoil her despite Helen's constant warnings that he was dangerously over-indulgent.

The babble of talk in the operations room centred upon the bomb at West Drayton, but Dan allowed it to wash over him. Helen would be miles away at London City Airport, safe and secure. And Janice Wilkins was only yards from him.

He stopped at the door and gave her one last grin. She looked desirable even after the long flight, striking jet-black hair, intense blue eyes and wide sensual lips glistening with pink lipstick. She gave him a quick smile in return. It was all she could allow while on the company premises, and was far less than she had given during the overnight stop in New York.

He took the shuttle bus to the long-term car park and recovered his bright blue Porsche. He was about to turn the ignition key when he heard Janice calling him.

"Dan," she shouted breathlessly as she ran across the tarmac towards him. "Dan, wait."

He released the key and leaned back in his seat. As she came closer, he heard her shout, "I've managed to change my roster. I'm now on the Miami run next week. One of the girls wanted to swap."

Mayfield grinned mischievously. He was already rostered for the Miami run and Janice knew it. He nodded to her to get into the car. "I hope you didn't do anything too obvious," he said.

"No, of course not. You know me."

Only too well, he thought. But he said nothing.

"No one suspects anything, Dan. I would soon get to hear about it if people were talking." She leaned across to him and wrapped her arms round his neck. "Honestly, darling, it's just our little secret."

Mayfield smiled and allowed himself the short pleasure of succumbing to the embrace. When their lips parted, he saw that she was glowing with satisfaction. There was also a look on her face that expressed relief that she had been able to grab that last moment of togetherness before he returned home to his wife.

"You'll be able to come and see me in a couple of days?" she asked softly. Her expression of childlike innocence — the gentle play of coyness that flittered around her mouth — tugged at his more rational intentions and made him nod in return.

"I'll call you tomorrow," he said. "I promise."

"What will Helen say?"

"Helen won't know. There'll be enough going on at home for me to get away for a while."

"Make it early. In the afternoon I want to pop down to Southampton to see my parents and spend a day or two with them."

He kissed her again and ran the palm of his hand gently across her breasts. "I must go." He gently eased himself loose from her grasp.

"You won't forget to call me early tomorrow." Her puckish face, dominated by her round pleading eyes, was angled towards him in such a way that he would have found it hard to refuse had he wanted to. For the moment he had no intention of refusing.

"I promise. We'll arrange to do something in a couple of days. Things always go flat after a while at home." He turned in his seat and reached for his seatbelt. It was his signal for her to leave.

"I'll miss you, you great hunk." She climbed out of the car and gave him one last smile before she slammed the door.

"Sure, you will."

As he drove away, he wondered why he had not met that smile until after he had married Helen. If he had to choose between the two women in his life, he wasn't too sure at that moment which way his decision would go.

*

Squiffy Quilley handed over control to his tea relief, pulled out his headset plug and ran down the length of the control room to the watch manager's desk. He was certain now that things were far more serious than he had at first believed. If he was right, someone had to act quickly to avert a major incident.

As he approached the manager's desk, a senior RAF officer ran into the control room from the direction of the RAF Distress and Diversion Cell. His face looked puffed and red. Senior RAF officers were even less prone to running than civilian controllers; it was a portent of a very weighty matter.

"It's the Royal Flight aircraft," Squiffy gasped, struggling for breath as he bumped up against the manager's desk. "It's been turned away towards London City!"

The watch manager looked up from a lengthy telephone conversation, paused with a puzzled look on his face, and then slammed the telephone back onto its cradle.

"What are the guys over at Heathrow doing?" he asked.

"They're not talking to us at the moment. At first they told us everything was in order. Then, a few minutes ago, I called them again and there was some guy on the supervisor's line talking gibberish. Don't know who he was. Now they're not even answering the phone. And that message I showed you on the television display is still there."

The RAF officer took up a stance beside the civilian watch manager and listened intently to Squiffy's report. "We think the Royal Flight aircraft is in trouble," he eventually interrupted. His voice was measured, almost pompous. "According to our operations people at Benson, Heathrow have told the crew they have a bomb on board. The pilot is diverting into London City Airport."

"Oh God. Not another bomb!" The watch manager's hand dived back towards the telephone on his desk. He selected the direct line to City Airport and listened for a response. There was none.

"Damn! They're not answering, either. What are your people doing about this?" he snapped at the military officer.

The officer was wrong-footed and hesitated before replying.

"We're trying to find out what's happening. I've got my people working on it as a matter of urgency."

"Well, I hope to God they know what they're doing. We need to find out what's going on."

"What exactly is—" the RAF man began.

"There's something very wrong here," the watch manager snapped as he selected another line. This was a direct link to the headquarters of the Civil Aviation Authority. He gritted his teeth as he waited for a reply.

Squiffy looked at the RAF officer and raised his eyebrows. "I have one hell of a nasty feeling about this. Very nasty!"

*

Peter Elliot watched intently. The British Aerospace 146 four-engine jet transport was specifically designed to get in and out of airfields with limited runway lengths, and it sold on the strength of its low level of noise disturbance. Once the runway at London City Airport was lengthened, it became a regular visitor there. But London City was a unique airport and the 146 had to operate under very strict conditions in order to land safely on the dockland site. In all probability, the pilot of the royal baggage aircraft was not briefed on those conditions; he would be concerned solely with getting on the ground as quickly as possible.

The aircraft, wearing its distinctive Queen's Flight livery, sank out of the cloud. Elliot checked the desk instruments in front of him and then he keyed his radio transmitter. "Kitty One, you are cleared to land. The wind is two five zero degrees at ten knots."

"Roger, Tower." The reply was terse. "We'll be evacuating the aircraft on the runway immediately after landing."

"Good luck," Elliot acknowledged.

The telephone line from Heathrow buzzed and Elliot answered it. He said, "Okay," to a short message and then turned to the gunman behind him. "There are four people on board the 146."

Without answering, the Geordie gunman pulled a walkie-talkie from his jacket pocket and strode to the front window of the control room. He keyed the transmitter and said, "Raider One."

"Go ahead."

"Four on board. Kill three. Not the pilot."

"Okay. Kill three. Not the pilot."

Elliot felt a nervous twitch rattle through his arm as the gunman walked back to a position behind him. He noted the cruel curve of the man's mouth and he registered the sour grin which was reflected in his face. Everything seemed to be happening according to their plan, even down to killing the crew of the 146.

"I should have the fire crew on a local standby," Elliot said.

"No. They stay at their fire station," the answer came back sharply.

Elliot shrugged his shoulders. He was powerless. There was nothing more he could do to help the crew of the 146. He glanced round to the rear of the VCR where Helen and Charlie Kent were standing under the menacing cover of the second gunman. Helen was biting her lip but, otherwise, she seemed remarkably calm. Kent, on the other hand, was visibly shaking like a leaf on a windy day. He held a lighted cigarette in one hand and took frequent, short drags.

The anemometer needle flickered as the wind gusted. Elliot reacted immediately by keying his transmit switch. "Wind-check. Two five zero degrees gusting to fifteen knots."

"Roger, Tower," answered the pilot.

A quick scan down the runway told Elliot that it was still clear for the landing aircraft. He wondered if the pilot could see the prone figures in the grass strips either side of the landing area. Each of the terrorists lay facing the runway with his rifle at combat readiness.

The aircraft was only a mile from touchdown, but it was too fast for the runway length and the speed brakes were only just coming out.

"Oh, God!" Kent's voice in the background caused Elliot to turn. Kent was trembling violently and his face was deathly white. The second terrorist had his rifle rammed tight against Kent's chest while he hissed, "Shut your bloody trap. You hear?"

The BAe146 was over the threshold, the pilot still trying to pull off the speed for a landing. On the grass area either side of the runway, the terrorists rose up from their prone position, and they edged closer to the tarmac. Elliot reached his hand towards the transmit switch, noticed the look of warning in the terrorist leader's face, and quickly retracted it.

"You say nothing more," the gunman hissed. "Nothing."

"For God's sake, Peter!" Kent's voice bellowed out from the rear of the VCR. It was a reaction to his pure animal fear. "Warn him! Warn the pilot!"

"Be quiet, Char—"

The rifle barked before Elliot could finish his sentence. A red fountain of Kent's blood spurted out from his chest as the bullet struck home, splashing the clothes of Helen Mayfield beside him. Shot at such close range, Kent was dead before he hit the floor. Elliot watched, mouth agape, as the body rolled over and came to rest face up. The dead eyes were wide open.

Helen drew back and threw her hands to her face, stifling a shriek of horror. The nearest gunman turned towards her, waved his rifle threateningly and then snorted, "You're next if you make one more sound!"

Elliot turned reluctantly back towards the runway. The aircraft was just touching down. It was still travelling fast and an eddy of smoke from the brakes billowed out as the pilot tried to slow down. Elliot found himself grasping the edge of his desk so tightly the wood dug into his flesh. The 146 had always been a marginal bet at the City airport, even with the extra runway length.

As the aircraft passed them, each of the terrorists out on the airfield rose to his feet and ran forward onto the runway, his rifle at a hip-firing position. It was too late now for the pilot to start an overshoot, his speed was dropping off as the brakes took hold. Elliot thought he saw flames amidst the smoke coming from the brakes and he held his breath.

An emergency hatch opened, even though the aircraft was still moving too fast for anyone to jump out, and a uniformed figure was clearly visible inside. Still the 146 continued to slow down, with less than half the runway length to go.

"We're about to start abandoning the aircraft," the pilot announced.

"Roger." The word was out before Elliot remembered he was ordered to remain silent.

As the aircraft's speed dropped off, the brakes took a firmer grasp. Only a quarter of the runway left, but the speed was well down now. A figure jumped from the emergency hatch and another jumped from the opposite side of the aircraft. Both ran blindly and unknowingly towards the waiting gunmen.

Rifles cracked and one of the figures fell to the ground, then the other.

"No!" Helen screamed. She stopped abruptly as an Armalite barrel was pressed into her body.

Elliot closed his eyes and tried to think of some sort of response to this dreadful attack, but his mind refused to cooperate. He was the aerodrome controller, he told himself, it was his responsibility to do something. But what? What possible action could he take to save those poor people still on board the royal aircraft? One more was about to die at the terrorist's hands.

"Tell the pilot he is not to leave the aircraft," the nearest gunmen snapped.

"But... the bomb!"

"Do as I say."

Elliot breathed in sharply. Things were getting worse by the minute.

*

Patrick Toome leaned against the watch supervisor's desk in the Heathrow control room, and he waited. And the waiting got on his nerves. Any moment now, if all was going well, there would be an ATC tie-line call from the City Airport to tell them that the Queen's Flight aircraft had been taken. It was a vital part of the

72

operation. If it failed, they would have problems getting the bomb out of Britain when the government gave in to their demands. They needed *both* aircraft at City Airport.

Toome was not used to public displays of failure. The fact that his brigade had been selected to lead the attack on the Heathrow control tower was, he had been assured, an honour. Well, he told himself, his part had gone exactly to plan. Now everything depended upon the people at London City Airport.

What would Roisin O'Steafin have made of this? Would she have been proud of him? He hoped so. She had been a slim, dark-haired girl in her late twenties, somewhat younger than him. Not exactly an attractive girl; she had a wide mouth and prominent teeth that protruded when she laughed. But, in the eyes of Patrick Toome, she radiated personality. She seemed to be as deeply committed to the Republican movement as anyone in the Belfast organisation.

They became lovers because it seemed the natural thing to do, even though they hid their relationship from their own brigade members. Roisin had a flat near the Belfast markets area, and Toome came to regard it as his home for the few months they had together. In the tiny bedroom, she confided in him about her life on the country farm her parents owned in Sligo.

He, in turn, told her about his brother, Danny, and how he died at the hands of the Brits. She listened and encouraged him to continue talking openly about those thoughts. In one sense she was the cleansing agent he needed to scour out the deepest horrors still lurking in his mind and bring them into the open.

At one time, he had thought there might be some future for him with Roisin O'Steafin, but he was wrong. He had forgotten that, in Belfast, there could be no future for any of them. In the lectures given to new Provisional IRA recruits — lectures he should have known by heart — the message was hammered home that each of them was destined either for the Republican plot in the Milltown cemetery or Long Kesh. He should have had that in mind when he began his association with Roisin O'Steafin. But the message had been lost somewhere along the line.

It was a wintery Saturday night when an assassination squad came for the girl. She and Toome were lying in bed, quietly embracing one another after making love, when they heard a loud knocking on the door of the flat. Roisin sat up suddenly, looked at her watch and slipped out of the bed. She donned a dressing gown and said, "Just stay here while I see who it is."

In the intensity of their relationship, even she seemed to have forgotten her innate sense of security. He heard her open the door, heard her scream, heard the loud explosion of the gun. By the time he ran to the door, still naked, the attackers had gone and she was dead in a pool of blood. Her face had been blown apart.

The hurt and pain of Roisin's death never faded and they fuelled his acts of revenge. In time, all he felt was hatred. He never admitted openly that he hated those acts of revenge almost as much as he hated Roisin's killers because there was no way he could back out. All he could do was kill in the name of Irish Republicanism. Or be killed.

Toome passed a hand across his eyes and forced himself to ignore the conflicting feelings whirling about inside his head. He had to concentrate on the scene inside the emergency control room. He had to keep his concentration on what was happening here and now. If the leader cocked things up, the leader would have to pay. It was the law of the jungle.

He glanced at his watch. He should have had the message by now. What was happening at the City Airport? There was, of course, no bomb on board the Queen's Flight aircraft. That was just an idea Joe Dillon had thought up for diverting the flight from its planned destination. Toome trusted Joe, not totally, but more than he trusted some of the people he had to work with. Joe had some degree of intelligence and he knew about aircraft and air traffic control.

The tie line to City Airport rang abruptly and Toome moved towards the controller who sat near it. He waited while the man took the message.

"It's the royal flight," the controller said. "It's on the ground. They say it's been taken." His face was pale as he spoke.

Toome breathed a sigh of relief. Then he tightened up his expression and snapped, "Good." It wouldn't do to let the Brits believe he was human. Better to keep his cardboard expression of hardened bitterness. It was what they would expect.

He noticed a young girl sitting in front of a desk that looked different from the controller's desks. She had no radio headset and he guessed she would be an assistant, not a controller. She looked frightened, which was good because it meant she would be unlikely to cause trouble. Right now, he didn't want any trouble. He strode towards her.

"You!"

The girl turned, her eyes wide.

He spoke with a deliberate harshness. "You've got tea or coffee round here somewhere?"

She nodded. There was something about her that unnerved him. As if he was looking into the face of a kitten he was about to drown. He turned away as he said, "Go and make enough for everyone here."

She rose slowly, looking pleadingly at the people around her. Most of them were too busy to even notice her plight, and the ones who did notice seemed reluctant to do anything. Maybe they were too frightened. God, why does war have to hurt young girls, young people like her? People like Roisin?

Toome felt a spasm of frustration.

"Hurry up, girl! Unless you want a bullet in you!"

What a stupid thing to say, he thought. He couldn't put a bullet into the likes of her. Unless he first covered her face.

Chapter 7

Jennifer White's hand slipped as she offered a cup of coffee to the terrorist leader. She froze, her arm outstretched, as some of the hot drink spilled onto the floor and the cup rattled loudly on its saucer. Her shoulders were bent and her head was inclined downwards. She dared not glance up at him.

"Put it down there!" she heard him snap angrily.

She obeyed hastily and turned away as soon as the saucer was settled firmly on the supervisor's desk. She had never imagined how psychologically painful fear could be. Real fear. Fear that was painful enough to affect her mental balance. Her eyes had difficulty in focussing, as if a translucent film were glued over the lenses. At the same time, a lunging sensation in her stomach made her want to vomit. She felt her heart pounding so hard she had difficulty breathing. And she desperately needed to visit the lavatory, although she dared not ask for permission.

As she approached Simon Hudson, she saw a look of deep concern in the controller's face, a look made more dramatic by the way he stared at her. She suddenly realised that his concern was a result of her own behaviour and appearance, and that made her feel even more frightened. Although she was only a teenage air traffic assistant and he was a fully qualified controller, she knew him well enough to trust him.

"You okay?" he asked quietly.

She tried to nod, but her head was riveted into a forward-bent position and she was unable to release it. Hudson reached out and touched her hand. It felt reassuringly warm. Finally, she looked up. His nearness was so reassuring, she tried desperately to think of a reason to remain there, close beside him. But the reason evaded her.

"Th... there's... sugar... in the jar," she said, struggling to allow each word to escape.

Hudson smiled, a forced, unreal smile, but better than nothing. "Keep calm," he whispered. "If we stay calm, no harm will come to us."

"I need to go to the loo," she replied. She felt trickles of sweat creeping down her back, and the clammy sensation of her blouse sticking to her cold, wet skin.

Hudson glanced round the room. "We'd better ask them," he said. Then he looked at her and grinned awkwardly. "Can't have you doing it on the floor."

She tried to smile back at him, but her facial muscles refused to comply with her mental will. Her mind was turning blank. She tried to think lucidly but the thoughts refused to appear in her head. She opened her mouth to speak and felt her lips quivering uncontrollably.

Hudson turned towards the supervisor's desk and raised one hand like a schoolboy attracting the attention of a teacher. The gunman called Paddy was bent over the desk giving instructions to Vince Trewin, talking in a low, gruff voice. He stood up for a moment, rubbed his neck and then appeared to notice Hudson's gesture. With a grim expression, he strode towards the radar console.

"Well, what is it?" He glared at the girl as he spoke and she again lowered her gaze to the floor.

"She needs to go to the toilet," Hudson stated calmly. Jennifer marvelled at the way he kept his voice level and measured. It was as if he had no fear of the terrorist, although she was certain that he was inwardly as frightened as the rest of them.

"No one leaves the room." The response was accompanied by a cruel twist of the man's mouth.

"But—" Hudson's attempted argument was cut short by a swift upward movement of the man's Armalite. The barrel cracked against Hudson's ribs and forced him back in his seat.

"I said no one leaves the room!" This time his voice barked loudly, causing others to turn towards the source of the disturbance.

"You don't need to shout at us." Hudson stared fixedly at the Irishman until he turned his face away, as if unsure how to reply.

The gunman paused for a moment, grunted at them and then turned towards Jennifer "Don't stand so close!"

She instantly took a step back.

"She's frightened," Hudson said softly. "She needs to go to the lavatory."

"I said *no!*" The words were aimed directly into Jennifer's face.

Hudson's cool manner suddenly snapped. "For chrissake! Do you want her to pee on the floor? Is that the way you people treat frightened young girls?"

Paddy's head again swung round towards him, but this time he avoided Hudson's gaze. For a couple of seconds the weapon dug deep into the controller's ribs, then it was pulled back. The gunman's cruel mouth opened and then closed again.

"Please," Hudson whispered, his gaze now fixed on the weapon.

The Irishman turned away. He walked back to the desk and then he stopped and looked over his shoulder at Jennifer. She felt her pulse racing and she raised her head fractionally to see a strange look in his face. It was almost as if he felt sorry for her, but she quickly told herself that couldn't be right. While she watched, he picked up the desk telephone and dialled a short internal number. Then he spoke into the receiver.

"Where's McGovan?" A pause and then, "Well, tell him to get himself along here to the radar room. Now!" He put the telephone down on the desk and gave Jennifer a black, angry look. As dark a look as she had ever been given.

"You've got two minutes," he said. "Just two minutes!"

"Thank you." Her lips quivered.

"And I'll shoot *him* if you don't come back." The Irishman pointed a finger at Simon. "You hear me, girl?"

"Yes, I hear you." She heard him and she believed him.

She ran from the room before the man could change his mind. She felt both thankful that she was permitted to leave, and anxious for Hudson's safety after his brave confrontation. But, of the two, the thankfulness far outweighed her anxiety.

*

McGovan burst into the radar room in a flurry of blustering movement. Toome looked at him with a feeling of detestation. Of all the men in his brigade, McGovan was the one he would most like to get rid of. The trouble was, the Scotsman had influence in the Republican movement, relatives in Ireland holding high office. Before he moved to Northern Ireland, he had been active with the Scottish National Liberation Army. There was a rumour he was the one who sent the letter bombs to Thatcher and Princess Diana. Only rumours, but they were likely to be true.

"There's a girl just gone to the women's bogs," Toome snapped with more than a hint of annoyance. "Make sure she doesn't do a runner."

McGovan gave him a surly look. "The women's bogs, you say?"

Toome could smell the whiskey on his breath. He replied, "That's what I said. Have you been drinking again? I don't want you drinking at a time like this."

The little Scotsman laughed. "Piss off."

Then he turned and shuffled from the room.

*

After relieving herself, Jennifer stood in the ladies' washroom and stared into the mirror. She looked a mess. Her make-up was streaked with rivulets of sweat and traces of poorly hidden tears. Her deep brown eyes were bloodshot, something she had never before seen in her own reflection. And her dark hair looked straggled and messy and refused to frame her face in its usual manner. She sniffed, damped her handkerchief under a tap and wiped it across her forehead.

She wondered whether news of the terrorist attack had reached the outside world, whether it was being broadcast on the radio. If it was, her parents would be worried for her safety. Her father was weakened enough by his chronic bronchitis — the aftermath of years of chain smoking — and he would suffer most. Her mother would suffer inside, but she would hide her pain in order to present an image of strength. Her father would both expect that and need it. When it was all over, they would probably try to persuade her to give up this job.

"There's plenty of other work for a clever girl like you, Jennifer," her mother was likely to say. "You don't have to continue working at West Drayton."

Jennifer imagined herself trying to explain to them how she normally enjoyed being an air traffic assistant. And this attack hadn't happened at West Drayton anyway. Then she remembered what *had* happened at Drayton and her mind fell to pieces. Besides, she knew that both of her parents would fail to understand, whatever she told them.

Jennifer sniffed again and stood up straight. She felt better now, almost ready to face the problem in a rational manner. Even the thought of escape began to seep into her thoughts. Escape... she was on the ground floor and there were numerous windows large enough for her to climb through. Not here in the washroom, the window here was far too small, but along the corridor in various offices and workshops. Was she brave enough to chance it? Or would she simply return to the radar room and face the crisis with her friends? She bent forward again to give her cheeks a last brush with her handkerchief. Behind her, the washroom door burst open.

"Paddy said I should check on you." A harsh Scots voice crept up on her.

When Jennifer turned, she saw a short, stocky, middle-aged man leaning against the door. Unlike the other terrorists, he had removed his white overall and was dressed in grimy denims. His eyes were dull, almost lifeless, as if he was affected by drugs or in some sort of trance. But there was nothing trance-like about the way he rubbed his hand across his stubbly chin, only partially hiding the traces of a leering grin. There was something about the leer, the way it creased the corners of his mouth, which caused Jennifer a sudden surge of panic.

"Paddy said I was to make sure you don't do anything stupid, like running away. He said I was to keep an eye on you." The man moved away from the door and ran his hand across his mouth once more. "You know we're in complete charge of this place, girl."

Jennifer shuddered. "What do you mean?"

"I mean that I'm in charge of you now, and you're going to do what I tell you. Didn't you hear me?" He advanced towards her, slowly and menacingly.

"I don't understand..."

"You soon will. And you won't be the first one, girl. Not by a long way."

Jennifer felt a shockwave thunder up through her body. "I've finished here," she said. Her voice sounded like the distant echo of another person.

"Not yet, you haven't." The man's broad, Strathclyde accent grated against her senses like a thick rasp. He continued to step towards her, dragging the Armalite behind him so that the stock scraped loudly on the tiled floor.

"You know what's going to happen," he grunted. "You're not stupid, are you? You can either cooperate and not get hurt. Or you can put up a fight and I'll thrash the hell out of you."

"I'm going... going back to—"

"You're not going nowhere. Not yet."

Jennifer shuffled backwards until she felt herself pinned against the cold white ceramic tiles of the washroom wall. The man's pot belly was close against her, almost touching her. She flinched at the stale smell of drink and smoke on his clothes. Then she realised why his eyes were so dull. He was half-drunk. He wasn't incapably drunk. Surely, even the IRA wouldn't take an incapable drunk with them on a raid like this. No, he was still sober enough to be able to carry out his terrible threat and he was sufficiently affected by drink to want to do it.

She tried to cry out, but her throat was dry and soundless. With her hands drawn in front of her, she sank down the wall until she was crouched in a small bundle. Her lip quivered as she realised that there was no escape in retracting into a ball.

"Get up!" The man's voice snapped.

She looked up and watched, dumbfounded, as he set his gun against a washbasin and began to loosen his belt.

"Get up! Or you'll regret it."

Jennifer noticed for the first time that his teeth were blackened and broken. She wanted to retch, but her whole body was frozen with fear, unable to move. He grabbed her violently and dragged her to her feet, the tightness of his grasp shooting spasms of pain through her arms. But still she was unable to make any sound.

As she came to her feet, his trousers crumpled to the floor. His rough hand grasped her thigh and pulled her skirt upwards. This was it! This was the moment when he would take her. She was not the sort of person who could react bravely in the face of danger. She could only react instinctively. She had no idea how the process worked, only that it brought out a sudden and unexpected reaction which was beyond the realms of her understanding.

Her knee came up violently into the man's groin with such unexpected force that he was caught completely off guard. He screamed with pain and staggered backwards. In the same instant Jennifer barged forward, rammed herself against his chest and knocked him off balance. As the man fell to the floor, she raced to the washroom door and pulled it open without a single coherent thought in her mind, just an urgent and instinctive need to get away.

She hesitated out in the corridor and tried to force some rational thoughts back into her mind. If she went back to the radar room now, she would be pursued by that evil little man, and there was no guarantee that anyone would be able to help her. Shaking violently, she hurried towards the entrance lobby with no clear idea of what she might do next.

Someone was standing at the main entrance; she could see the outline of a figure through the smoked glass partition that shielded the main entrance doors. Holding her breath, she raced on, hoping to be out of sight before the figure could come round the partition. She stopped farther down the corridor adjacent to a lift. It was bigger than the lift in the entrance lobby, big enough to carry equipment up to the higher levels.

A quick glance around told her that no one had yet seen her. Knowing that the evil little man was sure to come into sight very soon, she pressed the lift button and groaned as the doors opened instantly. Sheer panic was in control of her brain as she dived in and jabbed at an upper floor button. The door closed and the cage began to rise straightaway.

She felt a sudden mixture of semi-relief and horror. Her entire body was trembling uncontrollably, and she put a hand to her mouth as a sickly feeling rose in her throat.

The lift stopped, she wasn't too sure at what floor, but it had to be near the top of the building. Now almost blind with panic, she ran out onto the landing. Once she began to run, the mental impetus continued and she scampered on down the corridor and through the fire doors at the stairwell.

Where next?

A brief moment of lucidity returned. She would find no obvious cover here. Then panic took over once again and a previously unknown agility carried her down the stairs at breakneck speed to the next floor. She burst through the next set of fire doors and continued halfway along the corridor, stopping at a random door. It was numbered five hundred and something — her eyes couldn't quite make out what — and that told her she was on the fifth floor. A low moan escaped her lips as she twisted and pulled on the handle, but it was firmly locked. She continued to the next door, heaved it open and dashed into the room with no thought for what she might find.

She slammed the door behind her, leaned against it and breathed heavily. Her heart was now thumping as though it might suddenly erupt from her body, and her mind was an explosion of vivid pictures, impressions of violence.

She stood, unmoving, for several minutes until her heartbeat began to subside and her thoughts began to melt into more reasoned images. No sounds came from beyond the door. Nevertheless, she knew it would be foolish to believe that the gunman would not pursue her, and that he would determinedly find her. And then...

She gave little odds for her chances.

The room appeared to be some sort of office. One wall was lined with metal filing cabinets, and another was almost hidden behind shelves laden with documents. In the centre of the room a single desk held a computer workstation. A door led into the adjacent office, the room which was locked from the corridor. Near the door was a serving hatch, obviously used for passing documents from one office to the other. Jennifer found her thoughts coming more clearly now and she searched round for some obvious means of escape. She spent some minutes walking around, wrestling with conflicting ideas until, suddenly, she picked out an ominous sound.

A bellowing voice reverberated outside in the corridor. Jennifer recognised it at once, and she shivered. How did he know to follow her here? He must have seen the lift go up to the sixth floor. Perhaps he had followed in the other lift. What then? Once he reached the sixth floor, he would be working on pure guesswork. Maybe he had been close enough behind to hear her running down the stairs. He was probably searching every corridor from the sixth floor down. The sound of banging doors told her that he was checking each unlocked room as he approached.

She ran to the connecting door that led to the adjacent office, but it was locked like its counterpart in the corridor.

Another wild scan round the room revealed nothing that could give her any hiding place, and then her mind began to swirl again, sinking into the mists of raw fear. She ran across the room for no reason and then back again. Desperately searching.

The hatch!

She pressed against the hatch doors and almost sobbed when she discovered that they also were locked. Sheer unbridled fear made her push again, and this time she felt the catch give under the pressure of her weight. She pushed harder, mustering up every ounce of strength until she felt the doors to begin to give way. Then they suddenly burst apart, flying open into the inner office.

The terrorist's bellowing was very close now. She had little time to spare as she pulled herself up into the narrow hatch and wriggled through the opening. The door hinges caught her legs. She felt something sharp scratch painfully against her calf and rip the skin. She fell into the room, landing awkwardly on a small table and then slid down to the floor.

There was no time to consider her injuries. She leapt up and rammed shut the hatch doors. The catch was on the inside and still intact, despite being forced open. Her fingers fumbling, she locked the doors and stood back, breathing heavily. Then she waited.

*

Hudson jumped as the telephone line to London City Airport rang with a sudden belligerent sound. He leaned forward, picked up his headset and selected the appropriate switch.

"Hello?"

"Do you have someone there called Paddy?" The voice at the other end of the line sounded worried.

"Yes. You want to speak to him?"

"There's a message for him from his comrades here."

Hudson looked towards the terrorist leader. If he were prudent, he would call the man across the room, but he was feeling less than prudent. He was feeling increasingly angry. Besides, this was an ideal opportunity to find out what was happening at London City.

"Okay. I'll pass the message on to him. What is it?"

"You're to tell him that the Queen's Flight aircraft is down safely and the pilot is being held hostage."

"Has anyone been hurt?"

"Yes... people have been killed over here. There's at least two dead bodies out on the airfield, probably three. And another here in the tower."

"Who was killed in the tower?"

"A guy called Charlie Kent. You know him?"

"Shit! That old bugger! Yes, I know him... *knew* him."

Hudson replaced the handset and beckoned to the gunman as he reset the telephone switch.

"It's a message for you from City Airport," he said as the Irishman came towards him. "They say that the Queen's Flight aircraft is down safely and the pilot captured."

A smile spread across the gunman's face. He turned to his companion. "You hear that, Joe? The plan's working. By God we're going to do it."

The other terrorist grinned briefly and then returned his attention to the controllers. His reaction was both subdued and dispassionate. It gave Hudson a further clue to the man's mentality, a clue that he carefully filed away in his mind for future reference.

He had already formed a certainty that Paddy, the leader, was not as strong and self-assured as he pretended to be. Hudson's look into the man's eyes had shown him an image of poorly concealed fear. He knew that it did not make the position of the controllers any easier because that fear could spark off a spontaneous burst of violence.

Hudson swept his gaze around the room once more. All the controllers looked strained, a result of both the terrorist attack and because they each needed a relief from the task of controlling aeroplanes. Air traffic controllers tended to 'burn out' at a relatively young age anyway. Without periodic breaks from their work, they would simply burn out very much quicker.

Apart from the F27 and the Royal Flight, no flights had been diverted because the terrorists refused to sanction it, so the radar controllers worked on. But the morning flow was slowing. Was it possible that the traffic rate had now slowed enough for Hudson to cope with it again? Would anyone allow him to even try, after the airmiss he caused? He steeled himself for the test.

He stood up slowly, ensuring that his hands were visible and clear of his body. He wanted no mistakes made over his intentions.

The man called Paddy stood at the supervisor's desk, his body arched over as he pointed to a sheet of paper which Trewin was reading.

Hudson coughed lightly.

The Irishman swung round and raised his weapon in one swift motion.

"Hold on." Hudson raised his hands protectively. "I only want to speak to you."

The man grunted and bared his teeth while he kept his rifle aimed at Hudson's chest in a theatrical gesture. The full horror of the situation in the radar room ensured that Hudson took the gesture seriously.

"The controllers are getting tired." Hudson waved towards his colleagues. "They all need a break. My job isn't as essential as theirs, so I could close down the Thames Radar service and relieve someone else."

The man eyed him closely, as if an inner distrust was influencing his thoughts without any conclusive result. He seemed to be weighing up reasons why he should, or should not, allow the controllers to relax, and why he should permit Hudson to provide that break.

"You stay where you are," he snapped suddenly. "I may need you there later."

He turned back towards the supervisor's desk. After some moments a stray thought seemed to enter his mind and he swung round to where Hudson was edging back to his radar display.

"You!" he barked. "What happened to that girl? The one who wanted to go to the bogs."

"I don't know." Hudson looked round. He had not seen Jennifer since she left the room. If anything happened to her... He suddenly felt guilty.

"She should have come straight back here!" the terrorist leader snapped.

Hudson remained outwardly impassive. Inside, he felt a cold hand of horror clawing at his chest. The Irishman said he would shoot him if Jennifer tried to escape, and he had already shot other controllers in this room.

Chapter 8

Jennifer clasped a hand to her mouth when she heard the gunman burst into the outer office. She stood with her back against the adjoining wall, forcing herself into it tight enough to feel the pressure over every inch from her heels to her shoulders. She held her breath and the effort brought a pounding sensation to her ears.

"Hell!" she heard the man swear, followed by the sound of something falling to the floor. After a moment's silence she caught the louder noise of a chair toppling over. Then another short silence.

Was he gone? She had heard no sound of the door closing. Perhaps he had left and not bothered to close the door. A soft hiss of breath passed between her lips as she began to mentally wind down. The pressure of the wall against her back eased, and she raised one hand to her throbbing temple. The stale smell of her own sweat rose to her nostrils and she suddenly realised that her clothes were soaked in perspiration. She pulled the front of her blouse away from her breasts and felt dribbles of sweat run from the garment onto her hand. It didn't matter, she tried to tell herself. As long as she had evaded the gunman, it simply didn't matter at all that she needed a wash. She almost laughed with relief.

A sudden sharp crack brought her back to reality. It was the sound of a boot thrust against the connecting door. Then the agitated rattle of the handle.

Oh, God! Don't let him in!

Jennifer felt a constriction rise in her throat as she watched the handle moving up and down. Please don't let him in! She grasped both hands to her head while her mouth hung open wordlessly.

*

Something about the girl stuck in Patrick Toome's mind. It wasn't the fact that she hadn't returned from the toilets because there was no way she could escape once he had sent McGovan to keep watch on her. If anything, he was more worried about McGovan cocking things up. He was troubled by the way the girl looked at him, frightened, scared out of her tiny mind. As if he really was the vicious terrorist he pretended to be. She reminded him of an incident he had almost forgotten.

It was after Roisin's death. His brother, Danny, and Roisin were both dead then. God, there had been a terrible vengeance in his heart. His plan had been to eliminate one of the loyalist paramilitary leaders from the Ulster Defence Association. By now, he was almost certain the UDA had been behind Roisin's murder. The gossip down the Falls Road suggested this very man had pulled the trigger.

It was a dark evening and they had no trouble getting into the area with the explosive and setting the booby trap. He took with him one other man to drive the getaway vehicle while he planted the bomb. When the trap was set, they retreated to a nearby side street to wait. After a while, hearing no explosion, Toome went to the junction with North Queen Street and peered round the corner. Within minutes, the loyalist's front door opened. Two people came out of the house. One was their target, the UDA leader. The other was a girl. She climbed into the passenger seat while the man got behind the steering wheel.

Toome heard his companion creep up behind him and he looked back with a feeling of unease. "We didn't plan on two of them."

"It doesn't matter. There's enough explosive to take out both of them."

The engine started with a short roar and the car began to move. Then the mercury switch made contact and the vehicle leapt into the air on top of a violent flash. A split second later the sound of the explosion erupted between the tightly knit houses. The blast reverberated down the street, shattering windows and punching down doors as it rolled along like a huge thunder peal.

Toome waited until the roar of the explosion subsided before he ran out into the street and raced towards the wreckage. Debris and burning remains littered the area. A wheel with its tyre aflame rolled across the street and bounced against the front wall of a house. One side of the car was split open like a discarded tin can, and the girl's upper torso was spilled out onto the pavement. Blood poured out of her multiple wounds and both her arms were bent at impossible angles, but she was alive. God knows how, but she was still alive. Her head moved and she cried out in agony.

Toome shivered as he melted into the background. He felt a hand on his arm. It was his companion, drawing him back towards their own car.

"It's done, Paddy," the other man said. "Let's get away quickly."

"I didn't know there was going to be a girl involved," Toome gasped.

"For chrissake, leave it, Paddy! The job was a success. And the girl's only a Protestant."

Only a Protestant. Toome jabbed his shaking hands into his pockets. Protestant or Catholic, what did it matter? It was a waste of a young life. Like Danny and Roisin.

"You want me to try to find the girl?"

Toome shook his thoughts back to the present. "What was that?"

The controller who sat at the supervisor's desk spoke again. "Do you want me to go and find her?" He was leaning towards Toome, waiting for a response. A straight question, but it took Toome some seconds before he could find a straight answer.

"No." Toome pulled himself upright. "She's only... only a young girl. She'll not cause any bother."

*

Dan Mayfield let himself into the house and made straight for the kitchen to prepare a pot of tea. The stuff they served on the flight was no substitute for his own expensive Darjeeling tea, not that he really expected it to be. While the kettle was boiling, he went into the study and flicked through the pile of letters left on his desk. He isolated the bills from the letters he intended to enjoy reading later, and he set them back in two neat stacks. Then he ambled back into the kitchen and prepared a tray with a pot of tea and a plate of biscuits.

He set his tray onto the coffee table in the lounge and idly switched on the radio. He wasn't sure what channel it was tuned to, but it seemed to be delivering reasonably sane music. At the first sign of jarring guitars and screaming pop idols he would flick over to another channel. The music provided a pleasant background while he sipped his tea and allowed his thoughts to wander at will.

Janice Wilkins slipped into his mind as easily as she had slipped into his bed in the New York hotel. As easily as she had slipped into his bed in other foreign cities.

At first he had harboured a considerable sense of guilt over his betrayal of Helen's faith in him, but much of that had passed away in time. The strangest part of the whole business was his understanding that Helen was the better of the two women in lovemaking. She was more vibrant, more adventurous and infinitely more caring towards his enjoyment. Janice was soft and warm in bed, like a young kitten that has still to learn how to behave, but was all the more loveable for its immaturity.

A change in the radio programme began before Mayfield had time to register what had happened. Once he was aware that a flash news bulletin was being broadcast, he re-tuned his mind towards the radio.

"...we are only getting preliminary reports of the incidents at the moment and we will bring you further details as soon as they are available. First reports indicate that both Heathrow and London City Airport control towers have been taken over by hijackers. There are no reports of casualties as yet, although shots have been heard at both airports. As I said, we will bring you more news as soon as it comes in. In the meantime, I'll hand you back to your regular morning programme..."

Mayfield was on his feet before the bulletin ended. He jumped towards the telephone, the tea spilling onto the carpet as his cup bounced off the side of the coffee table.

"Hell!" His hand trembled as he dialled Helen's office number. He danced around as he listened to the buzzer ringing out. There was no reply. What the hell was happening at the airport? He pressed down the cradle and dialled the London City Airport exchange. While he waited for the number to ring out, he felt his whole body shaking. Gunshots, the radio reporter had said, there was the sound of gunshots!

Again there was no reply to the call.

*

Janice Wilkins let herself into her Kensington flat, threw her outer clothes onto the settee and ran herself a hot bath. Within five minutes of arrival, she was languishing in the perfumed, sudsy water, considering what she was to do about Dan Mayfield.

The problem, she reflected, was a common one. In fact, it was all too common in aviation relationships. She wanted him for herself, but he was married. She wanted him totally and permanently, but he had given her no indication that he would even consider a divorce. He had to be made to see reason.

She lay in the water for ten minutes and then made a sudden decision. Not even bothering to dry herself, she ran into the lounge, picked up the telephone and dialled Dan's home number. She stood, dripping water onto the carpet, while she waited for an answer.

If his wife picked up the phone, she told herself, she would quickly ring off. But if he answered, she would say... she wasn't too sure exactly what she would say, but she would let him know that he was constantly in her thoughts. Give him an indication of her true feelings. Make him think about that divorce.

But there was no reply.

She replaced the receiver thoughtfully. He ought to have been at home by now. She would try again this evening, when she would feel and sound more attractive after a good sleep. She yawned and made her way towards the bedroom, still dripping water across the carpet.

*

Helen Mayfield stared out of the large glass windows of the City Airport Visual Control Room to where the terrorists were transferring a container from the F27 to the BAe146. She puzzled over the heavy guard they had posted to protect the cargo. Whatever it was, they were taking no chances over it. But what were they up to? As yet no one had given any indication of the reason behind the attack on the airport. It was something big. But what?

Voices drifted up from below and then two men pounded up the stairs. She had seen them leaving the F27 earlier. One was dressed in full combat gear and the other wore an expensive suit.

The old, fat man in the suit puzzled her. He carried an air of authority within the terrorist group, as if he was in command of the operation, and yet he seemed to have a nervous tic affecting one side of his face. With a quick look around the VCR, he went straight to the leader of the gunmen already occupying the tower and spoke quietly to him. The man in military uniform joined them, turning it into a three-way conversation. The brief discussion ended when the man in military gear stood back and then turned to Helen.

"You!" He stabbed a finger in her direction and spoke in a broad Belfast accent. "Get downstairs!"

Helen paused for a moment and then stepped towards the VCR door. More voices drifted up from below and she waited while several other men pounded up the stairs. They were all heavily armed.

Behind her she heard the old, well-dressed man speak in an affected upper-class English accent. "I'll take over up here, Mc-Quarrie. You know what to do with the woman."

"You want her brought back here?" the Ulsterman asked.

"No, of course not. I don't want to see her here again." His nervous tic had got worse.

The Ulsterman called McQuarrie gestured Helen to continue down the stairs. She moved slowly while she racked her brain for some way out of her predicament. She had no illusions about the limit to which the gunmen would go. Charlie Kent's crumpled body was still lying on the VCR floor as a testimonial to their murderous intent.

On the lower levels of the building, other gunmen were posted at strategic points and Helen began to count them, realising as she did so that this was an operation of major proportions.

As they walked out onto the apron, McQuarrie pointed towards the Queen's Flight aircraft.

"Just walk towards it quietly," he hissed. "One false move and you're dead."

Helen kept to her slow pace. She was in no hurry to become a posthumous heroine.

"Is the pilot still alive?" she asked.

"Aye, he's still alive, but only because we choose to let him live. We have a job for him later."

"Your men killed one of my staff," she said.

"Too bad."

She stole a short glance at the gunman. He spoke as if he had no feelings, as if the victims of this dastardly deed were an irrelevance. Was that the nature of armed Republican politics? The end justifies the means?

"Why do you want me on the aircraft?" she asked. "Isn't one hostage enough for you?"

The Ulsterman laughed out loud this time. "Hostage! You're not a hostage, woman. You're going to be our messenger. They might not believe us when we tell them what we have here, but they'll believe you."

The laugh frightened her. She felt certain there was something evil about it.

"Of course they'll believe you," she replied. "They know who you are and what you've done."

"They know who we are?"

"They must do. You're the Provisional IRA, aren't you?"

For a moment there was no reply as they continued in close step towards the aircraft. Then the Ulsterman snapped abruptly, "Shut your mouth and keep walking."

They walked past the F27, where armed men were striding around with seeming impunity, and headed towards the BAe146, which was stopped on the runway just short of the final turnoff. Two armed men stood at the main entrance hatch while others were visible at various points around the aircraft.

Helen was pushed roughly aboard the aircraft, stumbling into the cabin ahead of her captor. Almost immediately she came up against a metal container lying in the centre aisle close to the entrance. She looked down the length of the aircraft and saw an RAF uniformed officer under the guard of another armed gunman. Probably the pilot, she guessed, and turned her attention back to the container.

"Take a very close look at this." The gunman came up behind her and pointed towards the container. "Take a long, hard look because the British security forces will want a detailed description of it."

The device was about four feet long, two feet wide and two feet deep. It seemed to be a simple metal trunk from the outside, but when the gunman bent over and opened the upper lid, he revealed an array of electrical objects inside.

"What is it?" she asked.

"A bomb." He spoke with a forced lack of concern.

"It doesn't look like a bomb."

"Well, it is. Study it carefully because we're going to set you free so that you can describe it to your security forces. Just to convince them that we mean business."

Helen leaned towards the container and said, "You'll have to explain to me what I'm looking at. I don't know much about bombs."

"You don't need to. As long as you remember what you see."

"But how does the thing work? Where's the explosive? And how much explosive does it have?"

"There's more than enough explosive power in there for our needs. If we have to detonate it, we all go up with it. You. Us. The whole of bloody London."

Helen stood up slowly and tried to isolate the meaning behind the words. Surely, she reasoned, it would take a much larger bomb than this to blow up London. And Republican terrorists were not known for deliberately setting out on suicide missions.

"You wouldn't kill yourselves," she said, buying time while she tried to think.

"Wouldn't we? That's what they said about Bobby Sands. Wouldn't starve himself to death, so they said. Well, they were wrong. He died in pain." The man paused and wiped his lips. "If we have to go, we go quickly. No pain. We won't even know it's happened."

"The whole of London?"

"Of course." He spoke slower now, trying to appear casual but having difficulty in achieving the right balance between clarity and an easy tone. Helen stared at him as she waited for the punch line she knew was coming.

"Look at the thing." he said, "It's what they call a two-man portable tactical weapon. It's a nuclear bomb."

Chapter 9

Commander FitzHugh shifted uneasily in the rear seat of a police Rover. He was on his way back from Central London to Heathrow after a meeting with Sir James Heatherley. FitzHugh was worried, very worried, and there seemed little he could do about it. The terrorist activity was divided between Heathrow and City Airport, and there was no way he could be in two places at once.

The car accelerated suddenly along the busy M4 motorway towards Heathrow, then slowed equally suddenly. FitzHugh was forced to sit and glare at the back of the driver's head, containing his frustration with bad grace.

Long lines of traffic stretched ahead of the car, moving painfully slowly. Nothing abnormal, but highly inconvenient. FitzHugh grasped his seat belt as the car suddenly swung violently across the lanes to move into a faster traffic flow.

"Sorry, sir," the driver groaned. "Didn't see the gap in the traffic until the last moment."

FitzHugh levered himself upright and brushed a hand across his crumpled jacket. "You do know this road, don't you?"

"Yes, sir. But the traffic gets worse every day. Shall I use the siren?"

"Not yet. Wait until we hit a suitable gap in the outside lane, then use the siren, and put your foot down."

The driver nodded but said nothing.

FitzHugh reached for his briefcase. There was so much to read about this case, and so little time to do it.

"A call for you, sir." The driver grabbed his attention as he reached across the seat back with his radio phone. "It's from the Yard."

FitzHugh took it impatiently.

"Yes," he snapped into the mouthpiece with barely concealed

aggression.

"There's a message from the Commissioner, sir." The voice in the telephone was weak, scratchy. He instantly identified it as a junior liaison officer, a young, irritating man who sounded somewhat complacent, as if the message contained little of concern. "He wants you to go to London City Airport. Something important seems to be brewing over there."

"Hell's teeth! We're on the wrong side of town."

"Yes, sir."

"Why does he want us to change tack now?"

"We're not too sure exactly what's going on, but we think there may be something very important developing at the City Airport now that the Royal Flight aircraft has landed. The Commissioner agrees."

"Something important? Like what?"

"There are too many terrorists over there for our liking. We think it may be the hub of the operation. Heathrow may be just a side show."

"Hell!" It wasn't what he expected to hear, but there was an element of logic in it. City Airport was close to the heart of the City of London, the centre of the country's commerce. "All right," he snapped.

"Where are you at the moment, sir?"

"On the M4, and stuck in traffic."

"I could alert the local traffic police."

"Well, bloody well do it, man!"

"Yes, sir."

FitzHugh shook his head and lowered the telephone. "Turn round at the first opportunity. We're going to the City Airport!" he bellowed at the driver. He braced himself as the brakes came on suddenly.

*

Sir David Myers, Commissioner of the Metropolitan Police, was having difficulty containing his bad humour. Things should never have got this far out of control.

At two minutes past eleven, he was one of four men hastily ushered into a conference room at the Home Office. He noted how the other three looked anxious as they took their seats in the long, ornate room. They arranged themselves around one end of a gleaming mahogany conference table. The other dozen or more leather-covered seats were empty, making the room appear hollow and underused.

Sir James Heatherley, Permanent Under Secretary at the Home Office, was seated at the head of the table. Myers took a seat to one side of him.

Directly opposite Myers sat Herbert Morgan-Jones, the Director of Military Operations (Ground Forces) from the Ministry of Defence, and alongside him was Piers Templemore, the Cabinet Secretary. It was Templemore who would have the task of reporting the outcome of the meeting to the Prime Minister. Myers resolved to watch Templemore's reactions carefully.

Heatherley opened the meeting with a brief introduction and then invited Myers to speak.

"The first thing you'll be asking," the Commissioner said in measured tones, "is, who are these buggers? And the next question will be, what do they want? Before I attempt to answer either question, let me fill you in on a little piece of background detail."

He cast his eyes steadily around the group, inviting interruption before continuing. There was none.

"It seems almost certain," he said, "that last night's bomb at West Drayton was connected with the attacks on Heathrow and City Airports. We think there's a pattern to the whole thing. And we suspect something really bad." He emphasised the word 'bad'. It was in his nature to divide the world into wholly good or wholly bad, with no grey areas between.

"You have concrete evidence?" Sir James Heatherley asked, his tone suggesting scepticism. Myers knew that Sir James was not too pleased at the timing of the attack. He had been invited, with his wife, to attend a dinner this evening at Number Ten. Undoubtedly, it would be cancelled.

"Not conclusive, but we're working on it." Myers stood his ground with a frank expression. "We think the bomb at Drayton was planted by a young Irishman who took a job there as a cleaner. We're trying to get a lead on him but he seems to have gone to earth."

"So, you think this is the work of the Provisional IRA?"

"Well, let's face it, those buggers have to be the prime suspects although we won't be certain until they contact us with their demands."

"You think there will be demands?" Sir James kept his insistent tone.

"Of course there will! This isn't just a Provo mortar attack designed to frighten us, you know. This is the real thing."

"What was the purpose behind the West Drayton bomb?"

"We think the aim was to get the controllers who deal with Heathrow and London City aircraft moved across to the emergency control room in the Heathrow control tower."

"Why use such desperate means to do that?"

Myers sighed. Wasn't the answer obvious? "West Drayton is primarily an RAF base, with a lot of military as well as civilian staff. It's a big site and well-guarded. These buggers wanted to take over the air traffic control system around London, and it's easier to overrun the tower at Heathrow than the West Drayton complex. A lot easier. And it would take a helluva lot less gunmen to do it."

"So this was a well-planned operation," Heatherley observed.

Myers nodded. "Looks like they've achieved what they set out to achieve, so far. They now control the ATC system around Heathrow and City Airport." The Commissioner coughed loudly before looking directly at the MoD man opposite him. "I think, Herbert, it would be advisable if you would bring the Regiment into the area and have them on readiness."

"We're doing that anyway," the Director of Military Operations replied. "In the meantime, I've sent in covert military reconnaissance groups to both Heathrow and City airports. Under the direct control of the Anti-Terrorist Squad, of course." Herbert Morgan-Jones was a man of few words who believed in action rather than deliberation.

The Commissioner compressed his lips. He should have been told about any military squad sent in to help the civil police. He made a mental note to guard against any hint that he might hand over control to the military before he was good and ready. He had long held a suspicion that Morgan-Jones was a little too rash for his own good; it was the behaviour of a career civil servant who had aspirations of much higher office. Sir David Myers was determined not to be overawed by him.

The Cabinet Secretary was busily taking notes to assist his briefing of the PM. He looked up at the Commissioner and asked, "Just how are you dealing with this at the moment, Sir David?"

"At the moment... at the moment all we can do is to suck it and see. That's all anyone can do until we know exactly what these people want. Andrew Metcalfe, my Assistant Commissioner, is on his way over to the City Airport right now. In the meantime, I've got a heavy concentration of men on the spot, sitting tight and waiting."

"Mr Metcalfe will take charge once he gets there?"

"He'll have overall control, but Commander FitzHugh is also on his way to City Airport and he's effectively going to be the brains on the spot."

"FitzHugh?" The Cabinet Secretary creased his eyes. "The Irish fellow? I thought he was retired. Didn't he go early?"

"He is... *was* retired. But he's a damn good man where anti-terrorism is concerned and he knows more about this sort of thing than anyone else. All the right experience for this sort of business. He's been dragged back out of retirement."

"Yes, but..." The Cabinet Secretary bit his lip and held back on the words in his mind. "So you're setting one Irishman to catch a few others?"

The Commissioner ignored the remark. It was not worthy of a reply.

"And is there any indication yet of what these terrorists want?" Morgan-Jones chipped in.

"No," the Commissioner replied abruptly. "Not yet. But they'll tell us when they're ready."

"The Prime Minister will want to know," the Cabinet Secretary went on, "about the level of danger to the public."

Sir David Myers raised his eyebrows. "Tell the PM that we will do our best to minimise any risk to the public, but we can't properly assess that risk until we know what the hell these loonies want."

"Not loonies, Sir David." Sir James Heatherley looked at him fiercely as he rejoined the conversation. "Whatever else they are, they're not loonies. They're dedicated terrorists with all the resources and knowhow to mount an operation to take over two of our major airports. Misguided, yes. Ruthless, yes. Psychopathic at times, yes. Out and out evil if you really want to be pedantic. But loonies... no!"

*

Mickey Kearney's voice sounded urgent on the telephone. "You'd better come out here, Paddy. They've got the whole bloody police force gathering across the road."

"Shite!" Toome slammed down the phone and hurried along to the entrance lobby, bumping into the uniformed gunman who stood at the side of the reception desk.

Kearney put a hand to his peaked security guard's cap and said in broad Liverpool accent, "Steady, Paddy. It ain't yer own funeral you're going to."

"Where are they?" Toome gasped.

"Across the road, Paddy. There must be a dozen or more of them behind the bus shelter."

Toome moved forward to the tinted glass screen that sheltered the main entrance from the rest of the lobby. Kearney had left one of the glass doors open to allow a better view of what was happening across the road. The STRICTLY NO ENTRY sign had fallen to the floor. Toome put a hand above his eyes although there was no glare to be shielded. "I don't see them," he snapped.

Kearney moved up to join him. The scene outside had changed over a period of ten or fifteen minutes, but with no obvious excitement. The usual bustle at the bus station had gradually subsided, buses and coaches had been quietly driven away and the people had melted off into the background.

"Watch closely, Paddy," Kearney said, "Look! Over there... see that uniform moving past the side of the bus station building. And that one over there behind the shelter."

"Oh, yes." Toome whistled softly. "They're wearing flak jackets."

"Some of them are, but not all."

"Well, this is what we've been expecting." Toome gritted his teeth and turned to his guard. "Has anyone tried to get in here?"

"Not since they cleared the bus station."

Toome began to edge back into the lobby. "The balloon's gone up now, for sure. You'd better keep well back from the door in case anyone tries to take a pot-shot at you."

"Don't worry about me, Paddy." Kearney grinned, showing a mouthful of discoloured teeth, "You should know by now that I'm pretty hard to knock out."

"That's true, Mickey. But watch yourself all the same."

Toome trusted the Liverpool Irishman. Kearney had spent time banged up in Long Kesh. By the time he was released, he was a full graduate of the University of Terror. When Patrick Toome joined the Irish Republican Army, it was Kearney who taught him how to use an Armalite.

"Look! Over there!" Kearney put a hand to Toome's shoulder as he pointed to a gap between two sections of the bus shelter across the road. "That's a senior policeman, for sure. And he isn't wearing a flak jacket."

Toome inched forward. "There'll be a lot of senior policeman out there, Mickey."

"I could pick him off from here." Kearney looked inquisitively at Toome and reached for an Armalite leaning against the security desk.

"You'd have to hit him with the first shot. Reckon you could do it?"

"No bother." Kearney winked at his senior and waited patiently while Toome made up his mind.

"All right, Mickey." Toome moved a step backwards. "Knock him out."

Kearney took careful aim through the open doorway. The uniformed figure had stopped in partial view, apparently studying the control tower building through binoculars. His head and chest were clearly visible as Kearney's finger squeezed the trigger. A sharp, loud retort reverberated round the lobby and the distant figure collapsed to the ground.

"Got him!" Kearney lowered the rifle and edged back into the inner area of the lobby.

"They know now that we really mean business," Toome observed.

"I reckon they already knew that, Paddy."

"I imagine they did, Mickey. But there's now no doubts left in their minds."

*

Jennifer White remained rock still for some minutes after the noise at the office door ceased. Her heart continued to thump uncontrollably, but she dared not move a fraction of an inch for fear of being discovered. She thought she heard the sound of a door slamming shut in the adjacent office, but her brain was so disorientated that the noise could have come from anywhere. It might, she suddenly thought, even have been a trick to make her reveal her hiding place. With that horrifying possibility in her mind, she stood, petrified, silently grasping her head and wishing the nightmare had never begun.

A clock on the wall opposite ticked away the minutes. It was now eight minutes past eleven. Surely, she reasoned, the dreadful man must have gone by now. She took an investigative step forward, bent her head to the door, and listened. There was no apparent sound in the next room. From outside the building came the sound of an aircraft applying reverse thrust as it landed. Despite the hijack, the air traffic at Heathrow seemed to be still moving.

Jennifer relaxed marginally and looked round the room again, suddenly homing in on a telephone on the desk. She eyed it for some minutes, but she knew that it would demand considerable courage for her to speak out loud into it. Any sound from within the room might alert the terrorist to her presence, and yet, it was probably the only way she would be able to summon help. If only she could be sure that there was no one in the next room.

She tiptoed back to the hatch and bent her head to the minute gap between the doors. It was impossible to see between them so she inclined her ear to the hatch and listened.

Nothing.

Another glance at the clock. Twelve minutes past eleven. She would wait another ten minutes and then use the telephone. Yes, that was her plan. Once she had confirmed it in her mind, she felt better. She crossed to the desk and sat in the plush swivel chair behind it, carefully testing the seat's reaction as she lowered herself into it. There were no squeaks so she relaxed, just a little. Only ten minutes, she told herself, and then she would call for help. She looked closely at the clock and studied the minute hand. It moved so slowly that she was certain the clock must be faulty.

Suddenly she jumped.

"I'll give you five minutes to show yourself, girl! If you don't come out now, you'll regret it."

Jennifer felt her body go rigid as the voice bellowed out from the public address speaker which was fixed near the top of one wall. There was a similar speaker in every office so the evil little man could be certain that he was getting through to her. Even though she had escaped his presence, she hadn't escaped his voice.

"Five minutes, girl. Come out and show yourself now."

Her hands went straight to her head and covered her ears, and her body began to shake once more.

Not again. Dear God, not again!

*

A gaggle of police vehicles was parked in the London City Airport car park. Walking slowly towards the vehicles, Helen Mayfield noted several clusters of furtive figures. The uniformed policemen seemed to be gathered together in one organised group, well clear of the airport buildings. Helen forced herself to walk calmly towards them.

Ahead of her, the policemen warily watched her approach. And yet she knew she was under close scrutiny from the gunmen behind her. The thought came to her that she carried a message of great moment, as momentous as the message Moses carried on tablets of stone down the mountainside. And, just like Moses, she was piggy in the middle. He had God above and the children of Israel below. She had the police in front and terrorists behind.

She crossed her fingers and continued walking slowly.

"Hold your hands up, love." One of the uniformed policemen shouted to her as she came closer. She obeyed instantly, noting with alarm that some of the men were armed and their guns were aimed at *her*.

"I'm the ATC Executive Officer," she called back. "I've been released to give you a message."

"Okay, love." The policeman's voice was calm and measured. "Now just stop where you are and turn around."

She halted about ten feet from the nearest policeman, the one who was speaking to her, and she slowly turned.

"I'm not armed," she said, "They haven't planted anything on me."

"We can't take any chances, love."

"I have an important message to pass on. Is there a senior officer I can talk to?" She finished her turn and addressed the group.

"What's the message?" A tall, bearded man moved to the front of the group. Wearing plain clothes, he spoke with a soft brogue, much mellower than the brash Northern Irish accents she was accustomed to hearing on news broadcasts. She had no idea who this man was, but he carried an air which marked him out as more senior than the uniformed men.

"I have to talk to someone in authority," Helen said. "But I can't talk out here. It's too serious a matter."

"You can talk to me."

"Who are you?"

"Commander FitzHugh."

"Alright, Commander FitzHugh. But not out here. Will you let me come in now?"

The bearded man studied her closely through dark, penetrating eyes. Then he nodded and stood aside to allow her into the protection of the police gathering. She felt a wave of relief break over her as she walked on.

"I must talk to you privately," she said, "It's extremely important. I have a message from the terrorists."

"All right. Come with me." FitzHugh took her arm and guided her quickly towards a Range Rover parked a short distance away from the other vehicles. He made no attempt to question her until they reached the Rover, by which time only one other plain clothes policeman was within hearing range.

FitzHugh pointed to a small cassette recorder in the other man's hand. "The chief inspector... the officer here... will be recording everything you say. Now, you are..?"

"Helen Mayfield. I'm the ATC Executive Officer."

"And you were taken prisoner inside the control tower."

"Yes."

"Right. Tell us all you know, Helen."

She coughed to clear her throat. "The Provisional IRA are in complete control inside the tower and out on the airfield."

"It's definitely the Provos?"

"Yes. No doubt about it. And the situation is far worse than you probably imagine. They have a bomb on board one of the aircraft." She gritted her teeth. "It's a nuclear bomb."

"A nuclear... Oh my God!" FitzHugh's composure visibly collapsed. "Are you sure?"

"Yes. They showed it to me. They called it a two-man portable tactical weapon, whatever that means. They wanted me to see it in order that you would believe me."

"Which aircraft is it on?"

"The 146, the Queen's Flight jet. They flew it in on the F27 and then carried it across to the 146. I don't know why."

FitzHugh's eyebrows arched upwards as he digested the information. "I hope for all our sakes," he said, "that this is one big bluff."

*

Vince Trewin picked up the supervisor's telephone and listened for the dialling tone. His gaze was concentrated on the sheet of paper in front of him, the paper he had been studying for some fifteen minutes or more while he waited for the order to make the call. During that time he had racked his brain for some way to outwit his captors, but his brain refused to come up with an answer. He was sure there had to be such an answer, and he was annoyed with himself for being unable to find it.

He was privately surprised that he felt no fear of the terrorist who stood alongside him. There was every reason to be afraid when four of his immediate colleagues had died in acts of violence. He would have no reason to feel any shame had he been scared out of his wits. But his hand remained steadily calm as he grasped the telephone receiver, and his brain remained alert even if it was short of suitable ideas.

"Get on with it." Paddy's voice grated hard on Trewin's senses. It was a coarse, aggressive voice and it suggested to him that the terrorist was acting on the basis of gut-reaction politics rather than well-reasoned argument. That annoyed him.

He dialled 9 to get an outside line, then the Home Office number written at the top of the sheet of paper. The call was answered straightaway. Trewin licked his lips, raised the piece of paper, and asked to speak to the senior civil servant whose name was also at the head of the page. There was a short pause while the call was put through. When the civil servant spoke, Trewin responded with a short message, which included the coded name *Seamus O'Donnell*, to indicate that this would be an authorised Provisional IRA statement.

"This morning, a combined force of Provisional IRA operational brigades took over the control towers at Heathrow Airport and London City Airport," Trewin read out. "In the same operation, a nuclear bomb was taken into the City Airport."

He paused to take a breath, sensing that the control room had suddenly turned quiet around him and faces were turned in his direction. He looked round at the disbelieving controllers and almost immediately he felt the barrel of the gunman's rifle jab into his ribs. Hastily, he continued.

"The bomb will be detonated at four o'clock this afternoon, GMT, unless certain demands are met. These demands will be dictated in the next message you receive."

Trewin lowered the page and looked at his captor. There was a pregnant silence from the other end of the telephone line, then the civil servant's voice asked, "Who am I speaking to?"

Trewin replaced the receiver without replying.

"Why don't you make your demands now?" he asked, keeping his face away from the gunman.

The reply was strangely positive without being aggressive, as if the gunman was allowing his normal human behaviour to come to the fore. Maybe he was getting a little overconfident.

"It'll keep them guessing. Have them running round in circles wondering what we're up to. They'll know the game we're playing, but it won't make them feel any better."

"When will you want me to contact them again?"

"You won't be contacting anyone." The big Irishman glanced at his watch. "They'll get the next message from someone else in an hour or more."

"To keep them wondering about who's running the show?" Trewin suggested.

"Something like that."

Trewin tried to settle back, but his thoughts wouldn't allow it.

He asked, "What will be in the next message?"

Toome smiled for the first time, a broad harsh smile. "The British government will find out in due course. Whether *you* find out will depend upon whether you're still alive when we make the announcement."

*

Sir James Heatherley, the Permanent Under Secretary at the Home Office, and one of the four senior officials who had been in discussion, rose slowly from the polished conference table. His head was filled with questions as he made his way towards the door, questions no one present could possibly answer. The voices of the other three were suppressed with small talk as they too made for the door. Each man would undoubtedly be anxious to get back to his own office. There was important work to be done.

Before any man reached it, the door opened suddenly. A young woman wearing a very worried expression came into the room. She whispered into Sir James's ear and then handed him two flimsy sheets of fax paper.

Something in the woman's expression told Sir James this was something serious. He motioned the rest of the group to sit down again, adjusted his spectacles and then silently read the notes. When he looked up, tension filled his whole body.

"I have just received some very important information," he began, glancing down to study the flimsy notes once more. A growing sense of disbelief caused his voice to quiver. "The terrorists have made contact with one of our senior officials here at the Home Office. It *is* the Provisional IRA, as we thought." A subdued groan ran around the room. Sir James ignored it and went on, "They claim to have flown a nuclear bomb into London City Airport."

An immediate electric reaction brought the room to attention.

"A nuke!" Myers, the Commissioner, gasped. His mouth hung wide.

"Only a claim, of course," the MoD man said tersely.

"Yes." Sir James Heatherley looked up sharply and picked up the second fax sheet. "But we have confirmation from City Airport. Someone in the control tower — one of the ATC staff — was actually shown the bomb."

"How big is it?"

"We don't know." Sir James paused while each man took in the news. Then he went on, speaking slowly and deliberately, "These are desperate people, and I think we must take this as a genuine threat until we know otherwise."

"And their demands?" the Commissioner asked.

"Not yet known." Sir James removed his spectacles. "Gentlemen, there is a set procedure we have to go through in the event of any nuclear threat..."

Chapter 10

Jennifer White heaved a heavy desk across the room and positioned it beneath the public address speaker. The legs made a scraping sound as she dragged the desk across the floor, but there was little she could do about it. In any case, the terrible little man was clearly not in the next room. His verbal threats had ceased for the time being, but she wanted to ensure there would be no further messages. She was just able to reach the speaker by standing on tiptoes on top of the desk. When she leaned forward and put her full weight onto it, the apparatus fell away from the wall, speaker, wires and a large area of plaster to which the device had been screwed. She breathed a short, heart-felt sigh.

Her mind was working more positively now, thinking more clearly about how she might escape. Escape! The mere thought gave her the courage to act decisively. She pulled the desk back into the middle of the room and replaced the telephone on top of it. Then she sat down, grasped the receiver tightly with both hands, and dialled the airport exchange. When the operator's voice answered, she whispered, "Police... quickly please."

Within seconds she was talking to a police officer.

At first Jennifer whispered into the telephone and the man at the other end had difficulty in hearing her. He spoke with the clear authoritative tone that she expected of a policeman, but he kept telling her to speak up. She couldn't. Instead, she continued to whisper a brief account of what had happened.

"I can't hear you, love, you'll really have to speak up."

She paused and tried to bring reason to bear. She had already made enough noise moving the desk, so why was she whispering?

"I'm sorry," she said just a little louder, "Can you hear me now."

"That's a bit better. Now tell me all that again. Tell me who you are and what has happened?"

She repeated her message. This time he seemed to get the gist of it and he left her for a few moments while he went to speak to someone else.

"I'm going to put you on to an army officer," he said when he came back to her. "He needs to know about those people up in the control tower, so you tell him everything you know, will you?"

"Yes," she said.

The voice at the other end ceased, replaced by the muffled sound of the receiver being moved into different hands.

"Hello, Miss White? Jennifer? Can you hear me?" It was a new voice. A dark, commanding voice with an edge of calm determination.

"Yes."

"Good. My name is Captain Stenning. I understand you've seen the men who attacked the control tower."

"Yes. I was in the radar room."

"I see. I want to talk to you about the men you've seen up there. The terrorists. I want to ask you some questions. All right?"

"Yes."

"Good. Now, how many terrorists have you actually seen inside the building?"

Jennifer forced her brain to think. "Four, I think."

"Good. Now tell me where they are. Exactly."

"Two are in the emergency control room. They're standing guard over the radar controllers. One is in the main entrance lobby, at least I think there's one in the lobby, I didn't get a good look at him. The other one is the horrible man who chased me up here."

"Where is 'here', Jennifer?"

"Somewhere on the fifth floor. I'm not sure exactly which room I'm in."

"Okay, we'll come back to that. Now, how many people have been hurt by the gunmen?"

"Four. They shot the supervisor and the watch manager... and two of the radar controllers." She shivered. "It was horrible—"

"Yes, I'm sure it was. Who did the shooting?"

"The leader, they called him Paddy."

"Paddy? I see. We need to know more about these men in the radar room. What do they look like?"

This time Jennifer had to pause to collect her thoughts.

"Are you still there, Jennifer?" Stenning asked.

"Yes. I was thinking."

"Speak up, Jennifer."

"I was thinking," she said in a louder voice. "There's the big man called Paddy, the one who seems to be the leader. He's Irish. And there's a smaller man who seems to know a lot about air traffic control. He sounds Irish as well."

"I see. How are they armed?"

"They've both got rifles."

"And what do these men look like, Jennifer? Describe them to me."

"They're both horrible, absolutely horrible." She hesitated for a few seconds, unable to find the words to describe her feelings or impressions.

"I need something more specific, Jennifer. Try to think carefully. Picture them in your mind and tell me what you see."

"I can't... it's all too dreadful... I can't."

"All right, Jennifer. Don't worry about them for the moment. What about the man who chased you. What's he like?"

"He... he tried to rape me!"

A very brief pause followed, and then, "I'm sorry. Did he actually rape you?"

This time she had to take a deep breath and then compress her lips. She closed her eyes and tried to prevent the memory from returning, but nothing could wipe it from her mind. "No. I got away from him. I hit him and ran away."

"Good. Well done on getting away, Jennifer. It's all right now, you seem to be safe where you are. But you must tell me more about these people. I need to know more about them in order to stop them. Do you understand?"

"Yes."

"All right then. Tell me more about the man who attacked you."

"He sounded Scottish and smelled of drink."

"I see. Where were you when he tried to rape you?"

"He... he caught me in the ladies' toilets... I managed to kick him and get away. Then he chased me up here. I'm hiding in an office."

"Good girl. You've been very brave, Jennifer. But you must be brave a little bit longer. Now, I want you to think very carefully... have you any idea how many more terrorists there are in the control tower?"

"No... I don't know. I haven't seen any others."

"All right, love. You've been a tremendous help so far. I'll want to speak to you again shortly and I'll need to ask you some more questions. So keep the telephone line open. Okay?"

"Yes."

"Right. I'm going to put you back to the policeman on duty here while I talk to my men. Just stay calm, don't do anything to attract attention to yourself, and don't you worry. We'll get you out of there."

A rustling sound followed as the telephone was handed back to the policeman. Then the authoritative policeman spoke again. "Hello, Jennifer."

"Hello," she replied, her voice suddenly dropping to a whisper.

"You've no need to worry now," the voice said. "The army boys will get you out safe and sound."

"I hope so. I'm frightened."

"Of course you are. Can you tell us exactly which room you're in?"

"No. I told the other man that. I haven't been in here before."

"Never mind, let's see if we can work it out. Go to the window and tell me which way the room is facing. Tell me what you see outside."

She set the receiver carefully on the desk and walked to the window. Inside, a small kindling of relief was beginning to sparkle into flames. They would get her out. They *had* to get her out of here.

116

*

Angela was sleeping, the nurse told him. She had been restless and needed more painkillers, but she seemed quiet now. FitzHugh took the news with some sense of relief.

He stood apart from the general melee in the City Airport car park, facing a blank wall as he spoke into his police radio telephone. He did not want others to see the look of concern on his face as he made the call. They might see the cracks in his outward façade of determination.

"Tell her I called when she wakes," he said to the nurse. "I'll try to call again in an hour or so."

When he disconnected the line, his thoughts were still centred on Angela and the catalogue of difficult times that had brought them to this sad end to their lives together. He stood for a moment, facing the wall, forcing his blood pressure to steady itself. It was a story that always made him angry, a story made all the more difficult by Angela's mother. She had never understood that there was a legitimate life outside of her own small sphere of knowledge.

Angela's mother was a small, wiry woman, her back half-bent from years of drudgery and heavy work. Living in a small, rented two-up, two-down terrace in one of Belfast's poorer Catholic ghettos, she had been widowed many years, when FitzHugh and Angela were married. Angela continued to live with her mother while FitzHugh was at sea so, for much of the early part of their married life, she continued under her mother's thumb, just as she had since birth. FitzHugh resented it, but he was at home only for short periods.

They had three children in as many years and it was Angela's mother who took immediate and total control of the children's lives. The problems became magnified when FitzHugh, then a Commander RN, left the navy and joined the RUC at a time when Catholics lived in fear of their lives for such a perceived sin. Things got much worse when FitzHugh announced that he and Angela were leaving Northern Ireland to live in London.

"You'll do no such thing!" Angela's mother responded. "I'll not have a daughter of mine living in London! You can go, but Angela stays here with me."

"We are *both* going," FitzHugh told the old lady. "You cannot stop us. This is our life and we will do as we choose."

Angela suffered as the one caught in the middle.

They left Northern Ireland and set up home in a small, detached house on the leafy outskirts of Wimbledon. At first it wasn't easy but, in time, they grew to understand one another in a way they had never previously found possible. And, in time, they began to relax in the knowledge that their lives were their own. They even began to believe that things were better for them on a permanent basis.

But they were not.

Angela was just fifty-two when she was diagnosed with breast cancer. Two years later, when they thought it had been finally cured, she went into relapse. This time, they were told, there was no chance of a cure. She was going to die in England, far removed from her family in Ireland.

*

Helen nursed a cup of coffee as she watched FitzHugh talking on his police telephone. He was standing apart from everyone else and seemed to be in some sort of dilemma as he spoke, as if he ought to be in two places at once.

He had been thorough in the way he had debriefed her, thorough but human, and she respected him for that. She, in return, had trusted him and told him all she could remember about the terrorists inside the control tower.

"Sorry to keep you waiting, Helen," he said as he got into the vehicle beside her. "I was just checking on my wife. She's been ill for some time. They have a nurse at the house looking after her, but I still like to keep checking."

"I understand, Commander. How ill is she?" It came as no surprise to her to discover he had a human side.

"They say she'll probably see the next couple of weeks. After that..." FitzHugh bit his lip as he settled back into the driver's seat. For a brief second his beard quivered.

"I'm so sorry." Helen turned in her seat to face him. "That must be hard."

"We've been together a long time." He pulled at his beard as he spoke and his eyes took on a faraway look. He went silent for a couple of seconds and then added, "I'd got into the way of thinking that she would always be there. That's something you risk taking for granted, you know. That someone will always be there. Except that one day she won't be."

Helen wondered whether to put a comforting hand on his, but decided against it. She didn't know him well enough.

"I'm upset at the thought of losing her, Helen," he went on. "And I'm sorry if it shows. I can't be sure I always did the right things for her when she was fit and well. Does that make sense?"

Helen put down her coffee on the top of the dashboard and looked at FitzHugh's stark silhouette. The capital city was threatened by a nuclear bomb and yet his thoughts were essentially with his wife. Either he was the wrong man for the job... or the best.

She said, "You don't strike me as the sort of man who would have cause to harbour such thoughts."

"Why? Because I look honest? Or because I look callous?"

"You'd better tell me about it," she said. "There's something you have to get out of your system and you'd better do it now, while you have the chance."

He leaned forward and clasped his hands together, searching for the right way to express himself. "I hardly know you. Why am I telling you this?"

"Who knows? But if that bomb goes up, you'll never get it off your chest."

He sucked in through his teeth and stared into the distance. When he next spoke, it was to tell her about the problems in the early years of his married life. He spoke slowly and deliberately, as if his words were chosen with care. When he finished, he sat back, his face pale.

"It's a sad story, but you lived through it," Helen said. "You overcame the problems."

"Yes. Yes, we did. But that's not the point. You see, I should have handled things better right from the start, and I didn't. I let them grow."

"But you loved her despite all of that trouble?"

"What do you think?"

"And your children?" She picked up her cup and lifted it to her lips.

He turned to face her and she saw a dampness in his eyes. "They grew up happy enough. We tried to give them a decent home, a happy home."

"But now those insecurities are coming back? Surely, Angela is not going to turn against you now. Not now."

"No, of course not." He stabbed at his eyes, a hurried gesture. "Now I worry that she's dying in a country that's well removed from her own home and family, and all because of me."

Helen sighed. What a mess this man was. She moved closer to him, her voice calm and easy. "It sounds to me like the home you gave her here was the real one."

"Maybe. Let's hope to God we all have homes to go to after this business." For a second FitzHugh smiled back at her. Then he pulled at his beard and his face went serious again. "Masks?" he snapped, so suddenly she was caught unawares. "How many of the terrorists wore face masks or balaclava helmets?"

Helen shrugged. "None that I saw. Is that important?"

"Vital." FitzHugh pulled at his beard. "If you were a terrorist, would you want your identity exposed? What about gloves? Did any of them wear gloves?"

She shook her head thoughtfully. "I don't think so."

"So they can be easily identified, and they don't mind leaving their prints all over the shop. What does that tell you?"

"I hadn't thought about it."

FitzHugh leaned back in his seat and exhaled long and low. "It means they're supremely confident of getting away, probably to some country where we can't touch them. Or else..."

"Or else what?"

"Or maybe they intend to destroy all the evidence. Maybe they plan to blow it up. Including themselves."

*

Dan Mayfield pulled up at a police road block as he approached the City Airport. It took ten minutes of careful persuasion to convince the police constable at the barrier that he had a legitimate reason to speak to a senior officer. It took a further fifteen minutes to convince the officer that he had a right to be concerned about his wife's safety.

At the back of his mind he carried a growing suspicion that Helen meant more to him than Janice Wilkins ever had, or ever would do. That brought with it feelings of guilt and the dreadful thought that he might lose her — might already have lost her. It was too much to bear. God, he had actually wondered why he hadn't met Janice Wilkins first!

He shivered as he waited.

Eventually he was escorted to where Helen stood beside a police Range Rover in the airport car park, surrounded by a melee of activity. She was quietly sipping coffee from a plastic cup and she looked up inquisitively as he approached. Mayfield ignored the policemen nearby and ran the last few yards towards her, a deep sense of relief washing over him.

"Dan!" Helen placed the cup on the Land Rover's bonnet and held out her arms to embrace him.

"Thank God you're safe." He pulled her close and kissed her with no regard for the watching policemen. He didn't deserve this from the woman whose love he had betrayed, but he clasped her tightly.

"What happened to you?" he asked when he felt ready to release his hold on her.

"Nothing to cause me any harm. The terrorists captured me in the tower along with two controllers. One of my staff was shot."

"Shot? Oh, my God! But you're unhurt?"

"Yes, Dan. I'm quite safe."

He noticed for the first time how pale she looked. Pale and tired.

"What did they do to you?" he asked, "I mean, why did they let you go?"

"They took me outside to an aircraft on the runway, then they showed me what was inside, and then they released me. Honestly, Dan, I haven't been hurt. Not a scratch."

"Oh, thank God. I was so worried about you."

She grinned. "You know me, Dan. Tough as old boots. They couldn't hurt me."

"It's no joke, Helen. What about the other controllers? What about the one who was shot?"

"He's dead."

Mayfield hugged her again. "It could have been you," he said. The more he held her with visions of possible violence racing through his head, the more Janice Wilkins sank further into the back of his mind.

"Why did they release you?" he asked.

"They wanted someone to carry a message back here to the police. I seemed to be the logical choice." She put out her hand to his chest as she spoke, forcing a small gap between them. He sensed that there was more to be told.

"What was the message?" he asked.

Before she answered, she drew away from him completely and wrapped her arms about herself. "I'm not sure I can tell you..."

"Helen!" He pulled her back, grasping her arm tightly. "What is it?"

"They showed me something... something on the aircraft. And they told me to describe it to the police."

"What? What did they show you?"

Helen looked towards FitzHugh who was standing nearby, listening in the background. He nodded almost imperceptibly.

Shaking her head sadly, she said, "It was a bomb. A nuclear

bomb."

"Jeez! A nuke!" He stood rock still for a moment, stunned by the revelation, before he continued in a more hesitant tone. "What... What do they want?"

"I don't know. They've not said yet."

"Can you guess?"

"Hardly." She glanced again at FitzHugh who now had his back to her. She lowered her voice and nodded towards the commander. "The police know more about it than they're telling me. I was just a messenger, you know. Do you know who that man is, the one over there?"

"No."

"Commander FitzHugh. You know, the anti-terrorist man. We've seen him being interviewed on television. We've been chatting and he's quite a normal person, really. A nice man. I was quite surprised."

"Seen him on the television? Have we really?" Mayfield sounded far less than interested as he turned away from the airport scene and nodded in the direction of the approach road. "I think we'd better go. You've had enough for one day."

"No, Dan. I can't go." Helen held back while holding onto his hand. "It's a matter of security. I have to stay here. They probably won't let you go, either. Not now that I've spoken to you."

"Why the hell not?" Anger was surging inside him now. He had not slept since that rough Atlantic crossing and the strain was beginning to show.

"If we walk away from here, the press will get their teeth into us pretty damn quick. And once they get onto the story, they won't give up until they get something out of us for the front page."

"Hell! But why—?"

"That's life, Dan."

For a moment he was on the verge of rebelling and forcing his way out of the area along with his wife. But he knew that he wouldn't get far, not in a crisis situation involving a nuclear bomb. Neither would there be any gain in confronting the commander and insisting that they be allowed to leave. This was no simple hijack, this was big. Really big.

Helen nudged him and nodded towards a large unmarked van parked at the rear end of the car park. "See that van?"

"Yes?"

"Something is going on over there. I wondered if it might be the SAS. It would be pretty odd if they weren't here and that van seems to be the focus of some sort of activity. Notice how they've parked a few cars in front of it to make it look less obvious from the terminal building."

"Are there any more soldiers around here?"

"Probably. But it's difficult to tell." Helen swept her gaze around the surrounding scene of activity. "Have you noticed how many civilians are working here with the police? I think they know what they're doing, probably too well to be genuine civilians.

"Do you think they'll storm the terminal?"

"No." Helen shook her head and turned towards the source of the drama. "They can't do that. Not with a nuclear bomb over there."

"I suppose you're right. Thank God you're out of it." He grasped her hand tighter and tried to smile. Helen kept her face turned away, as if she had something else on her mind, something she was not revealing.

*

Jennifer sat at the desk and studied the telephone handset, willing someone to speak to her. A quarter of an hour had passed since she had last spoken to anyone and she was getting nervous again. Now that the initial sense of shock had worn off, she wanted nothing more than to get out of the tower as quickly as possible. As soon as the man called Captain Stenning came back on the line, she would ask him to get her out. She didn't much care how he did it. In fact, she had no idea how he might do it. She simply wanted out.

She picked up the receiver, listened to a distant sound of

muffled voices from the other end of the line and said, "Hello?" There was no reply. They seemed to have their receiver sitting on a table, or something, with no one actually listening for her. That made her feel vulnerable again. She had no immediate access to anyone, no direct means of summoning help until the policeman picked up his handset.

There seemed to be no point in sitting at the telephone when no one was listening for her, so she stood up and walked to the window. She could see no obvious sign that an emergency situation existed, except that no vehicles travelled along the airport roads in front of the terminal buildings. The other, distant roads seemed clogged with traffic, but not the nearest one. Groups of people were gathered outside the terminal buildings but, closer to, the bus station was empty. Almost empty. She could see armed policemen darting from one hiding place to another.

Just below her she could see the large wooden cross of the airport chapel, looking incongruous in the middle of the busy township that was Heathrow. Even the little paved garden that surrounded the cross looked out of place. She raised her head and saw the large advertising sign for a Korean electronics manufacturer, a huge hand grasping a flickering torch. What use was a flaming torch when she was incarcerated inside the control tower building? In the farther distance, an Air France Airbus climbed away behind the ugly structure that was the Number Three terminal building, carrying a lucky band of passengers who were escaping from Heathrow.

She turned her head slightly and noted more policemen in front of the Number Two terminal building. Then she dragged her attention back to what was happening at the front of the control tower. She could see only a small area to the side of the building and that seemed to be very quiet. She suddenly realised that the pavement below was quite empty. No public, no police, no army, no... anything.

Then she saw a British Telecom van parked only yards from the base of the tower. Her imagination began to take hold of her thoughts and translate the sight of an innocent vehicle into a dramatic rescue attempt. Maybe there were soldiers inside the van watching her through powerful binoculars. She half-raised a hand to wave, then pulled it back self-consciously. Of course it was all just wishful thinking, how could she be so stupid?

Her heightened senses picked up the sound of a distant voice, and she hastened back to the desk and picked up the telephone. The seeds of hope told her she had to be ready whenever her rescuers called. When the policeman did speak, she eagerly pressed the receiver closer to her ear.

"Jennifer? Are you there?"

"Yes. Yes, I'm here." Her voice came out more confident now, no longer strained.

"Good. The army captain wants to speak to you again."

She waited for the expected changeover, and then felt a mounting excitement as she heard the army officer's voice.

"Hello, Jennifer. This is Paul Stenning again."

"Hello." Anticipation was beginning to take over.

"I'm sorry to keep you waiting so long. I had to discuss what you told me with my men."

"Yes, I understand. That's all right," she lied.

"I've a few more questions I must ask you."

She felt a sudden minor sinking feeling, nothing serious, just a disappointment that the rescue plan was not discussed first.

"I understand," she said.

"Good. I want you to think very hard about everything the men in the control room said. We must find out where the terrorists are stationed around the building. Can you think of anything that any of the men said which might give us a clue?"

"No. Honestly, I can't think of anything."

"Think again, Jennifer. Are you absolutely sure?"

"Yes. I told you!" Her voice was raised now, a growing desperation filling her responses.

"Okay, Jennifer. Not to worry. Let's go back to your description of the leader of the gang. I want you to picture him in your mind.

Can you do that?"

"Yes. I think so."

"Good. Now tell me what he looks like. Take your time over this because it is important."

"He's... he's Irish. He's got a red face... and he has a rifle... and he's sort of... sort of... well built."

"Is he tall?"

"No. Not very tall, but he's..."

"Thick set?"

"Yes. And he's got black eyebrows. They meet in the middle."

"That's good, Jennifer. You're doing well. Now, his height. How tall is he?"

"Hmm. Reasonably tall."

"Can you be more precise? If I said he was about six foot, would that be about right?"

"Shorter. About five foot ten. That's how tall my dad is."

"Excellent. Now let's go back to his face. You said he has a red face, and black eyebrows which meet in the middle. What about his hair?"

"Pretty normal, I suppose. Black. I think it's black."

"And is he clean shaven?"

"Yes." She was more positive now.

"That's very good, Jennifer. Now I'm going to give all this information to my intelligence people. So that we can positively identify the gang leader."

"You know who he is?" she asked.

"We think so. I'll come back to you in just a few minutes. Okay?"

"Okay."

In fact, it was a full five minutes before he came back on the line. When he did, his voice had changed. It was more sombre and a little reticent.

"You've been a great help to us, Jennifer. We know now who we're up against. But we can't get you out of there just yet. Not until we know exactly where each of the terrorists is stationed inside the building."

This time she was ready for the disappointment, half-expecting it. "All right," she replied.

"It's very important that we find out exactly what is happening in there, Jennifer. These men are desperate and they've already shot one policeman across the road from the control tower. The lives of all your friends in the tower are at stake, as well as the lives of people at City Airport."

"What's happened there? At City Airport?" It was her first real indication that a drama was being played out elsewhere in the London area.

"The IRA gunmen have captured the control tower and an aircraft of the Queen's Flight."

"Oh." She felt a dullness which came with the realisation that her own safety was probably not of prime importance at that moment. In fact, she probably ranked pretty low in their order of priorities.

"However, someone else is looking after that side of things," the army officer continued. "My job is to work out how we can deal with those jokers in the Heathrow control tower, and how to rescue the controllers in there."

"I see." She noticed that he had said 'controllers', omitting to mention the other staff inside the building. Like assistants. Especially young female assistants.

"Like I said, Jennifer, we must find out more about what is happening. Where are the terrorists located? What are they all doing? We must have the answers to these important questions. You can see that, can't you?"

"Yes." But she spoke the word with a sense of dread beginning to form in her mind.

"I want you to think hard. Is there any way we can find out exactly where each of the terrorists is right now?"

"I don't know."

Stenning's voice came back with a more insistent edge. "Think, Jennifer. We can't just rush into the tower without knowing. Too many innocent people would be killed. Think hard."

He was right, of course. He had to know. It was patently obvious. But how on earth could she help him?

"You'll need to talk to someone in the radar room," she mumbled. "One of the controllers. One of them will know what's going on."

"You know that's not possible. The gunmen have cut off all outside contact. But you are right on one point. We need someone inside the radar room to tell us what's happening."

"You mean me, don't you!" She raised her voice unwittingly as the implication sank in. "You want me to go back in there and find out for you. You do, don't you?"

"I can't force you to do that, Jennifer. It would be very dangerous."

No, he couldn't force her, but it was what he wanted. That was obvious now. He wanted her to go back to where Simon... Oh God! She had forgotten the Irishman's last words to her, but they came back to her now.

She clasped her hands to her cheeks. "Oh, God, no! One of the controllers... Simon Hudson... They said they'd shoot him if I tried to get away."

A soft voice came down the telephone line. "You didn't mention that before."

"I... I forgot..."

There was a brief pause before Stenning spoke again. "It sounds like Simon Hudson's life is in your hands, Jennifer."

That was unfair. He was putting pressure on her. But she already knew the outcome. She couldn't let them shoot Simon. Not him. "I don't have any choice, do I," she wailed. "Oh, God. I have to go back there or they'll kill Simon. They'll kill him because of me."

"You're a brave girl, Jennifer." That was all Stenning said in reply, and she hated him for it.

"But, I'm frightened!" she sobbed.

The army officer's voice was more determined now. "Of course you are, but I'm going to rely on you. I want you to find out what's going on down there, and then find a way to get a message out to me."

Jennifer held the telephone away from her ear and turned her head. A trickle of tears was working its way down her cheek and she didn't want anyone to hear her crying.

*

The atmosphere at London City Airport seemed to come more alive suddenly — almost as if an electric shock had been delivered into the crowd of police officers littering the car park. Helen sensed rather than saw the change and she felt herself go tense as a familiar figure hurried towards her. Commander FitzHugh had been called away after a brief introduction to Dan, leaving them both in the custody of his juniors. He came back in a hurry, his face looking grim and ponderous.

"We've got problems." He hurried up to the Range Rover where they were standing.

Dan Mayfield scowled. "I thought that was pretty obvious."

Helen suppressed a feeling of alarm that her husband might lose his cool.

"It's the press." FitzHugh ignored him and turned to Helen. "They've got hold of the story and they know about the bomb."

"How did they learn about it?"

"I don't know. Probably a mole somewhere inside the Home Office. The bloody civil service is full of informants ready to make a quick buck from the press."

"The press were bound to find out sooner or later."

"True. But it would have helped us if it had been later. Now the hounds are clamouring for information. Worse still, they're likely to scare the public."

Helen tried to sound calm. "The public have a right to know what's going on."

"That's debatable, Helen. Can you imagine what's going to happen when the public find out that a band of nutters have threatened to explode a nuclear bomb this close to the city. It's bound to

130

cause panic, the like of which we've never seen before."

"Slap a D-Notice on them," Dan interrupted.

"Come off it, Mr Mayfield. With a story like this, do you think we can keep it secret just by slapping a D-Notice on it? No, it's going to get out so we may as well try to control the information instead of suppressing it. But God help us all when the public start to panic."

Chapter 11

A young WPC came round with a tray of hot tea in plastic cups and a tray of sandwiches. A clear sign, Helen thought, that the police were under no illusions about how long it would take to sort out this enormous mess. She took a tea for herself and grimaced when she found it tasted like dishwater. She ignored the sandwiches which were wrapped up in cellophane and sealed with adhesive tape.

"Do you have any coffee?" she asked.

"I'm not sure..."

"Go and see if you can rustle up a cup for me and my husband, will you?"

The WPC wandered off with a resigned shrug.

Dan Mayfield seemed to ignore the whole question of food and drink. The strain of the occasion coming right on top of a tiring Atlantic flight showed in deeply creased lines across his face. Helen felt concerned. She could see an incipient irritability crawling into the foreground, with the risk that he might blow his top soon.

They sat inside the police Range Rover, half-listening to the burble of chatter on the radio, and half-immersed in their own thoughts. Although the vehicle doors were shut, it felt cold. Helen wore a borrowed coat, her own outer clothes still inside the control tower building. She reflected that in calmer circumstances she and Dan would be thinking of wrapping Judith's birthday presents.

"They must have demanded an awful lot," her husband mused, stroking his stubbly chin. "To go to all this trouble, they really must want a lot by way of ransom. What do you think is behind it all?"

"Haven't a clue. But I think there's more to it than just ransom."

Helen stretched her arms and directed her eyes towards the terminal building. "I mean, they wouldn't go to all this trouble just to make themselves a few quick bucks or get some of their mates out of gaol, would they?"

"Judging by what they've done already, they're a pretty determined bunch." Dan stifled a yawn.

"Yes, I suppose so. But the IRA don't strike me as being fully up to this sort of game."

"You're probably right." Dan put his arm over the back of the seat and sipped at his drink. "So what's this all about? Has your friend FitzHugh been filling you in?"

"Not really." Helen paused for a moment to recall that FitzHugh had 'filled her in' only on his own domestic problems. "Based on what I've read about the IRA, I'd say they're not the sort of professionals who could organise something like this."

"You mean they're more in the mould of a parish council? Tea and biscuits, Vicar? Would you hold the Semtex while we prime the bomb?"

Helen laughed. "Mrs Billington-Smythe will now blow up the village hall unless we all donate towards the church organ fund." She became suddenly more serious. "But I still say that getting hold of a nuclear bomb has got to be way beyond any Irish terrorists. There must be someone else involved. Someone with real influence, somewhere or other."

Helen was, in part, turning over thoughts in her mind and, in part, trying to analyse those thoughts by verbally airing them. It didn't seem to bring any real answers. Just guesswork.

"So, who do you think is really behind the bomb?" Dan asked.

"God knows." Helen jerked herself back into a more active state and threw the remaining dishwater tea out onto the tarmac. There was no sign of the coffee she had asked for. "We'll find out in time, I suppose."

"It's a bit of a bugger, isn't it?" Dan put a hand to his head and closed his eyes, fatigue ripping out of him.

"You look all in," Helen observed. "How would it be if I ask

Commander FitzHugh to find you somewhere to get your head down? This business is likely to go on for some time."

"I'd rather go home... I know, I know!" He raised his hands defensively. "They can't let us go in case we get nobbled by the press. Okay, let's see if your policeman friend can find us somewhere more relaxing than this bloody cop car."

They found FitzHugh at the centre of a buzzing group of uniformed policemen gathered near a mobile police control room. Helen edged her way into the throng, with Dan following at her heels. The Commander looked up and pulled at his beard as he watched them approach.

"I need a quick word," she mouthed across the huddled gap between them.

He nodded and indicated into the control room. The atmosphere inside was more organised. Policemen and women, working in shirtsleeves, went about their duties quietly and efficiently, a contrast to the melee outside.

FitzHugh removed his hat. "Sorry to keep you hanging on, Helen. I haven't forgotten about you, you know."

Dan crammed himself into a corner of the room beside Helen. "We wondered whether there is somewhere else we can go," the pilot said simply. "Somewhere a bit more comfortable while we wait for you to sew things up here."

FitzHugh looked at him silently for a few seconds, considering his reply. His hand went to his beard in a telling gesture. "You look tired," he said eventually. "I believe you were flying the Atlantic last night."

"Yes. It was a bit of a rough ride."

"He's feeling whacked," Helen explained. "He hasn't slept."

"I can see that. All right, Mr Mayfield. I'll arrange somewhere secure for you to get your head down for a few hours. I'm sorry about all this, but you do realise that Helen has to stay here. We need her." His tone hinted at more than had previously been said.

At the same time, Helen detected a change in her husband's manner and she saw him glance in her direction. Without hesitation, she butted in, "I'm sorry, Dan. I'll have to stay here. But you go and get a couple of hours sleep. I'll be alright, honestly."

"What exactly do you mean? Why do you need her here?" Dan looked sharply at the commander.

FitzHugh looked at them both, chewed his lip pensively and again pulled at his beard before he replied. "Your wife represents the only real contact we've had with the terrorists over there. We tried to set up a telephone link with them in the control tower but they've refused to allow it, so far. We're working on it, but it's giving us a real headache."

"But what's that got to do with—?"

FitzHugh put up his hand to the protest. "We need to have Helen nearby just in case we get the chance to make contact. In case they eventually decide to speak to us."

"Why Helen?"

"Because they know her. She's the only one they might trust if they try to call us."

"You mean you may want to make use of my wife as a go-between?" Dan's thinly-suppressed anger began to bubble to the surface.

"We have to be prepared for an approach from those people over there. Any sort of approach. You see, this really is a major incident, Mr Mayfield. This is not just a run-of-the-mill piece of IRA troublemaking. This threat puts the lives of millions at risk. We have to be prepared for what comes next."

"Just a phone call? That's what you expect?"

FitzHugh stroked his beard slowly. "Any sort of approach. Whatever it takes."

Helen turned her head away, fearful that Dan might recognise her own misgivings. A phone call might be the least of her worries.

*

Yesterday, the Right Honourable Nicholas Horton MP had been happy to hear the media refer to him as an up-and-coming government minister, a future leader. Today he suffered severe reservations at being pushed into a higher public profile.

He leaned back in his seat and ran a hand through his thin, snowy hair. He glanced anxiously around the group of men sitting at the conference table. His mind weighed up all the points made by these men and found no answers to the most important questions. He needed those answers if he was to convince the Home Secretary that his up-and-coming status was still justified. After some moments, he eased himself forward and drummed his fingers on the wide, mahogany table, still thinking.

Three men sat opposite him. George Elsmeer, the Secretary of State for Defence, was in the centre. On either side of him sat Herbert Morgan-Jones, the Director of Military Operations (Ground Forces) at the Defence Ministry, and Sir William Bessbrook, the Director General of MI5. On his own side of the table, Horton had the support of Sir James Heatherley, the Permanent Under Secretary. Right now, he felt very much in need of that support.

Sir William Bessbrook, the Director General of MI5, was looking impassively grim, a sure sign that he was not pleased with the way the meeting was going. His department had goofed in not having any prior warning of the Provisional IRA's nuclear capability — real or otherwise — and he would have to carry the can on that score.

"What you seem to be saying," Horton ceased his drumming and shuffled forward in his seat to address Bessbrook, "is that your people have no idea whether this threat is real, or just a bluff."

Bessbrook hedged uneasily. "I wouldn't put it that way. We have opinions, of course. But, dammit all, it's impossible to be sure." He spread his hands expressively. "We can't really be certain until someone gets close enough to examine the thing. You see, this is a classic case of contradictory improbabilities."

Horton screwed up his face to indicate his lack of comprehension. Why the hell couldn't the man stick to simple words?

"On the one hand," Bessbrook went on, "we have had no evidence, until now, that the IRA has the means of obtaining a nuclear device, or the skills to handle one. Nor have we had any clue that they were casting their eyes in that direction. Not one single hint. In fact, if you had suggested it just twenty-four hours ago, I would have laughed out loud."

"So it looks like a bluff?"

"No. That's the contradiction, you see. They have nothing to gain by bluffing. Whatever their demands are, they must know that we won't give in to them on the basis of an unproven threat. An operation like this will only work if the threat is real."

"So, now you're suggesting that the bomb is a genuine device."

"I'm not suggesting anything," Bessbrook replied forcefully. "Real or bluff, it just doesn't make sense."

"All right. So what is your personal opinion?"

Bessbrook's eyes slanted down at the corners. "Personally... if you really want to press me, then I think that, on balance, the thing is real."

"But you just told me..." Horton was getting angry now and his hand waved across the desk and scattered a pile of documents. "You suggested that there is no evidence it could be real."

At this point George Elsmeer, the Defence Minister, intervened. He was a brash young member of the cabinet, and Horton hated his guts. Elsmeer's career would take him over the dead body of any colleague he cared to knife in the back. He was a threat to all the old guard within the cabinet.

"What Sir William is trying to tell you, Nicholas, is that the IRA couldn't, *by themselves*, get hold of a nuclear bomb." Elsmeer's gaze flashed threateningly as he spoke. "At least, not in his opinion. Or mine." He paused and sat back to let the words sink in. Then he went on, "But other organisations might have that capability, given the right circumstances."

Horton threw himself back in his seat. "Who?"

Elsmeer simply shook his head silently.

"God!" Horton raised his hands in a gesture of frustration. "That really puts us in one hell of a spot, doesn't it? You're telling me the thing is probably a real nuke, but you don't know whose finger is on the button. Meanwhile the PM has asked the Home Secretary to put one of his junior ministers in front of the television cameras to say it's a bluff. The PM wants to play down the threat. Tell the population that it's all a hoax."

"I suggest you recommend to the Home Secretary that he should do just that, Nicholas." Bessbrook drew in a deep breath as he re-entered the discussion. "We don't want a national panic, do we?"

Horton compressed his lips. This discussion wasn't giving him the answers he needed, the answers the Home Secretary and the PM would be looking for.

Heatherley, the Under Secretary, shifted in the seat alongside him and came back into the conversation with a curious tone of delicacy. He stared across the table at Bessbrook. "Could you tell us, Sir William, why your people were unable to pick up any warning of this?"

"No, I can't." Bessbrook went immediately on the defensive. "We can't predict everything the IRA does."

"But this isn't everything, is it?" Heatherley smiled grimly. "This is the biggest threat to the City of London since the Second World War. Bigger even. Surely this is something MI5 should have ferreted out before it got this far."

"Oh, no! I can't accept that," Bessbrook snapped. "What do you want from us? Miracles? In a free society you just can't put tabs on everyone. You can't find out everything everyone is doing."

"I see," the Under Secretary replied expressively. "So there could be other threats like this in the offing and you wouldn't know about them, either." He forced a long breath through his nose and wrote speedily onto a notepad resting in front of him.

Bessbrook crossed his arms and looked to the Defence Minister for support. But there was none.

Horton stared silently across the table at the group opposite him, his gaze running rapidly from one to the other. Eventually, it came to rest on Herbert Morgan-Jones, the Director of Military Operations at the Defence Ministry. He had been silent for too long.

"What exactly is the state of readiness with the Regiment?" he asked as he fixed Morgan-Jones with a heavy stare. Horton always referred to them as the Regiment, never the SAS.

The DMO shuffled some papers on the desk and then replied cagily. "They have a team in place at Heathrow, and another team at London City Airport. My information is that the Heathrow team are preparing to re-take the control tower."

"That's a feasible proposition?"

"Yes. Provided that they can cut all the IRA's communication links between Heathrow control tower and London City Airport. So as not to let the bastards at City Airport know—"

"*All* links?"

"We'll keep our own lines of communication open, obviously. First rule of the game is to keep on trying to talk to these people if we can. But we'll have to take out all the links between the two groups. We'll even disable all citizen band radio frequencies in the area. Could cause a lot of problems to other people, but it has to be done."

"The emergency services?"

"We can keep their radios on line."

"And what are the Regiment at City Airport doing?" Horton butted in.

"They're being held back because of worries by Sir David Myers and Commander FitzHugh. They both seem to be afraid that the IRA at City Airport may take fright if they get one hint that we plan to send in the Regiment." His words held a hint of a sneer, as if he held the opinion in contempt. "They're both worried that the PIRA might—"

"Blow us all to kingdom come? Probably a wise precaution on the part of the Commissioner and Commander FitzHugh," Horton said evenly. He sat still for some seconds, thinking, then he jerked his head towards Heatherley. "What time do I see the PM?"

Heatherley glanced at his watch. "A little over twenty minutes from now, Minister."

"Right." Horton became decisive. "We need to know exactly what sort of threat we're facing. The PM will certainly be looking for positive answers. So, between us, we must find some way of getting a look at that device to determine whether or not it's real. I suggest that the MoD gets together with the police and sorts out an answer quickly. Then perhaps, George," he fixed Elsmeer with a hard look, "you and I can get together again in an hour or so to work out our next strategic move."

Elsmeer nodded silently.

Horton allowed the silence to last a full ten seconds. Then he stood up suddenly and the other men followed.

"Obviously we're in the dark and we must play this one very softly..." Sir William Bessbrook began.

"I don't care how you do it," Horton cut him short. "One way or another, we have to know exactly what sort of threat we're facing. Get someone to take a close look at that bomb. Find a way to do it! It's vital. And for God's sake find out who's really behind it!"

Horton signalled to Sir James Heatherley to wait behind while the other three men left the room. When they were alone, he asked, "Your man, FitzHugh, has he come up with anything positive?"

"Not yet, Minister."

"You'll tell me when he does come up with answers." He hung his head and glanced at his watch. "We don't exactly have all day to sort out this business, do we?"

"That is understood, Minister."

"You trust this man, FitzHugh?"

Heatherley nodded. "We must trust him. There is simply no one else with the experience to handle this."

*

Simon Hudson rubbed a hand across his eyes and then sat up straight to focus on what was happening in the Heathrow emergency control room. All flights into and out of City Airport were now halted because of the aircraft stopped on the runway. Hudson's job was now limited to controlling the few light aircraft and helicopters flying around Biggin Hill and the dockland vicinity. He guessed that most — if not all — were either police or military reconnaissance flights, but the callsigns were strictly civilian so he kept his suspicions to himself.

His workload was now light enough for him to concentrate his attention on what was happening in the room. Jennifer had yet to return and he was becoming increasingly concerned for her — and his own — safety. He looked around at his overburdened colleagues and the two terrorists.

Paddy, the leader of the terrorist group, was seated on the edge of the supervisor's desk, smoking continually. The smaller man was standing behind the Heathrow controllers, covering them with his rifle. Rather pointless, Hudson thought. Now that the F27 and the BAe146 were both on the ground at London City Airport, the terrorist had no reason to continue monitoring the radar controller's work. Vince Trewin was no longer at the desk. He had been sent upstairs to the Visual Control Room to relieve one of the hard-pressed air controllers.

The telephone line from City Airport rang frequently now and Paddy took all the calls himself, putting on an outward show of confidence which probably fooled no one. Hudson listened carefully to each call and began to piece together a picture of the terrorist plan. One telephone conversation caused him more concern than the others. In it, Paddy made the comment, "We'll be picked up one hour before the deadline. If the bomb goes off, we don't want to hang around here, do we?"

Hudson was casually turning things over in his mind when Jennifer came in through the corridor entrance. He noticed that she was pale and disturbed, as if she had been under some pressure.

"Where the hell were you?" As soon as he spotted her, Paddy jumped to his feet, threw his cigarette on the floor and bellowed in the girl's direction. "Who said you could bog off like that?"

Jennifer cowered back against the door, her frightened face looking drawn and pinched, even in the subdued light of the radar room.

"Someone attacked me," she whispered.

The Irishman advanced towards her. "Someone did what?"

"Someone attacked me in the ladies' toilets. It was one of your men. He tried to... he tried to... to rape me."

Hudson swung his seat round suddenly and was half-risen to his feet before the barrel of the terrorist's Armalite was swung in his direction. He sat down again slowly.

"He tried to rape you? You must have led him on," Paddy said accusingly. His face grew black, as if he was suppressing an inner anger.

"No, I—"

"Did he actually rape you?"

"No. I ran away from him."

"Where did you go? Where the hell have you been all this time?"

"I hid," she mumbled. "In one of the offices."

"Did you, by Christ! And you thought it would be safe to come back here now, I suppose?"

Jennifer nodded imperceptibly. The Irishman stared at her for a full minute before he backed away. He called over his shoulder, "Get back to your job, girl. And if you disappear again, I'll personally take you apart piece by piece."

A few seconds later he added, "If I once get my hands on you, you'll wish you had nothing more than a simple rape to worry about. Do you understand me, girl?"

This time she nodded fiercely.

With that, the Irishman returned to his stance at the supervisor's desk. To Hudson, quietly watching, it was almost as if the man was afraid to say more to the girl.

Jennifer went back to her assistant's desk and avoided looking anywhere but down at the flight details in front of her. Hudson thought he saw her shaking and wondered whether she was crying. He decided that she probably was.

As well as his concern for the young assistant, Hudson also harboured worries about the fatigue he observed in his colleagues. He wondered whether they would be fed. While he was pondering the problem, Jennifer left her seat and brought some flight progress strips across the room to him.

"These are for you," she said as she handed him two strips. She avoided his gaze as she spoke and passed on quickly to the other controllers.

Hudson set the strips onto the desk in front of him. One showed the details of a light aircraft wanting to route through the airspace around the City Airport. The other had nothing written on it. Hudson puzzled over the blank strip and looked back at the girl. She had returned to her desk, and sat with her shoulders hunched over her work. He shook his head and pulled the paper strip from the plastic holder, a normal reaction to any strip that was no longer required. He was about to throw it away when he saw something written on the reverse side. It was a small, neat script — the writing of a tidy female hand. He read:

> I telephoned the police from an office. An army officer spoke to me. He wanted me to find out where all the terrorists are and what they are doing. Please help me.'

Hudson felt a sudden shock punch through him. He read the message again, and then screwed the strip into a ball and threw it into a waste bin beside him. This put a whole new complexion on things. When he glanced again at the girl, she was looking in his direction. He raised his eyebrows as a sign of understanding, and then turned away before anyone else saw the gesture.

One thing was for sure: if he was to help her, he would have to get away from the Thames Radar suite. That was technically possible with so few flights on his radio frequency. The problem lay in finding an excuse.

When Hudson made his move, he acted decisively in the hope that it would appear to be more than a servile gesture by a frightened man. He placed his headset on the radar console in front of the screen, coughed loudly to draw attention to himself, and crossed his fingers.

"Excuse me," he called across to the terrorist leader as he stood up. "I wonder if I might have a word with you. If you don't mind." His heart thumped loudly inside his chest, but this was something he just had to do.

"What the hell do you want?" The big man turned to face him, his rifle levelled from the hip.

Hudson spoke evenly. "It's about the staff here. They haven't had anything to eat all morning. And it is lunch time."

"So?"

Hudson took a hesitant step forward. "Well, I thought you might ask for some food to be sent in."

The gunman stood looking directly at him, his face twisted into an expression that could have been thoughtful puzzlement or outright hatred. It was difficult to tell in such a face as his, and Hudson was left unsure whether his action had been wise or extremely foolish.

Chapter 12

"The problem," Commander FitzHugh mused, "is that we don't really know if this is a real threat or a bluff."

"I did see inside the bomb," Helen replied. She was sprawled back in a rather wobbly plastic seat inside the police control room. She was on the verge of asking why the police couldn't afford better seating, but held the remark in check.

FitzHugh was perched on the edge of a desk and seemed to be enduring an equal share of bodily discomfort. "Yes. I know. But was it the real thing? Or just a convincing mock-up of a bomb? We need a far more detailed description."

"I've told you all I know."

"Yes, and we appreciate all the help you've given us. But, right now, the Home Office is causing a bit of a stink because we're still not too sure about the device."

Helen smiled grimly and said, "I understand. The man at the top wants answers and you have to get them for him."

FitzHugh leaned forward and took a deep breath. "It's one hell of a thing to ask you, Helen. But, would you go back there and take another look at it? We'll get someone to tell you exactly what to look for, so that you can examine the really important bits."

A momentary shudder ran through her, causing Helen to scrape the chair legs several inches across the floor. She had been prepared to talk to the terrorists on a phone line, but this... this was asking too much. And yet, deep down, she had known all along that they might want her to do this. She remembered FitzHugh's words, "Any sort of approach. Whatever it takes."

"That's asking a lot, isn't it," she muttered hastily, recomposing herself. "I mean, I was prepared to talk to them, but..." Her words trailed off before she added, "They haven't actually asked for me to go back over there, have they?"

"You're right, it is a lot to ask." FitzHugh averted his gaze in apparent embarrassment. "And no, they won't be expecting you to go back. You'd be on your own."

"There's no one else?"

"No. If anyone else tried to go over there, they would almost certainly be killed."

"And the risk to me?"

"High."

Helen considered the request with a growing sense of horror. Dan would undoubtedly have tried to prevent her from going back into the terrorist lair, but FitzHugh had arranged for him to be given a room at a local hotel. By now he would be catching up on his lost sleep.

"Is there any point in me refusing?" she asked.

The commander gave her a deep deprecating look and replied, "You have the right not to help us, if you so choose, Helen, but the lives of millions of people could be at stake. If this bomb is genuine, it really will be millions. So I would prefer to think that you will help us willingly."

"I see." Helen shrugged her shoulders. She saw a look of pain in the policeman's eyes, a look that told her he hated himself for putting such pressure on her. But he had no other option, did he? She drew in a deep breath and clasped her hands together to keep them from shaking. "In that case, it looks like I'm about to go visiting."

"Thank you, Helen. I hoped you would see it our way." FitzHugh looked away, hiding his emotions as he slid down off the desk. He indicated to the door. "Would you like to come and meet our nuclear bomb expert?"

You bastard, she suddenly thought. You had it set up all along, before you even asked me. But she said nothing of her feelings as he led her out of the control room and towards the unmarked van at the rear of the car park. What was the point?

"I thought that van was something to do with you," she said. "I told Dan you probably had the SAS in there."

"A reasonable guess," FitzHugh replied. "But wrong. The lads from Hereford are holed up somewhere far more secure than a van in the car park. They have to stay well out of sight right up until the moment we authorise them to attack. We mustn't alarm the people with their fingers on the button, must we?"

"So the SAS regiment is nearby?"

"Near enough. But for the moment we're trying to keep this as a purely civilian matter, at least as far as the IRA are concerned. Once the SAS become involved, we will probably get into a shooting match, so we're keeping them hidden until we've exhausted every other possibility."

"They're the last resort?"

"Here at City Airport, yes. The very last resort. We think we can use them sooner at Heathrow, once we've cut the communications links between the two groups, but not here. Not yet." FitzHugh came to a halt on the steps of the van. "This is just another bit of office space for our own use. At the moment we've got a nuclear physicist from Aldermaston holed up in here. He's the man I want you to talk to."

From the outside it looked like a fairly nondescript van of un-certain vintage. Inside it was fitted out with office furniture and radio communication equipment. FitzHugh gave Helen a helping hand up the steps and quickly followed her, slamming shut the door behind him.

The physicist turned out to be a rather overweight, middle-aged man with a balding head and thick-rimmed spectacles.

"Professor Miles," FitzHugh said with a wave of his hand, "this is Mrs Mayfield."

"Ah, Mrs Mayfield." Miles held out a podgy hand and beamed at her through his owl-like spectacles. "Just the lady I need to talk to."

"You were expecting me?" She glanced at FitzHugh. He averted his gaze and said nothing.

"Mrs Mayfield *has* agreed to help us, hasn't she?" Miles looked inquisitively at the commander.

FitzHugh nodded.

"Good." Miles indicated a built-in seat at one side of a small table. Helen squeezed into it.

"You know what this is all about?" the professor asked as he levered his heavy bulk into the facing seat. He adopted a serious expression as he looked at her through his heavy lenses. He reminded her of an owlish school teacher.

"Sort of," Helen hedged, not sure how much she was supposed to know. It was clear to her that there was still a lot to be divulged.

"Well. The thing is, we would like you to take another look at the device and, in particular, try to study the detail of the important parts. If this thing is for real, we want to know how sophisticated it is, and how much of a hole in the ground it's likely to make. We also need to know more about the people out there on the aircraft."

"Aren't you the best person to go and take a look at the bomb?" Helen asked. A pointless question, she knew, but it gave her some small satisfaction to ask it.

He shook his head firmly. "Come off it, Mrs Mayfield. You know damned well what sort of people we're dealing with. They killed one of your staff and three of the crew of the 146. They killed a number of people in the tower at Heathrow. And the police are pretty sure that this is tied up with the deaths of fourteen people at West Drayton. What do you think they would do if I walked over there and asked to see their bomb?"

"Sorry. Carry on, Professor."

"Right. The only thing we have in our favour is that they know you and they were prepared to use you as a messenger. We really do need to know more about the bomb and the people we are dealing with."

"They're the usual sort of Republican terrorists, as far as I could tell."

"No. Not them, Mrs Mayfield. If this is a real nuclear device, you can be sure the IRA gang are only pawns in a much bigger game. If that device is a real nuclear bomb, it wasn't put together

148

or provided by them. Someone else is behind this business and we want you to look very closely at everyone over there to see if you can figure out who it is."

Helen adopted a thoughtful expression. "There was one man... he came into the tower just as they took me out."

"What was he like?"

"Quite old, in his mid-seventies, probably. But smartly dressed. Very high-class English accent. That's about all I can tell you, except that he was short and fat." She paused, and then added, "Oh, and he had a nervous twitch. Could that be important?"

"It could be, if he's in charge. The last thing we want is someone with a nervous disposition in charge of a nuclear bomb. Would you recognise him again?"

"I don't know. I didn't get much of a look at him. Anyhow, what exactly do these people want? And why have they planted the bomb here in London?" Helen looked from the professor across to FitzHugh. Each shook his head.

"There are a number of possible reasons..." Miles began, "but at the moment it would only be speculation on our part."

"Okay. As I see it, you haven't a clue who is behind this threat, or why. On top of all that, you don't even know if the bomb is real."

Miles smirked. "We don't know much, do we?"

"Doesn't seem like it. But, whatever they want, will the government give in to them?"

"I very much doubt it."

*

Hudson kept his face deceptively straight as he listened to the terrorist leader telephoning a demand for food to be sent into the control tower. He had eaten little that morning, but the stress of the situation had dulled his appetite. He thought, however, that his colleagues on the radar suites would probably be feeling somewhat different. Anyhow, it was a good excuse.

Paddy put the telephone down heavily and glowered at him. "They're sending in some food, so they are. You can help carry it round the building." He picked up the receiver again and dialled an internal number. "McGovan! Get yourself over here to the radar room!"

"Thank you," Hudson said calmly. He tried to maintain an outwardly relaxed stance. He had read somewhere that, in a hostage-taking situation, it was important to keep cool and try to build up some sort of rapport with the attackers. Maybe that wouldn't be possible with these people, but he was willing to try. "Can I have one of the assistants to help me carry the food? If they send in enough for everyone, it'll probably be more than I can carry."

The terrorist leader waved his hand with an indecisive gesture and then replied, "Just don't try any tricks, you hear?"

Hudson nodded. He turned towards the assistant's desk and said, "Would you give me a hand please, Jennifer? I'm going to carry some food around the building."

At first the girl looked wary, probably unhappy at the prospect of leaving the relative security of the control room for the possible dangers that might lie out in the uninhabited corridors. Hudson instantly recognised her fears and felt sorry for her. But it had to be done. It might be the only possible opportunity to talk to her.

He rustled up a smile. "Don't worry, I'll be with you all the time."

Privately, he felt at least as worried as the young assistant. It was not in his nature to carry out acts of bravery, nor had he ever thought of himself as being in any way heroic. The memory of that morning's airmiss incident also sat heavily in his mind, reminding him that he wasn't even an ace at his own job, let alone suited to the unknown and dangerous work of counter-terrorism. But — he tried desperately to convince himself — someone had to assist the police and army who were outside the building. And, at that moment, there didn't seem to be anyone else.

A gasp of alarm from Jennifer brought his thoughts back to reality. The door had burst open and the repulsive little gunman called McGovan, still trailing his Armalite rifle, strode purposefully into the room. He grinned lecherously as soon as he saw the young girl.

"You little bastard!" he growled and advanced towards her. "I've been looking for you!"

Hudson instinctively stepped in front of Jennifer. "Hold on. There's been enough violence in here, let's keep it cool... eh?"

"That sodding bastard's going to get what's coming to her." The man pointed a finger at Jennifer, using his other hand to level his gun at Hudson's middle.

"Cut it out, McGovan!" The terrorist leader's voice echoed loudly across the confrontation and carried with it enough authoritative weight to hold the stocky gunman in check. The short barrel of McGovan's Armalite wavered upwards in front of Hudson's chest, painting an unsteady trace. He had the stock folded and was using the weapon with one hand as if it was a pistol. It gave him the rather pathetic image of someone playing at cowboys.

"Take those two outside to the main entrance," the leader snapped. "The Brits are sending in some food. Give some of it to the prisoners down the corridor and bring the rest in here." He paused and then added, "And keep your bloody hands off that girl."

McGovan swivelled slowly on his heels and waved Hudson and Jennifer towards the door. He kept his gaze on the girl as she passed him. Once they were out in the corridor, he put his hand roughly to her shoulder and pulled her back against the wall.

"You'll pay for what you did," he snarled.

Hudson darted forward without a second's thought and he levered himself between Jennifer and the terrorist. "Leave her alone. You heard what your boss told you."

McGovan swung the narrow barrel of his weapon round so that it came to rest against Hudson's neck, tight under his chin. "Bugger off," he hissed. "Or you're a dead man."

The stale smell of tobacco and alcohol drifted angrily into Hudson's nostrils.

"Paddy doesn't want any trouble," he insisted. He had to draw the man's attention from Jennifer to himself. As he consolidated his position between the two, he felt her begin to slide away. A deep tremble rippled along his spine. "Your leader doesn't want anything to spoil his plans now that he's in a strong position." The gunman seemed only partially convinced, so Hudson pressed on. "You don't cross a man like Paddy and get away with it, do you?"

"What do you mean?"

"I mean that Paddy's in charge here. And he told you to leave the girl alone."

McGovan stepped back, scowled and spat on the floor. He raised a finger to Hudson's face. "Don't get clever with me, sonny."

Then, with some apparent reluctance, he motioned them on down the corridor. Jennifer moved away quickly, taking care to keep Hudson's body between herself and the gunman.

Hudson manoeuvred himself into a protective position as they walked steadily towards the main entrance lobby. He also tried to keep up a façade of calmness which would, he hoped, fool both McGovan and Jennifer. He might even fool himself.

The terrorist who had donned the security guard uniform was seated at the desk, calmly watching the television screens in front of him. He nodded to McGovan. "What's happening along the corridor? Don't tell me. You've a thirst on you and Paddy wants you to get a few pints in?"

"You watch your tongue, Kearney. Paddy says we're to collect some food and give it to the Brits," McGovan grunted and he spat on the floor once more.

"They've already delivered the stuff," Kearney responded.

Hudson turned to where two cardboard boxes had been left outside the glass doors of the main entrance. The police outside must have had the food ready, he decided. Perhaps they were now playing the delicate game of giving the terrorists a sense of security. He shivered when he saw another gunman standing well within the cover of dark shadows inside the building, a Kalashnikov automatic rifle levelled towards the entrance doors. There would be no chance of making a run for it.

McGovan motioned to him to walk towards the food boxes.

"No tricks!" he snapped menacingly. Hudson nodded and kept his hands in clear view as he walked out into the real world of freedom. He had a sudden impulse to run, to escape the madness inside the control tower. But the thought of the gun aimed at his back, and the timid figure of Jennifer, held those thoughts in check.

Apparently satisfied that no trap had been laid, McGovan ordered Hudson to bring in the boxes, one at a time. All the while he kept half an eye on Jennifer who stood as far from the man as she could without provoking an angry outburst. Once the boxes were safely inside the building, McGovan led Hudson and Jennifer away from the entrance lobby and directed them towards the telecommunications equipment area.

One of the rooms was crowded to capacity. Some of the prisoners stood idly within a semi-circle of maintenance control desks, while others were seated on the floor between the desks and banks of grey metal equipment cabinets. The coloured warning lights that littered the front of each of the cabinets were almost hidden behind the mass of bodies.

McGovan motioned Hudson to leave one of the boxes just inside the door where an armed guard stood with his ubiquitous Armalite. A second gunman stood at the far end of the room holding a Kalashnikov. Each had his rifle directed into the heart of the group of hostages. Each looked likely to kill at the first provocation.

The small group then made their way back towards the radar room with the remaining box of food. As they walked down the silent corridor, Hudson noticed that McGovan was hanging back. Something was wrong, he sensed it and it frightened him. A sudden scuffle behind him caused him to turn. McGovan was restraining Jennifer, one hand firmly gripping her arm.

"Simon," she whimpered.

"Let her go," Hudson said evenly. "You don't want trouble, any more than we do."

Jennifer stood wide-eyed with fear. Her mouth hung open as

she gave Hudson a desperate begging look, pleading for his help.

Hudson stood immobile, uncertainty filling his mind. The narrow barrel of the Armalite wavered towards his chest, and the look in McGovan's eyes told him that there was a real intention to use the weapon.

The gunman had stopped adjacent to the lift that Jennifer had used earlier in the day. He barked at Hudson. "Turn round and keep walking to the radar room!"

"Paddy said no trouble," he reminded the gunman.

"Keep walking!" McGovan's hand wavered and the Armalite barrel drew large circles in the air.

Hudson stared at him for a few seconds before he turned and paced slowly forward with indecision and mental anguish chasing each other round inside his brain. He was almost at the main lobby again when he heard Jennifer cry out. He dropped the box, spun round, and just caught the movement of the terrorist and the girl as they disappeared into the lift.

*

Nicholas Horton, the up-and-coming government minister, had spent an uncomfortable fifteen minutes with the Prime Minister. The questions — which he was still unable to answer — were exactly as he had predicted. It was what he learned from the PM that shocked him. By then his patience was wearing as thin as the PM's.

Horton had just arrived back at his office when Sir James Heatherley hurried in with unaccustomed haste, his face grim.

"We know now who is behind this," the minister said firmly before Heatherley could speak. "The PM has been contacted by the Kremlin."

"The Kremlin? Yeltsin himself?" Heatherley gasped aloud while still striding across the room.

"Seems like he was sober enough today." Horton adopted a wry look. "One of their embarrassing guests has escaped from a psychiatric hospital in Moscow."

"Surprise me." Heatherley came to a halt in front of the minister's desk.

"It's Murdoch. Peregrine Fraser-Murdoch." Horton waited for a response before he revealed more. Tension was taut inside him.

Heatherley flinched visibly. "Murdoch? I thought he died in a Russian mental hospital."

"No. Burgess, Maclean, Philby and Blunt are all dead. Only Murdoch, the fifth man, is still alive. An old man now, in his mid or late seventies. He was in a secure psychiatric hospital, but he's been spirited away. He's left Russia within the past few days, without saying goodbye. We figure he's got to be here in England, and in charge of this business."

"A mental patient in charge of a nuclear bomb?" Heatherley's face paled.

"Doesn't bear thinking about, does it?"

"He couldn't have managed this by himself," Heatherley said. "He must have had friends over there to get him out, friends in high places."

Horton hissed through clenched teeth. "Of course he couldn't have escaped without help. The brains behind it... maybe it's not wise to use the word 'brains'... the *people* behind this are the hawks in Russian Intelligence. The hardliners within the SVR. People with little in the way of moral judgement. Whoever they are, they spirited Murdoch out of the hospital and out of the country. And they supplied him with the bomb."

"Their aim?"

"The usual. To provoke us into retaliation. They want a Third World War."

"Why Murdoch? Why did they choose him?"

Horton shrugged. "He's an Englishman with a grudge against his own country, he knows all there is to know about nuclear bombs, and he's expendable. He's also unstable, of course. Mad enough to do something like this."

"Oh God." Heatherley took a step back. "What's Yeltsin's line?"

Horton forced himself to reply calmly. "He knows who got Murdoch out of the hospital and he'll try to plug the gap at his end. He didn't say so outright, but it seems likely the perpetrators won't be alive by the end of the day. If they're caught. But that doesn't help us, does it? Murdoch and the bomb are now on our patch and we're going to be hard-pressed to deal with it."

"I'd better get this information to FitzHugh as quickly as possible."

"I've already ordered a briefing file to be sent to him. He'll need to be brought back up to speed on Murdoch's history."

"What about the Provos?" Heatherley asked. "If Murdoch is in charge of the bomb, how do they fit into the picture?"

"They're just pawns in a game that's well beyond their mentality." Horton sighed deeply and waved a hand to reflect his annoyance. "The worrying bit now is that the Russians haven't acted quickly enough to contain everything at their end. Someone inside the Kremlin has already sent out leaks to a few unstable countries. Very shortly the world's press will know the full truth, that we have a madman here armed with a nuclear bomb. That's when full-scale panic will set in."

"How are we going to play it with our own press?" Heatherley asked.

"Get in first and give them our version of it." Horton glanced at his watch. "We can go public in time for the one o'clock BBC news, if we work quickly. But we must get this right."

*

Toome left the emergency control room clasping a small transistor radio. He strode down the corridor, stopped in the entrance foyer and asked, "What's happening to the food, Mickey?"

"McGovan and the two Brits carried it down to the radio workshop," Kearney replied easily. "I hope they intend to come back with some for me."

"You'll get your share, Mickey." Toome nodded and stepped into the lift. He rose quickly to the top floor and then climbed up into the Heathrow Visual Control Room. When he reached the top of the steep stairway, the burst of light caused him to blink furiously. His eyes had become too much accustomed to the low level of ambient light inside the radar room and he had to pause to allow some adjustment to the brighter environment at the top of the tower.

He nodded to the gunman who patrolled the outer area of the control room, then he stepped up to the central dais where the two air controllers sat. Toome pulled forward a tall stool and sat down. Directly in front of him, the air controllers sat at desks raised above the base level of the control room. One controlled the arrivals landing on runway two-seven-left, and the other man controlled the departures taking off from two-seven-right.

A long line of aircraft was queued along the taxiways leading towards two-seven-right, the departure runway. Wide-bodied jumbos waddled along between smaller aircraft which they seemed to overshadow in length and girth. A much lesser number of aircraft seemed to be landing on two-seven-left, and all seemed to be taxiing off in the direction of Terminal Four, an ugly building with bright yellow tubular walkways issuing from it like tentacles. It was well remote from the control tower in the central area, a safer place to unload.

Toome looked across to the departure runway as a 747 taxied into position for take-off. He watched the aircraft for a few seconds before turning back to the tower occupants. They all appeared to be carrying out their routine duties. He shook his head grimly.

The bomb would be detonated at four o'clock if the British government did not give in to Murdoch's demands. Toome fervently hoped they would concede quickly. There was, of course, a real risk they would not concede and then the consequences would be terrible. Most of the PIRA brigade would then be on their way to Eastern Europe in the very same aircraft that carried the bomb into London. What happened to the Brits left here shouldn't worry them.

But it worried Toome.

He had taken part in too many raids, killed too many people, seen too many mangled bodies to treat this matter as anything but potential mass murder. He hoped to God the Brits would see enough sense to give in to the demands.

He looked down at a digital clock mounted in the control desk directly in front of him. It was just coming up on one o'clock GMT. He switched on his radio. The first cackle of sound was the end of yet another report on the closure of so many deep coal mines. Typical British ability to get their priorities wrong, Toome told himself. Then the newscaster's voice became suddenly more grave.

"We have just received breaking news from a Home Office spokesman concerning this morning's attacks on Heathrow and London City Airports. These attacks were carried out by active service units of the Provisional IRA. A message concerning the terrorists' demands has been received by the British government. According to a statement issued by the Home Office just minutes ago, the terrorists are demanding that all Irish Republican prisoners should be immediately released. The terrorists refer to them as prisoners of war. If this demand is not agreed to by four o'clock this afternoon, our time, a nuclear bomb will be detonated at London City Airport.

"The Home Office spokesman has further told us that the matter is being urgently investigated to determine the credibility of the threat. At the moment the government does not believe that there is any nuclear device at London City Airport, which is in London's docklands, and there is no danger to the population. However, as a matter of precaution, houses in the vicinity of the airport are being evacuated. We're now going over to our reporter at Heathrow Airport where the attack began this morning."

The voice changed as the reporter came on the air, the sound distorted as if it were transmitted over a telephone link.

"Despite the horrific bomb at West Drayton last night, which was initially thought to be an equipment fault, the police were apparently not expecting any follow-up action today. However, early this morning a group of Republican terrorists, believed to be an IRA active service unit, entered the control tower here at Heathrow and took over the building. The building is now occupied and all the doors are booby-trapped with grenades. The terrorists forced the air traffic controllers — who had moved across from the bombed

158

building at West Drayton — to guide two aircraft into London City Airport. We understand that the first aircraft was used to carry the nuclear bomb, if indeed there is a bomb. There is some doubt about the reason for diverting the second aircraft. Sources in Whitehall are stressing that this is in all probability a huge bluff and that no bomb exists..."

The reporter's voice was cut off in mid-flow and replaced by the main newscaster who spoke quickly and off the cuff.

"We're interrupting that report from Heathrow to bring you more news from Downing Street. We understand that a minister from the Home Office will be making a national broadcast on BBC radio and television and ITV at two o'clock this afternoon. We believe... I'm still getting news coming in and... we believe that a junior minister, Douglas Stewart, will go to the BBC studios to make a television statement on the situation. In his broadcast, he will make a national appeal for calm in this emergency. Government sources are stressing that there is no genuine cause for alarm, but an emergency telephone number has been set up for anyone wanting information on people who have been evacuated from the docklands area. I'll be giving you that number in a moment. In the meantime I'll hand you over to our political correspondent for his assessment of the events."

The voice changed yet again.

"Well, the news from Downing Street is hot off the press and we are still trying to assess its meaning. The repercussions of this terrorist activity are quite considerable..."

Patrick Toome sighed as he switched off the radio. He had no wish to hear any more. The sooner the whole thing was over and finished, the better it would be for him. As far as he was concerned, all that mattered was the successful completion of their part in the operation. They had taken the bomb into London, and they had brought the whole country to the edge of disaster. If the Brits gave in and released all IRA prisoners, that would be enough to justify their actions.

He dreaded the consequences if things did not go according to plan, and the bomb was detonated.

*

FitzHugh fingered a set of files sent to him from the Home Office as he approached the police car where Helen Mayfield waited. He recognised these files. Some of the material bore his own signature.

"You look surprised," Helen said. She sat in the front passenger seat.

FitzHugh stopped at the driver's open door and peered inside. "Not surprised. Just disappointed that I didn't spot the connection before," he replied.

"What connection?"

"The IRA and the SVR."

"SVR?"

"Russian Intelligence."

"You mean the KGB?"

"No." FitzHugh shook his head. "The KGB was dissolved four years ago, Helen, after a coup attempt against Gorbachev. The people I'm talking about are called the SVR. That's the *Sluzhba vneshney razvedki*. Try saying that with false teeth."

"What does it mean in English?"

"It translates quite simply as the Foreign Intelligence Service."

"Spies and the like?"

"Sort of. They are responsible for all intelligence and espionage activities that take place outside the Russian Federation. Their connection with the IRA is what this all boils down to, you see." FitzHugh sat down in the driver's seat and patted the uppermost file. It was labelled: IRA LINKS WITH RUSSIAN INTELLIGENCE. "We have a working relationship with the Russians these days, better than you might think. Pity it wasn't always so. Anyway, the Prime Minister has had a call from President Yeltsin warning him about an Englishman called Peregrine Fraser-Murdoch."

"The name sounds familiar."

"He spied for the Russians all through the Second World War. He defected to Moscow when his cover was blown a few years ago.

160

It was in the news at the time."

"You mean... the Cambridge spy? I've heard of him."

"I'm sure you have. He was the enigmatic fifth man. Burgess, Maclean, Philby and Blunt were the famous four. Then there was the fifth man who turned out to be Murdoch."

"You really think he's behind this?"

"Almost certainly. I'm going to describe him to you in a moment, and I want you to look out for him when you go back to the control tower."

"You think this bomb is Russian?"

"Certain of it. The telltale markings will be removed, but there will be some clues we'll want you to look out for."

"So this is really a Russian attack?"

"No. It's not really a Russian attack as such. Good heavens, that's the last thing Yeltsin wants right now. It's all to do with dissidents in Russian Intelligence. You see, there are hawks inside the SVR who don't like the way Yeltsin is running the country. They'll stop at nothing to change the regime."

"And the IRA? Where do they fit in?"

"They are just pawns paying the price for previous Russian help. There's a long history of links between the IRA and Russian Intelligence."

"Supplying weapons?"

"Yes, the first consignment of Russian arms to Ireland was delivered by a Russian intelligence-gathering ship, the *Reduktor*, as long ago as 1972. It was authorised by Yuri Andropov, who later became General Secretary of the Soviet Communist Party. When Fraser-Murdoch defected, he became friendly with Andropov."

"What does Andropov do now?"

"He died in 1984. But his cohorts in the KGB and now SVR keep in contact with the IRA. They still send them the odd bit of help, and now they expect something in return. Today, the SVR is riddled with hawks who want a full-scale shooting war in Europe, and that's what this is all about." He slapped a hand down on the top file. "Helen, I think this is a far more serious matter than we ever imagined."

Chapter 13

Jennifer White felt the world spinning as the blood pounded inside her head. McGovan was staring fixedly at her across the lift cage as it rose. His gaze moved up and down, scanning her body, then her face, and then back to her heaving chest. Suddenly and without warning, he rammed his fist against the emergency stop button and the lift cage juddered to a halt halfway between the fourth and fifth floors.

His eyes were blazing now, as if his obsession with her overrode any pretence of rational behaviour. He raised the barrel of his Armalite until it was level with her face, barely an inch from her open mouth.

She pressed herself back against the wall of the lift, her heart thumping, her body shivering violently. She gasped at the vile stench of the man's breath against her face, and she whimpered as his free hand fumbled heavily across her chest. Fear held her body rigid as his fingers rubbed side to side across the front of her light blouse and then curved round each breast in turn.

"I said you'd pay for what you did," he rasped. He pulled his hand away and reached into a hip pocket for a metal flask. She watched through hazy eyes while he put the flask to his lips and drank deeply. Then she turned her head away and felt the heat of his breath in her ear. The cool wall of the lift cage was still pressed hard against her back, and she could feel the throb of her heart struggling to pump blood to her numb limbs.

"You thought you'd get away, didn't you?" His voice was low, like the hissing of some repugnant reptilian horror. "Well, no one gets away from me, girl. Not from me."

He took another long draw from his whiskey flask before returning it to his hip pocket. A trickle of liquid meandered down from his lips to his chin.

Jennifer wanted to cry out, to make a frantic call for help, but her throat was dry and constricted. No coherent words would come, just a hoarse gasp of pain as, once again, he reached out for her and his nails dug in through her thin blouse.

"No!" Her voice returned with a sharp cry as his hand made a sudden violent downward movement. In an instant he ripped her blouse away from her body. She brought her arms up in front of her breasts, but McGovan knocked them aside as easily as a child pushing aside its play bricks. His rough fingers grabbed at her bra and yanked it so hard it tore apart. A distorted laugh escaped his mouth. He took a step back to look at her, and his laugh quickly turned to a grunt of animal desire.

Again, Jennifer tried to wrap her arms across herself in a futile act of self-protection. And, again, McGovan's free hand reached out and pulled them away. In the same movement he used his other hand to jam the barrel of his gun up under her chin.

With his gaze riveted into her eyes, he hissed, "Keep still girl, or you're dead!"

Jennifer's whole body froze.

She felt sick as his rough-skinned fingers crawled across her soft skin. A terrified spasm punched into her belly as he laughed at her.

Oh God! This could not be happening to her.

"At least you've a good pair of tits on you," he said slowly and with emphasis. "You should have given in the first time, girl. It would have been quick and simple the first time. Now it's going to be slow and—" He hiccupped suddenly and unexpectedly. "By God! You're really going to pay."

His hand slid down to feel for the belt of her skirt.

Her stomach heaving, she shook her head from side to side. "No! No!" The words came out hoarse and feeble, held back by the oozing sickness that clogged her gullet. This could not be real. It had to be a nightmare from which she would soon awake. "Oh God! No!"

McGovan jammed the gun tighter under her chin, his lips

compressed together as he fumbled until the belt buckle snapped. Then he grinned again as the skirt fell to the floor. Jennifer wanted to sink down with it, but she was held upright by the force of the Armalite's barrel. Dizzy lights began to flash before her eyes. She shook violently.

"Please stop! Please!" she begged.

But there was no stopping him now. He was too deeply crazed with a mixture of desire, drink and revenge.

Jennifer sobbed and frantically pushed her tight fists against him. But her raw fear seemed only to arouse further lecherous desires inside his animal brain. All she wanted was some way of escape, any escape... even if it resulted in her own death. She was beyond all reasoned thought.

"Bend over and get your knickers off, bitch!" With his gun pressed against her face, he forced her down to her knees. "I said bend over! Bitch!"

Moments later his fist smashed against the side of her face and she fell into a heap on the floor. Partially concussed, she tried to sit up, tried to make sense of his ranting voice, but it was too much for her brain to cope with.

"Do you hear me, girl?"

Slowly, her eyes began to focus on the beast hovering over her. Cogent thought began to seep very slowly back into her brain. Tears streamed down her cheeks and her lips quivered uncontrollably. She was as good as dead now, life could hold nothing for her after this.

McGovan thrust his head towards her, eyes dull and mouth wide. For one short minute, she felt hatred, pure and undiluted, crowd her brain. But that was quickly wiped away by renewed fear.

She stood up slowly, feeling her muscles come back to life, feeling the blood pulsing madly through her throbbing head, feeling the violent pounding of her heart.

The enormity of the danger she still faced was lost beneath the horror of the despicable act he had in store for her. Suddenly, she no longer cared that her life was at stake, no longer cared that he might blow her head from her body at any moment.

McGovan momentarily released his grip on her as he fumbled with his trousers. In that short second Jennifer reacted with a sudden burst of subconscious inner reserve. Only partially aware of what she was doing, she swung her arm outwards to push the rifle away from her head. At the same time she leaned forward with the whole weight of her body to topple the man backwards. His face showed a momentary look of comic surprise that she had dared to repulse him, and he gave a short, high-pitched cry of alarm as his feet crumbled beneath him.

Jennifer saw his surprised look as he fell backwards. Then she heard a loud crack as his head banged against the wall of the lift cage. He crumpled to the floor unconscious. His rifle clattered down beside him.

"Oh, God! Please help me!" Jennifer pushed herself back against the opposite wall, her body tense and shaking.

He wouldn't remain unconscious for long, and when he recovered she could expect no mercy whatsoever. She stretched out her hand towards the lift control panel, sliding her fingers soundlessly across the cage wall until they felt the buttons. She pressed one without noting which. It didn't really matter which way the lift went as long as she could get out. Immediately, the lift began to move upwards.

At the same time, McGovan started to groan.

Jennifer watched him rise to his knees and put a hand to the back of his head. He groaned again, tried to stand, but he seemed to have difficulty in controlling his legs. With a sharp cry of pain he sank back to the floor. Seconds later the lift came to an abrupt stop and the doors opened.

Jennifer's first reaction was to run, but McGovan lay across the floor in front of her and she hesitated to step across his prostrate body for fear of him grasping hold of her legs. The corridor outside was deserted, an invitation to escape back to her secret hideout, if only she could get away from McGovan.

"You little bastard," the terrorist said thickly. He rose to his knees again, one hand still held against his head. Her hopes of escape would disappear fast unless she acted now.

The gun! The Armalite rifle was lying on the floor between Jennifer and McGovan. She had no idea how to use it, had never used a firearm in her life, but if she could just get hold of it, she might be able to force her way past him.

Her hands reached down to grab the rifle before McGovan could stop her.

"Give me that!" McGovan recovered his senses sufficiently to pull himself up against the opposite wall of the lift cage. His eyes were blazing and his teeth were bared. Jennifer held the weapon in trembling hands, the barrel pointed at McGovan's chest. She knew that she would not be able to shoot him, she lacked the courage to actually pull the trigger, but perhaps the mere threat would be enough to allow her to escape.

"I said give me that gun!" His hand reached out to grab the barrel and pull the weapon towards himself. Jennifer struggled, wrestling with him to keep control of the rifle. It was no longer a matter of immediate escape, it was her life!

She knew that once McGovan had possession of the gun, she was as good as dead. She tightened her grasp, suddenly realising her finger was on the trigger. Then she felt the blast and sharp kick of the weapon as it fired.

*

Sitting high above the runways at Heathrow, Toome looked out at the long, empty expanse of runway two-seven-left. He turned and watched as Trewin, the controller who had been directing the landing aircraft, leaned back in his seat and removed his headset. All arriving flights had now suddenly and unexpectedly ceased.

Toome struggled to contain his annoyance. He had given orders for the traffic to continue to flow in and out of Heathrow as normal. Someone had deliberately disobeyed his commands. He knew full well that it was not the work of the Heathrow controllers; they were at the end of the chain of the air traffic control system. They had played no part in the decision to divert the arriving aircraft. It had to be the work of the British government.

He was in a quandary. His own active service unit had fully succeeded in its task. But he had to keep applying a degree of pressure from the Heathrow control tower in order to keep the Brits on their toes. Murdoch was depending on that. He also needed that pressure to be maintained in order to ensure their escape from Heathrow before the deadline.

The escape plan depended upon Murdoch bringing the F27 across from City Airport to collect them, and whisk them off to safety in Eastern Europe. Toome couldn't afford any degree of complacency. Was this the time, he wondered, for him to turn the screws tighter on the British government by threatening the life of one of his hostages.

He turned through one-hundred-and-eighty degrees to where a long queue of aircraft had built up along the taxiways leading to the departure runway. All the crews and passengers would be anxious, he guessed, to get away from London. Rats deserting the ship. The 'departures' controller was working hard to get the aircraft airborne as quickly as he could, and the tension showed in his face. As Toome watched, the hard-pressed controller called across to Trewin and asked, "No more inbounds, Vince?"

"No."

"In that case, can we get some of these outbounds away on two-seven-left?"

"Fill your boots," his colleague replied and wrapped his headset back around his ears.

Reluctantly, Toome held back an inclination to intervene, something to show he was still in charge. There was nothing he could do that would add to his remaining control over the situation. He strode away noisily and climbed back down the steep metal steps to the seventh floor. There he summoned a lift, the smaller of the two, the one which would take him directly to the entrance lobby. As the cage descended, he heard a sudden gunshot.

A short moment of panic was followed by a few seconds of reasoning and lucid thought. If there were shots in the control tower, they would have come from his own men. The likelihood was that someone — probably McGovan — had loosed off a shot by accident. Nevertheless, he compressed his lips and held his Armalite rifle in a state of readiness as the lift reached the ground floor. He stepped out into the lobby with the weapon held out defiantly, probing the air ahead. But there was no sign of trouble here where Kearney still kept watch. Toome gave him an inquisitive look, walked over to the reception desk and stared at the security television displays. There was no sign of anything untoward. He relaxed marginally.

"Did you hear a gunshot, Mickey?" he asked.

Kearney shook his head. "Not down here."

"Well, I heard a shot while I was coming down in the lift."

"Which floor did it come from?"

"Dunno. Let me know if you hear anything."

"I'd do that anyway, Paddy."

Toome grimaced and walked on down the corridor to the emergency control room. Here, the atmosphere of tense activity had been diluted in the short time he had been upstairs. The controllers' job was now limited to departing aircraft, the stream of arrivals having been diverted elsewhere. Most of them leaned back in their seats, their headsets draped around their shoulders.

The room had assumed an air of unusual calm. Joe Dillon, who had been left guarding the controllers, had pulled up a seat behind the bank of suites, and was quietly smoking. Toome looked to him for some comment.

"We knew they'd stop the arriving flights sooner or later," Joe said, a plume of smoke wisping from his nose.

Toome nodded and strode across to the supervisor's desk. He thought carefully for a minute and then picked up the telephone. He selected the direct line to City Airport.

It was dead.

He jiggled the cradle button. It made no difference so he returned the receiver to its rest.

"Damn!" he swore quietly.

There was now no one seated at the City Radar suite so he

walked across the room and picked up a headset. He pressed one of the earphones to his head and again selected the direct line to the City Airport. Again, the line was dead. He was tempted to try an outside telephone line, but guessed the only people who would answer would be the Brits outside. He was now cut off from London City Airport.

He swung around quickly with the first intent of calling to Joe. Then his better judgement came into play. At that moment Joe and the air traffic control staff were acting calmly and if he alerted them to the fact that something was wrong, it could spell real trouble for all of them. He tried to think. Why were they cut off from City Airport? Presumably to stop him from telling Murdoch what was happening at Heathrow. Or was it to stop Murdoch contacting him. What the hell were the Brits planning?

If something was going to happen — an attempt to re-take the control tower, maybe — they could be in real trouble. He knew from experience what the SAS were capable of and, privately, he wasn't too sure of his chances of containing the situation. As long as they had the support of Murdoch at City Airport, there was no problem. The mad Englishman had only to make a threat and the British would back off. But, with no way to get through to City Airport, how could he now enlist that support?

And what about their escape plan? Would it suffer because of this?

The F27 should take off from City Airport one hour before the four o'clock deadline and land at Heathrow to pick up Toome's unit. Only a small suicide squad — McQuarrie and four other men — would remain at City Airport to guard the bomb.

Toome stared at the dead telephone lines and clenched his fist. Damn! He should have been ready for this. If he had planned the whole thing, he would have made sure there was no chance of this sort of cock-up. At the same time, in the back of his mind, was the niggling realisation that he should have thought of this anyway. Could this be his first real error of judgement? If so, it was time for him to get out of the whole damned business!

*

Helen saw the gunmen close in behind her as she walked back across the apron towards the BAe146. What they would do as she approached them was a calculated gamble on the part of Commander FitzHugh. He, however, had the advantage of remaining behind within the relative protection of his own police force. Helen's consoling thought was that such protection was not something to be highly rated when they were all within close proximity of a nuclear bomb.

As she came closer to the 146, she spotted the man who had been in the control tower with her. It was the Ulsterman who had shown her the nuclear device on the aircraft. She knew now that his name was McQuarrie, an IRA activist who had been under close police surveillance for some time. The surveillance had not been close enough, Helen thought, and it gave her no comfort. FitzHugh had shown her police photographs of the man, and he had described him as a ruthless and cold-blooded extremist. Even looking at those photographs had done little to help her flagging courage.

"What the hell do you want?" he shouted at her as she drew nearer.

"I need to speak to you."

"We didn't tell you to come back here," McQuarrie's face creased into an angry expression.

Helen continued at her steady pace. It wouldn't do to show indecision or hesitation at this stage. "They don't believe you," she responded.

As she spoke, the expression of annoyance in the man's face turned first to disbelief and then to outrage.

"You'd better not try fooling around with me, woman! Who doesn't believe us?"

Helen came to a halt just a yard from him, her face passively directed towards his. "The police. They said you were bluffing. They told me to tell you that they think the bomb is just a mock-up. They said you could never get hold of the real thing. They said the IRA doesn't have the money or the contacts to get hold of a real working nuclear weapon."

McQuarrie's mouth hung open as he stared at her, his face burning as if he had been dealt a stomach punch. "You're lying!"

"What have I got to gain by lying? They don't believe you and they sent me across here to tell you so. They said it's not a real nuclear weapon. It's a bluff."

"Who said that?" he asked. "Who did you speak to? What's his name?"

"Commander FitzHugh. He used to be Head of the Anti-Terrorist Squad. He seems to be in charge of this business. I also spoke to a nuclear physicist from Aldermaston. He agreed with FitzHugh."

"You're lying!" McQuarrie repeated. He raised his hand and, for a moment, Helen thought he was about to strike her. But he allowed the hand to fall again when she flinched.

"Would I risk my life to come out here if I had only lies to pass on to you?" Helen felt her nerves tremble. "Think about it."

McQuarrie considered the comment and then pointed towards the control tower. His voice dropped as he said, "You'd better come with me. I need to speak to someone."

"Who?"

"Never you mind. Keep your mouth shut and follow me."

*

When Jennifer and McGovan disappeared into the lift, Hudson felt the dull ache of fear reach out and grab him. Not a fear for his own life, but for the safety of the girl. He kicked the box of food to the side of the corridor, ran back to the lift doors and hammered on the call button.

Nothing happened.

God, what should he do now? He darted his gaze from side to side, frantically looking for an answer. There was another lift in the main entrance lobby, but it was in sight of the gunman on guard there. So, also, were the stairs. His only hope was to wait until this lift came back down.

He focussed his gaze on the floor indicator. The lift climbed almost to the fifth floor before it stopped. It sat there, refusing to answer the call button. Hudson waited, his hands bundled into tight fists and his muscles tensed.

Ten minutes passed.

At one point Hudson thought he heard a gunshot, but he wasn't sure. It might have been just a sharp thud made by someone dropping something in the engineering section. He heard a voice from the direction of the main lobby and instantly pressed himself back against the far corridor wall. It was the man they called Paddy. Somewhere along the line, someone had used the name Toome. The IRA leader stepped out of the second lift, the one that opened directly into the lobby, and spoke to the guard, but Hudson was unable to make out his words. Eventually Toome walked away.

Hudson continued to press himself firmly against the corridor wall for some time after Toome strode off in the opposite direction. He wondered how long the Irishman would wait before sending someone out to find the missing food.

A sudden humming sensation from the lift made Hudson flinch. The indicator began to unwind back to the ground floor. He heard the cage whine to a halt and he stepped forward anxiously.

The doors parted.

He started towards the lift and then jerked to a halt, shocked.

Two things stunned him.

The first was Jennifer, leaning heavily against the back wall. She was half-naked, wearing only her panties and shoes. Her face was contorted with pain, and the front of her body was splattered with long globules of blood that rolled down her breasts, her stomach and her legs in ugly red rivers. The crimson splashes stood out boldly against her pale skin. She seemed to be looking into a distant scene with a glazed expression, as if all reality had departed from her.

The second source of Hudson's shock was McGovan's body, spread across the floor. At first he thought the gunman was simply unconscious. No more than a second passed before he took in the horrifying red mass which had once been McGovan's head.

It was blown apart.

"Oh, my God!" Hudson made the one loud exclamation before clasping his hand over his mouth as he remembered the gunman in the main lobby.

He felt his heart thumping and his head went light and unearthly, as if it was spinning on his shoulders. Gradually, in the space of seconds that felt like hours, some degree of clarity returned. He stood back and took a deep breath. Then he forced himself to move hesitantly into the lift cage.

In the forefront of his mind was an overwhelming fear that Jennifer had been badly injured. God forgive him if the girl had been hurt! He carefully avoided the dead body and reached out to grasp at Jennifer's bloodied hands. Although sticky and dripping red, they felt icily cold. At first he thought the blood was hers, and he looked closer for the injury. But there was no obvious wound, just a tender young body tainted with ugly gore. A rushing hope drove into his mind: perhaps she was physically unhurt. His brain worked at lightning speed now. The impact of what he saw caused his body to pump out adrenaline at a much raised level and, within a minute, his thoughts began forming into crystal-clear decisions.

He pressed an arbitrary button to take the lift back upstairs, anywhere away from the lower corridor. He had pressed the button before he noted that they were headed for the third floor. Then he pulled off his jacket and wrapped it around Jennifer's shoulders.

"Are you injured?" he asked softly.

She did not answer at first, instead her eyes remained fixed on the far wall of the lift cage. Slowly she turned to face him. Finally, as if the question had taken all that time to sink into her conscious thoughts, she shook her head.

"Are you sure, Jennifer?"

Her only response was a quivering lip and a glazed expression fixed in his direction. She looked so young, so defenceless, so incapable of coping with such trauma. Suddenly, she burst into silent sobbing and reached out to hold him, wrapping her arms about his neck. In the process, she wiped blood onto his shirt, but that was the least of his worries.

"All right, Jennifer... all right." He held her tightly. "Just tell me, where's the office you hid in before?"

She released her tight hold and looked at him blankly.

"Think, Jennifer. The office. The telephone you used. Which floor is it on?"

"Fifth. I think." Her voice was dull and flat.

Hudson continued to hold her tightly. God, what an ordeal for such an innocent! And he had been the one to ask her to leave the radar room and come with him. He sensed some shivering motion as she slowly began to unwind, and then he felt the rhythmic movement of her body as she sobbed quietly on his shoulder. Finally, she began to weep out loud. He knew then that she would recover... eventually. The shock would pass, even if she was left with a deep-seated stain in the roots of her mind.

The doors opened at the third floor and Hudson peered out. No sounds reached him from the deserted area outside.

He released his hold on the girl and bent towards the dead body. He turned it over and immediately felt a gagging sensation in his gut. Blood and brain tissue oozed across the floor.

Forcing himself to ignore the sickening gore, he pushed the body out of the lift. It took a trail of blood and tissue with it, painting the floor red.

"If they find him here, they'll be less likely to look for us up on the fifth floor," he said. Then he threw out Jennifer's blood-stained clothes, scattering them around the body. His mind was running sharply now, and he knew that he had to get rid of anything that might leave a trail of blood behind them when they hid themselves in the office on the fifth floor.

As the lift continued upwards, Jennifer kept her eyes averted from the blood that remained on the floor. Hudson's heart went out to her. When they arrived at the higher floor, he removed her shoes. They were covered with the dead man's blood and would leave a telltale trail. Then he helped her out of the lift, holding her tightly so that she avoided stepping in any bloody pools. Out on the dry floor, he checked again that neither of them was leaving behind any bloody marks.

"Where's the room with the telephone?" he asked.

Her hand trembled as she pointed down the corridor. Hudson clasped his arm tightly round her waist and led her in the direction she indicated. He felt her whole body shaking as she continued to sob quietly, her head inclined onto his shoulder.

The office door was slightly ajar — she had obviously forgotten to close it when she left — and Hudson hurried her inside. He followed up with a backward kick of his foot to close the door.

"Is this it, Jennifer? Is this the office?"

She shook her head and pointed to the serving hatch doors.

"Through that hatch?" he queried.

She nodded.

Cunning, he thought. He began to understand how she had managed to escape from her attacker on that first occasion. He helped her across the room and pressed against the hatch doors. Like the office door, they had not been fully closed, and they sprang open to his touch.

"Well done, Jennifer," he said.

He glanced around the room, his eyes coming to rest on the door to the adjoining room. "Hold on one moment."

Leaving her propped against the wall, he first checked the door. It was securely locked. He then crossed the room and made a quick rummage through the desk drawers in case a set of keys was left behind. There were none apparent. Almost certainly they were held by whoever used that office. If he couldn't easily open the door, neither could the gunmen, he decided, so the next room would be their best bet for a hiding place. It had to be. God help them both if they were discovered now!

Chapter 14

Helen Mayfield looked around, surprised that an air of casual inactivity hung around the London City Airport Visual Control Room. Peter Elliot sat quietly at the aerodrome control desk with his headset draped around his neck. One of the gunmen stood by the window, covering Peter with his rifle while watching the scene outside. And there was one other figure in the room.

He was the old, fat man, the one she had expected to see here. He wore an expensive suit that was smartly cut, but creased through continual use. He held a hand telephone and quietly shook his head. A nervous twitch invaded one side of his face.

"The direct line to Heathrow is dead," he announced with a precise emphasis to each word. "We should have expected this. Why did you not plan for this eventuality?"

He spoke with the cultured tones of a man who had been schooled in the finest education system that money could buy. Helen locked onto the accent and she knew straightaway that this was the man she had been sent to find. If Commander FitzHugh was right, this would be Peregrine Fraser-Murdoch, the man in charge of the operation.

McQuarrie appeared not to hear the Englishman's question. "They don't believe us!" he snapped as he followed Helen into the room, jabbing his rifle barrel into her back. "They don't believe we've got a real bomb out there."

Murdoch turned and eyed the big terrorist with a look of disdain. "Calm yourself, McQuarrie. Who doesn't believe us?"

"Them! The English cops out there." The Ulsterman pointed in the direction of the car park.

"And how do you know that they don't believe us?"

"This woman." McQuarrie was becoming more agitated. "She's the stupid bastard I released, like you said to do. She's just come back to tell us they think we're bluffing."

Murdoch walked across the room towards Helen and stopped just inches in front of her. He screwed up his eyes as he studied her closely so that she felt a twinge of fear spark across her thoughts. Despite his age, despite that twitch, he had the sharp voice of a dedicated professional. And yet there was something dull and unfeeling about his behaviour, as if he was not entirely in control of his actions.

"You say we are bluffing?" he hissed.

"Yes, but—" She got no further before Murdoch's hand whipped out towards her and caught her across the side of her face. She fell backwards under the impact of the blow.

"You were sent over there to convince them we are *not* bluffing!" he bellowed.

Helen recovered her stance and put a hand to the side of her face. For a few seconds her vision went fuzzy. Then she recovered her voice. "That was the message—"

"You're the ATC Executive Officer?" he interrupted her in a firm but even tone.

"Yes." Helen struggled to keep a steady bearing.

"You should have convinced them. Who gave you this message?"

"A policeman called Commander FitzHugh. He is, or was, the Head of the—"

"FitzHugh! I've heard of him. Who else did you speak to?"

"A man from Aldermaston called Professor Miles."

"I see." Murdoch started to turn away and then halted. "And they asked you to help them play for time. Is that it?"

"I don't understand," she said.

"Yes you do." He was smiling now, the forced, unreal smile of one who was trying to maintain an upper hand. "It's just a game, isn't it? They sent you back here to try to sow some seeds of doubt in our minds. What else did they tell you to do?"

Helen tossed her head nervously so that her blonde hair rippled about her cheeks. Then she licked her lips and said, "They asked me to get a closer look at the bomb because they think it's just a dummy. They want me to give them a better description of it."

Murdoch gave a short staccato laugh. "Do you take me for a fool? If they really thought it was a dummy, they wouldn't need anyone to take a closer look." He walked away to the window, shaking his head. Then he turned on her once more. "However, since they see fit to play games with us, I'll let you take a closer look. As close as you wish. In fact..."

He stopped, as if considering his next move, his eyes gleaming wickedly. The twitch was gone now and Murdoch looked more menacing because of it. "I think it would be a good idea if I showed you exactly what we have out there, and how we intend to use it."

*

Jennifer cowered into a corner of the office. She sank to a crouching position and her eyes took on a dazed look that told of deep inner terror.

"Tell me again, Jennifer," Hudson said. He knelt on the floor in front of her, one hand making contact with her arm. "Have you been hurt? Have you been wounded?"

She shook her head.

"Were you..." The words stuck in his throat.

This time she shook her head more slowly and her body went suddenly rigid. "Almost," she mumbled. "Then I..." Her voice trailed away.

Hudson put his arms about her, wiping more gore from her chest onto his shirt. He didn't know if it was the right thing to do, but he could think of nothing else. He felt his blood suddenly run cold with the enormity of what had happened. She needed help — they all needed help — and the only way to get that help was to make contact with the outside world.

He got to his feet and picked up the office telephone. He checked for a dialling tone, then stabbed out the number of the Heathrow Airport police.

The reply came back almost immediately. "Jennifer, is that you?

We've kept this phone line active for you."

"No, it's not Jennifer," Hudson rasped.

"Who is that?" The voice at the other end of the line had the sort of firm edge that he expected from a policeman.

Hudson identified himself in as few words as possible. "And I want to speak to a man called Stenning. The one Jennifer spoke to earlier."

"I see. Hold on." A short delay followed while the soldier was called to the telephone. Then a commanding voice said, "Yes?"

"Is that the officer who spoke to Jennifer White?"

"That's right. Captain Stenning."

"You're the person who told her to go back up to the radar room?"

"No. That was her decision. She knew that one of the controllers would be shot if she didn't go back."

"She told you that?"

"Yes."

Hudson felt his anger towards Stenning subside.

She went back because of him! She had put her own safety in jeopardy because of him.

"That was... me," he said, the words almost sticking in his throat. "It was me who would have been shot." He sensed that all emotion was drained from his voice. "She went back because of me... and she was viciously attacked."

"She's hurt?" The officer's voice sounded concerned, but Hudson wondered how real that concern was.

"Yes. She's terrified. She was almost raped!"

"She was what?" This time Stenning's voice indicated he was genuinely concerned.

"You heard what I said. Thank God she was able to defend herself, but it's been a terrible ordeal for her."

Stenning's voice went suddenly calm. "She managed to get away?"

"Yes. Fortunately for her, she got away. Fortunately for her, she wasn't killed." Hudson allowed the words to sink in. "There was a struggle and the attacker had his brains blown out by a shot from his own rifle. I don't know exactly how it happened, but I do know that he's dead. Anyhow, Jennifer is here with me at the moment and we're hiding out in an office on the fifth floor."

"I'm sorry about that... what did you say your name is?"

"Hudson... Simon Hudson. I'm an air traffic controller."

"Yes. I remember now. She told me you were threatened." Stenning's voice went back to its previous commanding tone. "I suppose you've seen most of the men involved in this attack?"

"Yes. I've been downstairs throughout the affair, at least until we went to collect some food," Hudson said. "I went with Jennifer to the front entrance to collect the food. I was trying to help her to find out how many other gunmen are in the building."

"You did? Good. Tell me what you saw." The officer's voice suddenly carried a hint of undisguised satisfaction that Hudson found rather tasteless.

"As far as we can tell, there are not too many of them. In fact, I would guess not more than seven or eight."

Stenning's reply hinted at further signs of enthusiastic satisfaction. "Good. That's very good. I need to know exactly where each of the terrorists is at this moment."

Hudson launched straight into his answer, keeping his tone level and objective. "There are quite positively only two of them downstairs in the radar control room. One is the lead man. He's called Paddy. I think his name is Toome. The other one knows something about air traffic control. He's called Joe. I don't know his second name. I haven't been up in the Visual Control Room, but I guess there's at least one of them up there." He paused for a quick breath.

"Go on."

"There are two men in the telecommunications workshop. They're holding all the telecommunications and office staff as hostages. They've bundled all of them into the one room so that they can mount a guard over them. Then there's one man in a security guard uniform near the main entrance. And I also saw one other man near there when we brought the food in."

"You're quite sure there are only two of them downstairs in the telecommunications workshop?" Stenning responded.

"Pretty sure. As sure as I can be without going back down there."

"Right. That's a possible seven of them accounted for. Any others?"

"Yes. You've forgotten the one who attacked Jennifer." Hudson stole a quick glance at the girl still cowering in the corner. "He's dead now. Remember? The top of his head was blown off by his own gun."

"Yes. I'm sorry that happened. To the girl, I mean. How is she now?"

"How do you think she is, for chrissake! She's in shock. But she's with me so I'll take care of her until you can get us out of here. It's the least I can do for her."

"Right." The officer's voice was subdued now. "So the likely total is seven terrorists still alive in there. I'm going to have a quick word with my people and I'll come back to you in just a few moments. Hold the line open, will you. We've closed down some of the phone lines, so don't try to contact us any other way."

Hudson placed the receiver on the desk and went over to Jennifer to offer her some small comfort. He crouched down beside her and held her close. Neither spoke, but the degree of intimate feeling between them extended beyond any words.

When he picked up the telephone again, he immediately heard Stenning calling, "Hello... hello..."

"I'm here," Hudson responded. "I was just looking after Jennifer."

"Right." Stenning's voice snapped at him firmly. "Now listen carefully. We're going to take the control tower at two o'clock. That's fourteen hundred GMT exactly. On the dot. There's going to be a ministerial broadcast on radio and television at the same time and we're hoping the people on the tower will be watching and listening. A bit of a distraction, you see. The air traffic is already being diverted into other airports, and we've cut all telephone links to London City Airport. We're going to take out the terrorists on the ground floor first. It'll be a stealth attack so that we don't alarm the guys upstairs. After that we'll move up to the Visual Control Room."

"Sounds like you've got it all sewn up," Hudson answered cynically.

His tone seemed to be lost on the army officer. "I'm telling you this because I want you to help us," the distant voice responded.

"Me? Oh no, it's all your show from here on!"

"Mr Hudson, you must! It's very important that you do one more thing to help us. I want you to nip down to the lifts and jam something in the doors. Both of the lifts. That will prevent anyone upstairs from using them when we take the men at the bottom. It will also reduce the risk of anyone downstairs from escaping upwards. We don't want these boys running off when we attack. Can you do that job for us?"

"Well... I suppose I can do that." Hudson replied, only a shade reluctantly.

"Good. Don't do it yet, Simon. Someone might discover what has happened if you do it now. It might also give away your hiding place."

"So, when..."

"In about twenty-five minutes. We go in at fourteen hundred GMT, remember? And I'd like you to spike the lifts about four or five minutes before that. Once you've done the job, get back inside that office and keep out of the way. Things might get a bit hot."

"All right. Watch the man called Paddy. He's killed four people already."

"We know all about him, Simon." Stenning's voice was strangely calm now. "In fact, we have a pretty weighty document on Patrick Toome. He's a professional and he's good. Leave it all to us and keep your head down when the shooting starts."

Hudson bit his lip thoughtfully and then said, "Good luck."

He replaced the receiver and turned to the girl who was now curled up into a ball on the floor at the corner of the room. For the first time he noticed she was sitting in a pool of urine. Poor kid! She was frightened out of her mind. She badly needed someone to help her and Hudson desperately wanted to give her that help.

"How are you doing?" He knelt beside her and put his arms about her. She eagerly buried herself in his grasp.

*

McQuarrie seemed to sink into the background once Helen was introduced to Murdoch. Watching the apparent transfer of authority, Helen began to see the truth of Professor Miles's assertion that the IRA gunmen were only pawns in a much bigger game. Murdoch was clearly one of the major pieces in that game. Possibly *the* major piece.

He led Helen back on board the BAe146 and gestured towards the nuclear device. It sat on the floor of the aircraft cabin, just as before.

"This is what you came to see. Take a closer look, woman." He waved his hand dramatically as he opened the lid and pointed. "You know what to look for now? Eh?"

Helen nodded dumbly.

"Have you ever seen a nuclear device before?"

"No, but..."

"But they told you what it should look like?"

"Yes."

"Well then, look!" The cultured voice became insistent and the twitch returned. His hands shook as he crouched beside the container and pointed. "That's the detonator, it's connected up to the batteries over here through this timer box. The detonator is just a plastic explosive. The main ball of uranium 235 is inside here, and this..." his finger wandered across the device, "...in here, is where the detonator fires the uranium rod into the mass of the 235 to make the whole thing go critical."

"And the initiator?" In truth, Helen had little idea what the purpose of the initiator was, but that was what Miles had told her to ask.

"Lithium and polonium," Murdoch responded, just as Miles had predicted, "to set the whole thing off with a bang. Are you taking mental note of all this?"

Helen nodded again. She looked carefully at the devices that made up the bomb, noting how closely the whole arrangement came to Professor Miles's description.

"Do you have a Geiger counter here?" she asked.

"To check the radio activity level?" Murdoch grinned, a lop-sided grin with one half of his face now in fierce spasm. "No, we didn't think we would need one."

"I see." Despite that lack of conclusive evidence, Helen felt convinced. She still had no absolute guarantee that it was not an elaborate hoax but, on balance, there could be little doubt.

It wasn't just the physical evidence of the bomb itself. Helen had been briefed by Miles to judge the behaviour of the man in charge. Murdoch was more than convincing.

"Over here," the Englishman continued, "is the timing mechanism. See how it has two switches inside it."

Helen directed her attention towards the timer. It was a black metal box, about four inches square and three deep, apparently riveted to the inside of the main container, with wires trailing out towards the detonator. The lid was open and Helen took note of two rocker switches inside the box, one black and one red. Mounted on the open lid was a digital keypad with ten numbered buttons. It looked not unlike the keypad of a telephone receiver.

"These are both spring-loaded switches." The man's shaking finger hovered over the red switch inside the small box. "This red one is for detonating the bomb instantaneously. Press it, and we all go up in one big flash of light. You don't want me to demonstrate, do you?" He grinned wickedly, causing Helen to shrink backwards.

She shook her head involuntarily.

"This black one," he went on pointing to the adjacent switch, "simply connects the detonator to the timer which is basically a digital alarm clock — you can see it down there at the bottom of

184

the timer box. It's just a small device, but still an alarm clock. The timer is already set to switch in the necessary triggering charge at four o'clock this afternoon. So, if I press down the black switch and then release it, I ensure that the bomb will go off at four."

Helen leaned closer. She made out the shadowy remains of writing that had been partially erased from below the switch. It looked Russian. She leaned back and sighed loudly. "Where did you get this thing?" she asked.

"I worked with the people who built it," Murdoch replied, his face betraying a look of self-assured smugness. "Gave them a lot of help in the process. But you don't need to know any more than that."

"I see. And how big..."

"How big a hole is it going to make?"

"Yes."

"Tell your friends that it is a one hundred and fifty kiloton device. They will know what that means." As he spoke, his smugness seemed to penetrate his whole body. "Now, just a word of warning. Once I close the timer box, it will be secured by a booby trap linked to the keypad on the lid. If anyone tries to open the lid without first keying in the right code number, there will be an instantaneous detonation. It's quite a simple form of booby trap."

Sweat was now trickling down Helen's neck. She breathed deeply and moved back away from the device.

"You hear me?" Murdoch said, his face still twitching alarmingly. "You hear what I am telling you?"

"They won't let you get away with this." Helen felt quite faint from the clever enormity of the plan, yet she still had the courage to argue with the man. "They won't allow you to get away from here."

"Of course they will." He was smiling broadly now. "They don't want to risk me detonating the bomb. They will give in to whatever I demand. They will allow me to leave shortly."

"So you'll not stay here with it? You won't stay right to the end?"

"No. Why do you think we went to the trouble of having two

aeroplanes at our disposal? By four o'clock most of us — myself and most of these brave Republican freedom fighters — will have flown out in the F27 and we will be far away from here."

"And the other aircraft?"

"A small suicide squad will stay with the bomb. They will fly it out of the country if the British government capitulates to our demands. But if the government doesn't give in..."

Helen felt a tightening sensation across her chest. "Your aircraft won't be allowed to get away!"

"You think anyone would dare stop us when we have a nuclear device in our possession? Of course it will be allowed to go."

"And the suicide squad?"

"They're dedicated people. They call themselves the 'Bobby Sands Squad'. After the Irishman who starved himself to death for the Irish Republican cause. These men are all ready to die if they have to." Murdoch stood up, looking satisfied. "Incidentally, only two people know the code for opening the timer box. Myself and McQuarrie. He will lead the suicide squad. You understand what that means?"

"I'm not sure."

"It means it would not be a good idea for the British army to kill either of us."

Any doubts in Helen's mind suddenly evaporated. She now felt a total conviction that the bomb was for real and that there was a genuine intention to use it.

"Convinced?" Murdoch asked.

She nodded. "How can we be sure you will disarm the device if the government agrees to your demands?"

"You can't. You just have to trust me, don't you?"

"And these other people, the IRA suicide squad, do they know how to disarm the device?"

"What do you mean?" His voice became suddenly cold.

"You say that you are going to leave them here to guard the bomb. The man called McQuarrie knows the code for opening the timer box, but does he know how to stop the detonation?"

186

Murdoch jerked his gaze away from her. His speech rose to a higher pitch, the words coming out too fast, as if his tension had suddenly boiled over. "Of course! He only has to press down on the black switch. Now, that's enough questioning." He continued to look away.

"Press down on the black switch?" she queried.

"That's what I said." His hands shook as he spoke. He clasped them together, but the shaking continued.

In that brief moment, it became clear to Helen that she had touched a raw nerve. She wasn't at all sure why or how, but there was something wrong about the plan to disarm the bomb. Something very wrong.

Murdoch stood up as he continued, "I'm going to let you go free once again so that you can report all of this to your friends across the way. Are you sure now that this is a real nuclear bomb?"

Helen bowed her head and answered truthfully, "Yes. I'm quite sure."

"Good. I wouldn't want your friends to get the idea that this is just a childish game." He leaned towards the device and allowed his hand to hover hesitantly over the two switches. "It would be a pity if all those people were to die just because someone thought we were bluffing. I'm going to arm the bomb now."

He leaned forward, hiding his action as he pressed down on the switch. Helen heard the click as it connected up the electrical circuits inside the box. When Murdoch straightened up, Helen saw that both switches were now back at their starting position. The deed was done and yet there was nothing to indicate the bomb was armed. Nothing to record such a terrible action.

"Four o'clock," Murdoch said coldly. Then he closed the timer lid. It clicked shut with a distinctive sound.

*

Simon Hudson felt yet another dull nauseous sensation deep in his stomach. The odour of bile rose in his throat. Yet more fear filled his head. Fear for himself and fear for the frightened girl. If only they could both stay here until it was all over, until the night-mare was ended. But that was now impossible. He had to leave Jennifer alone while he went down the corridor to spike the lifts.

For the past twenty-five minutes he had been holding her tight-ly, talking to her, calming her. Now it was five minutes to two, time for him to go. Time to take another risk.

He stood up and removed his shirt, still heavily stained with blood, the blood of a man who deserved to die. Blood that could mark Hudson as the killer, if he was seen. He hoped the grey T-shirt he wore beneath it would not look too out of place if he met someone in the corridor.

"I'm going to be away for a few minutes," he said, noting how the girl looked at him with an appealing expression that begged him to stay. "You know I have to do this, but don't worry. I won't be long, and no one will find you here."

"You don't look right without your shirt and jacket," she mumbled. "Someone might see you. One of the terrorists might see you..."

"The blood on my shirt would be even more of a giveaway," he replied. "Especially if they've discovered the dead body."

"I don't want you to die because of what I did." She sat up and wriggled out of the jacket he had given her. Her voice was cracked with hesitancy. "You'd better take this. It would be safer than going as you are."

"You'll be cold without it."

"You could be in worse trouble if someone sees you like that, Simon." She handed it up to him. "Please take it."

She was right, of course. The inside was stained, but that wouldn't be seen. And a few small blood stains marked the front of the blazer, but they were almost invisible against the black serge. With some reluctance, he put it on.

"I won't be long. I promise."

Her mouth opened to speak again, but no sounds emerged.

Hudson bent down, patted her shaking hand, and then turned away. Once again, the smell of bile reached up into his throat.

When he had crawled back into the outer office, he made sure that the hatch doors were firmly closed. Now, everything seemed too quiet out here, too remote from the horrors being perpetrated elsewhere within the building. Given half a chance, he would have gone back to the office where it was safe. He knew he was no hero, and he couldn't hope to survive a conflict with any of the terrorists. And if his courage failed him now, the story would be bound to get out. What would Michelle think of that?

It was the first time he had thought about Michelle since the incident began. There had to be some significance there, he thought. If she saw all this on the television news, she would be worried out of her mind. Fortunately, he had left her at her mother's place. She would need a good deal of parental support. Curiously, Hudson was not as concerned about Michelle as he knew he ought to have been. His real worry was for the frightened young girl who awakened in him feelings that were more than simple compassion. He needed time to sort out exactly how far those feelings extended.

He crept out into the corridor and headed towards the lift, taking constant cautious glances from side to side. Even here, it seemed unnaturally quiet. He pressed the lift button, and was momentarily puzzled when the doors failed to open immediately. Then he heard the gentle whine as the cage came to a halt at the fifth floor. The doors opened and he was left staring directly into the face of Patrick Toome.

For a second both men were taken unawares. Then the terrorist snapped himself together and brought his rifle into an aiming position. Directly into Hudson's heart.

Chapter 15

Too late, Mickey Kearney saw the British soldiers approaching the main entrance door. He had moved towards the front of the lobby area, standing beside the screen which sheltered the door, and was attempting to focus his eyes on activity to the right of the bus station.

There were many more people moving about behind the bus shelters now, as if they were building up to some sort of concerted retaliation. Before he alerted Toome to what was happening, Kearney decided to take a closer look and he stepped out of the cover provided by the screen. It was his first and final mistake.

The combat-uniformed figures were closing from both directions, no more than four in each group, all moving low and swift across the open road. Kearney felt his pulse racing as he saw the black balaclava hoods and the HK assault weapons. SAS! One soldier flung himself to the ground and raised his gun to firing position.

The initial shot took Kearney in the chest just above his heart. While he was still falling backwards, the second shot slammed into his forehead.

*

Two policemen escorted Helen straight to the mobile control room where she met FitzHugh, Miles and the Assistant Commissioner. Aware that her voice quivered at times, she struggled to recall every detail as she briefed them on her meeting with Murdoch. She ended by adding her own conviction that the bomb was genuine.

"That's it, then," FitzHugh said sadly. "We must treat this thing as real, regardless of what the Home Office say."

"At least you know what and who you are up against," Helen observed.

FitzHugh pulled at his beard. "You're right, but it's not a lot of consolation, is it? A mad Englishman with a nuclear bomb, guarded by Irish terrorists. Can you think of anything worse?"

Helen shook her head. How could there be anything worse?

While FitzHugh made his way to a meeting with the Commissioner of the Metropolitan Police, Helen and Professor Miles were escorted back across the car park to where a crowd of uniformed officers was assembled to watch the Home Office minister's television broadcast. A portable television had been set up inside another mobile control room, its aerial precariously balanced on the roof. Similar aerials had sprouted from the tops of various police vehicles scattered round the car park. Everyone wanted to see the broadcast.

Despite the density of the gathering, a heavy silence hung over the small room, broken by just an occasional cough and a shuffling of shoes. The only other sound came from the tinny-sounding television loudspeaker. The picture showed a view of the Houses of Parliament. A television reporter stood in the foreground holding a microphone, talking in a low, dramatic voice, the sort of voice television reporters habitually reserved for serious occasions. His tense facial expression added to the effect. As the picture changed to the BBC studio, someone leaned forward and turned up the sound.

The Home Office minister sat, tight-lipped, behind a green topped desk, his hands clenched in front of him. He wore a sombre grey suit, and his face was impassively set — an image plainly designed to convey a pictorial message of formal severity. A caption at the bottom of the screen superfluously announced the name: the Right Honourable Douglas Stewart MP.

He spoke calmly and deliberately.

"As most of you will be aware, this morning the control towers at Heathrow and London City Airports were hijacked by groups of armed IRA terrorists. I am sure you have all heard varying reports about what is going on and you have probably heard some horrifying stories about what the terrorists have demanded and what they

have threatened to do. That is what I want to talk to you about.

"I am in constant contact with the police at Heathrow and London City Airports. I have also just telephoned the Prime Minister at Downing Street. He has instructed me to tell you that he is fully aware of the concern being felt by the public. Furthermore, he has asked me to reassure you and to calm any fears you may have.

"Firstly, I must tell you that we do have a serious situation on our hands and we are taking every step we can to deal with it. I tell you this so that you don't imagine that we are being complacent in the face of what is happening. However, I can assure you that we are quite certain that at the moment the public is in no immediate danger."

In the middle of the broadcast, Commander FitzHugh hurried into the room. A junior officer stood up to offer him a seat. The Home Office minister's broadcast continued unabated.

"The attacks at the two London airports were mounted by IRA terrorists who are known to the British security forces. The group at London City Airport is holding hostage the pilot of a Queen's Flight aircraft. They also claim to have a nuclear bomb in their possession, which they say they have placed on board the Queen's Flight aircraft. I can now tell you that we have positive information that this is not true. There is no such bomb. The IRA does not, and never has had, the ability to threaten us with a nuclear device."

At this point he leaned forward to emphasise his words. His gaze pierced firmly into the television camera.

"However, we do take seriously the fact that these people hold British hostages at both airports. It has always been our policy to resist terrorist demands, whatever the cost, and this policy will not change. We will do everything in our power to ensure that terrorism does not succeed, now or at any other time. In the meantime, I must ask you to remain calm and not to do anything that might help the cause of the mindless monsters who are perpetrating this horrific crime. Any signs of panic on the streets of London will give the IRA the sort of publicity that terrorists habitually look for. There is no need for panic and we must ensure it does not happen.

"I repeat again that you are in no danger provided you stay calm. Don't let the terrorists bully you into reacting with unnecessary fear. That would only help their cause. We, the British people, and especially the people of London, have come through terrifying ordeals before and have resisted aggression with firmness and fortitude. We stood up to the nightly devastation caused by German bomber aircraft. If we now resist the demands of the IRA terrorists who set up this outrage, in the end we must triumph."

The camera made a slow zoom in towards the minister's face.

"I rely upon the British public to show that neither the IRA nor any other evil group will cause us to give in to terrorism, whatever their threat."

The scene faded to be replaced by a short caption. Then followed a sudden cut to a view of the inside of a London television studio. The camera zoomed in on a reporter who sat in front of a large map of the city.

"That was a broadcast to the nation by the Right Honourable Mr Douglas Stewart. Here in the studio at television centre, we will be looking at the background to the serious incidents which..."

Someone stepped forward to turn down the television sound. Heads turned, directing worrying expressions around the confined space. Feet were shuffled and a low murmur of voices began to buzz around the scene. Gradually people rose from their seats, as if it had taken some minutes for the enormity of the situation to sink into their minds. Even though the police officers present were aware of what was happening at London City Airport, they were shaken by the broadcast. Perhaps, Helen thought, it was because they knew more than the people at the Home Office were willing to reveal to the nation.

They knew the truth.

*

Commander Colin FitzHugh stood up and gathered up a bundle of blue-coloured files. He had come in halfway through the broadcast but it was enough. Seated nearby, the Assistant Commissioner, Andrew Metcalfe, gave him a grim look and shook his head.

"He wasn't very convincing, Colin."

FitzHugh stopped suddenly. He looked at the now silent television screen and said, "You're right, of course. Douglas Stewart is not the best man for this sort of emergency. Not decisive enough. The PM should have made the broadcast himself. He's still in London?"

"Yes, the royal family have been held back at Balmoral, but the PM is still here. He wants to play the whole thing down," Metcalfe spoke slowly, deliberately. "Putting Stewart in front of the camera downgrades the emergency in the eyes of the public."

"Maybe. Anyhow, we've more important things to get on with. I'll study these straightaway." He tapped the bundle of files under his arm before turning away and stepping out of the mobile control room. He closed the door carefully behind him.

He had made his report — his opinion on Helen's inspection of the device — as clearly and concisely as he had been able. But there had been too many unanswered questions at the end. FitzHugh hated being plied with questions by senior officers at the best of times. What he needed was positive answers. This was certainly the most dramatic case in which he had ever been involved. It might possibly be the last, and not because he would immediately return to his retirement. It might possibly be the last dramatic incident for many people if the situation got any further out of hand.

He dropped his gaze to a note he had been handed while he was briefing the Assistant Commissioner. The SAS assault on the Heathrow control tower had commenced at the exact moment the broadcast began. There was no word of how the operation was progressing, or whether there had been casualties. Detailed reports would come later. God help them all if it went badly. The important point now was the shift of emphasis from Heathrow to London City Airport.

The decision to retake the Heathrow control tower was made without too much debate, the main questions being 'when' and 'how'. The Regiment would try to capture Toome alive, but there seemed little chance at the moment of capturing Murdoch.

He was the man FitzHugh really feared.

One strong thought filled FitzHugh's mind, a growing conviction that the operation might well involve a double cross against the IRA as well as a threat to the British Government.

He recalled Helen Mayfield's description of the bomb and her assessment of Murdoch. Especially her opinion of Peregrine Fraser-Murdoch. It was time to ferret again into the file on him. It was a thicker file than FitzHugh remembered.

He stopped near a police Land Rover and set down the bundle on the bonnet. The top cover of each file was labelled RESTRICT-ED and in the upper right-hand corner there was a security reference number. The first file was numbered GD109/1.

Halfway down the page was the file tile: THE CAMBRIDGE FIVE.

FitzHugh flipped through the first few pages and then stopped at a closely typed A4 sheet, a general resume of the file's contents. He read:

The Cambridge Five was a ring of spies recruited by a Soviet spymaster called Arnold Deutsch. The five were responsible for passing information to the Russians during World War II. Their spying activities continued into the 1950s.

The five consisted of:
Donald Duart Maclean who used the code name Homer
Kim Philby who used the code name Stanley
Guy Burgess who used the code name Hicks
Anthony Blunt who used the code name Johnson
Peregrine Fraser-Murdoch who used the code name Cicero

These five men were recruited during the course of their education at Cambridge University during the 1930s.

After the war, Philby joined the British Embassy at Washington DC, where he learned that British and US Intelligence were close to identifying Burgess and Maclean. He alerted them and in 1951 they defected to Moscow.

In 1961, Philby came under suspicion after he was identified by a Russian defector, Anatoliy Golitsyn. Philby subsequently escaped to the Soviet Union from Lebanon.

Blunt was identified as a spy in 1964 as a result of American Intelligence. He came clean and was given immunity in return for secret Soviet information he was able to feed back to British Intelligence.

Murdoch was the youngest of the five and turned to communist ideals while he was at Cambridge shortly before the war. He was identified through Blunt's confessions, but he escaped to Moscow before he could be arrested in 1964. He was a brilliant physicist who worked at Aldermaston and gave the Soviets highly valuable information on British atomic weapons programmes. However, of the five, he was the most unstable and, by the time of his defection, he had already been removed from top secret work. By 1980, his mental stability had deteriorated further and he was known to be held in a psychiatric clinic in Moscow.

Tired by the stress of the situation, FitzHugh blinked and cleared his mind again. It was important not to allow history to cloud his current objectivity. Having digested the basic information on Murdoch, he put the file aside and opened another.

The blue cover of this next file was referenced GD215/1 and was titled: PATRICK TOOME. If all went well at Heathrow and Toome was captured alive, FitzHugh expected to have the opportunity to interview the Irishman. The more he could discover about the background to the attack, the better placed he would be to deal with it. He opened the file and flicked straight to the bottom sheet which, in the Ministry of Defence filing system, was the first page. He quickly scanned the first few lines and then read:

Patrick Eamon Toome was the commanding officer of the Provisional IRA Second Battalion in Belfast. Prior to that, he was second-in-command or adjutant of a PIRA Battalion at a time when the PIRA mounted a considerable number of attacks against security personnel. He is believed to have successfully restructured the battalion after the setbacks in PIRA strategy caused by E4A...

FitzHugh stopped at that point and made a quick mental cross-reference. E4A had been a volunteer unit of the RUC based at Gough Barracks in Armagh. They were trained by the SAS and carried out similar style operations which led, eventually, to widespread allegations of a 'shoot-to-kill' policy by the RUC. If Toome had been able to overcome the setbacks caused by E4A, he would be a formidable enemy. With a sharp intake of breath, FitzHugh looked back at the page, skipped a couple of paragraphs, and read on:

...Toome became closely attached to Roisin O'Steafin (see ref 312/1, page 12) and was probably in the woman's flat when she was gunned down. He then turned militant...

Turned militant! What in hell's name were these idiots writing about? Toome was a militant as soon as he took the IRA oath of allegiance.

He read on.

In 1984, Toome became the contact between the Provisional IRA and certain hawks in the KGB. In 1985, he made one brief journey to Switzerland where he secretly met the Russian agent, Viktor Bolinov. Bolinov was strongly implicated in the defection of Peregrine Fraser-Murdoch in 1964.

There it was! The link between Toome and Murdoch was there all along. And Bolinov was still a high-ranking hawk within the

SVR. A man who would cold-bloodedly take the whole world into a nuclear war.

Damn!

FitzHugh slammed shut the file and crammed both documents under his arm. He swept away from the Land Rover in a cloud of suppressed annoyance, bordering on anger. At the unmarked van he stopped, forced himself to recompose his thoughts and scratched his cheek. This was going to be the biggest test ever for SO13, the Yard's Anti-Terrorist Squad. If they failed... well, he had led a pretty full life.

Inside the van, Helen and Professor Miles were deep in conversation over a small table. Most of the other police officers had dispersed and the television was now tucked away into a cupboard. A constable was quietly coiling up the aerial cable. Helen and the professor both looked up as FitzHugh entered.

"Well?" Helen queried.

FitzHugh rolled his eyes. "We're certainly being kept on our toes." He wiped at a layer of crumbs littering a vacant seat and sat down gingerly. "The important thing at the moment is that the SAS have launched an attack on Heathrow control tower. The next thing is to try to open up a dialogue with Murdoch. He's a very dangerous man. Our negotiators are presently being briefed by the senior police officers over in the mobile control room. Shortly we'll get them to try to make contact with Murdoch."

"And then?"

"Then we play for time. Try to get the deadline moved back. If we can persuade him to delay the time of detonation, and find out how he does it, we may be in with a chance."

Helen creased her face, "He says he plans to fly out of here with most of the IRA gunmen an hour before the deadline."

"Hardly the action of a true fanatic, is it? He'll leave others to die for their cause."

Helen sat back in her seat and thought for a while. Then she asked, "What exactly is Murdoch after?"

FitzHugh pulled his ear and looked up at the ceiling. "The

release of all IRA prisoners, so we've been told."

"That's what the IRA want, and they haven't a hope in hell of achieving it. But what does Murdoch get out of this? What does *he* want?"

"He's a pawn, just like the IRA. In a way, they're all disillusioned pawns in a game that's not of their making. The real force behind this whole setup is a group of dissident hawks in the SVR. This is their Princip moment."

"Princip?" Helen frowned.

"The man who killed Archduke Ferdinand, sparking off the First World War. He was the catalyst for that war. Murdoch will be the catalyst for the next one."

"You know this for sure?"

"Oh, yes. Like I told you, the PM has spoken to Yeltsin." Fitz-Hugh sighed. What was the point of holding back the rest of the story from Helen Mayfield? She was in this up to her pretty little ears. "You realise what this means? It means the bomb will go off regardless of whether or not we give in to their demands. The SVR dissidents want a full-scale nuclear war in Europe, and this is their way of starting it."

"And the IRA? Do they realise what's really going on?"

"Of course they don't. That's why we need to talk to them, especially their man, Patrick Toome."

"Do you really think Murdoch will go through with this? Blow up millions of innocent people?" Helen asked softly.

"What do you think?" FitzHugh retorted, "You've met him."

Helen looked him in the eye, her expression serious, and nodded slightly.

"That's what I think, too."

*

Hudson froze. Somewhere in the distance, two gunshots rang out while, in front of him, the Provo leader aimed an Armalite rifle directly at his chest. Hudson sensed instinctively that the terrorist was trigger-tense. Any sudden move on his part and the gun would be used. He caught a fleeting mental picture of McGovan's body lying on the corridor floor with half his head blown away. That could too easily be a picture of his own body.

"Shite!" Toome's eyebrows arched as he also registered the gunshots. He darted his gaze from side to side, seemingly checking whether Hudson was alone. His face carried a frightened expression, the look of a man who was the victim rather than the aggressor.

Hudson went rigid. Then, gradually, he felt his thoughts crystallising into some semblance of clarity.

"I'm alone," he said, trying to keep his voice as calm as his nerves would allow. He silently prayed the Irishman would not notice he no longer wore a shirt. Would the grey T-shirt be enough?

"Where's McGovan, and the girl?"

Hudson looked down at the bright red pools of blood on the floor of the cage. "I don't know," he answered in a level voice. "The man... the one called McGovan... he took her away. I think he intended to rape her."

Toome studied him with staring eyes. "Where did they go?"

Hudson shrugged his shoulders. "I last saw them down on the ground floor when your man dragged the girl into the lift. I don't know where they went. I've been searching the rooms up here but there's no sign of them."

"Hell!"

"If he's killed her—"

"Shut up!" Toome jabbed at Hudson with his rifle, and then swung his head around as if in search of an answer to his problems. "Get in the lift!" he suddenly snapped.

"Why?"

"Don't argue!

Hudson sidestepped the gory mess on the floor and stepped into the lift. He had to play this as cleverly as anything he had ever done in his life. The longer he could keep the terrorist leader guessing, the greater his chance of survival. He glanced at his watch and cursed his bad luck. It was two minutes past two — the attack on the control tower should have started already. Maybe the gunshots—

Hudson breathed in sharply. He hoped that the soldiers who carried out the attack would recognise that he was not one of the terrorist gang.

Toome seemed puzzled by what was happening. His hand hovered indecisively in front of the lift buttons, as if he was unsure what move to make next.

"Maybe your man went upstairs to the rest room, or the Visual Control Room?" Hudson suggested cautiously. The last thing he wanted was to be taken down to a lower level, straight into the face of the British soldiers. He guessed that they would be specialists in this sort of situation, but even so...

"There's something afoot. Something wrong," Toome replied dully. He suddenly swung round and raised the barrel of his Armalite again. "What are you up to?"

"Nothing!" Hudson reacted. "I told you what happened. I was looking for the girl."

"There's something going on. They've cut the phone lines to the City Airport. And they've diverted all the Heathrow aircraft into other airports when we told them not to. What do you know about it?"

"Nothing!" Hudson kept a straight face as he replied, but his pulse was racing now. As long as Toome was suspicious, he was dangerous. "Look, the best way to find out what's happening is to ask them. Why don't you use an internal phone here to call the airport police and ask them what's going on?"

Toome's hand hovered for a moment longer while he weighed up his options. Then he pressed the button for the sixth floor. Hudson allowed himself the barest sigh of relief.

*

Taff Windsor sat back in his seat and allowed the tight feeling of stress to drain down from his aching head. He had never before known such continual pressure. Now, almost without warning, it was all ending. It was also clear that something important

201

was happening, or about to happen. Taff didn't really care what it was, only that it was imminent. For the past six hours he and his colleagues had handled the twin stresses of the high level of Heathrow air traffic and the presence of armed terrorists in the control tower. To cap it all, they had been given not one single break to rest their tired minds. They were all now at the limits of fatigue.

In the background, Taff was vaguely aware of other controllers and assistants shuffling around the room. They had been working at their peak capacity for a long period and now they were suddenly left out on a limb.

Taff slid his headset down around his neck and stared at the radar display. The scene around Gatwick was horrific, aircraft diverted from Heathrow were swarming round the Gatwick holding stacks like bees round a honey pot. Their radar echoes crisscrossed and merged as the pilots waited their turn to land on Gatwick's single runway. He glanced across at an adjacent screen and saw a similar picture around Stansted.

The ATC digital clocks at Heathrow showed 1403 GMT when the control room door burst open. Taff's head was still turned towards the disturbance when the bark of a single shot echoed about the room. His eyes were still trying to focus on the rapidly developing scene when the wiry little Scottish gunman dropped to his knees, clutching his arm. Within seconds, combat-uniformed figures wearing black balaclava-type helmets were racing through the room. It took Taff many more seconds to register the fact that he had been rescued.

*

"I'm under orders to keep you here, just in case," FitzHugh apologised. "And in a matter as serious as this, I'm as much a victim of orders as you are."

Helen sighed and accepted the mug of coffee he offered her. She seemed to have been drinking endless cups of coffee since this business began and she wondered where it all came from. And why was it such bad coffee? Did the police have a greasy-spoon canteen somewhere nearby?

"Will I be allowed out before the four o'clock deadline?" she asked. "I am an innocent civilian, you know."

FitzHugh declined to answer and Helen decided not to press the point. She knew she would not like the truth if she heard it.

They were standing outside the van, casually watching the activity fermenting around the mobile control room. To Helen, it all appeared strangely remote, as if this were not happening to her at all. It might even have been a dream.

"I have a young daughter," she said slowly. "She will have to be collected from school at three thirty."

"Yes. We know." FitzHugh spoke quietly as he leaned back against the side of the van. "One of our WPCs has already collected her from the school and taken her to your mother, down in Winchester." Just a trace of a smile darted into his eyes and then disappeared equally quickly. "It seemed to be the right thing to do."

"You've got it all sorted out, then?" she said, pointedly.

"Sort of."

"What about your own family? Your children?" she asked. "Are they still in London?"

He looked at her thoughtfully for a moment, as if some great pressure was weighing on his mind, something which was beyond the scope of the emergency and which was hidden behind a mask of duty. She wondered whether he was able to express his true emotions when he was at home.

"My sons both live in the Midlands," he said. "My daughter works for British Atlantic Airways as a stewardess. She should be on a stopover in the States at this moment."

"You'll want to see your wife again. If things are going to be as bad as you think. You'll want to say something to her. Maybe explain how you feel?"

"It's a matter of finding time, Helen." Then he quickly changed the subject. "You can go down to the hotel to see your husband, if you wish. It's less than a mile down the road. I can get a constable to drive you there."

"Your chief won't object?" she asked, making no effort to suppress an air of cynicism.

He allowed her a short-lived smile. "It may surprise you to know that I'm not actually employed by the Met any longer. I've retired. That being the case, I don't acknowledge any bosses, and I make decisions to suit myself."

"If you're retired," Helen asked, "why are you here?"

He grinned wryly. "A sense of duty. A need to do the right thing. Or something silly like that."

"I see. In that case, Commander, I accept the offer."

FitzHugh pulled himself away from the side of the van and gestured towards a young constable who stood beside a nearby police patrol car.

"I may have to call you back here, Helen. Probably at very short notice," he said.

"I understand." She turned away, wondering if she would see him again.

The police patrol car pulled up at the front entrance to the hotel, barely three minutes after leaving the London City Airport car park. Helen checked with a policeman who stood near the reception desk and discovered that FitzHugh had already telephoned ahead to warn of her arrival. She felt even further convinced he had little faith in winning this particular battle.

She let herself quietly into the hotel bedroom, trying to avoid disturbing Dan who was asleep beneath a voluminous duvet in a large double bed. The curtains had been drawn, but sufficient light seeped through to allow Helen to navigate her way across the room. She sat on the edge of the bed for a few minutes, looking down at Dan's sleeping form. He looked too peaceful to warrant disturbance and she reflected that it would be a good state to be in when the end came.

She quietly slipped out of her clothes, dropping them on the floor at her feet. Then she slid in beneath the duvet and wrapped her arm around her husband's warm body. It gave her a glowing sense of comfort, a feeling which relaxed her mind and sent a tingling signal through her body. Less than twenty-four hours before, he had probably been in the arms of Janice Wilkins, but she tried to put that thought from her mind.

Only hours before, his infidelity had mattered, she reflected. But not now. Not when this might be their last day together.

When Helen had first learned about Janice Wilkins, through the gossip channels of the company's social scene, she had been deeply hurt. Those gossip channels had a tendency to embellish the truth with graphic details. Listening to the enhanced accounts of her husband's behaviour, she had wanted to leave him, to take Judith away and set up a home on their own. But then she had met Janice Wilkins at a company Christmas party and her extreme anger had subsided into annoyance.

She hadn't realised at first who the girl was, until someone had had the lack of prudence to introduce them. Janice Wilkins, Helen soon discovered, was not a real person. She was a shallow, immature figure with little personality and few original thoughts. She was, Helen decided after only a short period of strained conversation, a humanised cuddly teddy bear, someone to keep Dan's feet warm while he was away from home. A sex doll which happened to be alive. When the truth dawned, she felt a little sorry for the girl.

Helen cuddled up closer and felt the full warm touch of Dan's skin down the length of her body. If this was to be their last time together, any thoughts of Janice Wilkins should not be allowed to spoil it.

*

The lift stopped at the sixth floor.

Hudson's first sight, when the lift doors opened, was of a group of soldiers wearing black balaclava hoods. Toome saw them in the same instant. He reacted suddenly, diving into the corner of the lift and thumping his hand against the 'door close' button. Hudson flattened himself against the lift wall as the doors began to enfold on them again.

For Hudson, there was a real fear that he would be mistaken for a terrorist. Much as he wanted to be rescued from the clutches of the IRA, he did not want to be the recipient of an ill-timed bullet from a British soldier.

Toome pressed the ground floor button. He was shaking, his eyes wide and staring at the blank wall in front of him. His face had turned parchment white. He grasped his Armalite tightly against his chest and breathed deeply.

Hudson watched the floor indicator and tensed himself as the lift descended. Just before it whined to a halt, Toome took two giant steps across the floor and jabbed the barrel of the Armalite into Hudson's face.

"You do exactly what I tell you! D'you hear!"

"Yes."

"Right! Stand over there by the doors."

Hudson moved forward while Toome stood behind him and placed the narrow gun barrel against the back of his head. Hudson knew that he could afford no false moves.

The doors opened.

Outside, the scene was one of hurried confusion. Uniformed police and soldiers were mingling with civilians, all seemingly anxious to be doing something or going somewhere. Farther down the corridor, a group of tired controllers was led away from the radar room. They were either talking animatedly or walking quickly with a distinct air of purpose. For a moment, no one noticed Hudson and Toome as they stepped out of the lift.

"Move!" Toome hissed in a sharp, cracked tone.

Hudson stepped forward with short hesitant steps. At first they seemed to be just another part of the general melee of figures, but gradually Hudson felt a heavy silence level over the scene. As they passed on into the apparent confusion in the main entrance lobby, all eyes swivelled onto the Irishman and his prisoner.

"I'll blow his brains out if anyone makes a move to stop us!" Toome's voice grated across the heads of the watchers. "Tell them I mean it!"

"He means it!" Hudson spoke out loudly. His palms felt clammy with beads of sweat, and his lip quivered. "He's killed four people already. Don't try to stop him, please."

"Good." Toome's eyes darted from side to side. "I want someone to bring a car to the main entrance. Now!"

"Hold on there." A senior police officer stepped forward to block their exit from the building. "Who are you and why do you want a car?"

"Tell them!" Toome snapped and prodded his rifle into Hudson's back.

"He's the leader of the IRA terrorist group. He's killed already. Do as he tells you and get him a car, please."

"All right, son," the policeman answered. "Take it easy."

Behind the policeman, Vince Trewin stood watching the scene with a look of intense anger. Hudson caught the shocked expression in his colleague's eye as Trewin shook his head in desperation.

The police officer walked away to a group of men in military uniform standing at the main entrance. They spoke in a low whisper for some seconds and then the policeman came back towards the fugitive terrorist. "We'll get you a car as quickly as we can. But you'll have to wait until it can be brought through the traffic congestion."

One of the soldiers hurried out of the building and signalled to someone outside. Hudson watched him for a few seconds before his attention was taken by the road traffic. An endless stream of vehicles was headed towards the airport exit tunnel.

"They all want to get out of here as quickly as they can," the policeman explained. "There's a long queue from all the central car parks and each of the terminal buildings. Passengers, aircrew, airport workers, they all want to get out. Panic, you see."

Toome bared his teeth. "Be quick about it. I don't care how you do it, but do it quickly!"

"Why don't you come and wait in the rest room." The policeman tried to raise an encouraging smile but failed. "We'll tell you as soon as the car is ready. I promise."

"I don't trust you," Toome grunted.

"But you have a hostage," the policeman explained as he looked at Hudson with a faint expression of sympathy.

*

Dan Mayfield lay on his back, breathing gently while Helen was sprawled across his chest with her ear close to his heart. She could hear its regular beat like the rhythm of a grandfather clock, and she felt unreasonably satisfied.

"I disturbed your sleep," she whispered, wondering if his eyes would be open or closed.

"You shouldn't visit men in hotel bedrooms." He put his arms tight around her. "It's not considered decent."

Helen bit her lip. Janice Wilkins had visited him in hotel bedrooms.

The bedside alarm clock showed twenty-five minutes past two. A little over one and a half hours before the terrorist's deadline. She moved to the edge of the bed and said, "I'm going to take a shower. You lie there and relax."

"That's what I had in mind," he responded. "Unless you want to get me excited again."

"Not now." She stood up and turned towards him. "You should learn to quit after you've played the winning ace."

She turned on the shower in the en-suite and then walked across to the washbasin to pick up a tablet of soap. In the mirror she caught sight of a three-quarters view of her naked body. If Janice Wilkins could still boast a figure like that when she was thirty-one, and had a six-year-old child, she would be better placed to steal someone else's husband.

Helen mentally gave herself a credit mark and smiled to herself as she turned away. It seemed a little superfluous to be cleaning herself when, in a short while, she could be blasted off the face of the earth in one almighty explosion that would leave behind nothing of her existence. But cleanliness was a personal habit that refreshed her mentally as well as physically, and she needed that little boost before she went back to the London City Airport crisis.

She was relaxing under the steady spray of hot water when she heard the sound of voices in the bedroom and she paused for a second to identify the speakers. When she realised that Commander FitzHugh had intruded into their brief respite, she grimaced to herself and continued with her shower.

She walked back into the bedroom, wrapped in a hotel bath towel, and found FitzHugh sitting on the side of the bed. Dan was hurriedly dressing. The looks on the faces of both men told her immediately that there had been a serious development.

"What's happening?" she asked.

FitzHugh leaned forward and studied his hands. Then he looked up and said, "I'm afraid something has happened while you've been here. A shooting."

Helen moved closer to Dan and grasped his arm. What had this to do with her husband?

"They must have been jittery," FitzHugh continued. "I think they're all a bit uptight at the moment. Anyway, we had a marksman down near the airport fire station and one of the terrorists loosed off a round at him. There was a short exchange of fire which spread to other areas on the apron and a few people were hurt. A couple of the terrorists were killed."

"Murdoch?"

"No. He's safe, thank God. But one of the victims was the pilot of the F27. That means Murdoch and the IRA have no one to fly them out of the country."

"Fly them where?" Mayfield asked.

"We don't know. We only know that they are desperate for a pilot to get them away before the bomb explodes."

"What about the pilot of the Queen's Flight 146?" Helen asked.

"He's on board the 146, under heavy guard. We think they need him to fly that aircraft, along with the bomb, to wherever they plan to take it. If and when the government give in to their demands."

"Will the government give in?"

"Almost certainly not. The PM is adamant and there are precious few wets in the cabinet willing to argue for prudence. Besides, if we're right about this, it's going to be detonated anyway, whatever the government say."

"And so?"

FitzHugh made a wry face. "The important thing, as far as you are concerned, is this problem over who is to fly the F27."

"If I read you correctly, you want..." Helen turned her head towards Dan.

FitzHugh nodded and also turned to face the pilot. "Murdoch has demanded that we get someone to fly that aircraft, and just at the moment we think it would be prudent to do as he says. We want you, Mr Mayfield, to fly it. We could ask someone else but you're already involved and you know something of what to expect."

"You can't force him," Helen pointed out, doubtfully.

"No more than we can force you to help us, Helen. But this is a crisis."

Helen felt a sudden change of heart, a surge of hope for Dan's chances of surviving the attack. If he flew the F27, he would get away from the vicinity of the bomb. He had to take the chance that was being offered to him, whatever the consequences for her and the others left behind.

"There is one other thing, I'm afraid," FitzHugh continued. "And neither of you is going to like this."

Helen focussed her mind on the policeman's words.

"The suicide squad want their own hostage to give them a lever once Murdoch and the rest of the gang have left. Some insurance that they'll be allowed to leave London City Airport aboard the 146 and fly off to wherever, without being shot down."

"But they have the bomb!" Dan argued. "They don't need any hostage."

"Someone out there seems to value his own life. Interesting in a suicide squad, don't you think? Maybe they really do think they'll be allowed to get away safely. The point is, they want a human hostage to guarantee their escape. They want someone they can threaten without risking their own lives."

210

"You mean me, don't you?"

"Yes. There are other hostages in the control tower, but they've specifically demanded that *you* should go out there. And they want you to go with them if they manage to get away."

*

FitzHugh left Helen and Dan in the hotel room. He had no doubt they would have a lot to say to each other. In their shoes, he would have much to say to Angela. And with that thought he wished he could find the time to get back to her. Maybe talk to her one last time.

He walked out to his waiting car with slow, laborious steps. His driver was leaning against the side of the vehicle, reading what appeared to be a tabloid. His face was masked by a look of horror.

"Have you seen this, sir?" he queried as FitzHugh came closer. "The local daily. It's an emergency edition. Just hit the streets."

"What's it got to say about all this?"

"You won't like it, sir."

"Show me."

FitzHugh frowned as he took the paper and skimmed the headline. Anger rippled through him as he read the article that was splashed across the front page.

NUCLEAR DRAMA AT DOCKLANDS AIRPORT
By our Defence Correspondent
There were scenes of panic in London this afternoon when it became clear that a group of dedicated terrorists has planted a nuclear bomb at City Airport. The terrorist group are believed to be the IRA. The government is remaining tight-lipped about what is actually happening and still denies there is any risk to the public. However, according to sources within the Metropolitan Police, the bomb is a 150 kiloton device. We bring you this exclusive information about what would happen if the bomb was to be detonated so near to the heart of London.

THE EFFECT ON LONDON

The terrorists have said that the bomb will detonate at four o'clock this afternoon. This gives the government insufficient time to evacuate the city and there will be no effective shelter from the blast, so casualties will be very heavy. It has been suggested that London will be devastated like Hiroshima or Nagasaki, with many thousands of people being killed. We look at how the bomb will destroy people and buildings second by second.

After one second, a huge blast wave will be created and it will blow out to a distance of nearly half a mile from the airport within that first second. Nothing will be able to resist that blast. Silvertown and North Woolwich will immediately be affected and virtually all buildings will be totally destroyed. The concrete and bricks from the destruction of these buildings will create a huge mass of rubble with bodies buried beneath it. There will be a fireball which will reach out to nearly a quarter of a mile but it will be relatively unimportant as the blast wave will already have killed most people in the area.

There will be no survivors whatsoever within that range. Every living creature will be killed. People who are out of doors will die instantly and those who are inside will die as buildings collapse on top of them.

After four seconds, the blast wave will now have reached one mile from the airport. Within this area, all buildings will be destroyed or severely damaged. A few buildings may remain standing at the extreme edge of the area but the insides will be shattered. Any fires which are caused by the fireball will be immediately blown out by the shock wave. People who are inside buildings will be killed by flying debris and collapsing buildings. People who are outside will be killed either by the blast wave if they are in line of sight of the bomb or by collapsing buildings. Others will be seriously injured. At this point up to a quarter of a million people will have been killed or badly injured.

After ten seconds, the blast wave will stretch out to two and a half miles from the airport. It will now cover much of the heavily populated areas, reaching Poplar and Millwall. Reinforced buildings will be affected but private homes will be more heavily damaged. There will also be many fires started. By now about half a million people will have been killed. The blast wave will still kill or incapacitate people who are out of doors and are not in some way protected. People out shopping and children playing out of doors will have no protection against the blast.

WHAT CAN YOU DO?
It is estimated that more than a million people will die immediately from the blast. Up to eight million will die subsequently from burns and from the effect of radioactive fallout. There is only one way to avoid possible death, and that is to leave the London area...

FitzHugh threw the paper to the ground and raised his face to the dark sky above. This was the one thing the government had hoped to avoid. The one thing certain to lead to panic, looting and acts of desperation.

"The stupid idiots!" he roared. "Don't they understand what panic means?"

"Sir?" The driver looked taken aback.

FitzHugh glared at him. "Do you live in London?" he snapped.

"Yes, sir. Millwall."

"Family?"

"Wife and three kids, sir."

FitzHugh breathed out long and loud. "Take me back to the airport. Then get home and take care of your family. Get them away from London."

The driver demurred. "Not sure I'd be allowed to do that, sir. I'm allocated to you throughout the emergency."

FitzHugh snorted loudly. In the back of his mind were thoughts of his own family, his own wife. "If you're allocated to me, you do what I tell you! And I'm telling you to look after your family."

"Yes, sir."

Chapter 16

Tension rose as they waited for the car to appear at the Heathrow control tower. Eventually someone shouted, "Here it is!" and a police Rover appeared at the main entrance.

Toome pushed and prodded Hudson into the driving seat while the police and army looked on, seemingly helpless. Hudson started the car and gave them a forlorn look. From here on it was just him and the IRA leader.

Hudson drove the car out into the stream of traffic in Control Tower Road and was immediately caught in a noisy queue. Horns blared all around the police vehicle as he attempted to get out of the Heathrow central area. The snaking tailback of traffic snarled and squeezed its way towards the airport exit tunnel. Drivers hammered their horns and waved angry fists as they tried to get away. The police seemed unable to sort out the confusion.

As Hudson eased into the tunnel, the echoes of angry horns reverberated down the confined tube. When he finally drove onto the M4 motorway, the situation was even worse. All lanes leading out of London were blocked with slow-moving traffic, even the hard shoulder had been pressed into use as an extra lane.

"You know the way through London?" Toome asked.

"Depends where you want to go." Hudson kept his voice level. "Looking at this mess, I would guess that most of central London will be blocked solid, wherever you want to go."

Toome thought for a few moments. Then he breathed sharply. "Shite! You'd better head out towards the M25. We'll go that way."

"If you say so."

Hudson eased into the long queue, forcing a space for himself by pushing the nose of the Rover in between a sleek sports car and a slow-moving articulated lorry. He thought the fact that they were in a police vehicle might help, but it didn't. The lorry driver waved a fist at him.

"Shall I use the siren?" he asked.

Toome shook his head in frustration. Moments later, he changed his mind. "Okay. Give it a try."

The siren and the flashing blue strobe light caught the attention of the drivers in the vehicles ahead and behind them, but no one moved aside to let them through. The jam was too tight for anyone to turn or give way. Hudson switched off the alarm and followed the general mass of traffic in its slow exodus out of London.

Across the central reservation he noticed very few cars heading towards central London. An occasional police or military vehicle raced eastwards, and one or two fast police cars sped westwards on the empty eastbound carriageway, their flashing lights stabbing the air about them. There was an eerie sense of unreality about the whole scene.

Hudson noticed a helicopter hovering over the motorway at five hundred feet, about a mile ahead of them. The fuselage nose was pointed directly at them, as if someone was watching. Hudson put a hand to his eyes and tried to determine the registration, but the chopper was too far off and the registration letters were on the unseen sides of the fuselage. As they eased closer, the helicopter turned and sped away westwards. Seconds later, Hudson saw another helicopter flying low over the adjacent fields. It was a police machine, without doubt. He made out the shape of someone watching them from the bubble cockpit.

"What the hell is happening?" he asked.

"Panic." Toome's voice seemed calmer now that they were away from the immediate vicinity of Heathrow. "People are panicking."

"But why?"

"You'll find out when we get to where we're going."

"It must be something pretty big."

"It is. Just shut up and drive."

Hudson glanced across to the vehicle in the adjacent lane, a well worn blue Sierra with a replacement driver's door which didn't quite match the body colour. Inside, the driver grasped the wheel tightly while a woman in the passenger seat hugged a small baby. They looked silent and frightened and the woman pressed the baby close to her as if some terrible catastrophe was about to overtake them. But what catastrophe?

When they came to the M25 interchange, the already slow pace of the traffic reduced to a crawl. More vehicles crowded onto the M4 from both north- and southbound lanes of the M25, all trying to head west with the same sense of frantic urgency. One family had abandoned their car on the hard shoulder, exacerbating the traffic jam. They ran along the grass embankment at the side of the motorway and were soon well ahead of their vehicle.

Very few cars filtered off the M4 onto the orbital motorway going northbound. The majority seemed to be too hell-bent on making their way west. Hudson breathed a sigh of relief when he was finally able to swing the police car onto the M25 slip road and gun the speed up to sixty. In different circumstances, he thought, he would probably have experienced some sort of thrill in driving the powerful police vehicle at speed, but the presence of Toome in the passenger seat precluded that. After the slow crawl along the M4, he felt a strange sense of escape as he opened up the throttle.

He shuddered when he suddenly noticed the police helicopter still tailing them at low level, with someone now hanging out from the cockpit, watching. He thought the watcher might have been using a camera, but it was only a guess. The helicopter was pacing them accurately, locked in a position just in front of the car's side window post. Hudson bit his lip, looked to the almost empty outside lane, and rammed his foot to the floor. The helicopter pilot reacted instantly, maintaining his position with uncanny precision.

Toome's rifle was settled across his lap with the barrel pointed towards Hudson. The terrorist's finger was still cocked around the trigger and Hudson guessed that the slightest touch would send a hail of bullets in his direction.

"Where now?" he asked, although he had a pretty firm suspicion where they were headed.

"Just keep driving. I'll tell you when to turn." Toome's face was grimly set. He gave Hudson a sideways look. "Have you been to City Airport before?"

"Once or twice," Hudson replied. The question told him what he wanted to know.

"Good. Keep your foot down."

Hudson pressed hard to the floor and saw the speedometer needle swing up past the eighty mark, still moving.

As the outside lane opened up in front of them, he looked down at the car clock. Five minutes to three. Almost an hour since the Heathrow control tower had been taken by Stenning and his men. Undoubtedly, the attack had been successful, judging by the scene in the main lobby. So what was causing the terrible panic among the public?

And Jennifer? Had someone found her? Even in his confused bundle of thoughts, he had time to hope that she was now being well cared for. As he thought about the girl, he stamped his foot harder on the accelerator and the needle passed the hundred mark.

*

Murdoch felt only the merest twinge of guilt as he prepared to leave the City Airport. He gave his final orders to McQuarrie, and then he hastened across the apron towards the F27, leaving the suicide squad in sole charge of the bomb.

The lives of the IRA gunmen didn't really matter. The inevitable deaths of the suicide squad caused him not a second of remorse or concern.

He climbed the steps of the F27, took a last look around the apron and strode into the cabin area. The rest of the IRA gunmen, the ones who would escape with him, were seated, all except for a single man who stood near the entrance to the flight deck. His Armalite was pointed towards the pilot, a man called Mayfield. All that remained was to collect the idiot, Toome, and his men from Heathrow.

Murdoch strode up to the cockpit door and pointed a steady finger at the pilot. "Start the engines!"

Dan Mayfield studied the F27 cockpit layout. He had flown on the flight deck of an old Friendship once before, not as the pilot but as a passenger allowed to sit in the co-pilot's seat. He allowed the 'presence' of the old lady to creep back into his mind, soaking up the feel of a bygone age, a feel that was primitive, beautifully primitive. He placed his hands on the control column which was well worn, then he leaned across to touch the equally well-used throttles, and he forced himself to think twin propeller.

The panel looked positively archaic and, after his experience in 747s, reassuringly bare. The aircraft had those rudimentary instruments that were required by law for flight on airways: VOR, ILS and the radio receivers. But it had no on-board flight-management computer, no inertial navigation system, nothing that would take any length of time to master. It was just a straight-forward flying machine.

Murdoch entered the cockpit and eased himself into the right-hand seat. His face was grim and he carried a revolver which he pointed in Mayfield's direction.

"Start the engines," he repeated brusquely, sounding tense now that the moment of truth was little more than an hour away.

"You're the boss."

Mayfield glanced sideways. Although Helen had told him all she could recall about Murdoch, her description contained little of the 'presence' the terrorist carried around with him. It was an uncanny aura that Mayfield was unable to define or ignore. He turned away and concentrated on starting up the F27's engines.

The twin Darts whined into life reassuringly. To Mayfield they sounded toy-like, the two together delivering just a fraction of the power of only one of the four turbofans mounted on a 747.

The 146 had also been started up and was taxying clear of the runway to allow the F27 to depart. As Mayfield released the brakes and eased the throttles forward, the old lady began to move.

"What callsign shall I use?" he shouted across to Murdoch.

"Call yourself *Nemesis*," Murdoch replied.

Mayfield looked puzzled and then pressed the radio transmit switch. "Tower, this is *Nemesis*. Do you read me?"

"*Nemesis*, this is the Tower. Pass your message."

"Tower, *Nemesis* is taxying for runway two-eight."

"Roger *Nemesis*. The QNH is one zero one two, the wind two seven zero at ten knots."

"Roger, Tower."

Mayfield kept his vision focussed on the taxiway as he allowed the lumbering old lady to trundle towards the runway.

"What's the meaning of *Nemesis*?" he called across to Murdoch.

The gunman stared straight ahead and snapped, "Shut up."

Mayfield lined up the Friendship into wind and ran up the engines against the brakes. They seemed to be running smoothly.

"Where do we go after take-off?" he asked evenly.

"Heathrow."

Just as he had expected. Mayfield shook his head and then pressed his radio transmit switch. "Tower, this is *Nemesis*. We are ready to roll."

"Roger, *Nemesis*. You are cleared for take-off. The wind is still two seven zero degrees at ten knots."

Mayfield released the brakes and levered forward the throttles. He felt the old lady lift up her skirts and begin to run, slowly at first and then faster as the propellers bit into the air more keenly. Once they were airborne, he retracted the undercarriage and settled into a slow climb.

"I'll stay on this heading and climb to one thousand feet," he called across the cockpit, waiting for Heathrow's parallel runways to come into sight.

"Call the Heathrow control tower," Murdoch suddenly snapped. "Tell them to get the IRA men out near the runway. Make sure they're waiting for us."

"Okay." Mayfield reset the VHF frequency selector and keyed the transmitter. Murdoch's plan was becoming clearer.

"Heathrow Tower, this is *Nemesis*. Do you read me? Over."

The reply came back almost instantly from a tired voice. As

220

if the old Friendship was expected. "*Nemesis*, this is Heathrow Tower. Pass your message."

"Heathrow, we are an F27 en-route to you from City Airport. We request a straight in approach. Over."

"Standby for joining clearance, *Nemesis*." A short pause, and then, "What is the purpose of your flight?"

Awkward question, not what he expected. Mayfield looked across at Murdoch and asked, "What do I tell them?"

Murdoch's face twitched. He continued staring ahead. "I told you! I want those bloody IRA men out near the runway, ready for us!"

"Okay." Mayfield pressed the transmitter switch again. "Heathrow, we are coming to pick up the IRA group from your control tower. You are requested to ensure they are allowed out near the runway, ready for boarding when we arrive. Over."

"Roger, *Nemesis*. The..." The transmission stopped dead.

Mayfield waited a few seconds and then asked, "Say again, Heathrow."

"Roger..." Another pause. "You... you are cleared to join on a long final for runway two-seven-left."

Mayfield gave Murdoch a brief glance. Something was amiss at Heathrow, he was sure of it, and he hoped to hell Murdoch was not going to react unpredictably.

*

FitzHugh settled himself in the passenger seat of a police Land Rover in the car park at London City Airport. The files which he now had on his lap were buff coloured, and each was clearly labelled SECRET. He closed the Land Rover door, set one file on the seat beside him and studied the other. It was referenced, in the top right-hand corner, GA035/6.

He read:

*The IRA connection with the KGB and later the SVR was en-
hanced by the work of Patrick Toome. Although not on the*

army council, he is an intelligent man and is regarded as something of an amateur diplomat. He rose through the ranks of the IRA Belfast brigade in the early 1980s and became one of their most important brigade leaders.

Information from army intelligence suggests that the main thing which held Toome back from higher office within the IRA was an (unpublished) Sinn Fein suspicion regarding his true affiliations and his reliability. Although he was apparently doing a good job for the IRA, Sinn Fein made adverse secret reports on him to the IRA army council. (See intelligence reports in doc GD215/1, ref 312/1, page 12. See also the briefing given by McGuinness to the IRA army council August 1986. Ref GR534/3, page 27.) Intelligence reports from our agent, Stevenson, who at one time managed to get very close to Toome, are clear in...

FitzHugh stopped and cast his mind back to the fate of agent Stevenson. Not one of his own staff, Stevenson worked for Military Intelligence. Even so, he knew enough about the agent's work through his military contacts to be shocked when Stevenson was killed at the hands of Sinn Fein.

Was there anything useful to be found in Stevenson's link with Toome? He flicked over the page and ran down until he picked out the heading *The Stevenson Reports*. He turned to a lengthy preface page stapled to the front of the reports and read quickly through the document.

Rosemary Stevenson was a British counterintelligence agent seconded to Northern Ireland to investigate the matter of the IRA's links with Russian Intelligence. She was killed by Sinn Fein when they broke her cover. At the time of her death she was also exploring the role of Patrick Toome. Her British connection was never published by Sinn Fein, nor did they ever claim responsibility for killing her. In fact, they laid the blame for her death at the door of the Ulster Defence Association.

This move was important to them while they attempted to discover the full extent of her contacts inside the IRA Belfast organisation. Fortunately, they never did fully break her ring of contacts and her true identity was never openly published. Sinn Fein still have the jitters on that one as they cannot rule out the possibility of other moles deep inside the Belfast brigade. Who caused her cover to be blown is not known but there is strong evidence that she was killed by a known IRA/ Sinn Fein intermediary (see page 16, para 9). Toome was almost certainly not aware of her British Intelligence role at the time of her death. There is even evidence to believe that he came under suspicion from Sinn Fein as a direct result of his association with Stevenson. Under her cover name of Roisin O'Steafin, Stevenson made a number of valuable reports on the Russian connection. She discovered Toome's rising role in that area and she also confirmed the degree to which the SVR hawks still support the IRA. These reports are detailed in Appendices B/34 to B/36.

He shook his head and looked again at the page in front of him. A thought began to grow deep inside his mind. What about Stevenson's death? Was that important? Who had fired the shot that killed her? On an impulse he turned to page 16.

And there it was. Just what he needed to know.

FitzHugh closed the file and sat for some minutes staring out through the front windscreen of the Land Rover. One major thought filled his mind. It was now almost certain that the bomb was going to be detonated on British soil, regardless of what the government agreed to. If only he had been able to get his hands on Toome — alive — then maybe he would have had a chance of stopping the unthinkable carnage of a nuclear explosion. Maybe the Irishman would have been persuaded to give them a way out of this. FitzHugh tapped the file in front of him. He now had the information he needed to pile on the pressure, to make Toome talk. But it was too late.

He was still deep in thought when the Land Rover's police telephone suddenly rang. The emergency services communications network was still intact. He picked it up and snapped, "Yes?" in a brusque tone.

A police control operator spoke back unemotionally. "Commander FitzHugh?"

"Yes."

"An urgent message for you, Commander. I'm connecting you now to your home."

He barked, "Well, what is it?" and then waited until another voice replied.

"I'm sorry, Commander...." He immediately recognised the voice. It was the nurse tending Angela.

"No, it's all right. I'm sorry," he said in a calmer tone. "I shouldn't have snapped at you."

"That's all right." The voice paused. "Commander, I think you should come home as soon as possible."

"What's happened?"

"Angela was sleeping and I thought she was comfortable, but then she woke up in some pain. And... and I don't think..."

"How long?" he asked, saving her the agony of finishing the sentence.

"Maybe a few hours. I don't know." Then she added, with genuine regret, "I really am very sorry to have to call you."

"It's all right. I should have expected it." FitzHugh looked at his watch. Hell! What a dilemma: his wife or the lives of millions of others. He said, "I'll get there when... as soon as I can. It may not be straightaway."

*

Janice Wilkins was unable to sleep. She dozed for a while and then tossed and turned in the bed. Too many demanding thoughts floated through her mind. Eventually she gave up and went out to the kitchen to make a cup of coffee. While the kettle was boiling, she stood at the kitchen window and looked out on the road below. It was unusually busy.

224

A large Bedford van was parked outside the building and people were loading furniture into it. The men heaving heavy objects into the van were strangers, but she recognised the Swansons, her immediate neighbours. They were a young couple with an unreasonable taste for loud music. Both were busily lifting boxes of possessions into the rear of the van. Either side of the Bedford, cars were stacked with personal possessions. And to cap it all, a stream of vehicles paraded steadily down the road, each heavily loaded with people and luggage.

Puzzled, she shook her head and sipped her coffee.

She went to the bathroom to run a bath and then came back into the lounge with the sound of running water following her. She idly switched on her radio and searched round the room for her comfortable jeans. With her mind still not fully awake, it was some minutes before she realised what was coming from the radio. It was a news flash... the most horrifying news broadcast she could imagine. She stopped to listen and a sense of panic slowly took hold of her throat and began to strangle her.

Oh God! A nuclear bomb! That was why the people were loading up and leaving. What should she do? There was no one she could turn to... no one she could ask for help.

She had a sudden flash thought — to telephone Dan Mayfield. He would know what to do. She rushed to the telephone and jabbed at the keypad with a trembling finger, but there was no answer from Dan's number. Who else? Who could she call? She ran through her telephone directory and, on a sudden impulse, she called her parents in Southampton, but got no reply from them, either. She sank down to the floor, the sound of running water making a grim background to her blind panic.

*

The old F27 Friendship's main undercarriage kissed the Heathrow runway with all the grace of a precision landing. Mayfield felt a short burst of personal pride.

He keyed the radio telephone and said, "Tower from *Nemesis*, we are going to backtrack to the end of the runway. Please have the

IRA group sent out to us."

"Roger, *Nemesis*... standby."

The little Friendship turned just a short way down the long Heathrow runway and made its way back to the take-off point. When Mayfield glanced across the flight deck at Murdoch, he detected definite signs of agitation. The nervous twitch was getting worse. Murdoch shifted constantly in his seat and his gaze swung from side to side as if he was in fear of imminent attack.

Once the F27 was lined up at the take-off point, Mayfield sat back to relax and wait. The twin Dart engines were at idle and the R/T was silent. There was no need for him to do anything until someone else made a move.

"The British are up to something," Murdoch snorted, his neck turning red. "Toome and his group should have been here, waiting."

Mayfield gave him an enquiring look.

"Call them again," Murdoch said, "and ask them what the delay is."

Mayfield adjusted his headset. "Tower from *Nemesis*. What's the delay?"

"*Nemesis*, there's a slight problem. I'll call you back in a moment."

"Hell!" Murdoch was getting more agitated by the minute. He leaned forward to look out of the side window. Then he jerked back, startled. "What the—"

Mayfield jumped as Murdoch waved his gun hand wildly and jerked his other hand to the port side of the aircraft. Outside, vague figures moved towards the F27. A closer look showed they were armed men in combat uniform.

"Get out of here!" Murdoch's voice erupted into a roar. "Quickly! Get us airborne!"

Chapter 17

They didn't hear the gunshots; the sound of the fast-running turbines obliterated all outside noise. The first they knew they were under fire was when the side window alongside Murdoch suddenly shattered. Murdoch screamed loudly and Mayfield thought he had been hit, but it was only fear. Pure animal fear.

Mayfield pulled back on the control column, urging the aircraft into the air before it reached take-off speed. Protracted, heavy seconds passed before the F27 finally lifted off the Heathrow runway, still leaving a long, empty stretch in front of it. Sweating profusely, Mayfield heaved the aircraft round in a climbing turn and asked, "Where to now?"

Getting no reply, he glanced across at Murdoch. The old man was silently pressed back into his seat, his head withdrawn below the level of the instrument panel.

"I'm turning onto an easterly heading," Mayfield called out. "I'll take us south of London City, out towards the east."

"Yes. Go east. That's right." Murdoch raised his head and peered out through the shattered side window. Jagged cracks spread out from the gaping hole. After some moments, he leaned back in his seat and breathed heavily.

"You'll need to be more specific about our destination," Mayfield said.

Murdoch grunted. His face looked drawn, filled with the strain of a retaliation he clearly had not expected. The twitch continued. Sweat dribbled down his puffy cheeks. After a minute, he pulled a topographical map from inside his coat and opened it on his lap. He stared at it blankly, shifted its position and then looked closer. He studied the map, breathing heavily, before folding it into four and handing it across to the pilot.

"Here." He leaned across the flight deck and pointed to a spot on the wider part of the Thames estuary. "There's a long, flat meadow here alongside a narrow road. It's marked by that cross. When you get there, you'll see some vehicles parked at the side of the field with headlights lit. You're to land there and offload the passengers."

"All of the passengers? Including you?"

"No. Just a few of the Irish. There are some who don't want to go where I'm going. They'll be on their own after we drop them."

"Where will they go? Their faces are now known. The police will be out in force looking for every one of them."

"They'll be in safe houses long before the police know what's happened. When all this has died down, they'll escape to some other place abroad. They knew from the start they were destined for exile and they all accepted it." Murdoch grunted. "Now, do as you're told and find that field!"

Mayfield made a play of checking the map. "And where will *you* be going?"

"Wait and see. You'll be taking me there, after we offload the Irish."

"Back to Moscow, I suppose?"

"I said wait and see." Was that a resigned look on Murdoch's face? Resignation for what might await him when he returned to Russia? Mayfield mentally filed away the implication; FitzHugh might get something out of it.

"Will your Russian friends allow us to enter their airspace without shooting us down?"

"Of course. Now shut up and fly!"

When Mayfield levelled out at two thousand feet, the F27 was flying in IMC — Instrument Meteorological Conditions — and he was unable to see anything but the thick enveloping cloud. He had no visual contact with the ground below, nor any sight of the blue sky above. Only the aircraft instruments told him roughly where he was and where he was headed. If he were to encounter another aircraft in that cloud, he had no means of seeing it in sufficient time to avoid a collision.

"I'll have to climb to a higher altitude," he said keenly. "The cloud is too thick at this level and the cloud base is too low for us to get down below it."

"No! I want you to stay down at this altitude." A measure of self-confidence returned to Murdoch's behaviour as he leaned forward to inspect the altimeter. "We'll run out of radar cover once we get east of London, and ATC won't be able to track us to the landing field."

Mayfield frowned at the level of understanding Murdoch was displaying. "It's not safe. We could be in some danger of collision."

"It's safe enough. What's the matter with you? Haven't you flown low level before?"

"Not in a Friendship."

"You'll do as I say. Stay low."

Mayfield shrugged his shoulders. "If you say so. We'll be passing south of London City Airport in a few minutes. You want me to call them?"

"No! Call no one!"

*

Squiffy Quilley had taken a long lunch break and was again seated at a radar suite in the En-route Control room at West Drayton. And he was annoyed. After all the help he had given to the en-route controllers, he figured he deserved the first 'early go'. Historically, no one was too sure how the 'early go' tradition began in air traffic control. It was an unofficial fiddle that allowed a number of controllers to slip away from work before the end of the shift.

Squiffy wanted to play a round of golf before he attended a parent-teacher meeting at his son's school, but he had been warned that the 'early go' list had been curtailed because of the extra workload brought on by the crisis. Instead of heading off towards the golf course, he was now working like a one-armed paper hanger with far more aircraft inbound to Gatwick than the system could handle. The Gatwick holding stacks were both full and he was now using the Heathrow holding stacks for his Gatwick arrivals. And, to cap it all, something had just taken off from Heathrow and was wandering east through the thickest area of radar congestion.

"Who the hell is that?" he turned and growled at the support controller seated alongside him. He stabbed an angry finger at the offending radar echo. The aircraft which appeared to have come from Heathrow was transmitting no 'squawk code' which would identify it. "Can you find out for me?"

"Okay. You guard the frequency. I'll do the phones." The support controller picked up his telephone and prodded a button on his keyboard. Moments later his finger closed over the wild aircraft's radar echo and he announced, "It's the F27 that landed at London City Airport earlier. The one that was carrying the bomb. Try to track it as long as you can."

"Bloody hell!" Squiffy exploded. "Don't you think I've enough to cope with already?" He launched into a series of instructions to the various aircraft milling around between Heathrow and Gatwick. He vaguely noticed the stray radar echo disappear among the melee of others in its vicinity. He hoped it was flying low because there was far too much traffic already in the area. A wild aircraft at the same altitude could be lethal.

*

The Twin Otter was flying from Norwich to Bristol. The pilot had originally flight-planned to make his first landing at Gatwick before continuing on to Bristol. But, with so much congestion in the Gatwick area, he had decided to cancel that landing and continue directly to his destination. It was a commercially prudent decision and, besides, Bristol would be well beyond the effects of a nuclear explosion in London. First, however, he had to fight his way through the congestion inside the London Control Area.

The pilot levelled off at two thousand feet and selected the Thames Radar frequency. There was no reply. He would be passing close to Biggin Hill airfield so he decided to change to the Biggin Hill frequency. It all seemed to be a bit of a pig's ear down on the ground and he felt annoyed that no one had explained to him the full extent of the problem. His head went down into the cockpit to check the Biggin frequency on his UK Air Pilot Chart. His eyes then flicked across to his VHF instruments as he changed the radio frequency selector. In that same moment a sudden explosion of sound ripped apart the rear end of his aeroplane.

*

Mayfield was studying the VOR radio beacon receivers, trying to determine their exact position by cross-cutting from two ground stations. It wasn't a difficult task, just more fiddly and more time consuming than using the on-board computer that was standard kit in a 747. A glance at his watch told him it was 15:25. They had passed south of London City Airport and were now heading somewhere out towards the Thames estuary. Thirty-five minutes left to get clear of the bomb. But exactly where were they? His head came up just a split second before the Twin Otter came into view, filling the front screen. With a muffled cry, he instinctively heaved on the control column.

The F27 began to swing away from the smaller aircraft, but less than a second later the starboard wing carved into the tail of the Twin Otter with a wild scream of tortured metal.

Mayfield's razor sharp senses detected a change in the feel of the Friendship as he heaved the control column round. He still had aileron response and the engine power was unchanged, but the aircraft felt wrong. It had lost a sizeable portion of the front edge of its starboard wing!

The Friendship had lost some height in the steep turn away from the point of collision. As he eased the wings back level, Mayfield noted that the altimeter read just fifteen hundred feet. He levelled off, easing back gently on the control column in case there was some damage to the control lines. Then he ran his eyes across the instrument panel, mentally running a rapid check on each dial. He gave Murdoch only the briefest of glances, enough to register that the man was sitting rigid in his seat, petrified by the shock of the collision. Then he looked back at his panel again, noting that all the navigation instruments appeared to be reading accurately.

The airspeed indicator, the altimeter, the turn and bank indicator, the artificial horizon... they were all registering correctly.

Only the fuel gauges looked wrong; he was losing turbine fuel from the damaged wing. Severed fuel lines were ruptured, he guessed. He would have to land the aeroplane as quickly as possible. Not only was he losing fuel, he had no idea of the extent of the structural damage. His hand went out to the radar transponder switches to select the emergency 'squawk code', a reflex action which was a part of his flying instinct.

*

The Twin Otter had no chance. The control lines parted like a string sliced by a sharp knife. Stripped of elevator control, the aircraft nosed over into a steep dive.

With the entire tail section ripped away, it plunged towards the ground totally out of control. The pilot wrestled vainly with his controls amidst a raging crescendo of noise as his aircraft began to break up in the air. He had no positive impression of what had happened, nor of what he could do. There had been another aircraft, he had caught sight of it just after they hit, as the Twin Otter nosed towards the ground. But he had no clear idea of what it was... no clear idea of anything! Ahead he could see the ground spinning round as if he was looking at a revolving picture. He continued to struggle with the aircraft controls.

As the aircraft went inverted, his body was thrown sideways and he found himself looking back down the length of the passenger cabin. He saw a mass of arms and bodies waving about the rear part of the fuselage, some hanging from their inverted seats. One or two were flying loose... unrestrained.

*

A flashing SOS signal lit up beside the rogue echo on Squiffy's radar screen. At first he thought it might be an incorrectly cycled code. But it remained for several sweeps of the radar head and then he knew it was a real emergency.

"That's the F27 out of London City!" he shouted, grabbing the support controller's arm. "He's in trouble but he's not talking to me."

The other controller leaned towards the radar screen and simultaneously grabbed at his telephone. "Have you got anyone else in that area?"

"Anyone else? For God's sake! I've got a whole bloody screenful of aircraft! Can't you see?"

"I mean, have you any other aircraft at that low level?" The support controller pointed to the height read-out on the emergency aircraft. It was the first indication they had of how low the aircraft was flying.

Squiffy forced his mind to think. Think. What other aircraft did he have down there?

"There was a Twin Otter going through the area, but he left my frequency some minutes ago."

As a forlorn gesture, he called the pilot of the Twin Otter, but there was no reply.

*

Toome felt a blinding urge to make the car go faster. It was half past three and they had only thirty minutes left before the deadline. Could they get to City Airport in the time left to them? He stared at the young Englishman sitting beside him and gritted his teeth. He was convinced now that his only hope of escape from the country lay in getting to the City Airport in time to get aboard the captured Queen's Flight aircraft. He had briefly considered escaping directly into the English countryside, but that was a risky move with a helicopter closely following their progress along the motorway. Whatever happened at four o'clock, there would be a massive police search for known IRA sympathisers. The risk of capture was too great. He would be better dead than caught.

Of course, he couldn't be too sure exactly what would happen when the deadline ran out — that would depend largely on the British response. But he fervently hoped the British government would capitulate. If they did, the bomb would be flown out, and he would be on board the aircraft. It really was the only hope left to him.

The car swung off the M25 onto the M11. They still had a chance provided they weren't caught in any traffic jams. Toome's thoughts turned back to the fiasco he had left behind at Heathrow. After all his previous successes, the prospect of utter failure hung heavy on his mind. Equally heavy to bear was the knowledge that he had run away in the face of that failure, and he had left the rest of his brigade to face the consequences. His actions were unpardonable and he would certainly face severe censure from the army council. Assuming, of course, that he escaped from this unholy mess.

God, what an unholy mess!

Doubts began to crystallise in his mind. Doubts about the whole reason behind his IRA membership. If only Danny had not been killed. If only he had not been there to see his brother sliding into death on waves of agonising pain. If only he had refused to listen to the persuasive arguments Sinn Fein had used in the aftermath of the killing. He recalled the hours he had spent listening to their vindictive rhetoric, drinking in the horror of their lurid descriptions of other people's deaths and other people's pain at the hands of the Loyalists and the British Army. In the end, what did it all mean? He had killed and maimed just as wantonly as any of them. And for what? Revenge? Was that all it boiled down to? Was that the sum total of his life's aim? Killing aimlessly in return for someone else's aimless killing? Killing because of Danny... and because of Roisin.

Dear, sweet Roisin.

The car raced on.

In a sudden flash of recall, he caught a brief picture of the day he had taken Roisin out for a drive in his own car. It had been a lovely summer's day and they stopped for lunch in a small fishing village on the County Down coast. It was nestled between a green hill to the landward side and a rippling green-grey sea to the other. There were few boats about at that time of day, so they left the car on the harbour and walked on across a golf course to a small hollow which overlooked the water. Toome spread his coat on the grass so that they could curl up together and be at peace with one another. It was one of the few occasions when he really felt at ease, sufficiently at ease to relax and talk about their future.

They watched a group of children run across the grass towards the water's edge, young moon-faced children with dark expressions of determination. When they reached the water, they started a game of soldiers and freedom fighters, using the rocks by the shore as hiding places. Toome noted that it was a prominent feature of the game for all the soldiers to be killed. The freedom fighters cheered each time a soldier died. The underlying message would probably remain with the children for life.

He pointed them out to Roisin. "You see what those children are doing? Kids too young to know any better, acting out their parents' hatreds. That's the root cause of Ireland's trouble, you know, and it's bloody well self-perpetuating."

"It's the way things are, Patrick." Roisin seemed unmoved by the children's game and she commented that when she was married she wanted four children. Toome laughingly promised her at least four. At no time had he asked her to marry him, nor did she ever press him to. There was no need because marriage was something for the future, a future when every logical reason should have told him that they had none.

A future when he could soon be burned to an atomic crisp!

He looked across the car at the English controller and asked, "Are you married?"

"Yes."

"Any family?"

"No. We had a baby but she died."

"Oh." He was momentarily caught off guard. "What will your wife think about all this?"

The Englishman stared straight ahead, and Toome saw his hands tightened their grip on the steering wheel. After some moments, he said, "She'll be upset. She's not in very good health. She's... quite ill."

"I'm sorry."

Sorry! The word was out before he realised what he had said. In an effort to justify his position he added, "People get hurt in wars. Sometimes the wrong people."

"But this isn't war. This is cold-blooded terrorism." The controller spoke more sharply now.

"What's terrorism?" Toome looked ahead at the seemingly endless motorway as he spoke. "It's just another kind of war. One side has all the weapons, power, money, the sort of things only governments enjoy. The other side has to make do as best they can with homemade bombs and guerrilla tactics. But it's still a war."

"And innocent people get hurt."

Toome felt his anger returning. "Innocent people always get hurt in wars. You British bombed the very soul out of Germany, killing thousands of innocent civilians: men, women and children. Do you think that's a better way to conduct a war?"

"It was the only way," the young man replied. "The Nazis had to be stopped."

"You think we've any other option?"

"Yes. Everything you've done has made things worse for your own country. Because you kill your own people."

Silence fell between them for several minutes. Toome knew that he was trying to convince himself now. What the English controller thought was really quite immaterial. By the look of him, he was too young to have ever experienced life in a country at war, and he could never understand. He would never be able to appreciate what it was like to live in a country torn apart by bitterness, hatred... murder.

"My brother was killed," Toome said quietly. "He was sitting in a bar, minding his own business. And they blew him up."

"Who blew him up?"

"The loyalists."

"So your war is with them. Not us."

"You're all the same. English. Loyalists. British Army. You're all the same. For years your government propped up a corrupt Loyalist regime in Ireland."

"And you support a band of cold-blooded murderers. Psycho-paths who bomb innocent women and children. Vicious killers who would rape young girls. It doesn't say much for the people of your country, does it? I read somewhere that, long ago, Wilson's government wanted you lot expelled from the UK."

"We'd be better off today if he had expelled us." Toome stared through the window beside the Englishman and saw the helicopter move out of station. It pulled up sharply and then sped away in a wide, climbing turn. He wondered why.

*

Janice Wilkins left her flat and made her way to Kensington High Street underground station. An air of desperation was evident among the people who filled the streets. The crowd at the underground was stretched well back along the pavements, spilling onto the road. People were shouting and fights had broken out among those at the rear. Law and order was fast disappearing as mob rule took over.

Janice began to panic. The road was jam-packed with cars and there was no point in searching for a taxi. Neither was there any point in remaining at the tube station. The four o'clock deadline was only twenty-five minutes away and a deepening sense of futility was taking hold of the crowd. The mood grew steadily uglier. The sound of scuffles came from deep inside the underground and loud voices came drifting out from the entrance hall. She saw no point in staying, no point in dying with the crowd inside the station.

Janice backed away and retraced her steps to her flat. If only she knew who she could turn to! She was shaking as she stepped into the empty foyer and she only briefly noticed three men following her in.

They closed in on her when the outer door slammed shut, one on each side and the third behind. She stopped, startled. Instantly, the men on either side grabbed her arms and propelled her towards the lift. They were young, but well-built. Their hallmark was dirty clothes and aggressive behaviour. They smelled of drink and cigarette smoke.

"Don't cause us any trouble, darlin', " one of the men hissed, "an' we won't do you no 'arm. Okay?"

"What do you want?" Her voice was weak and squeaky. She felt sick.

"Yer valuables, darlin'. Show us where yer valuables is."

She tried to break away, but a sharp knife was pressed into her back.

They were looters! With the population leaving London in panic, the looters had moved in.

*

Helen felt a strange sense of detachment from what was happening about her. She was seated inside the 146 and the bomb was only a few feet away, but it might have been a million miles away.

At least Dan was now safely out of the vicinity and Judith was safe. What happened to her from here on was of lesser importance.

She swung her view around to the aisle and carefully studied the metal container. The lid had been left open and the timer box was clearly visible from where she sat. It was closed. She forced her mind to think about the layout of switches inside the box, conjuring up a mental image.

She pictured a single spring-loaded black switch — connecting the timer to the clock mechanism. And one red switch — that one was for instantaneous detonation. To disarm the bomb, McQuarrie had to press the black switch. Or did he? There was something suspicious about the way Murdoch had avoided that issue. Something that worried her. Was it another booby trap?

Helen studied the keypad on the outside of the timer box. If she knew the correct number sequence, she would have the key to opening that timer box. Without the combination they were lost. And the lock was certainly booby-trapped.

She looked again at her watch. Only twenty minutes left before the device blew them all off the face of the earth. She felt a sudden

238

short burst of regret because she would have liked to have seen Judith growing up into a young woman. She would have liked to have been with her when she explored those exciting teenage years, to have been her daughter's confidant and friend. She hoped Judith would understand when she learned of the part her mother played in trying to prevent the destruction of the nation's capital.

McQuarrie sat nearby with an Armalite rifle resting across his lap and a cigarette precariously hanging from his lip. He looked too calm for someone who was heading for oblivion. Maybe he thought that the threat would work and the British government would cave in at the last minute. She studied him thoughtfully. What could motivate a man like that into involvement with the mass destruction of so many people? Including himself! It was madness!

A babble of voices suddenly cut into the quiet atmosphere, raised voices outside the fuselage. One of the gunmen ran into the cabin, gesticulating wildly. "The aircraft's coming back!"

"What the hell!" McQuarrie threw aside his cigarette, jumped to his feet and raced outside.

In the midst of confused shouting, Helen caught the words, "...had a mid-air collision..." and her blood froze.

No one seemed to notice her at that moment, so she stood up and edged her way to the entrance hatch. Even when she was standing directly by the open hatch, no one seemed to pay any attention to her or, if they did, they didn't seem to care. They were more concerned with the returning aircraft and the implications of what was happening in the air.

Helen shielded her eyes and stared out along the approach path to runway two-eight. The F27 was on final approach. She felt light-headed and put a hand to her temple. What had gone wrong? Why was the aircraft returning? Why was Dan coming back into the danger area around the bomb? She turned towards the device and then looked again at her watch.

Sixteen minutes left.

*

Mayfield struggled to hold the F27 level as he throttled back on final approach. The old lady had lost much of her agility when the section of her wing was torn away; now she was acting with far too much infirmity. A section of the remaining upper wing surface was flapping loose. The aircraft would not stay airborne much longer.

In the right-hand seat, Murdoch stared silently at his watch. He had ordered Mayfield to put the aircraft down in a field. His high-pitched demands had been accompanied by threats from his pistol, but Mayfield had refused. It occurred to him that he could turn tragedy to good effect by taking Murdoch back to London City Airport. The bomb was at London City Airport, and Helen was at London City Airport. There was just a chance that he might be able to save her life.

Just a chance.

"You want to survive, don't you?" Mayfield shouted across the flight deck. "Well, this is your only chance!"

Murdoch was looking furious now, his nervous twitch working overtime. Mayfield ignored him. He knew that only minutes were left to tick away on the timer clock inside the bomb. If Murdoch was taken back to the vicinity of the bomb, there was a chance of getting him to disarm the device. It was a risk, of course. The terrorist might just blast him apart here in the cockpit, but that would mean killing himself, too. Mayfield suspected that the man had a more highly developed sense of personal survival.

"It's the only chance I have to get the aircraft safely on the ground," he stated forcefully as he pointed the F27's nose down towards the City Airport runway.

Murdoch's eyes were blazing. He waved his gun at the pilot and screamed at him. But then he backed off and withdrew into his seat.

As they came over the runway threshold, Murdoch leapt out of his seat and dashed back into the rear cabin. Mayfield continued to ignore him. He pulled off the remaining power as the main wheels touched the concrete. With the thrust levers closed, the nose wheel sank down to the ground and the aircraft began to slow as the brakes were applied. It was almost ten minutes to four. Mayfield taxied on down the runway and turned off towards where the 146 was parked.

*

Helen felt a painful burst of tension grasp at her stomach. She watched the Friendship come to a halt right alongside the 146 and she noticed a figure standing at the already open hatch. He was waving and shouting agitatedly to the terrorists nearby, but Helen was unable to catch his words. He jumped down to the ground just as the aircraft came to a halt. Helen gritted her teeth as she saw that it was Murdoch, and she cautiously moved back into the aircraft cabin and took a vacant seat — just opposite the bomb.

Murdoch burst into the aircraft cabin in a state of highly charged agitation. His eyes were wide with anxiety, his movements were sharp and swift. He dropped down beside the container and selected a combination on the timer lock. Helen caught only the briefest glimpse of the number, just a fraction of a second before Murdoch flipped open the timer box. Helen watched him reach out towards the two switches. She heard a distinct click as the terrorist leader pressed down on one of them. She couldn't see, but she assumed it had to be the black one. Then she heard the long, low sound of him breathing a sigh of relief.

It was six minutes to four.

*

Hudson had noticed for some time that he was being followed. The helicopter had long since disappeared, but he was still being tailed. There were two chase cars, a blue Rover and a silver metallic Volvo. They occasionally exchanged positions, always ensuring that one car was immediately behind the hijacked police vehicle. The second car sat farther back in the traffic, attempting to blend in with the few other vehicles on the M11 and later the A406. If the ploy was intended to fool Hudson, it failed miserably. He was an air traffic controller and trained to spot instantly the slightest unusual occurrence. It was almost second nature to him. Besides, there were simply not enough other vehicles heading towards London to make the ploy effective. Here, just as on all other roads, the heavy traffic was heading out of the city, clogging the northbound lanes for mile after mile.

Surprisingly to Hudson, Toome appeared not to have noticed the chase cars. Occasionally he glanced out of the rear window but he gave no indication of seeing either the Rover or the Volvo.

"What shall I do when we get to the airport?" Hudson asked calmly as they reached the end of the dual carriageway.

Toome darted a worried look at him. "I'll tell you that when we get there."

"Don't leave it too late."

The traffic on the roads into the dockland area became lighter, far too light for that part of London at that time of day. There were only two cars behind Hudson now, the Rover and the Volvo, and neither was making any attempt to disguise its presence.

Toome kept his eyes to the fore, still seemingly unaware of either.

"Just keep going," he snapped as they approached a road block. Groups of policemen stood at either side of a portable barrier while a further group of uniformed officers stood at the roadside nearby. Hudson wondered if they knew who was in the car and, if so, whether they would dare to intercept it. He was not too sure whether he would be better off being stopped or allowed to continue. Undecided, he kept his foot hard down on the accelerator.

With seconds to spare, the barrier was pulled aside. Hudson registered looks of concern on the faces of the policemen as he roared past them. As they raced on, he felt a sudden retrospective regret that he had not stopped the car at the barrier. It would, of course, have involved some personal risk to himself, with Toome pointing a gun in his direction, but Hudson was confident the police would have known how to handle the matter. Now he felt dismayed that he was still in danger, still continuing to... he had no idea where he was destined, beyond the general aim of reaching

London City Airport.

"What now?" he asked as he took the last turning towards the airport car park.

"Make for the terminal building."

"Then what?"

"Just do as I say!"

The police presence here was huge. Hudson noticed it instantly even though an attempt had been made to hide some of them from direct view. Toome was becoming increasingly nervous as he also detected the signs of a major police operation.

Hudson wondered if the Irishman now regretted coming to London City Airport instead of making a clean getaway into the countryside. The Irishman's gaze darted from side to side, his atten-tion distracted by the activity around them. His gun had wavered from Hudson's immediate direction and was only in-decisively aimed at the driver's seat. For a second it even moved around towards a large police gathering at the side of the road.

Hudson pulled his hand back from the gear shift and quietly released his seat belt. He wasn't sure exactly what he was going to do, but he was certain he would have to move fast. In the event, he acted more from instinct than planned intention.

The car was still travelling fast, too fast for the lie of the road. As he approached a sharp turn into the car park area, he swung the wheel violently over to the left and rammed his feet onto the brake pedal and clutch. Toome was taken completely off guard as the car rolled, lifted onto two wheels and then crashed back onto the road with a jarring thump which drove the breath from both of them.

The gun went off just as the car returned to an upright position. The bullet ripped through Hudson's flesh in the same moment that he pushed open the car door and fell from his seat.

Chapter 18

Helen's mind was confused, wrapped in a tangle of worry and puzzlement. She had seen Murdoch key in the coded number on the bomb's timing mechanism. It had been the act of an instant, just long enough for her to subconsciously register that important number, but not long enough to drag the information into her conscious thoughts.

There was something about that number, something which triggered off other memories. Every life was filled with a multitude of numbers so connections were inevitable. It happened all the time, so often that most times the connections were simply overlooked. But she couldn't afford to let this one pass. What was it? It was like an all-too-often-forgotten name which sat on the end of her tongue, refusing to be remembered. The answer was locked somewhere in her brain, if only she could get at it!

Murdoch sat back on his haunches, thinking deeply. He moved again suddenly and put his hand deliberately over the key pad, as if the action of just moments before could be wiped from the mind of anyone who saw it. Then he turned to his accomplices and said, "Watch the woman."

Helen was still fighting with her hidden memories when he strode purposefully out of the aircraft.

One of the terrorist gunmen advanced menacingly towards her and she hastily moved back into a seat some yards away from the bomb. She knew it was important that she should crystallise in her mind exactly what she had seen, but her subconscious memory was refusing to cooperate. No matter how hard she tackled her recall processes, she was only able to focus onto a generalised image of the timer, with Murdoch's hands manipulating the keys.

Helen shook her head and turned towards the window. The F27 was stopped alongside the 146 and she was able to take in the detail of the damaged starboard wing. Thank God, she thought, the collision had damaged the leading edge and left the flaps and ailerons intact. Even so, Dan was lucky to have been able to return the aircraft safely to the ground.

Fuel was spilling from a point close to the engine, a thin constant stream trickling down onto the apron. A shiver ran down her spine as she thought of her husband fighting to bring the aircraft under control after the impact. She leaned closer to the window and looked towards the cockpit, hoping that Dan was unhurt.

*

Mayfield let out a long sigh as he shut down the F27's engines. He released himself from his seat and leaned across the cockpit to look out at the starboard wing. Jagged ends of torn metal were bent and twisted like ripped paper.

Shit! What a hell of a mess to get caught in.

His hands grasped the worn framework of his seat. A lesser aeroplane would not have survived the impact, and Mayfield whispered a short prayer of thanks to the Fokker Aircraft Company. He looked out of the window again. Aviation turbine fuel — avtur — was still leaking from a ruptured fuel line close to the starboard engine, and it was spreading out into a widening pool under the wing. He double-checked that the cockpit fuel valves were secured and then turned towards the airport fire station. Nothing seemed to be moving in that direction.

A spillage of inflammable avtur was a serious matter, which should have brought out the airport fire crew — running. But the crew were probably stuck behind a barrier of Armalite rifles. In the meantime, the fuel spillage continued to spread, finger-shaped rivers meandering their way towards the 146. Mayfield consoled himself that the tank was almost dry and the flow of fuel would shortly cease.

Some bloody consolation.

He returned to his seat and pondered over his next move. Logic told him to get out of the aircraft quickly, but logic might just be inappropriate in the circumstances. He had taken a risk in bringing Murdoch back to London City Airport, one hell of a bloody risk! Anyone with an ounce of bloody sense would have got the hell out of it while he had the chance. But he had taken the risk.

What now? How would Murdoch react?

Mayfield moved back into the cabin. It was empty. His first thoughts were towards escape while he was out of the sight — and possibly the minds — of the terrorists. His head snapped up suddenly as he heard a shout from outside. Someone was getting worried about the fuel leak and he detected the words, "...hell of a lot of fuel coming out..."

He moved to one of the cabin's unusually large windows which marked out the old F27 from its successor, and looked across towards the 146. Helen would probably be on board. He could not run off and leave her while she was in the grasp of murderous terrorists. She had stood up to the ordeal well, displaying more courage than her job demanded. He felt a sense of pride in his wife's behaviour and he made a mental note to tell her so.

"Come on out, you!" A rough voice called to him from the main hatch. An irate-looking gunman prodded his Armalite into the cabin and gestured with a rough shake of his head.

"I'm coming." Mayfield moved cautiously towards the hatch. "What happens now?"

"Shut your mouth! Get over to the other aircraft. And no tricks!"

As he stepped down from the F27, Mayfield saw Murdoch striding purposefully across the apron towards the terminal building. Even that brief rear view told a clear story of anger boiling inside, anger which was bound to spill over onto someone.

Mayfield gritted his teeth.

*

"Toome is being airlifted over to you now, sir."

"Has he been talking?" FitzHugh felt his tension rise as he spoke into his police secure telephone.

It had taken him only three minutes to drive a police Range

Rover from City Airport to the hotel. He didn't even bother with a driver. Another three minutes enabled him to organise a suitable interview room. This was one confrontation that needed to be conducted away from the traumatic events at the airport. Everything could hinge on what happened here in the next few minutes. The four o'clock deadline had passed, the bomb had not been detonated, but the crisis remained. He had to get this right.

The voice on the phone sounded grim. "He's said nothing that's repeatable, sir. He's being tight-lipped about the IRA's part in the attack."

"We'll need to change his mind, won't we? Let me know if that young controller says anything useful."

"Of course, sir."

FitzHugh closed the connection and looked up, his mind still working fast when a police helicopter came into view. It landed at the far end of the hotel car park, touching down heavily on the cracked tarmac. The rotor blades were spinning noisily as Toome was hustled out. A police sergeant, who had been escorting him during the short flight, handed the Irishman into the custody of two constables. The sergeant hurried towards FitzHugh.

"Well? What's his attitude?" FitzHugh asked.

"Awkward, as you might expect," the sergeant replied. "We told him that the government was not going to capitulate to any terrorist demands, and he could bloody well die here with the bomb."

"And..."

"Reckon he's been shitting bricks ever since."

"Good."

"Are you ready to talk to him now, sir?"

"Too right I am. Take him into the hotel. There's an interview room already set up."

FitzHugh watched as Toome was hurried into building. Then he walked quickly back to the police Range Rover and recovered the Home Office file, the one labelled GD215/1 along with the name: PATRICK TOOME. He waited a few more minutes, sufficient to add to the Irishman's discomfort. With a final deep breath, he entered the hotel. Waving aside the two policemen who had brought Toome into the building, he strode purposefully into the interview room. It was the best he had been able to set up in the brief time available: an empty office into which a solid table and extra chairs had been hastily moved.

He slammed the door behind him and pulled at his beard. Everything could depend on what happened here.

Remaining on his feet, with the secret dossier clasped close to his chest, he stared at the Irishman now seated opposite. For the first time since the emergency began, he was in with a chance. Only a small one, but better than nothing. There was now no telling when the bomb might be detonated, but at least he had Toome in his grasp.

He glanced at his watch. So little time. He had to get this right.

Keep cool, he told himself, and don't get complacent. Years of training and experience had taught him that, in every problematic situation, there came a point where defeat might have to be accepted as an inevitable outcome. There was still the risk that defeat was now staring him in the face. But there was also the chance that he could use Toome to good advantage.

A young constable, a bright-faced lad with little experience of dealing with terrorists like Toome, stood near the door, the only other person in the room. FitzHugh had been offered a more senior man, but he had declined in the hope that the younger constable might present a lower visible threat, a contrast to his own image. In a situation like this, it was important to consider every possible scoring point. At the same time, he hoped the young constable was listening and learning.

FitzHugh said nothing at the start. The silence was oppressive because he intended it so. It was important that he should add to Toome's unease.

Eventually, Toome spoke, his face displaying a twisted mass of emotions. "Who are you? I've seen you somewhere."

"I am Commander FitzHugh."

A sudden flash of recognition lit up Toome's face. "You! Seen your picture in the papers, so I have. You're Irish."

"That's right. As Irish as you, Toome."

"A traitor, so you are. Workin' for the British. Nothin' but a foul traitor."

"That depends upon your point of view."

Toome turned his head away and spat on the floor. "There are IRA people who kill traitors like you."

FitzHugh drew a deep breath. This was getting nowhere. It was time to change the subject. "The problem we both now face," he said brusquely, staring into Toome's face, "is that we've been fooled by Murdoch and the SVR. You and me together. All of us."

"Fooled?"

"Like I said, all of us. You, me… and everyone else. Fooled by a gang of madmen."

Toome shrugged. "That's just bullshit."

For the first time, FitzHugh allowed a measure of anger to show in his voice. "For chrissake, man! We, at least, realise it. Why can't you?"

Toome shifted uneasily in his seat. His head had been bandaged, but a trickle of blood was beginning to emerge from beneath the bandage and creep down his forehead. He briefly shook his head, as if he had taken on a resigned attitude, knowing that his active part in the operation had been terminated.

"We know everything now," FitzHugh continued. "In fact, we know more than you. You might as well accept it."

He waited for the message to sink in.

"It was an abysmal plan and doomed to be an abysmal failure. When it failed, you pinned your hopes on Murdoch coming for you in the F27. That was one bloody failure also, wasn't it, Toome?"

Toome glared at him through slitted eyes. FitzHugh merely shook his head.

"When the Heathrow control tower was overrun, you came here hot-foot, hoping to get away from London on board the Queen's Flight aircraft, along with the man called McQuarrie. That's what you hoped for, isn't it!"

Toome's face held a confused mixture of expressions. Without doubt, he was trying to remain composed, and yet, at the same time, he seemed unable to resist the taunting words. FitzHugh saw the effect and felt a mild sense of achievement that a little crack was appearing in Toome's armour. However, it wasn't yet wide enough, not by a long chalk.

"You thought you had everything sewn up, didn't you? You thought the British government would simply give in and release all IRA prisoners. You thought you and your mates on the ground would be able to use the Queen's Flight aircraft to get themselves out of trouble. Christ, you're a bloody fool! You IRA people are so bloody naive, it's just too bloody laughable. Can't you see what those Russian hawks planned all along?" He took a deep breath. "That bomb will explode whatever happens!"

He hesitated before adding in a less demonstrative tone, "We're supposed to believe that we can prevent the detonation by giving in to your demands for prisoner releases, but we can't stop it like that."

Toome was looking at him keenly now, as if his mind was beginning to register the fact that there was more to the whole episode than he had first perceived. FitzHugh breathed deeply once again, and then went on, "Like I said, we've all been taken for fools. You and us."

The Irishman fidgeted with his sleeves and lowered his head. He seemed to be wrestling with his own thoughts, wanting to disbelieve FitzHugh, and yet finding conviction in the revelation.

"I suppose you expect me to believe all this rubbish," he said, a dry hoarseness encroaching into his rough Irish tones. He looked up cautiously beneath heavy eyebrows. "After all, it's your job to put one over on me, isn't it? But just for the record, what did they do to fool you?"

"Us? They really pulled the wool over our eyes. At first, anyway." FitzHugh walked to the window. The young police constable followed him with a staring gaze, digesting the detail with the same intensity as Toome.

FitzHugh swung round suddenly. "Oh yes, they really pulled one over on us. You see, it was all a very clever trick. It's been done many times before, but never as dramatically as this." He stared fiercely at the Irishman, noting the attention he had gained before he continued. "You know why the Russians pulled this stunt? It's because Yeltsin is succeeding in his efforts to turn the country into a Western-style capitalist state. The hawks inside the SVR don't like that. It weakens them. They think they can claw back their power by winning a nuclear war, but they won't be seen to be the ones to start it. That's why there's not a single Russian here on British soil. Just one mad Englishman and a bunch of naive Irish terrorists."

"So?" The single word was grunted out.

"So they want the bomb to explode and they want NATO to go onto a war footing as a result. Missiles and bombers will be armed and put on instant readiness, thousands of troops will be deployed, and huge armies will be ranged along fragile frontiers. And then, somewhere, a single opening shot will be fired. That's all it will need. After that the whole world will risk being plunged into a new nightmare. When that happens, the SVR hawks will push Yeltsin aside and bring the Russian Federation firmly back into their grasp." He pulled anxiously at his beard. "Even if it's only an extreme threat of war, even if the missiles are not actually launched, the hawks will still get their way and Yeltsin will be replaced."

"Huh. You make them sound like psychopaths," Toome sneered.

"Psychopaths?" FitzHugh shook his head. "Maybe they are. Who but a psychopath could possibly want to risk a full-scale nuclear war? And that's very likely to happen when the entire City of London is obliterated. That's the crux of the whole game: to kill every damned one of us."

"They won't do that!"

"Oh yes they will! But first they had to convince you lot that this was simply a way of freeing IRA men from gaol. That was the only way you would play ball with them, wasn't it? The only way to get you to bring Murdoch and the bomb here." FitzHugh shook his head sadly and lowered his voice. "The truth is, they've no intention of letting any of us off the hook. The bomb will go off later, whatever we do."

"You're making this up." Toome's voice was muted now, a clue to FitzHugh that he was at last getting through.

"No. They knew this was the only way you could be drawn in as their pawns. They fooled you."

Toome glanced at his watch. "So what happened? The bomb didn't go off."

"Murdoch was getting the hell out of here, but his aircraft was involved in a mid-air collision. The pilot managed to bring the aircraft back here to London City just a few minutes before four. It must have put the wind up Murdoch because he's stopped the countdown."

Toome's voice now held a quavering tone. "And where's Murdoch now?"

"He's somewhere out there on the airfield. But he won't stay for long. My guess is that he's now making further plans to get away. One thing's certain: he sure as hell won't hang around that bomb any longer than he has to."

"God, what a mess."

FitzHugh noted with satisfaction that Toome was now showing signs of accepting the reality that the nuclear bomb would be detonated regardless. Maybe there was more mileage to be gained after all.

He stroked his beard more easily and turned away from the terrorist. "So, at the end of the day, we're both dead men," he said. He gazed out of the window at the ugly mixture of old East-End houses which were left in violent visual conflict with the newer buildings. Soon it would all be gone, replaced by such a wasteland as had not been seen since Nagasaki. And who would benefit?

"Alright." Toome looked up suddenly. "Suppose... just suppose I believe you. What do you want me to do about it?"

FitzHugh turned and faced him. "I want you to help us."

"Help you?" Despite the obvious sneer in Toome's voice, there was a small hint of doubt underlying the surface tone.

"Think about it," FitzHugh continued. "You and McQuarrie are dead… and for what? You'll get nothing out of this whatsoever. Except the rest of the world's absolute condemnation for helping Murdoch bring the bomb over here. Your people will lose almost every bit of support you now enjoy. I doubt if any of your bigoted friends in Ireland will condone this one."

FitzHugh watched the man's face intently; he had to gauge his mood correctly now. The man's eyes showed fear, the mouth dropped at the edges. Did this new concept of what he had actually done cause him severe doubts? FitzHugh moved closer to him and pressed home his attack.

"You won't be around to see it, Toome, but it's going to be the end of Sinn Fein and the IRA. It's also going to mean the death of so many Irishmen living in London that scarcely a family in Ireland will not be affected. For God's sake, man! Can't you see that you've got to help us!"

"Help you!" Toome stood up suddenly and the young constable steeped forward to restrain him.

FitzHugh said calmly, "It's all right. Let him be." He raised a calming hand and the constable stepped back.

Toome looked about him, confused. "They killed him, they killed my brother. Years ago, the bloody Loyalists killed him. And they killed my girl. Why the hell should I help you?"

"Because…" FitzHugh put a hand to Toome's sleeve, "…because it's the only way to help your own fellow countrymen. *My* fellow countrymen, God damn you! The only way to stop the madness."

He lowered his head until his eyes were just inches from Toome's. Time to pile on yet more pressure. He gritted his teeth and spoke in a harsh whisper. "It is all madness, you stupid bastard. And one other thing, it wasn't the Loyalists who killed your girl. It was Sinn Fein. Someone working directly for Sinn Fein shot her. Did you know that, Toome? I bet you didn't know that!"

*

No one spoke as the lift rose to the third floor. Janice Wilkins stood rigidly between two of the men, her heart thumping loudly.

The third man, a West Indian, stood behind her with his knife pressed against her back. He was the biggest of the three, a giant with a bushy beard and tiny, piercing eyes. Despite their own beefy statures, the other two seemed to ride on the strength of the black man's enormous muscles.

When the lift stopped, Janice was pushed forward by the knife in her back. She looked from side to side, taking in the quiet, lifeless corridor. Everyone had gone. She was left to her fate. God give her strength.

She walked steadily towards her flat, her mind searching for some way of evading the three men. In all her training there had to be something that would help her. Something! After all, she was a stewardess trained to cope with emergencies. She wasn't the poor little dumb kid some people took her for. Or was she?

"Where's yer key, darlin'?" The man to her left held out his hand, a thick bucket of a hand.

She reached into her pocket and drew out a bunch of keys.

"That's right, darlin'." The man grabbed them from her fingers. "Do as we say an' you won't get 'urt."

Her mind was racing, searching for some way out. Maybe they would let her go once they had her valuables? No, of course they wouldn't. More likely they would kill her. Get rid of the evidence.

The West Indian unlocked the door and bundled her into the flat.

"Now, where do you keep yer money?" The man who spoke had short, spikey hair and pale blue eyes. His spotty face was almost cherub-like, round and youthful.

"I don't keep money here," she squeaked. She coughed to clear her throat and went on, "I keep it in the bank."

"Don't give us that crap." The man put his hand to her face and squeezed her cheeks between his powerful fingers. "Where is it?"

"I don't..." But even as she spoke, she saw his lip curl into a tighter knot and she felt his hand run down her cheek, her neck and grasp her breast.

"Tell me!"

"And the jewellery," chimed in the black man. "Tell us where the jewellery is."

"The bedroom," she croaked. "The jewellery is in the bedroom."

"You better be tellin' the truth!"

"It's in the bedroom."

"All rightee." The West Indian's face lit up, his gaze roved about the room as he spoke. He suddenly lit on a carriage clock sitting atop the mantelpiece. "Hey! Look at that, man! It's after four o'clock! See! I told you them guys was bluffin'. There ain't no bomb out there."

"Sure, there ain't no bomb. We know that. We figured it out all along, didn't we?" One of the other men spoke with barely concealed glee. "But they'll all come runnin' back when they find out. So let's get on with it."

The two white men grabbed at objects and ornaments which looked valuable. The men looked so huge and Janice felt so defenceless, so small... but their attention was directed away from her.

She turned suddenly, momentarily forgetting the man behind her. She crashed against his tall, bulky body and both cried out in unison. His voice was deep, angry. Hers was high-pitched, horrified. She pulled away again, slowly bringing her hands round towards her stomach.

"Ahhh! What—" Her words faded away as she saw a bright red stream bubbling over her clothes. The knife was deeply embedded in her lower abdomen, and blood, her own blood, gushed out onto the floor in an unstoppable stream.

*

FitzHugh stared across the table at Toome and wondered just what motivated the other man towards terrorism. Was he an idealist? Probably not. He didn't appear to have the dedication to a cause which marked out so many of his comrades.

He jolted back into reality when he suddenly found himself developing a degree of sympathy for the man in front of him. He couldn't allow that. It was time to tighten the screws even more.

Time to find out just what Toome was made of. He glanced down at the dossier, GD215/1, still cradled in one arm.

"Surprised, Toome? You never knew, did you? Never knew that Sinn Fein could kill your girl."

"Bullshit. You're bluffing."

"You're wrong, Toome." FitzHugh spoke calmly now, calmly but firmly enough to put emphasis into his words. "We've no need to bluff. You were under surveillance by one of our people. And you never knew that you were being watched by a British Intelligence agent."

"Bullshit, I said."

"Want to know what the agent's name was?"

"What do you mean? Why would I want to know?"

FitzHugh leaned forward, allowing himself a brief moment of satisfaction. "Rosemary Stevenson. That was her name, and she was in Ireland to keep a close eye on you and your Russian contacts."

"Never heard of her. Pull the other one."

"Oh, you knew her all right. You knew her as..." He paused for effect. "...Roisin O'Steafin."

"Roisin?" The word came out as a whisper.

"Yes, Roisin O'Steafin. Rosemary Stevenson. Know the name now? Sinn Fein found out about her and they killed her."

"They wouldn't! Besides, Sinn Fein's a political organisation."

"Don't give me that crap! We know exactly how she died, and that you were in her bed at the time. Want to know who Sinn Fein got to do their dirty work? Do you? Do you want to know?"

Toome stared down at the table, his mouth firmly shut.

"It was your friend Kearney, that's who!"

"Mickey? No! It's not true!" Suddenly Toome leaned forward, dragging himself to his feet. Then he sank back into the seat.

"It's true all right. She was one of our people and she sent back one hell of a lot of dope on you and your nasty little band. It's all in there!" FitzHugh threw the secret file onto the table. No point in keeping the dossier secret any longer.

"She was killed by the Prods," Toome snapped. He glanced up at FitzHugh, as if he suspected a trap. Then he looked down and opened the file slowly.

"Try page 16," FitzHugh said. "Stevenson was killed on the orders of Sinn Fein. Your people. And they never told you. Never told you that you were under suspicion because of your association with her."

Toome went silent as he read the file. When he came to the salient part of the document, he paused and ran his finger across the text.

The following transcript is taken from a telephone conversation between Michael Kearney and Desmond McGrew. The call was made thirty-two minutes after the assassination of Agent Stevenson. It was intercepted at GCHQ.

KEARNEY: "'Tis done, Desi. As neat a job as you'll ever see."
McGREW: "Good on yous. Did Patrick see it?"
KEARNEY: "Sure, an' he'd have seen the leftovers. Didn't do the pattern on the carpet much good. Poor Patrick. Wasn't the silly bastard after shaggin' the bitch just a few minutes earlier!"
McGREW: "But he didn't see yous?"
KEARNEY: "What d'you take me for? An amateur?"
McGREW: "Yous'd better stay away from the area for a while. We'll deal with Patrick when the time comes."
KEARNEY: "You'll not! The poor little shite doesn't have a clue about Stevenson even now. Thinks she's the real thing, he does. You'll not touch him!"
McGREW: "Someone may have to, Mickey. One day."
KEARNEY: "If anyone has to do that, it'll be me! Not you, Desi! You hear me?"

Toome looked up with a dull expression across his face. It was as if, suddenly, his whole life had become a waste. FitzHugh turned towards the young constable and nodded to indicate he wanted to be alone with the terrorist. The young man left quietly.

"You don't have a snowball's chance in hell, Toome. They plan to kill you one day. And you've now given them good reason. You might as well know it."

"Kill me?"

"Yes." FitzHugh stared into the dull eyes and bared his teeth. "You're dead, you bastard! Even if this whole attack stops right now, you're dead! Can't you see it? You made an absolute balls-up of things at Heathrow. You weren't even around when the SAS took the place. When your men were overrun, you were in the lift." He breathed deeply. "You fouled up and the IRA will blame you for everything. Look at that stupid car ride out of Heathrow. Trying to save your own skin, weren't you?"

Time to turn the screws even tighter.

"Think of what the Republican newspapers will say. Brave IRA leader deserts his fighters." He stood up suddenly and turned away, as if the whole matter was at an end. It was all a calculated gamble that Toome would react in the right manner.

"You bastard!" Toome was on his feet again. "You're setting me up, aren't you!"

FitzHugh continued to face away from the Irishman. He had to hide his own sudden fear that he had gone too far and ruined the only chance still open to him.

"Setting you up?" He turned slowly. "Hasn't the truth sunk into that thick skull of yours yet? You were set up by Murdoch and the SVR when you began this bloody escapade." He stepped towards Toome and noted a look of doubt in the man's face. "You've been used as a fool, Toome. You and all those men of yours. And Mc-Quarrie. God, can't you see that? I've no reason to set you up, in fact, I don't even want to see you again. I thought you might be able to help us to salvage something from this mess, but now I can see that you're no bloody use to us. No bloody use at all!"

He swung on his heels and reached for the door.

"Wait a minute!"

FitzHugh's hand hung over the door handle as Toome spoke.

He felt his heart thumping as he listened for the other man's reaction.

"That bomb. It really is going to be detonated? I mean, it really is going to go off regardless?"

"That's what I told you."

"You think Murdoch will really blow us up even if your government gives in?"

"That's his intention." FitzHugh faced Toome again and saw with relief that the man was scared, unquestionably scared out of his wits. "He'll have reset the timer by now and he'll be planning to get the hell out."

"You said..." Toome's voice was thick now, choked with the enormity of the crime he had committed. "You said Sinn Fein killed her... the woman."

"Stevenson? O'Steafin? Yes, there's no question about that. Sinn Fein gave Kearney orders to kill her on their behalf. You saw the transcript."

"And you said... that I could help you."

FitzHugh felt a small glow of hope begin to emerge.

*

Janice Wilkins was alone, lying on the floor. Consciousness drifted to and fro to catch her in its arms and then drop her back into the dark pit of an ever-widening void. There was something warm and sticky about her hands and her body. Every time she moved, there was more of it.

If only Dan was here. He would know what to do. He loved her. He was going to leave his wife... give up everything for her. She only had to ask him and he would...

She opened her eyes but the room looked dark and nothing was clearly focussed. It was easier if she didn't look. Easier to just drift... and wait. For Dan. He would come... soon... he had to... had to.

A vehicle started up outside and then drove away.

She was alone.

Chapter 19

The ambulance was being driven at breakneck speed away from central London. There were two people in the rear of the vehicle with Simon Hudson. One was a woman wearing the uniform of the ambulance service and the other a policeman.

"Where are we going?" he asked. He felt considerable pain through his upper body, but he tried to concentrate on what was happening around him.

"Just lie quietly," the woman said. "You're going to be alright."

Going to be alright. That's what they always said, Hudson thought. It didn't matter how badly hurt you were, they just told you that you were going to be alright. It was the biggest con trick in the book.

"I want to know what's happening," he insisted. "Where are we going?"

The woman looked at the police officer and then answered, "We'll have you in hospital shortly. You made a bit of a mess of yourself when you jumped from that car."

"But where? Why are you taking so long to get there? You're not taking me to the nearest hospital, are you?"

"Calm down," the woman said insistently. "You're out of it now. You're going to be safe. We're taking all the survivors to a military hospital outside of the London area. You're going to live."

"I don't understand," Hudson mumbled. "Survivors? What do you mean?" His thoughts returned to Jennifer White. Would she be taken to the same hospital? Someone must have found her by now.

"They'll want to talk to you afterwards," the woman continued, "to find out all you know. That's why it's important to take you to somewhere safe."

Safe. He felt another surge of pain. What was safe? For a while he lapsed into silence.

Would all of this be reported on the radio and television? He thought it most likely and he was certain that Michelle must have seen those news reports by now. He could picture her sitting in her mother's lounge, sprawled across the settee while her mother sat nearby, knitting. The television would be switched on in the background in order to give Michelle the comfort of voices in the room. Half-finished cups of coffee would litter the furniture.

Hudson groaned and twisted as a stab of pain ran down his left side. He saw the woman lean across to reassure him and he closed his eyes.

Jennifer.

He would have to make sure that Jennifer was safe. Poor kid. She had looked so vulnerable when he had left her, frightened and shivering and half-naked. She had been through one hell of an ordeal. It would have driven many a youngster out of her mind.

He had long felt a soft spot for Jennifer, although only in a platonic sort of way. What a pity it had been no more than that. Even in the midst of the pain which was racking his body he could remember the sensual outline of her young body. He breathed deeply and fervently hoped that she would be well looked after.

"There's a girl..." he began. But a soft hand was placed on his shoulder and he began to feel drowsy. He wondered if it was the effect of something they had given him.

*

Jennifer White heard people moving around outside; she even heard them try to open the two locked doors into the office. The sharp rattle of the doorknobs brought back memories of her earlier terror and she broke into another cold shiver. She dared not venture to the door in case her movements were heard by any-one in the outer office, whoever might be out there. She thought of using the telephone, but decided that the sound of her voice might be picked up through the office walls, so she sat silently staring into the blankness around her, and she prayed that no one would telephone her and force her to reveal her whereabouts.

Time seemed to stand still after a while. There was little more she could suffer that she had not already suffered, little more anyone could do to her that could increase the hurt she already felt. She wrapped her arms tighter about herself and waited.

She shook like a small fragile leaf when someone again rattled the handle of the outer door. Outside, several voices seemed to be in conversation, debating who or what was inside the office.

"You in there, love?" It was a deep, gruff voice and Jennifer mentally cowered at the thought of who might own it.

"Jennifer? Are you in there?"

They knew her name!

She looked wildly around the office. There was nowhere to hide if they broke in. Then she heard the sound of keys rattling. They had keys!

Shakily, she rose to her feet, her hands fumbling against the wall as she tried to steady herself. Her horrifying fear was turning into an enfolding numbness which she was no longer able to tolerate. She told herself that it had to stop now, one way or another. She raised her head and felt a morbid acceptance begin to creep over her. This had to be the end of everything; she could take no more. She stepped to the window and struggled with the catch. Behind her, she heard the sound of a key twisting in the lock, but she ignored it and pushed hard against the glass until the window opened. They would not get her now. Not now!

She hardly noticed the coldness of the air as she climbed out onto the window ledge. Beyond her was only open space. And safety.

*

Vince Trewin leaped out of the lift cage behind a young, fresh-faced police constable.

"She's in a room along here!" the constable called over his shoulder. "We'd never have known she was there if we hadn't seen her about to jump."

Trewin felt a shiver run up his spine and put an extra spurt into his stride.

"We called to her, you see, but there was no answer so we thought she must have got out a long time ago. Well, what else were we to think?"

Trewin said nothing. Only minutes before he had discovered that no one had bothered to check that Jennifer had been rescued from the locked room. Captain Stenning had been too preoccupied with the capture of the IRA brigade and had left the job of checking the offices to one of his NCOs. The officer in question made a perfunctory check, but he made no attempt to force open any locked doors. The detailed check, he had decided, could wait.

"She was standing on the ledge, just hanging from the window frame when someone saw her," the constable continued. "Half-naked and hanging from the window! I ask you!"

Trewin pushed past the young man as he came in sight of the office door where a small group of policemen waited, one kneeling close to the door and talking.

"It's all over now, Jennifer. The terrorists have been taken away and it's perfectly safe for you to come out." The man held up his hand to indicate silence as he listened for a response from within. After some seconds he turned to Trewin and said, "She's not answering. How well do you know her?"

"Well enough, on a working level."

"Try calling to her, will you. Maybe she'll recognise your voice."

Trewin moved closer to the door, coughed and said, "Jennifer. It's Vince Trewin. I've come to help you."

There was no response and he scanned across the row of anxious faces beside him.

"Try again."

"Jennifer. It's Vince. Vince Trewin. Can you hear me, love?"

*

Dan Mayfield put his hand on top of Helen's and felt the warmth of her skin. They were seated inside the 146, only two rows behind the bomb. The atmosphere was tense.

They had been left under guard for some time before Murdoch reappeared, storming angrily into the aircraft. At first he ignored them as he stood near the main hatch, talking in a low voice to McQuarrie, apparently trying to justify delaying the bomb's detonation. From where they sat, Mayfield could see that Murdoch was agitated, his nervous twitch working overtime. It led him to the conclusion that Murdoch's composure was cracked sufficiently to be prised apart completely if the right situation arose.

"He's got a big problem now," Dan whispered. "Does he try again to get the British government to give in? Or does he call the whole thing off?"

"He'll never call it off," Helen replied. "There's too much at stake."

"But he's lost the first round. He had to back down and reset the timer. In a sense we've lost as well because only God and Murdoch now know when it will go off."

Helen turned towards him and put her free hand on top of his. "Let's not get too uptight about it. At least we can thank God we're both alive for a little while longer," she whispered. "I know we're still in a hell of a lot of danger, but let's just play it as it comes."

Dan tried to smile in return. Privately, he still felt ashamed of his secrets, those occasions when he had been less than a perfect husband. He would have to do something about Janice Wilkins, and it wasn't going to be easy.

Helen put her cheek down on his shoulder and shuffled herself into a cosy ball beside him. He placed his arm tightly round her. It reminded him of their early days together, the days when he would no more have thought of infidelity than divorce. The days when he had been proud to be married to such an attractive woman.

"Penny for your thoughts," Helen interrupted his reflections.

"Nothing important," he lied. And he made a promise to try to put things right if they survived the ordeal ahead of them.

"I always know when you're thinking hard," she added. "You go all... sort of tense. It means you're worried about something and you can't get it out of your mind."

"I was thinking about you," he said.

She sat back in her seat and cocked her head to one side inquisitively. "Me?"

He felt uncomfortable and tried to find a way of changing the subject. "Murdoch is looking at us," he said.

Her voice changed, became hard as ice. "To hell with Murdoch. We may not have much more time together, so let's talk about us."

"Helen—"

"It's that Wilkins woman! You're really thinking of her, aren't you?" She drew away from him and folded her arms defiantly. In one brief moment all that quiet, wonderful empathy between them was shattered.

He felt the mental impact of a thunderclap suddenly roaring inside his head. His thoughts became confused, turned upside down by a violent and unexpected mind-storm.

"You knew?" he gasped.

"Of course I knew. Just what sort of wife would I be if I couldn't see what was going on?"

"I don't know what to say. I'm sorry..." The confusion inside his head continued to prevent his thoughts from sorting themselves into any semblance of order. "How did you find out?"

"Does it matter?" Her tone was abrasive, hurt. "If you really want to know, I overheard some stupid women talking at one of those company parties. Last Christmas, it was. They were laughing at you behind your back... called you a silly old fool."

"I would have told you."

"Would you?" She almost laughed, though her face was hardened into anger. "Would you really have told me, Dan?"

"Yes."

"Like hell you would! Unless she'd thrown you over for someone else and you wanted a shoulder to cry on. You really are the limit, Dan Mayfield! And a woman like that! A good screw, was she?"

"Don't talk like that, Helen. It makes you sound coarse."

"Coarse? Like her? Like Janice Wilkins? Is that how she talked when you were in bed together?"

"No!" He snapped at her with bared teeth before he realised what he was doing. Then he forced himself to stop and take a deep breath. "No, not at all."

"I wonder... well, if we get out of this alive, you'll have to do something about her. And quickly!"

"Yes. I intend to."

A noise in the background distracted Mayfield's attention and he glanced up to see Murdoch, looking thunderous as he strode down the aircraft aisle towards them. With his mind still recovering from Helen's outburst, he braced himself for the next assault, retaliation from Murdoch. Retaliation which he had been expecting since the F27 had landed. He felt Helen's hand suddenly grab his own. Somewhat surprised, he realised she was anticipating the same attack.

Their anger evaporated in an instant.

"Get outside, both of you!" Murdoch ordered. His voice had the cracked edge of a man who was close to desperation.

Mayfield shrugged his shoulders and replied, "What have you in mind now?"

"I have it in mind to shoot you both." Murdoch stood with his hands on his hips, compressing his lips tightly while the message sank in. The nervous twitch erupted again. "But maybe there is a better way of dealing with you. Follow me!"

He turned suddenly, stamping back down the aircraft aisle, and led them out onto the apron where several gunmen were earnestly studying the fuel leak. It had stopped pouring out of the ruptured fuel line, a sure sign the tank was empty. A large pool of avtur now stained the tarmac. Some of it had run underneath the front fuselage of the 146.

"I told you not to bring the aircraft back here," Murdoch hissed, his gaze swinging from side to side to check that he was out of the hearing of the gunmen.

"And I told you it was the only chance we had." Mayfield stood his ground, steadying his gaze on Murdoch.

"If you disobey me again, I'll have you shot!" Murdoch stood rigidly now, his arms clamped at his sides. "You may think you know more about aeroplanes than I do, but I know you didn't have to bring the aircraft back here."

"I bloody well did!" Mayfield bounced back. "It was the best thing to do. I couldn't put down in a field and I didn't have the necessary charts to get into any other airfield. And you wouldn't let me call ATC."

"Don't bullshit me!" Murdoch bellowed.

"All right, all right." Mayfield raised his hands to calm the situation. "Just what are you going to do now?"

Murdoch pulled a small pistol from his jacket pocket and whipped it up into Helen's face. "I ought to make you pay!"

"Easy." Mayfield kept his hands raised in a soothing gesture as he noted the look of horror in Helen's face. "You won't gain anything by harming her. For one thing, you won't get my services as a pilot if you shoot my wife."

Murdoch stood stock-still, silently threatening Helen, as he considered his next move.

"Tell me what you aim to do," Mayfield said. "You must have a plan of action."

Murdoch looked at him with a deep, penetrating stare, then he lowered the gun and Dan breathed easier. Murdoch turned towards the aircraft parking bays and pointed towards a Dash Seven which was sitting farther along the line.

"Have you ever flown one of those?"

Mayfield shook his head. "No. Never."

"But you could fly it if you had to?"

"I suppose so. I flew the F27 when I had to."

"Right! That's my plan! You will fly me out of here in that aircraft over there. The bomb is reset to go off at five o'clock and I want to be airborne by half past four. So you'd better start studying the flight manual."

Mayfield spread his hands once more. He was sure he could fly the Dash Seven. It wouldn't be as simple as the F27 but he could do it, given the time he needed to study the manual.

"You're the boss..." His reassuring response was suddenly interrupted by what he saw behind Murdoch. He felt his mouth harden into an expression of shock. Some yards away, amidst the pool of spilled fuel, one of the gunmen guarding the aircraft was smoking.

The errant Irish terrorist looked disinterested in all that was happening about him. He stood near the rear end of the F27 fuselage, his Armalite hanging loosely from his arms while he took long deep draws on his cigarette. A lengthy river of fuel was drawn out between him and a further group which stood some yards away beside the 146.

"I'll take a look at the Dash Seven," Mayfield said evenly, his attention only partially concentrated on Murdoch. As he spoke, he searched his mind for the right move to make next. If that fuel went up... if there was an explosion... with the bomb once again armed... they would not stand a chance!

"Don't get any funny ideas about escaping," Murdoch warned, trying to read Mayfield's mind. "I still have a gun trained on your wife."

Mayfield saw the pistol aimed once again towards Helen's head and he nodded. There was a careful balance to be drawn between the risk to Helen and the overall risk to millions of people who would lose their lives in a nuclear explosion. He pointed to the smoking gunman and said, "You'd better warn your friend over there about the dangers of cigarettes."

Murdoch looked round, cautiously at first, as if he suspected some trickery. His eyebrows shot upwards as he caught sight of the lighted cigarette hanging from the man's lip.

"Put that thing out!" he shouted angrily and waved his arms. But the man only looked puzzled by Murdoch's behaviour and started to walk towards the group, directly into the path of the spilt fuel. Mayfield reacted decisively. A fire in the vicinity of an armed nuclear bomb was too horrific to even contemplate. He pushed past Murdoch and beckoned to the gunman, calling out loudly. "Move away from there, for God's sake!"

The gunman looked bemused. He paused when he heard the shout from Mayfield and removed the cigarette from his mouth, as if he was totally ignorant of the danger he was creating.

"Move away, you fool!" Mayfield shouted. By now the gunman was standing with his boots in a shallow pool of avtur which formed a shimmering layer on the apron, a thin sea of highly inflammable liquid. The smoking gunman still seemed not to notice.

"Your cigarette! Mind your cigarette!" Mayfield yelled while Murdoch continued to gesticulate wildly.

The cigarette was smoked away to a small butt, and a length of hot ash hung from the end. As the gunman studied the shouting figures in front of him, a light of understanding suddenly broke into his consciousness and he raised the hand that held the offending object. He was grinning a silly, guilty grin. In that same moment, the hot ash detached itself from the body of the cigarette and fell into the pool of fuel. The sudden flash of flame engulfed him before he could cry out, reaching into the sky with the intensity of a giant funeral pyre.

Chapter 20

Mayfield caught a quick glimpse of Helen in the midst of the confusion. She was running away towards the terminal building, escaping from the terrorists' clutches.

Thank God she was free from Murdoch!

He swung round on his heels and raced back towards the BAe146. The F27 was completely engulfed in flames, a dramatic funeral pyre for the elderly lady. A terrible end for such a veteran flyer.

Murdoch was ahead of him and climbed up into the 146 cabin, pushing aside the gunman who stood wavering uncertainly at the main hatch.

"The bomb! Is it armed?" Mayfield shouted.

Murdoch turned suddenly and looked at him with wide and staring eyes. "Of course it's bloody-well armed. We've got to get it out of here. Quickly!"

"Can you disarm it?"

"I can disarm the timer. But the heat could set off the detonating charge. We must get it out!"

Mayfield grabbed a handle at the side of the container and lifted. It was heavy.

"For chrissake!" he roared. "Don't you have any safety devices on this thing?"

"Shut up!" Murdoch's eyes blazed. He was clearly frightened. He gestured to the gunman at the hatch to come and help, but the man refused. Equally shit-scared, he shook his head wildly, turned away and ran. The other occupants of the aircraft had also left.

"Grab hold of it, God damn you!" Mayfield shouted. "We can lift it out if you grab hold!"

Murdoch looked wildly around the deserted cabin before he bent down to grasp the container. The heat from the burning fuel was now wafting through the open hatch, creating a thick muggy smell inside the aircraft.

"Hold it steady!" Mayfield shouted as the two men edged their way towards the hatch. The flames had spread quickly. They licked fiercely around the 146 fuselage.

"Hurry, man," Mayfield shouted at Murdoch.

Dear God, what a mess! He jerked the container towards himself and Murdoch stumbled, trying to keep his footing.

The old man was sweating profusely. His eyes were widely dilated. The twitch gave him the look of a madman. Clearly, it had never been his intention to put his own life at risk.

"Come and help us!" Mayfield stopped at the top of the aircraft steps and shouted at the gunmen. They stood beyond the range of the burning fuel, and no one stepped forward to help. The enormity of the situation seemed beyond them.

"Someone must help us!" Murdoch croaked, acrid smoke beginning to choke him.

"Shut up and lift the thing!" Mayfield ordered. "Those bastards aren't going to help us now."

Murdoch trembled as he heaved on the bomb.

Grim-faced, the two men slid and moved the device out of the hatch and down the steps. Outside, burning fuel crackled and spat as it spread around the 146 like dancing waves. The heat felt painfully intense as it etched into Mayfield's raw skin through the metal handle. Pray God the heat didn't detonate the explosive inside. It alone would be enough to kill them. But if the bomb went up...

Mayfield bit his lip at the thought. Eight million people could be killed in an instant, incinerated in the biggest explosive attack this side of Nagasaki.

"Head towards the terminal building," Murdoch shouted in a hesitant voice, a voice thrown off key by his physical exertions. The old man took the lead as they staggered across the apron, breaking into a lopsided trot as they carried the container away from the burning aircraft.

They were halfway across the apron when the F27's port fuel

tank exploded with a sudden unexpected roar. The blast ripped into both men and threw them forward onto the ground. Mayfield felt his arms wrench in their sockets, felt his legs crumble beneath him. But he kept his grip on the container, instinct keeping his fist tightly gripped round the handhold.

But Murdoch tripped and fell, his arms flailing. His end of the bomb crashed to the ground.

*

Time: 1630
Thirty minutes to detonation

The IRA gunmen stood around in disarray, obviously unsure of their next move. This was not what McQuarrie expected of them. He held back in the lee of the terminal building and rubbed a nervous hand across his chin. He could have gone out onto the apron to help Murdoch, but what the hell! Why should he help them now? He had come here in the certain knowledge he might have to sacrifice his own life. What did it matter to him that Murdoch would die when the bomb went up? The British government had not given in — probably would not give in. So let the thing blow!

The F27 was totally engulfed in flames and thick, choking smoke. It was no longer possible to detect the damage caused by the mid-air collision, no longer possible even to determine the aircraft's colour or markings. An explosion in the starboard engine had blown the wing apart, but even that damage was no longer apparent to the observers.

The firemen were at a state of readiness to deal with the blaze, their appliances fully manned, but McQuarrie's men held them back. He had mounted an armed guard at the fire station early in the attack.

As the fire spread, the BAe146 began to burn. Rivers of flaming fuel ran under the fuselage and tortured the aircraft's metal skin. Then the flames reached inside the open hatch and grasped the inflammable seats and fittings within the cabin. After that, it was only a matter of minutes before the aircraft was fiercely ablaze.

Once the fire had caught hold of the 146, blazing fuel began to pour out of its tanks and spread across the apron.

McQuarrie spat on the ground and prepared himself for death.

*

Time: 1633
Twenty-seven minutes to detonation

FitzHugh saw the tall pillar of black smoke as soon as he left the hotel and a cold chill grabbed him. He bundled Toome into a police car and snapped at the driver, "Put your foot down!"

By the time they pulled up in the London City Airport car park, they could see the leaping flames that fed the smoke. FitzHugh shouted an instruction to his driver to guard Toome, then he raced across the tarmac towards a group of watching policemen.

"How did this happen?" he demanded.

"We don't know, sir." One of the police officers turned towards him with a grim expression. "We sent someone over there to take a look. He says he thinks the bomb is out on the apron, close to the fire."

"They haven't sent in the military?"

"Not yet. Waiting for orders."

"Christ, I hope to God they keep them out of it! We don't want the military starting a shooting match around that bomb."

FitzHugh hesitated for a few more seconds and then ran towards the terminal building. There was a possibility that someone might take a potshot at him, but that was a minor risk compared with the appalling prospect of the nuclear bomb being detonated.

A melee of gunmen wandered around inside the terminal, looking confused and frightened. FitzHugh guessed that most of them would have been on the F27 and were still confused by the mid-air collision. The return to London City Airport and then the fire would only have added to their bewilderment.

Someone shouted at him, but FitzHugh ignored the challenge and continued on through the terminal and out onto the apron. No one tried to stop him although more gunmen stood near the building, watching the blazing scene beyond. A figure rushed up to him and he noticed only at the last moment that it was Helen Mayfield. She was breathless and alarmed.

"It's Dan! He's out there with the bomb!" She pointed towards a small centre of activity halfway between the terminal and the blazing aircraft.

FitzHugh looked and gasped.

The bomb lay on its side, a badly-handled piece of air cargo, while Dan Mayfield struggled to pull it away from the aircraft. Murdoch was slumped on the ground nearby, grasping his ankle and groaning. Behind the two men, a river of burning fuel from the 146 was reaching out towards them. The devil's fingers were searching for victims.

FitzHugh suddenly felt the presence of another person beside him. Out of the corner of his eye he saw the uniform of a police constable and promptly ignored him. He had no time for mere constables when they were about to disappear in one giant nuclear flash. He tried to force his mind to concentrate on the bomb, but his thoughts were a whirl of contradictory ideas and half-formed decisions.

Godsakes, get a grip on yourself!

It took him some seconds to acknowledge the constable's urgent signals.

"What is it?" FitzHugh snapped.

"Toome, sir. He says it's best for all of us if he's released."

"What?" FitzHugh's mind quickly refocussed on the terrorist leader. He sensed a tingle of tension in Helen's stance beside him.

"He says you want him to help us, sir."

FitzHugh gave the man a short, desperate look and said, "Let him go."

The constable raised his eyebrows, started to reply and then thought better of it.

"You're letting Toome go? Surely not." Helen's voice was raised above the level of background noise. It niggled to be criticised by a woman who had no police training.

He swung on his heels and shouted, "For chrissake! Let me do my job, Helen!"

"All right! If you want to do your job, go out there and help them!" She stabbed a finger out towards where her husband was struggling with the bomb. Nearby, Murdoch continued to writhe in pain on the ground, and the flames were steadily advancing towards the metal container.

She was right, goddammit. They needed help!

FitzHugh stepped forward onto the apron with a suddenness that caught the attention of a group of terrorists standing nearby. He had gone two or three steps when a thick voice called, "Stay where you are!" and he saw one of the gunmen aiming an automatic rifle in his direction.

It was McQuarrie.

He raised his hands, paused and called back, "Look, they need help out there."

"Get back, policeman!" The gunman waved his rifle towards the terminal. His eyes were blazing, filled with determination.

"Don't be such a bloody fool. That bomb..."

"I said get back!"

FitzHugh grimaced and turned back to where Helen watched with disbelief.

"Someone's got to help him!" she cried out.

*

Time: 1635
Twenty-five minutes to detonation

"That's far enough. You stay here." Patrick Toome flapped a heavy hand at the policeman alongside him.

They were at the entrance to the terminal building and he thought it wouldn't do for the gunmen inside the building to see him escorted in by an English policeman.

Some of the IRA men should have been on guard outside the terminal, he told himself angrily, but there was no one. There was only a strange unreality about the whole setup here. It was as if

275

both the British forces and the IRA were in some disarray over precisely what was happening. It didn't bear the mark of the sort of well-organised campaign he was used to mounting in Ireland. Perhaps there was just as big a cock-up going on here as he had left at Heathrow.

"Leave me," he snapped again at the English policeman who seemed reluctant to leave him alone, and he strode across the hall towards a group of his own men. Everything was so chaotic around them, none of the sense of order and command that he expected to find. Just Irish volunteers standing around looking for some command decision from someone. Anyone.

He saw FitzHugh standing beside a woman, both of them looking at the fire out on the apron. They had their backs to him.

"Who's in command?" Toome shouted at a young volunteer. He recognised him, an eighteen-year-old straight from the Creggan Estate in Derry. The lad responded with a wide-eyed look and a shrug of his shoulders.

"Give me your gun!"

The youngster reacted instantly, handing over his Armalite rifle eagerly, as if he was glad to be rid of it. Toome swore at him and then strode purposefully towards FitzHugh and the woman.

"What's happening?" he bellowed as he came up behind them.

FitzHugh swung round sharply. "Murdoch needs help," he said evenly.

Toome caught his breath as he looked out onto the apron.

"That's the nuclear device," FitzHugh continued, "out there on the apron. We need to get it clear of the fire."

Toome stared at Mayfield and Murdoch. "Why is no one helping them?" He turned and waved a fist at the watchers nearby.

FitzHugh fumed. "Because no one is giving any orders. I tried to go out there but McQuarrie ordered me back."

"Where's McQuarrie now?"

"I don't know. He backed off and I don't see him, but he's got to be somewhere nearby."

Toome swore again. He swung round and raised a decisive finger towards a small group of gunmen.

"You!" he snarled. "Get out there and lift that bloody thing!"

At first the men reacted with some indecision, but they edged out onto the apron. Toome glared at them until they moved faster.

"They'll shift it," he said brusquely.

"God help us all if they don't," FitzHugh responded in measured tone.

Toome ignored him. He took a step forward and studied his men as they hurried across the apron and grabbed up the container.

"Thank God for that small reprieve." FitzHugh was speaking to Helen, but Toome picked up the remark and considered it.

"It's true, isn't it?" he said, interrupting. "Everything you told me. About the bomb going off whatever we do. It's true."

FitzHugh nodded. He pointed to where a man staggered towards them, supporting Murdoch. "That's the pilot, Dan Mayfield. He was flying the aircraft when it collided in mid-air."

Murdoch groaned loudly as the pilot lowered him to the ground in front of the terminal building. Following close behind, the gunmen set down the container and then anxiously melted away, leaving Murdoch to his fate.

"What now?" Toome asked.

"There's an aircraft at the next stand. Get me over to it!" Murdoch glowered at the group, gritting his teeth as he bit back the pain in his leg. His hand waved vaguely towards the Dash Seven nearby.

No one made a move in response.

*

Time: 1640
Twenty minutes to detonation

"No one is leaving now. Especially not you." FitzHugh fixed Murdoch with a purposeful look. So this was Peregrine Fraser-Murdoch, the so-called 'fifth man'. Close up, he didn't look much.

"I demand you get me to that aircraft!" His eyes blazed and he waved his hands violently, as if he were in a fit of madness.

"No." FitzHugh spoke calmly and quietly. "You've played your last card, Murdoch. Now you can stay here and sit it out with us. What time is it set to detonate?"

Murdoch stared wildly at the policeman.

"Tell us! What time?"

"Five o'clock." All sense of command had gone now. There was only pure fear in Murdoch's voice.

FitzHugh looked down at his watch. "You must disarm it," he said calmly. "Disarm it completely. It's the only way. You've lost this battle, Murdoch. Disarm the bomb and we'll protect you from any Russian backlash."

Murdoch's brows rose as the implication sank in.

"Toome!" Murdoch turned towards the Irishman. "Get me over to that other aircraft. We still have time. There's a pilot here and we can get away. You can get away with me."

Toome flinched. His hands curled tighter around the rifle, and his jaw dropped just enough to betray his own fear.

He shook his head. "They told me..." he whispered. Then he raised his voice and said, "They told me the truth about the bomb. You intended it to go off all along. The British never had a chance."

Murdoch's gaze swung back to FitzHugh. "Lies!" he roared. His hand swung suddenly upwards, aiming a pistol at FitzHugh's chest. "It's all lies!"

His eyes flickered, swept around the group and came to rest on Mayfield. "You'll fly me out of here!" he squealed.

Mayfield shook his head silently.

Murdoch's gun hand wavered, still aiming at FitzHugh's chest. "Tell him to do as I say!" he bawled, desperation wringing through his wavering tone.

"You've lost," FitzHugh said as calmly as he could. "Now defuse the bomb."

"No!" Murdoch's face was contorted by the extremeness of his twitch.

"He's right, Murdoch. It's no use going on with this." Toome stepped forward, his own weapon aimed towards the madman. "The only way out is to defuse the bomb. It's all over."

"No!" Murdoch's eyes were wide with alarm. "No one disarms the bomb. Not now!" His gun hand wavered again as he caught sight of the barrel end of Toome's rifle aimed at him. His teeth were clamped together as his pistol swung round suddenly towards Toome. In the same instant his eyes blazed.

"Hell!" Toome swore. The burst from his automatic rifle tore into Murdoch. Lifeless eyes still wore their last look of surprise as the old man crumpled to the ground.

"For God's sake!" FitzHugh leapt forward and put a hand to Toome's chest, pushing him back. "What the hell have you done?"

"He was going to shoot!" Toome lowered his rifle. "He was going to shoot me."

FitzHugh grabbed at the rifle and took it from the Irishman's hands. He knelt down beside Murdoch and felt for a pulse. There was none.

"He's dead." He stood up, shaking his head.

"He was going to shoot! I swear he was going to shoot!" Toome looked wildly about.

"You bloody fool," FitzHugh hissed. "He was our only chance." He swung on his heels and glared at the Irish gunmen who were now closing in from each direction.

Toome hesitated. "What should I do?" It sounded almost like submission.

FitzHugh reacted decisively. "You can get those bloody morons of yours to put up their weapons and let us tackle that bomb. But God alone knows if we can crack the thing in time."

Toome looked around him with glazed eyes.

"What the hell is going on?" McQuarrie suddenly appeared at the forefront of a group of armed gunmen. Emerging from cover a little farther along the terminal building, they strode towards the bomb.

"It's all over," Toome called out to them. Then he snapped his head up and shouted, "Stay where you are. Stay back and for God's sake listen to me!"

McQuarrie and the other men stopped.

Toome looked too impressive at this most decisive moment for them to ignore him. He shouted, "The bomb out there is timed to go off at five o'clock. I'm ordering you to stand back and let the Brits defuse it!"

"No!" McQuarrie led his men a few steps further forward. "We're not afraid to die. Let it blow!"

"For chrissake! It'll kill all of you and millions of innocent people as well! Do you know how many Irishmen there are in London?" Toome swung his eyes around the rest of the gunmen now emerging from inside the terminal. "Is that what the rest of you want?"

Looks of puzzled confusion remained in the faces about him. "I'm sorry, men. Put down your arms. This whole operation is a failure."

"No!" McQuarrie gestured angrily to his own men. "Don't listen to him." Before anyone could stop him, he raised his Armalite and fired directly at the group around the bomb. A policeman fell to the ground, dead.

McQuarrie fired again and then retreated a few steps. His men fell back with him. Within seconds they were all shooting at random.

*

Time: 1645
Fifteen minutes to detonation

The world had dissolved into a cacophony of noise. Armalites were firing at the small group now sheltered just inside the terminal building. SLRs were answering back from a platoon of soldiers who quickly appeared once the shooting began.

FitzHugh wondered who had given the order for the troops to advance into the building. Then again, what the hell did it matter now? Sure as shit, they were all dead!

Bullets ricocheted off the apron, bounced off the walls, shattered plate glass windows. In the distance FitzHugh saw two Puma helicopters moving fast across the horizon, low down, circling behind the terrorists' lines.

"We have to get to that bloody bomb!" he shouted above the crack of the guns.

Toome was crouched down beside him. "Better we get the thing in here, out of the line of fire."

FitzHugh turned to him. "You fancy fetching it?"

The bomb sat on the apron. Unconcerned. Almost innocent looking. Just a piece of air freight. Ready to blow millions of people to kingdom come.

A camouflaged soldier dropped down beside him. An officer. He had a boom microphone in front of his mouth and he was talking to someone unseen. Speaking all the time.

"That the bomb?" He pointed with one hand and set the other on FitzHugh's sleeve.

"That's it."

"My men are circling behind the enemy. How long do we have?"

FitzHugh studied his watch. "Twelve minutes."

"Not enough time. What's your plan?"

"Plan! I don't bloody well have one!" It was too late now. They were facing the ultimate horror and they had no plan to deal with it.

Chapter 21

Flames crackled and hungrily reached out into the blackening sky. Bright orange fingers. Smoke billowed upwards, choking and acrid. The sound of the gunfire was almost incidental.

Toome crouched down inside the terminal building. Shite! He was with the wrong side! He should be out there with the Irish volunteers. A bullet chewed up the ground just outside the departure gate. A British soldier lay flat on the ground and fired back towards the burning aircraft. There was a cry from beyond the pall of smoke. Toome winced. His own men were out there!

"We've got to get to that bomb!" FitzHugh was crouching down beside him, shouting.

"It's not my problem," Toome shouted in reply. He backed away, easing through a cordon of British police and soldiers. When he was clear of the departure gate, he stood up.

He stared at the group of people opposite him and felt an ache inside which was too much like horror. He had failed in the task he had been set and, worse than that, he had betrayed his own kind. But, worst of all, he felt an almost overpowering sense of horror that an act of genocide was about to take place.

Alone among the gunmen, he stood unguarded, almost as if he was one of the British security forces who now scurried around the airport terminal. All around the building uniformed policemen and soldiers appeared like buds suddenly springing into bloom after a summer storm, a multi-coloured spectacle of blue, khaki and combat camouflage where once there had been only a loose array of gunmen. They moved quickly, hastily, aware that they probably had only minutes left to live.

And, all the time, the gunfire continued. Armalites and SLRs in deadly combat. A clattering that might have been an industrial factory process. A clattering that was manufacturing death.

Toome turned towards the main entrance where a group of captured volunteers were being stripped of their Armalites before being herded into a fleet of military vehicles to be rushed from the area. They looked confused and dejected.

As he watched them, Toome felt the sickly claws of discomfort wriggling over his skin. The feeling grew more intense when a uniformed police officer stopped to ask him to identify certain volunteers. Toome told the policeman what he wanted to know, reluctantly pointing out and naming each of the men he knew by sight. He could have refused, but he was quite sure that it no longer mattered — they were all going to die anyway.

There was, of course, no hope for his own future. Even if the bomb was defused, he would almost certainly go to prison for a considerable number of years. Or he could become the victim of a revenge squad. But more likely he would die when the bomb exploded.

The small group of Irishmen standing near the main entrance were under the guard of two uniformed soldiers, both of whom were solely interested in getting their charges on board the vehicles. Toome recognised the men, knew them well. One, at the edge of the group, was nervously smoking the butt of a cigarette while his gaze darted furtively about the building. He looked up as Toome came closer and gave an angry nod towards his one-time colleague. Toome understood and accepted the implications with sinking heart. It was the law of the jungle that no true Irishman should betray another, and he had broken that law; he had collaborated with the British and persuaded the volunteers to lay down their arms.

This was the certain warning that, even if he escaped the bomb, the Republican movement would haunt him for the rest of his life, following him like a nightmare wherever he went. No matter how far he might run, no matter how cleverly he might disguise himself. He would never escape, and never be able to return to the life he had left behind when he took the Sinn Fein oath. It suddenly hit him that if he had to die, it would be best done now, quickly and cleanly by his own kind, not by the disgusting terror of a nuclear bomb.

He ran back towards the departure gate.

*

Time: 1652
Eight minutes to detonation

Simon Hudson was angry. It had taken him far too long to convince the attendant doctors, nurses and police officers that he should be allowed to speak to Jennifer. They seemed not to care that he desperately wanted to hear her voice, to know for certain whether she was safe.

When he first discovered that the police had been ignorant of her presence in the Heathrow Tower, he had exploded. The hospital was a hive of activity, and he seemed to be only a small part of what was going on, too small to merit more than the occasional contact with the uniformed officers milling around. He had fumed and shouted at the police and the nurses, until they had, finally, listened to him. Then they had promised to find out what had happened to the girl in the control tower.

Now — an eternity later — a sad-faced constable entered the ward to speak to him. "The young lady you were asking about. She's safe and well." The constable began, and then corrected himself as he consulted his notebook. "... at least, as safe and well as can be expected under the circumstances."

"Where is she?"

"They've taken her to another hospital."

"I want to talk to her!"

"Well, sir, I—"

"I want to talk to her!"

"I'll see what I can do, sir. I think we've got the telephones up and running again."

It took more agonising minutes before they brought a telephone to his bed. The same sad-faced constable dialled the number and waited while the call was put through to the hospital ward. Hudson twisted his hands together and looked at the clock on the hospital wall as the constable handed him the receiver. It was now six minutes to five o'clock.

"Jennifer?" His voice was hesitant and carried an edge of doubt.

"Simon."

"Jennifer. Thank God you're safe."

He heard a quiet sob from the other end of the line and he put the receiver to the bed cover as he waved the constable away.

"Tell me that you're alright," he said as he watched the officer tread lightly down the centre of the ward.

"I'm alright. I thought they were coming to get me... I thought it was them, the ones who..."

"I understand," he whispered.

"I was going to jump. From the window. But Vince Trewin came and stopped me."

Hudson felt a constriction in his throat. "How long were you in that office?" he asked.

"I don't know. A long time."

"It's all taken so long," he said sadly. He looked across at the hospital clock as he spoke, not quite sure why the time should matter.

"Why didn't you come back?" she asked.

"I was caught. By that man called Toome."

"Someone could have come." Her voice was weak, quavering badly. "Someone should have known I was there. Why didn't they come and find me sooner?"

"I don't know, Jennifer. I just hope to God it's all over now," he said heavily.

His eyes swept across to the window opposite his bed. Outside he could see the outline of a copse beyond the hospital boundary, and a thin evening sun beginning to emerge from behind a cloud. Somewhere in the distance a bird was singing rather forlornly, as if it were heralding some great drama.

*

Toome waved to the soldier who was crouched down beside FitzHugh. He didn't stop moving because there was no time.

"Come on! We'll drag the bomb in here!"

He continued out into the open air without slowing. The sky was blacker now, almost obscured by the smoke. Maybe it would give him cover. He reached the bomb before he noticed the soldier beside him.

"Grab that end!" he shouted. His foot skidded under him as he grasped the bomb container and pulled. It didn't look anything like a bomb, but what the hell!

The soldier dragged his end across the ground. Toome pulled from his own side and the device began to slide towards the terminal. Still the firing continued. The British soldiers were firing rapidly to keep the Republican men's heads down, but it was small comfort. How the hell could the Armalites miss from this distance?

How far to go now? Fifteen feet.

Beside him, the concrete erupted into a starburst of broken concrete splinters. He staggered, recovered.

"Pull, damn you!" It was the soldier shouting now. Face as white as snow. Shit-scared. Just like himself.

"Pull, you—!"

The man suddenly threw his arms into the air and crumbled to the ground. Dead. The weight of the bomb dragged Toome to a halt. He looked round wildly.

Ten feet to go.

"Pick it up!" It was the policeman. FitzHugh. Running to help him. And shouting. "Pick it up!"

"It's bloody heavy!" Toome responded.

"Shut up and heave the damn thing!"

They were moving again, leaving the dead body spread-eagled on the ground. Almost at the gate. Just a few feet to go.

Toome felt a flush of success. He cried out, "We've made—"

Stupid thing to say. The bullet hit him square in the chest. He felt no pain, just a greyness sweeping over him. Then darkness. Nothing, just darkness.

*

Time: 1656
Four minutes to detonation

FitzHugh released his hold on the bomb as soon as he was back inside the terminal building, just as his police mobile telephone rang in his pocket. He pulled it out and jabbed the receive button.

"Yes?"

"I'm sorry, Commander." It was the nurse. "I have some bad news for you."

He gulped. "When did it happen?"

"Just a few minutes ago."

"Was she in any pain? At the end."

"No."

FitzHugh briefly closed his eyes. Thank God for that small mercy.

*

Time: 1657
Three minutes to detonation

Helen shook her head as she bent over the bomb. It was safe inside the building, but they were no nearer disarming it. So what was the point of it all?

Alongside her, a bomb disposal man shook his head as he sat back on his haunches. After a moment's thought he pulled savagely at his chin.

Helen caught a hint of desperation in his eye. "I only caught a brief glimpse of the code. I'm sorry, I just can't remember what it was."

The man set a timer on his wrist watch and replied, "If we can get that box open inside the next three minutes, we can stop the detonation. If not..."

FitzHugh rejoined the group from the direction of a group of military officers. His face was pale and haggard. He had still not recovered from being under fire.

"Less than three minutes," he echoed as he came up beside the bomb disposal expert. "You have approval now to take any risk you see fit."

The man shook his head again. "It's booby-trapped," he said. "I could get round it, but that will take time."

"We don't have any."

"That's right, no time at all. And all we have is the information locked inside the young woman's memory."

The two men turned towards Helen. She felt the pressure of a lifetime fall across her shoulders and she winced.

"For God's sake, Helen. Think! You're the only one who's seen the timer box open!" FitzHugh's voice was raised by several octaves.

Miles was standing beside him now, white-faced and solemn, rubbing his sweaty palms together. Helen glanced into the scientist's eyes and saw only hapless indecision. She looked again at the combination lock. Four numbers. How many possible combinations? Ten thousand? And only one would open the timer box and allow them to disarm the device. If she got it wrong, the consequences would be catastrophic. Equally, if she came up with nothing at all, the consequences would be just as catastrophic.

Another thought suddenly caught her mind. Even if she remembered the combination, could they trust Murdoch's word that the black switch would disarm the timer?

FitzHugh bent over the box and looked again at his watch. "Two and a half minutes, Helen! Think!"

Helen scanned around at the sea of faces, pleading eyes all trained upon her. The bomb disposal experts, the senior police officers, the SAS soldiers, FitzHugh, Miles. All willing her...

begging her to search deep enough into her subconscious to seek out that vital information.

She closed her eyes and shut her mind against the distractions around her. All she needed to recall was that brief instant after Murdoch had opened the box, that split second when her eyes had come to rest on the combination.

There was something about those numbers that activated a trigger in her mind, something about the code which acted like a personal form of reminder. Something peculiar to her life. If only she could dig deep enough to bring out the clue.

She drew herself more deeply into her inner self.

"Two minutes, Helen."

It was something to do with her childhood, something about her parent's home. She opened her eyes.

The bomb disposal man had come forward from the crowd and was crouched alongside the bomb. He held a pair of wire cutters and was preparing to cut the cables that led from the timer box to the detonator.

"No!" Helen reached out a trembling hand. "It's booby-trapped, you said so! You'll trigger it off!"

All eyes turned towards her again.

"The number, Helen. The number."

She lowered her eyelids and pictured her parent's bungalow. The smart little home at the end of a small cul-de-sac. She used to play with her friends in a park nearby. There was one friend in particular, a girl of her own age. They often spoke for much too long on the telephone...

"Sixty seconds. We can't wait any longer." The bomb disposal pliers were inserted into the container and angled around the first wire.

"I think I've got it!" Helen jerked herself forward and reached for the lock. She placed her index finger on the first combination number and revolved it. Five. There was no time to let anyone else do this. The second number. Zero. It was the telephone which gave her the clue. One. The number was the same as her parent's old

telephone number. Eight. She was almost certain she had it right...
almost!

But there was no time left for doubts.

She grabbed the lock and pulled. It came open easily. There was a partial easing of the tension among the people around her. But they didn't share her doubts about the switches!

"The black switch! Press the black switch, Helen!"

"No!" Murdoch had been too uneasy when he had told her about the black switch. Something had been seriously wrong. She remembered how his hands shook as he spoke to her.

It was a trick! Murdoch had been supremely composed until she had questioned him about how McQuarrie would disarm the device. There was a trick!

"Fifteen seconds, Helen! Press the black switch."

She hesitated and the bomb disposal man reached forward, his fingers stretched out to the black switch.

"No! It's a trick!"

"We're running out of time, Helen! Ten seconds left."

The bomb disposal man tried to push her hand aside. She resisted him.

"I'll do it!"

The faces about her were frozen, ashen.

"Five seconds, Helen!"

She rammed her hand down on the red switch. There was a loud click.

Then silence as she released her pressure on the switch and it sprang back.

A second passed... two seconds. And then she heard the agonising thump of her heart beating loudly.

Another five seconds passed.

It was over.

Epilogue

The ground beneath Simon's feet was muddy, too slippery by far. Maybe they should have put this off until the storm passed over. Wind-blown rain stung sharply as it beat against his face, almost as if it was blaming him.

Why him?

He had not been responsible for Michelle's death. It was not his fault the heroin had taken her. It had always been a possibility, maybe a probability, that the drugs would kill her, but he never wanted it that way.

He glanced to one side where Commander FitzHugh stood close to the open grave, just beyond the aged priest. The policeman's head was bent sharply forward, his collar turned up against the rain. He would understand. Maybe he was, even now, thinking about his own sad loss. It was good of him to come to the funeral.

Simon appreciated the gesture. They had met only in the aftermath of the emergency, but the horror of what they had gone through had drawn them together. Given them a common aim to move on and put the ghosts behind them.

It was the same with the family standing at the opposite side of the grave. Helen Mayfield, her daughter and her husband were huddled together as if they would willingly spend their lives like that: close-knit, despite the trauma they had experienced. Maybe because of that trauma.

"You're shivering, Simon." A soft voice struggled to cut through the wind while a small figure pressed close against him.

He clasped at the girl's small hand. "I'll be glad when the service is ended." He stared down into her soft eyes. "I tried to help her, despite all the pain. I tried. It shouldn't have come to this."

"I know." She patted his hand. "It won't be like that with us. I promise you."

"Of course it won't." He shook his head. How could their future possibly be anything like his dismal past?

"New job, new life, new future together. We'll make a go of it." She was doing her best to comfort him, he understood that, and it heightened his feelings towards her.

"Of course we will, Jennifer. Of course we will."

He felt a smile creep slowly across his face. The rain continued to sting, but it somehow seemed not to matter anymore.

Prestwick by David Hough

Danger in the Sky (Book 1)

Four hundred frightened passengers
Two badly cripled aircraft
And nowhere to land

A freak mid-air collision cripples a trans-Atlantic 747 and a US Air Force jet. Against the clock and overwhelming odds, the planes' crews — or what's left of them — struggle to save the on-board survivors. Meanwhile an obsessed narcotics detective tries to pin drug smuggling and murder on two suspects on board the crippled 747.

As the weather deteriorates, most Scottish airports are closed, leaving Prestwick the only airport available for a safe landing. However, Prestwick has its own emergency to deal with, something that overshadows all other problems. Landing permission is refused and more than four hundred people are condemned to an almost certain death over icy, blizzard-swept seas.

Can things get any worse? They can — and they do...

David Hough whips his reader along in a roaring jet stream of action and high tension that buckles the reader to his seat. A breathtaking, whirlwind of a thriller.

Made in the USA
Charleston, SC
10 June 2016